Vows
&
Lies

Based on a True Story

Phoebe Leggett

Endorsements

The atmosphere of rage where Jessica lived, as well as physical violence that resulted in black eyes, bruises, and broken bones, was stunning. The abuse eventually escalated to include death threats and yet, broken, and afraid, she resigned to her fate. She tried to live the outward life of a pastor's wife and mother of three young children while hiding from everyone around her the truth of what she faced daily at home.

Perhaps one of the most heartbreaking parts of her story is that when she finally did begin to seek help, no one believed her. Not her family. Not her in-laws. Not even law enforcement. How could a man who was a pastor be abusing his wife?

Sadly, the author's narrative of domestic violence is hardly an isolated event. An estimated one in every three women worldwide will experience gender-based violence during their lifetime. Multitudes of women are abused daily—yes, even in Christian homes.

Changed hearts and the healing of marriages is the ideal. But in our broken world, that doesn't always happen. And when it doesn't happen, there comes a time when escape is imperative.

After years of adhering to the erroneous idea that divorce is an unforgiveable sin, Jessica realized her only hope of survival was to escape. Such escape takes considerable courage and an unshakable faith in God. She had both.

As she clung to the Lord for help, she discovered everything she needed to escape and survive was provided by his hand. He led her to a new place, one of healing and joy. And ultimately, he blessed her with a new marriage based on love and respect.

Jessica's story is the greatest of testimonies to God's grace I have ever known.

—ANN TATLOCK
2012 Christy Award Winner
Named by Booklist Magazine
as one of the Top Ten Historical
Novelists of the year
Award-winning, Author, Speaker
Conference speaker

My heart is on fire after reading Phoebe Leggett's exquisitely wrought novel. She has put the religious world on notice that even a pastor's wife can suffer years of torture at the hands of a zealot husband.

With an original voice, *Vows & Lies* is a startling account, a revelation of the sin embedded within a Christian man's soul. Battling her way out the darkness, Jessica emerged with her faith intact, and walked into a life that was calling her name.

—PAMELA KING CABLE
Author of *Televenge: the dark*
side of televangelism

Jessica married young, with hopes and dreams of life as a pastor's wife. But within days she discovered her dream was a nightmare. With vivid detail and heart-wrenching transparency, the author takes readers behind the scenes of physical, emotional, and verbal abuse at the hands of a volatile man who was both pastor and evangelist.

But her story is more than that of a battered wife. The author digs deep into Jessica's life, and peels back layers of childhood trauma, family loss, and health issues; then brings her story into an ending that is both revealing, and exquisitely glorious.

—VONDA SKELTON
Author, *Seeing Through the Lies: Unmasking the Myths Women Believe*

This is a powerful book about a very brave woman. The author chronicles life with an abusive husband and a chance at freedom with honest and clear writing.

Throughout the story she sprinkles poetry written during her time of terror and escape, as well as Scripture verses that helped to keep her strong. She shows us, through her story, that God is our strength and our refuge.

The second half of the book details signs and symptoms of abuse and depression so the reader can recognize these in herself, or in a friend or relative. The author also tells the reader what to do in these situations, how to get out, and how to heal.

Grab a tissue when you read *Vows & Lies*.

—PAM ZOLLMAN
Author, Speaker, Freelance Editor, Writing Instructor

Vows
&
Lies

Based on a True Story

Phoebe Leggett

Contents

Vows & Lies
Survival Guide
Part Two

Preface

When Jessica fell in love at the age of eighteen, the future looked sunny and bright. Her new husband was both charismatic and handsome, their marriage, a dream-come-true. But his representation as minister of the Gospel, devoted to both God and man, wasn't justified.

The truth of reality would soon shatter her vision, innocence, and religious beliefs after she realized her jump from the frying pan into the fire had been a horrible mistake. Yet she remained committed, and worked hard at making her marriage a success.

Over time, internal turmoil, the result of assaults, insults, and battering, began to slaughter the love she once had for her husband. But she remained true to her marriage vows.

What goes on in a marriage behind closed doors is nobody's business. Yet when the truth is revealed, families often refuse to believe their loved one is an abuser—or married to one.

Family is where one goes when bruised and battered. But not Jessica's. Due to religious pressures her reality remained hidden behind a façade of family disregard, church ineptness, and an overall lack of perception. The embarrassment she felt disguised as what appeared to be a marriage made in heaven.

Love hurts but should never be abrasive. From the pit of despair, a thread of hope for deliverance was born. But it required twelve years of deception to unravel the disillusionment, heartache, and despair that played havoc with her sanity.

After years of unrestrained cruelty, the facts of realism began forcing the light of truth to shine at the end of a compelling tunnel. Misery was then replaced by a sweeping desire for freedom, once forgotten and swept under the rug.

"My days have passed; my plans are shattered. Yet the desires of my heart turn night into day; in the face of the darkness light is near" (Job 17: 11-12)

Secrets of a small-town girl, now grown to woman living under the shadow of death, are revealed through the eyes of an innocent wife of youth. When everything in her life unraveled, God's perseverance provided a way of escape, and just in the nick of time.

"...on those living in the land of the shadow of death a light has sprung up" (Matthew 4:16)

"Do not be deceived: God cannot be mocked. A man reaps what he sows" (Galatians 6:7)

Vows & Lies is based on a true story. Names and locations have been changed, but the heroine remains a trophy of God's grace.

"No weapon formed against you shall prosper and every tongue which rises against you in judgment you shall condemn" (Isaiah 54:16)

Chapter One

Keeper of the Peace

The rain pounded its discontent as Jessica closed the door behind her husband. "I'm glad he's gone," she whispered, and breathed a quick prayer of thanksgiving.

She took a deep breath, trying to refocus, and prayed her battered nerves would soon calm down. After a long sigh she walked to her desk and absentmindedly reached for her journal. But tears shed the night before had drenched the book, and the pages were sticking together.

Anger, hurt, and remorse over the harshness of her reality again ignited, allowing un-restrained tears to flood her heart. Her brow then furrowed, her writing pen repositioned, and she surrendered the truth of her existence to the crumpled pages of a secret diary.

When Trey and I first married, we were happy. At least I thought we were. But the puzzle of a stable marriage has never quite fallen into place. The rigor of maintaining a calm environment keeps me anxious, stressed out, and frazzled to the max. When angry his violence conveys a serious lack of self-control.

His overbearing dominance keeps me busy making amends for everything wrong in his life. Our marriage is a complete disaster. But my prayer was answered. He did marry me. Is it my fault our marriage was on the rocks shortly after it began?

I feel trapped, paralyzed, and afraid. Other times I'm proud of my pastor-husband. His message of deliverance rings out as true. Everyone loves him and believes he's wonderful. People pray through to salvation under his ministry. He is handsome and charismatic, but his actions don't make sense.

His ability to minister is astounding. But his inability to appreciate me, his wife, is heartbreaking. Hiding evidence of his abuse to maintain the peace is an everyday affair.

Assaults at home are crushing, painful, and intimidating. But clues of his character reveal he will do whatever's necessary to make himself appear as one who cares. In the aftermath I remain a prisoner of fear and abuse. I want to run away. I want escape. But can I? Who can I trust?

Voices in my head scream isolation, despair, and hopelessness—even hell and divorce. Fire blazes through my body even though I'm not yet divorced. I know how the church feels, and how my family will react if we separate. But my life is nothing more than a lie.

What if divorce lands me in the bad place?

An embedded image of romance past softened her heart as she recalled moments when the word defeat could only be found in a dictionary. After a tedious sigh, she closed the journal, gazed far into the distance, and remembered the way it all began.

A short week-end visit with a friend, only months past high-school graduation, landed them both in church on Sunday. But a handsome man sitting across the aisle caught her eye and snagged her heart. His handsome charm kept her glancing in his direction. On the inside her heart pounded restlessly.

"Barbara—who is that?" she asked, aiming her finger at the man who had claimed her attention all morning.

She smiled and winked. "That's Trey, the man I was telling you about," she said. "He's an evangelist, and a pretty good preacher."

"Can you introduce us?" Jessica asked, her voice bubbly and excited.

Barbara hesitated, then complied. "Trey, this is my friend—Jessica, this is Trey."

"H—Hi Trey," Jessica said, but her face flamed, and she quickly turned away.

"Hello back to you," he said, followed by laugh. His

words dissolved her heart, and she melted beneath his gaze.

He reached out his hand, grasped hers, and slowly released. And so began her new life—the one she had dreamed about her entire life; or so she believed.

Chapter Two

Jitters

"Let's get married."

"But we've only been dating three months."

"Time is running out."

"Let's keep it a secret," Jessica said. I'm not even telling Barbara until the marriage certificate is in my hand." And with those words, the decision was sealed.

The following Monday, the day after Easter, was the planned day.

***

Early Monday morning, as the fragrance of spring surrounded them, Jessica and Trey sped to the courthouse, ready to exchange vows in a secret elopement ceremony. The judge, an elderly gentleman with a receding hairline, imparted words of wisdom after pronouncing them as married "Remember and put God first in everything you do," he said, and placed the marriage certificate in Trey's hands.

At that moment, all that mattered was young love, but held no true promise of happiness. Little did Jessica know her dream would soon begin to unravel. But she was in this marriage for the duration. Her commitment was solid, and firmly grounded. God would be her anchor, or so she believed. So, she brushed aside her fears, and quickly forgot her concerns.

***

After work one afternoon Trey pulled his jacket close and stepped back outside. In response Jessica pulled her own wrap on and followed close behind, shoes clicking and clacking on the uneven pavement in rhythmic accents.

"How long will you be gone?" she asked as the car door closed.

"Oh, probably a couple of hours," he said, and shot his famous smile back. "I'll be back before you know it. The pastor's meeting shouldn't last too long."

"I'll miss you," she said.

"I'll miss you too, baby," he said.

She stepped away from the curb, and mouthed, "See you soon," before jiggling her hand in slow motion.

"Come here a minute," he said, and jumped back out of the car to draw her close. "How about a kiss for the road?"

Leaning over, she melted into his open arms. As hot lips met, her mind began to drift. The next instant he pulled away.

"I really need to go," he said, "or, I'll be late." He jumped back in his car, waved good-bye, and sped away.

Her heart splintered as she gazed after him. But after car rolled out of sight she trudged back to their tiny bungalow and closed the door.

Once inside, she hugged herself. She was glad they were tight. Being Trey's wife was accelerating, and she relished every moment spent with him. Although sharing him with the church was inevitable, that was something she was willing to do.

***

She glanced at the clock once more, then let out a long sign. Where was Trey? The next instant a grinding noise from the outside caught her attention, and she jumped in quick response. Tires were spinning up the driveway. The car stopped, and he ran up the porch steps, and into the house.

"Hi, Trey—you're finally home" she said, reaching out. But instead of a kiss, he pushed her aside, threw his keys on a table, and strode to the kitchen.

"You don't need to worry about me," he said. His

words were acid.

"I'm just glad you're home," she said, hands still outstretched. But again, he turned away.

"I'm hungry," he said. "What's for dinner?" He jerked the refrigerator open, looked inside, then slammed the door closed.

"I made a casserole," she said. "It's cold, but I can heat it up."

Why didn't he kiss me?

"I don't like casseroles," he said, but sounded agitated. "What's in it?"

"Pasta and chicken," she said, proud of her accomplishment. "It's good—Mama's recipe."

"Never mind," he said, and a frown formed. "I'm going to Mom's and get some real food."

"What's wrong?" she asked. "I cooked this especially for you."

"I'm not in the mood," he said. "Now stay out of my way."

Never had Trey acted this way. Why was he mad?

"Just leave me alone," he said. "Where are my keys?"

"Don't leave. What happened at the meeting?"

"Nothing you need to know about," he snapped.

His words were troubling, so Jessica stepped aside; baffled with his attitude. But instead of apologizing, he turned, shuffled through some papers on the table, and then strode to the door.

"Please," she said, again reaching out.

But his eyes instantly glazed, and, with a hand of steel, he struck her across the face. Her back slammed into a table, causing it to slide hard from the impact. Her cheek flamed, and tender tears formed. "What did I do? What did I do wrong?" she asked, voice trembling.

"Leave me alone, Bitch," he hissed. "Just leave me alone."

She was stunned but quickly rebalanced and rubbed her reddened cheek. Then she brushed away hot tears. "I don't understand," she said, crushed.

A second punch landed, and her body fell backward, this time into a kitchen cabinet. "I'm leaving now," he said. His face was clinched and unreadable as he stomped to the door.

Confused, and still rubbing her jaw, Jessica pulled herself up and ran after him. "What did I do? Why did you hit me?" she asked.

He glared back, jumped in his car, and sped away. Understanding was impossible.

Should she keep Trey's actions a secret? He was, after all, a good preacher. Besides, she wasn't ready to wreck his reputation. Maybe she needed more time to learn how to be a better wife. He could change—with her help.

It was important, for the sake of the ministry, to remain calm, she reminded herself. Besides, his childhood had probably been difficult without a father in the home.

Confidence in herself filled her heart. "Mama always told me that being punished would make me stronger," she whispered. "Maybe I needed to be punched. The Bible says a wife is a husband's helper. That means I'm Trey's helper."

Shattered in body and perplexed in mind, she lifted both hands upward, then reached for her Bible, searching for words of consultation. When her eye rested on the third chapter of Philippians, verse thirteen, and she resigned herself to forgiveness.

"Brothers, I do not consider myself yet to have taken hold of it. But one thing I do: Forgetting what is behind and straining toward what is ahead, I press on toward the goal to win the prize for which God has called me heavenward in Christ Jesus"

Chapter Three

Puzzle Pieces

The following morning Trey was his old self again. After apologies, hugs, and kisses, his pleas of forgiveness were accepted.

Jessica was still apprehensive, unable to understand his rage. But she swallowed her pride—just happy things were back on track. Their planned trip to Hendersonville would be fun. She would make sure of that. He needed to meet her parents, and they needed to meet him.

Her father, as a welcoming gesture, displayed his collection of guns and rifles for his new son-in-law to examine. Trey's interest in one piece was motivation enough for her father to give them the rifle 'for safe keeping.'

"Let's buy some bullets," Trey said on the way home. "I want to try this baby out and see how good it shoots."

Panic seized Jessica's mind. Funny she'd never before noticed how high strung, self-centered, and flamboyant he was. For now, staying one step ahead of the game would be safest.

Once home, he was all about the gun.

"Let's put some cans on this old stump," he said after aiming at several trees. "They make good targets."

Several empty cans were placed in neat rows on the stump, and Jessica stepped back to watch. "Is that the best you can do?" she asked and tried to squelch a laugh. "You've missed half the cans, and the others are falling over."

"Shut up—shut up," he said, and moved his shoulders in circles as if to loosen them. He then reloaded and aimed again.

"I'll knock them all off this time," he said, the pitch in his voice rising. "Just watch and see." His face then reddened, and hers tensed.

"What if he turns the gun on me?" she whispered. But she shook off her apprehension and concentrated on the action at hand. She was, after all, in love. "And love covers a multitude of sins, right?"

***

More odd actions were beginning to surface, and Jessica couldn't understand why. What was happening to her marriage? Why was Trey pulling away from her? Did he regret getting married? In her heart she was beginning to think he did. But they both believed marriage was forever.

While dating they often discussed the importance of God's guidance in their lives. How God wanted him to preach. Dreams of speaking to large crowds while leading many to salvation had been foremost in his mind. In the past he prayed all the time. Now he rarely even prayed over their food.

Chapter Four

Christmas Gift

Jessica's first Christmas as a newlywed had to be special, if only a single box of ornaments and a few lights were in the budget. Christmas was her favorite time of year.

Days before the holiday, and shortly after Trey left for work, she pulled her jacket close, and prepared for action. But before she got busy, she glanced outside one last time.

Winter was in full swing. The chill of a blustery wind whistled through tiny holes and unsealed crevices in the outside wall and sounded ominous. On the inside windowpanes and shallow frames creaked and squeaked with each passing wind gust.

Committed to her plan she scurried about decorating their home for the upcoming season. An hour later a newly decorated tree sported colorful lights and assorted baubles ready for Trey's return home. "I'm so excited," she whispered as shivers of excitement ran up and down her spine. She could hardly wait for the big day.

Early Christmas morning, as daybreak flickered through the windowpanes, the newlyweds climbed out of bed, and meandered to the tree. One gift, lovingly swathed in reds and greens, was handed to Trey. "Hurry up and open this one," Jessica said, her words slurring in the excitement of the moment.

Trey grinned, reached for the gift, and ripped through the paper. The next instant a metal container full of assorted hand tools and accessories jetted across the room and slammed their newly purchased furniture.

The tools spilled, spreading a colorful array of metal across the floor. Chipped fragments of wooden debris from the headboard and bureau now littered the floor around them. "Who do you think I am—a handyman?" he asked, eyes his full of fire. "I'm a preacher, remember?"

Tears instantly streamed down Jessica's cheeks as she bolted to retrieve the gift. The tools were quickly gathered and placed in the container. When she glanced up, still holding the case, Trey's face was turnip red. "I thought you'd like my present," she said, meek and apologetic. "You didn't have any tools."

His glare made her shiver. "I—I'm sorry," she said. What else could she say?

Still angry he stomped from the room. But when enraged words of profanity filtered back, she dropped her head in confusion, and brushed away more tears.

She wasn't accustomed to cursing, or vulgarity. Neither had she observed course actions while growing up. She had never been treated this way, and sensed instant isolation, and rejection. This was unchartered territory, and she wasn't sure how to react, or what to do.

"I'll have to do better," she promised herself. "After all, Mama said keeping my husband happy was my responsibility."

***

An abrupt blast from the outside rattled Jessica's sleep, and she bolted upright. Seconds later more explosions echoed through the neighborhood, and she quickly climbed out of bed. "Oh, no," she said, clutching her head. "I forgot all about New Year's."

"Get the rifle," Trey said, grabbing his pants and coat. "I'm going outside and make some real noise."

Jessica sucked in her breath and stared outside through the closed window, waiting for him to dress. Bright flashes of fireworks glittered the sky as she watched, leaving a glowing residue; but reminding her of the gun. Did she dare speak her thoughts? Did she have a choice?

"Bullets aren't fireworks, you know," she said. Her words were spoken with caution.

"Who cares?" he asked. He jerked the rifle from the

rack, turned on his heel, and headed out the door.

"Please, come back inside," she said as gusts of frigid air flooded the inside through the opened door. "You might get in trouble." But when a shot ripped through the air, she decided to join him on the dimly lit porch.

Once outside, she pulled her robe tighter. "You really shouldn't shoot that gun," she said, and nervously twisted the tie around her waist.

The next instant an outside light illuminated, and a door across the street opened. A robust man, shaking his fist, stepped through the opening. "What do you think you're doing?" he yelled, looking in their direction.

He stepped off his porch and strode to the corner of his house. Trey looked dazed.

"You'd better go talk to him," Jessica said, urging him forward.

"Guess I can't hide from this one," he said, glancing around. "Guess I'll go see what I hit."

The neighbor's manifested anger continued as Trey sprinted across the road to join him.

Jessica said a quick prayer as Trey and the man examined the corner of the house. Minutes later Trey gaited back across the street, a grin on his face. "The man said it's alright," he said, panting. "Only nicked the corner. Told me not to shoot his house again, or I'd be in real trouble."

Jessica sighed, reached out, and touched Trey gently on the arm. "I'm just glad he's not mad," she said.

"He said if I did it again, he'd call the police."

She released another sigh, then held the door open for Trey, who slid inside.

"That was a close call," he said. He flopped down on a chair, glanced at her, and howled with laughter.

Chapter Five

Slammed

A few days past New Year's and Trey was again in a mood. After he returned home from a quick trip to the store Saturday evening, his eyes were flashing. Jessica winced in confusion. "What's the matter," she asked.

"Stop nagging me," he shot back, then hauled off and punched her in the face. And instantly her nose went numb.

Why did he hit me? Why is he so angry? What did I do?

"Please help me, God," she whispered. Her hands were now shaking and gripped in fear.

"Stay out of my way," he said. The next instant he was rummaging through a bureau drawer. He turned for a moment, glanced at her, then removed several of her childhood keepsakes; all the while snickering in a mocking way.

Dismayed, she watched in horror as he strode to the oil circulator, grabbed a cloth to cover the handle, and jerked the lid open. Still laughing, he tossed two figurines of Bach and Beethoven into the fire.

"Please stop. Please don't—" she said. In desperation she wrung her hands. "Those are my trophies—from piano recital. I earned them."

Instead of responding, he reached for their newly processed pictures, ripped them in half, and tossed the entire packet into the fire. A look of contempt filled his eyes, and he seemed to stare right through her as she cowered beneath his gaze.

"Stop, please—," she said, still frightened.

"Shut up. Shut up you ugly Bitch," he said.

More profanity rolled from his lips in words she'd never before heard from him. The next instant a fist slammed her face, her jaw popped, and she could feel the tightening of swelling flesh.

Will he ever stop hitting me? Why is he so mad? Maybe it's because I was a late getting home from the store. He might be jealous, or something. But why?

Circulated rumors of wives beaten by husbands were rare in Jessica's reclusive world. She recalled many punishments as a child, but never one of being hit with a fist. Well, her father's back-handed slaps were unforgettable, as were the many whippings she'd received throughout childhood. But Trey shouldn't get angry. He was a preacher.

Maybe he needs to vent. I guess it's okay for him to hit me. After all, I am his wife. But what I did I do that was so terrible?

All night long course words and tempered battering held her captive. When daylight emerged, tears no longer fell from her eyes. Having surrendered to exhaustion and pummels, she felt drained, emotionless, and withdrawn.

Exhausted, and still in a stupor, she dragged herself to a chair; curled up, and closed her eyes. But she opened them again at the sound of sopping.

"I'm sorry," Trey said again and again. "Please forgive me. You know I love you."

Words of remorse were again spoken as he slid down beside the chair and stroked her face. Jessica could only stare at him through swollen lids.

"I really am sorry I hit you," he said again, and his arm drew her close. "I didn't mean to hit you. I was mad. You know I love you."

The urge to resist was strong. Her nose was bleeding. Her lips were split, and her spirit was sagging. She was more than bruised. She was confused. What about all the things he had destroyed? She couldn't replace any one of them. What about her bruises? What about the rip in her heart?

Still, she wanted her marriage to work. And because

she was also embarrassed, keeping her mouth shut was essential—because the word defeat did not yet exist in her mind.

"I love you, too," she said—words spoken, but not felt. And, to keep the peace, a hug of forgiveness given, although forced.

"Are you okay?" a church member asked as, together, they climbed the church steps later that morning.

"I—I think so," she said. Her words were automatic, and she absentmindedly rubbed her tongue over a chipped tooth.

"Please, God, don't let anyone else notice," she whispered. "I don't want them feeling sorry for me."

They didn't.

***

Would life always be this way. All Jessica wanted was someone to truly love her. Now she felt trapped without the possibility of escaping her destiny. Her existence was more than confusing. It was a nightmare. Would it always be this way?

Childhood discipline and church training had long before indoctrinated her convictions. She was stuck. Her parents would disown her if she divorced. The church would turn her out if she left Trey. And, for some odd reason, all her friends had suddenly disappeared.

Already signs of Battered Wife Syndrome were visible yet ignored by those around her.

After taking note of skeptic reactions, Jessica realized disbelief was inevitable, and decided to keep Trey's actions to herself. Shame over the battering, fear of rejection, and apprehension of probable doubt allowed a decision of silence.

Three years into the marriage and a pattern of abuse was in place. Episodes of battering would begin with slaps to the face, then cumulate into kicks, and fist-impressions on head and arm. It wasn't every day, but frequent enough to be bothersome.

Trey, now the pastor of a church some distance from

home, but within driving distance, held an irreproachable and prominent stance. It was important, for the sake of church and family, that Jessica applaud and respect him as others did.

Although the church was tiny, this intermit would be the building blocks to his future. But she only a shadow of his increasing popularity and growing status among the congregants.

Her contributions were in the music department, yet often devalued, and perceived as less important than his. And she knew her place.

***

Late Sunday evening, after returning home, Trey stood solid in front of Jessica, and gritted his teeth. "Why did you stay and talk to Sister Rogers after church?" he asked.

All she could do was shrug her shoulders.

"You knew I wanted to go straight home and watch the game on TV."

This conversation wasn't going well, so she placed her purse on a chair, turned, and faced him. "I forgot," was all she could say. "I simply forgot."

A fist then rammed her face, and her legs instantly gave way. The force of impact landed her on the floor, where another blow caught her on the shoulder. "You never listen, do you?" he asked.

She refused to answer. Instead, she pulled herself up. But before she could again move, clammy hands were propelling her down the hallway.

It was futile trying to stay balanced, so she stumbled forward, tripping over her own two feet as she plunged headlong into the abyss. Trey's breath, hot on her neck, made her quiver; and she inhaled in staggering gulps of air.

"Please stop. Please," she begged. Her shoulders were now mush beneath his strength.

"Stay out of my way," he hissed, and formed a nubby fist for another round. "Now get up."

He lunged again and shoved a harden fist into her

head. "Get up, you mother-fucking whore," he said. His words were cold, and she was instantly scared of her wits.

How can he be a preacher, and beat his wife? How could he stand in front of church people and preach? And how can he give an altar call, and people come?

Terrified, she wrapped her arms around the top of her head as another blow knocked her backward. When she looked around from her spot on the floor, she realized there was no way to escape—no way out. The door to the outside was at the far end of the hall.

Shaken and demeaned, battered and beaten, she glanced down at several blood droplets spattering the top of her folded legs, and new terror gripped her by the throat.

"You're a stupid bitch," he said, degrading her with more profanity and foul language. His words, spoken through gritted teeth, also challenged, and were full of hate.

Uncertain of what to do next, she pushed herself into a standing position, reached inside the bathroom, and grabbed a towel bar for support. The next instant she was sprawled over the bathtub. When she tried to get up, cold porcelain held her hostage.

"You're an ugly bitch," he said again, his voice course and unrelenting. But as more degrading words erupted, she withdrew even farther into herself, and closed her eyes. All she could do was lift a silent prayer for guidance.

"I'll blow your fucking brains out, you ugly whore," he said, and she cowered beneath his gaze. Could she survive another terrorizing onslaught?

"I promise I'll kill you," he said, "and it will be soon." He again lunged, and his eyes blazed. "Now get up Bitch."

An angry boot kicked her sharply in the thigh, and she slumped forward. The sting of harsh slaps, and the throb of aching bones held her firmly at his command. His boot then met another intended target, bashing her upper thigh with blunt force.

The heaviness of hardened leather crushed her leg

as it was shoved deeper into her lower extremities.

"Oh, God—help me. Please help me. Please don't let him hit me again. Please—"

His fist again rammed her shoulder, but she sucked in the pain, and refused to verbally surrender. Although words of urgency were released, they were silent.

Oh, God—help me!

"If you ever try to leave me, I swear, I'll blow your fucking brains out," he said. His rage was ballistic.

"He's going to kill me," she whispered.

"You have nowhere to go," he said, laughing. "Besides, you'll never make it on your own." His boot again landed on her thigh, as added emphasis. He then turned, and slunk from the room, leaving her to suffer on her own.

"Please God—help me. It hurts," she said, struggling against the tub. Her body, drenched with sweat, throbbed, and ached with each labored breath. Once on her feet, she limped to the side, grabbed a hand mirror, and grimaced. A swollen face and purple eye stared back at her.

With an index finger, she traced an uneven path down her cheek where blood and tears had formed a trail to her breast. "I can't live like this," she whispered. "I can't do it anymore. I need help."

Balancing as best she could, she slid her torso along the wall to the bedroom and staggered to the bed. She eased down on the mattress, and let go—sinking deep into the cool, unruffled spread.

Fresh lesions and newly formed bruises throbbed incessantly. "Oh God, what is my purpose?" she cried out. "I'm the wife of a preacher who enjoys seeing me in pain."

Nothing seemed to please Trey, no matter what she did. It was time to talk to the police, or someone in authority. The church and her parents would be no help. She also had serious doubt about his family, although one of his sisters had recently noticed some injuries and questioned the reason. Perhaps she had an advocate after all.

Oh, God, how did get in this mess?

Chapter Six

Jail Bird

Monday found Jessica at work as Bookkeeper at a local radio station, although she was stiff and sore. But as the day progressed, she decided to tell Ashley, one of Trey's sisters, of his actions hoping for direction and sympathy.

After work, and barely able to walk upright, she managed to stagger inside the convenience store where Ashley, her favorite sister-in-law, was straightening shelves behind a mirrored counter. After a ragged breath and she tapped the surface to get her sister-in-law's attention.

"I turned Trey into at the sheriff's department," she said, and released a long sigh.

Ashley turned in an instant and looked her in the eye. "Did you really?" she asked, a shocked look on her face.

"He knocked me over the bathtub and cussed me out last night," Jessica said. "The last time you and I talked, you said I should turn him in to the police if he assaulted me again."

"Yes, I know I did," Ashley said, looking somber. "I just didn't think you'd do it." She sighed, turned away, and swiped a duster along the edge of the shelving.

"I didn't know what else to do," Jessica said, leaning forward, and resting her arms on the countertop.

"Well, Trey is my brother, you know," Ashley said as she straightened cans on the shelf. "Maybe you did the right thing. Maybe you didn't."

"Please don't be mad," Jessica said, and her lips drew into a thin line. "I thought you knew I'd do it."

"When is he getting arrested?"

"Today—after he gets off work," Jessica said. Her

stomach then tensed, and bundled nerves began to tie her flesh into knots. "I'm really not happy about any of this."

"When did you sign the warrant?"

"Today. I went to see a magistrate today."

"Well, you knew he would get arrested, didn't you?"

"Not at first. I only wanted to see what my options were."

Jessica's heart was now pounding, so she shifted into another position, trying to understand her sister-in-law's reaction.

Ashley turned and walked to a phone behind the counter. "Does anybody in church know besides me?" she asked.

"I don't know. How would they?"

"Does Mom know?"

"No."

"I'm calling her now," Ashley said, and lifted the phone.

"What will the church do if they find out?" Jessica whispered to herself. "Besides, my in-laws are closer than my own family. I certainly don't want to hurt them."

Beads of sweat suddenly encased her forehead, and she reached up to wipe them away.

Why did I talk to that magistrate? Maybe I should've left things alone and not said anything. What if Trey beats me up again for having him arrested?

A customer holding several shopping bags walked past, and Jessica stepped aside. The next instant her legs wobbled, and she grabbed the counter for support. Her lips were also dry, so she moistened them with the tip of her tongue.

Did I do the right thing? Well, maybe not. But Trey's been hitting me with his fist. He said I deserved it. Maybe I did. But no—I don't deserve being hit that way. I'm not a kid anymore. I'm an adult. Adults don't need to be corrected.

That evening, after returning home, Jessica heard a small knock at the door. Mrs. Williams, Trey's mother, was standing outside.

Jessica took a deep breath and opened the door.

Mrs. Williams smiled a half-smile, then stepped inside. Trey followed her inside and closed the door.

"How did you get out of jail?" Jessica asked, looking directly at Trey. Then she lowered her head. "Well, I guess I know," she said softly, and a large sigh escaped.

"Why don't you two make up?" Mrs. Williams asked.

"I'm sorry I hit you," Trey said, and huge tears filled his eyes. "I promise, I'll never do it again."

It was obvious he'd been coached. His crocodile tears looked staged. Then Jessica caught his eye. "You still have to go to court," she said.

"You can drop the charges, can't you?" He was begging.

"I don't know if I should."

"Please." And he fell to his knees. "I promise I'll never hit you again."

"I'll think about it," she said.

He is, after all, a preacher. I have to trust him, don't I? His reputation will be shot if I don't drop the charges. How could anyone survive a scandal like that? But the church is miles away from where we live. They'll never know anything happened.

"I guess I'll drop them," she told herself. Everybody wants me to."

Three months later she was pregnant with their first child.

Chapter Seven

Stones to Throw

Holding her side, Jessica hoisted ten-month-old Kayla to other the side, grabbed her purse, and stepped outside. "Thank God the doctor's office is only a block away," she said out loud. Writhing in pain, she walked a short trek to the doctor's office as fast as her legs would allow.

In the waiting room she dropped her purse on a bench, and gingerly positioned herself after sitting the baby down. She grabbed her back, hoping to ease the pain, then lifted her purse, and searched deep inside. The aspirin bottle was located, and she swallowed the remaining tablets without a second thought.

Where is that doctor? Why is he so slow?

When her name was finally called, she slowly dragged herself to the examining room.

"You look like you're in pain," the nurse said.

"It's killing me," Jessica said, rubbing her back. "It's worse than labor pain."

"I'll get the doctor right now, no more waiting," the nurse said, then reached for Kayla. "I'll take the baby with me, and leave her up front with the receptionist, if you like."

"Yes, thanks," Jessica said, grateful the baby would be safe. Lamaze breaths, used during labor, were then used—hoping to control the pain, but only reinforced an urgency to fight her way beyond whatever was causing the anguish. It was pointless calling Trey. He wouldn't care if she was in pain.

Minutes later, after several tests and excruciating positions on an x-ray table, Jessica was more than ready for the doctor's analysis. In fact, she was anxious to get up and go about her day if only the pain would stop.

"I'm giving you're an injection for the pain," Dr. Thomas said. "You'll feel better after the medication takes effect.

***

As she rested, the throbbing began to ease. But now she was dizzy—and giddy. Blinking to stay awake was barely working, and she struggled to keep her eyes open.

"Should I let myself go to sleep?" she whispered. "What about Kayla?"

"You have kidney stones," the doctor said when he returned. Jessica could only stare at him.

"I've called the hospital" he said. "Looks like the stones are too large to pass." Then he patted her on the shoulder. "They're waiting for you in Emergency."

"Where's my baby?" she asked but sounded as if encased in a jar.

"Up front with the receptionist," the nurse said. "We need to call someone to take you to the hospital."

"My husband is at work," Jessica said. Her words were slurred. "My, uh, sister-in-law."

"Do you have a number?"

Several digits were recited, and in what seemed like seconds, Ashley was standing beside her in the room. "I'll take Kayla home with me after I take you to the hospital," she said.

At least the baby would be in good hands. At this point Jessica doubted if Trey would care either way.

***

Fourteen days in the hospital was taking its toll. Depression was taking its toll—so much so that the staff psychologist was visiting Jessica on a regular basis. Stitches and scar tissue covered half the expanse of her body. And she felt more alone and isolated than ever before.

"I miss my baby," she said, words whispered every night as tears fell like rain. Already Kayla first steps were history. What else had she missed?

"You're going home today," the nurse said as she straightened the pillow beneath Jessica's head. She slipped a fresh straw into a Styrofoam cup on the tray and smiled.

"I am?" Jessica asked, and the beginnings of a grin shaped her lips. "Are you sure?"

"The doctor will be in shortly to release you," the nurse said. "Go ahead and make arrangements to be picked up. Today's your day."

At last Jessica was going home. Her heart raced with anticipation. She could hardly wait to hold her baby again.

***

"I'm taking the week off," Trey said as he rolled Jessica's wheelchair down a long hospital corridor. Her lap, piled high with flowers, magazines, and a small suitcase, was filled-to-capacity. The response to her hospitalization from family and church had been overwhelming.

"I'll be able to change your bandages whenever you need them changed," he said.

The chair came to an abrupt halt, giving Jessica a chance to reinforce her thoughts. But she chose her words carefully. "Remember what the doctor said." And, as a distraction, she straightened a magazine ready to slide off her lap. "My bandage needs changing several times a day. He said the incision would drain a couple of weeks."

"I'll be around," Trey said, and the chair was again on the roll. "Don't worry about a thing."

She reserved some doubt, but at least she was going home.

Poor Kayla. She hardly knew who Jessica was. As for Trey, his actions hadn't changed at all. His promise to assist had only been words.

As the week progressed, so did Jessica's workload, and Trey's outings. They were as detailed as a power map. But rude comments about surgical scars she could do without.

Reaching around her back, she taped another bandage into place. At least the tubes were producing less and less.

Trey's family believed he was helping her. And so did the church. But, again, he was fooling everyone.

She dropped another soiled bandage into the trash, and verbally released her anguish. Changing bandages was hard. After another pain pill she edged toward the bathroom. It was time to gather more soiled laundry. If she didn't keep the clothes clean, who would?

Grunting for energy and momentum, she shoved a ton of dirty laundry into the washing machine, and turned the dial. Meanwhile, Kayla was crying for attention.

"Oh, God. Please help me through this day," Jessica said out loud. Her words were strained as she inched along the wall.

Where was Trey? I wonder—did he take golf clubs or a tennis racket this time?

Chapter Eight

The Appointment

Six hours of labor through the night produced an eight-pound-five-ounce boy with auburn hair and blue eyes. Ayden's arrival early Wednesday morning brought new joy to Jessica's shattered heart. As she cuddled the new baby in her arms, Trey stepped in the room.

"Look what came in the mail," he said, and a huge smile covered his face. He waved a large manila envelope in her face. The return address read Superintendent of the Holiness Conference.

"I've been accepted as pastor of a church just across the state line—my second pastorate," he said.

"Well, I guess today calls for a double celebration," Jessica said, and forced a smile.

"I can't wait," he said. He reached for the baby, holding him for the first time since his birth hours earlier. "I'm riding up this afternoon to check out the church building."

"Are you coming by to see us again?"

"I'll swing by tomorrow," he said, and handed the baby back. "I'm doing some visitation too."

"Guess what happened after you left this morning?"

"What?"

"The nurse gave Ayden his first bath in front of all the new moms," she said. "He was the demonstration baby on how to bathe an infant. I was so proud of him, even though he didn't like his bath very much."

"That's funny," he said. "But listen. I found out the church is really excited we're coming."

Jessica was more focused on the new baby than a new church assignment.

"They're giving us a baby shower next week," Trey said.

"Nice," Jessica said, followed by a frown. Then she slid up higher in bed. "I get out of the hospital on Friday."

"I won't forget," he said.

Minutes later, as Trey fingered through a magazine, she dozed. When he bumped the tray table, her eyes instantly popped open. "I need to go," he said, and dropped the magazine on a table.

"How's Kayla?" she asked, as memories of bright blue eyes glimmered in her head.

"I think she misses you. At least that's what Ashley said."

"I hope she doesn't forget who I am again."

"Okay," he said, glancing at his watch. "I need to run. I have some things to do this afternoon before I go and see the new church."

After he left, the baby was breastfed, and fell asleep in Jessica's arms. "Having babies is easy compared to life at home," she said out loud. "Two babies and a new church assignment will keep this pastor's wife busy."

***

"You'll never be any help to me as a pastor's wife," Trey said, glancing at Jessica as they headed to the new church a couple of weeks later.

His words stung. Why was he so critical? Not only was she church pianist—required attendance—but wasn't her role as his wife also relevant?

Piles of sheet music and printed verse were kept ready, as well as ideas for the choir. Preparing lessons for children's church was also important. Even her janitorial skills were crucial. She couldn't justify his words. What exactly did he mean? But instead of responding, she stared through the car window, and remained silent.

"You're not wearing that ugly thing again, are you?" he asked. "You don't even know how to dress. Plus, you're fat now."

His words wrenched her heart.

Why does he say such mean things to me? Recovery from childbirth is still ongoing.

"You don't even know what to say to people," he said. "I have to tell you what to say, you're so stupid." His laughter whipped through the air. "You look like an old hag—you old hag."

He used to love me—told me I was beautiful. We used to be crazy about each other. Two kids later and I'm an old hag? What happened?

Looking down she couldn't help but note the out-of-style dress she wore that came to her knees. She didn't own pretty clothes. Extra money always bought updates for his wardrobe.

Neck ties of various color and design decorated the bedroom door. Suits of modern style and cut filled the closet. Crisp white shirts pressed and separately hung remained clean, neat, and ready to wear. Dress shoes, both brown and black, finished the collection, and stayed polished and fresh. Her job was simply making sure his clothing was immaculate.

Church doctrine in the seventies required women wear only dresses, as pants, and heaven forbid, shorts and swimwear were banned as sinful. Make-up and jewelry, even the wedding band, was out of the question. Clothing for women was simple, and basic. No frills to enhance their attire.

But what did it matter? She couldn't afford, or even find the time, to examine such extras. Life was simple at best. Babies and church—church and babies.

Caring for the children, although tiring, was enjoyable and fulfilling. Church work, on the other hand, was hard work. Not to mention living with a man who, at times, seemed to detest her.

The rules of Christian living listed severe disciplines if one strayed from church teachings. But that impossibility was laughable as sermons from pulpits across America dictated similar compliance on purity and chaste living—directed mostly at women.

The Amen corner often resounded with complacent

men who believed that wives should remain simple, and unadorned. But did aspiration control undisciplined eyes from lusting after women who were more modern? Well, probably not.

Life was what it was. Overcoming the rules of church leadership and family dictates had always been a challenge. It was also impossible to change them.

Jessica now realized the man she had married wasn't genuine, God-fearing, or true to his marriage vows. Commitment was a word yet to be defined in his mind. But in her eyes, the bonds of matrimony were to be honored— and celebrated.

Trey's hatred only intensified, slicing her heart to bits, and denying her one desire for true love and happiness. He despised his indenture, and was more ingenious, calculating, and destructive as time moved forward. His demolition began with personal possessions, and quickly escalated to body, heart, and soul.

Although fractured early on, Jessica remained committed despite numerous red flags indicating her dream marriage had long before ended. But alienation and manipulation began driving her to re-evaluate her desires and forcing her into action.

It was then she decided to no longer take the abuse. She would seek a way of escape and flee her abuser · permanently, realizing she could never return to a man who enjoyed carving out devastation and ruin in her life. Her heart had been deceived, and her sanity stripped away. Scars, both physical and emotional, remained as reminders of past trauma.

Once common sense returned, she was thankful God had not forsaken her.

"Be strong and of a good courage, fear not, nor be afraid of them: for the LORD thy God, he it is that doth go with thee; he will not fail thee, nor forsake thee" (Deuteronomy 31:6).

Belief in God, and trust in her core values, would see her though. She wasn't afraid to die. She no longer feared death as confrontation with that opposition was still ongoing. Trey's promise to blow her brains out had long ago destroyed that fear. It was implausible at any unexpected moment.

Her concern, from this time forward, was for the children. They were worth saving. With this in mind, she mentally prepared for what was ahead—her escape to freedom.

A release from her ruined existence would happen. Of this she was certain, or she would die trying. It was simply a matter of time.

Chapter Nine

Baby Times Three

Glancing down Jessica absentmindedly rubbed her stomach. "I think I might be pregnant," she said, and a hint of a smile formed.

"What?" Trey asked, then spun around to face her, fist in hand.

"I said, I think I'm pregnant."

"Get an abortion," he shouted, and his fist pounded the table with unexpected force.

"I can't. It's wrong."

"If you're pregnant I'll tell everyone that baby's not mine."

His words instantly ripped her heart to shreds. But maybe he didn't want his girlfriend to know he was still sleeping with his wife. In her heart Jessica knew he was cheating—long visitations, and late-night returns.

"Well, if I am, it was an accident," she said, but twisted her hands trying to stay calm. "I didn't plan it."

"Get an abortion," he said again, only louder. "I don't want more kids." He clamped both hands on the back of his chair. "Two are more than I ever wanted."

"You know I can't get an abortion. It's wrong."

"I don't care. Get one or get out."

"I haven't been to the doctor yet," she said, and her lips curved. "I just think I might be."

At that moment, she realized she would need to be careful. She recalled being punched in the stomach when pregnant with Kayla, and again with Ayden.

She didn't dare risk this pregnancy. But with a baby on the way, plans to leave the marriage would need to be laid aside. Without a support system in place, or money, any endeavor would be wasted. And yet, despite the risk, another baby would be exciting. Any diversion in her chaotic life must be a blessing. Perhaps even mend the marriage.

Trey's infidelity could be forgiven. If only he would be the man he portrayed himself to be—a dedicated minister of the gospel.

The following day Jessica left the doctor's office somewhat elated, but mostly subdued. Could she continue living with an abusive man who didn't want his baby? If only he would change. Her prayer was for things to settle down, and their new addition bring fresh unity to the marriage.

***

"Can you help me?" she asked several hours later. "Please?"

Trey turned, sauntered across the room, and stopped in front of her as she cowered on the floor. "What happened to you?" he asked.

Rubbing both ankles, she stared back as tears streamed down her cheeks. "I tripped over the thresh-hold when I went outside and twisted both ankles."

"Well get up," he said. "I'm hungry." He grabbed a chair and began tying his shoelaces. "I leave in thirty minutes."

Frightened, she inched over, reached for a chair, and tried to stand. Pulling up was impossible, and she again sank to the floor writhing in pain. "I can't walk," she said. "I don't even think I can stand."

"Well, that's your problem," he said, rocking back and forward, and causing his chair to lean precariously. "Just because you can't walk doesn't mean you don't take care of things around here."

"Shouldn't I see a doctor?"

"You shouldn't have fallen," he said. "Besides, I'm taking the car." He jumped up and jerked the refrigerator open. "Since you won't get up," he said, "I'll fix my own sandwich."

The next instant two-year-old Ayden tottered

through the kitchen and stopped. "Mama on the floor," he said.

"I know," Jessica said, but her attempt to smile died. "Mama's okay. I just fell and hurt my legs."

She again tried to stand, but her ankles were swelling, and screamed resistance. "What about the kids?" she asked.

"You had them. You can take care of them," Trey said, a snarl on his face.

She'd heard those words before. But why was he so mean hearted?

"I'm out of here," he said, and grabbed his jacket. "Where's my keys?"

"Right there on the table where you left them."

"I don't see them," he barked. "Now get up and help me find them. I'm going to be late."

"I can't walk."

"I need my keys," he said, and his voice rose in decibels with each accelerated word.

Frightened, she crawled to the table, and fingered the surface. And immediately a clatter of metal against metal jangled in her hand. "Here they are," she said, and lifted them up.

He reached over, grabbed them, and slammed the door on his way out.

Seven months pregnant, yet none of Jessica's responsibilities as wife and mother stopped. But no longer did she see herself as marriage partner, but more as caregiver. Trey's demeanor had long before turned sour, making her more responsible than before.

"Ayden, honey, go and get your sister," she said. "Tell her I need her."

What else could she do? She couldn't walk, but she could crawl. With that in mind, she drew a deep breath, and surrendered to her fate.

"Mama, what happened?" Kayla asked, staring down.

"Mama can't walk," Ayden said.

At least the babies cared. She wasn't alone after all.

After soaking her ankles, she wrapped them both—all the while praying the pain would ease. Soon she was crawling around on both knees, caring for her babies and her home. Although her bulging midriff made it difficult to move about, she persevered.

"Dear God," she whispered. "Please help the baby not be hurt. I know I fell hard. At least I'm not bleeding."

From sheer determination, she learned to manage from her knees—even climbing a tall wooden stool to reach the stove, and cabinets.

"Dear God, my ankles are throbbing," she whispered. But, maybe, it's a good thing. Staying on my knees keeps me humble."

"I'm a survivor," she told herself "If I can work while on my knees, I can do anything."

***

A couple of weeks later, after Jessica was able to walk, both sisters-in-law stopped by. "Come on." They were begging. "Go with us."

"I don't want to know," Jessica said.

"We've been talking," Ashley said, and nudged her sister. "We've heard some things. Something makes us very suspicious—"

"—that Trey's fooling around," Emily said, and finished the sentence.

"I don't want to know," Jessica said. "Probably don't need to know either."

"Well, we're still going to find out."

"Okay," Jessica said. "But don't tell me. I don't want to know."

She didn't have time to learn who Trey was having an affair with. She couldn't take care of herself, or the children, without him. She didn't have money of her own, or a job. Besides, she was pregnant. Seven months. What exactly were they thinking?

The following week as Jessica headed to Ashley's house, nervous reservations surfaced. "I hope everything goes smooth," she prayed. "I hope Ashley won't tell me what she learned about Trey." The children would be staying with her while she visited the gynecologist. At least they were excited.

"We're here," Jessica said, peeking through the screened door. "How's it going?"

"I thought you didn't want to know," Ashley said, and a smile emerged.

"I don't," Jessica said.

"Okay—then I won't tell you," Ashley said as she held the door open.

"Thanks," Jessica said.

"Hey, kids—who wants ice cream?" Ashley asked. And instantly they came running, voices babbling and small shoes pounding as they rushed to be first in line.

"Max has been excited all morning—since I told him Kayla and Ayden were coming," Ashley said, after they all scampered away.

"They love playing together," Jessica said, shifting in her chair. "I'm glad this family is close, and the kids have each other to play with."

"Me, too," Ashley said.

"Anyway, my doctor's appointment is at three."

"Eight months already, huh?"

"Eight and a half," Jessica said. "Seems like forever." And a small sigh erupted. "My stomach's as big as an elephant. I can't even see my feet now."

"I remember when I was pregnant," Ashley said, then pulled more popsicles from the freezer. "I'm glad it's you, and not me."

"Three kids are enough, although I'd love to have a dozen," Jessica said, and released a long sigh.

Ashley laughed again, closed the refrigerator door, and handed Jessica a frozen treat. "You know, when you're pregnant, you can eat as much as you want," she said, and both eyebrows lifted.

"Well, I guess—if you say so," Jessica said, and a small smile emerged. Minutes later she stood and reached for her purse. "I need to get on the road. Don't want to be late for the doctor."

"The kids will be fine," Ashley said, and held the door open. "Trust me. They won't miss you."

"See you later, then."

"Drive careful," Ashley said. "Don't rush and watch out for traffic."

"Thanks for caring," Jessica said. "You're the best."

Four weeks later, and shortly after midnight, Josh presented as an eight-pound redhead.

"Hot dog—another boy," Trey said before passing out in the hospital hallway.

But, again, Jessica was content. Mothering came natural for her. A baby at her breast and two tagalongs were the happiest days of her life.

Chapter Ten

Just Fix It

"Everything's your fault," Trey said, glaring at Jessica from across the room. More spiteful words, spoken in anger, rolled nonstop from his lips.

How many times had she been blamed for what was not her fault? She turned away and rolled her eyes in disgust. What had she done now?

"What's this?" he asked and threw a newly ripped envelope at her.

She caught the paper, and quickly scanned the contents. "Your decreased house payment hasn't been approved for the current year," she said, reading the letter. And she drew a sharp breath.

This could be costly, and we can't afford a higher payment.

Trey plopped down on a nearby chair and stared at her—eyes flashing. Then he raised his eyebrows. "Exactly what does that mean?" he asked.

Her words were repeated.

"What?" And he bolted upright.

"Read the letter," she said, and pointed to the paper in her hand.

"You're supposed to keep up with this stuff."

"I don't know what it means," she said. Then realizing his rage was rising, she again responded, this time in softer tones. "I'll call them and see what I can do."

"You'd better take care of this quick," he said, eyes still flashing. "And I mean today." He jerked his jacket off the back of his chair, grabbed his keys, and stomped outside.

As soon as the door slammed, Kayla and Ayden

came running. Thankfully they were too young to understand their dad's temperament. But by the time Trey was again home, Jessica's stomach was tied in knots. She dreaded relating the news, but truth is truth. "Our house payment is going to double," she said.

"Why?"

"Because we didn't file the proper paperwork this year."

"Why didn't you take care of this before it happened?" he asked and swatted at her.

"I—I didn't know," she said, but quickly placed the baby in his highchair for safe keeping and breathed a quick prayer for protection.

"You're supposed to know," he said, and his face blazed. "I don't have time for this."

"No paperwork came in the mail."

"You're supposed to take care of things like this," he said.

"I didn't know anything about it."

"Then get a job," he said, and a scowl replaced his frown. "We need more money."

"I can't get a job," she said. "We have three little kids."

"That's your problem, not mine," he said. The next instant he was pacing the floor, and his anger seemed to increase with each stomp of the foot.

Frightened, Jessica tried to redirect his rage, fearing yet another beating. "You promised I could stay home and take care of the kids," she said, cowering.

"I've changed my mind," he said, and his face turned red.

"If I get a job, the cost of daycare will take everything I make."

"I don't care," he said, and stomped even harder to emphasis his words. "I said, get a job. I can't keep supporting you, and the kids, on a church salary and my job."

"That makes no sense," she said, and grabbed a piece of scrap paper to write on. "Look at the numbers.

There's no way working a job right now will help anything. We have three pre-school age kids. Daycare would eat up my paycheck. Besides, we want the children to learn principals from us, and not a babysitter." Then she took a deep breath and waited.

"Well, we have to do something," he said, "or we'll lose the house."

"I'll—I'll talk to the bank again," was all she could say. But the answer was the same. They would be selling their home and moving to a less expensive house. Trey's salary wasn't enough to keep their heads above water.

***

Moving day was hectic as Jessica skirted about trying to keep the peace between three rambunctious children and a super-sensitive husband. Josh, now an active toddler, meandered among assorted items in his room ready for boxing up.

Kayla, toys piled in colorful heaps, sorted through various dolls and accessories for transporting to their new home. Trey, on the other hand, dragged two large suitcases into the living room, and sat them on end in the middle of the floor. He then left the room.

Minutes later Ayden darted through a wide opening between kitchen and living room in an attempt to leap over the cases. His terrifying screams brought Jessica on a run. A sharp piece of glass from the now broken storm door was embedded in one of his knees. Blood squirted from the wound, and covered his leg in streams of sticky red.

"Call 911," Jessica yelled. She grabbed Ayden, ran to the kitchen, and snatched up the phone. But Trey was nowhere to be found.

Phone in hand, she punched in 911. "Come quick," she said. "My three-year-old has a piece of glass in his leg, and blood is squirting everywhere."

A rescue team arrived in short order amid sirens and clanging bells. The glass shards were removed, and a compress applied. "He needs to go to the emergency room and get stitched up," one rescuer said, patting Ayden on the head. "We don't stitch wounds. We only stop the bleeding."

"I can't thank you enough," Jessica said, but her heart continued to pound. Seconds later Trey sauntered into the room.

"Why are they here?" he asked and pointed outside.

"You know those suitcases you left in the middle of the floor?"

"Yes?"

"Ayden knocked them over. He fell through the storm door, and it shattered." Her hands, wet with sweat, were rubbed together. "We need to take him to the hospital for stitches. He had glass in his leg. He's bleeding."

"You should've been watching him."

"Why did you leave those suitcases in the middle of the floor?"

"Shut up. Just shut up," he said, and made a fist. His words seemed to mock and criticize at the same time.

"Can you drive us to the hospital?"

"I'm not going anywhere," he said. "I'm busy packing. We're moving, remember?"

"Can you watch Kayla and Josh?"

"No. Take them with you."

Jessica knew better than to argue. "Come on, kids," she said. "Let's take your brother to the emergency room for stitches."

Chapter Eleven

Sandbox Debacle

Now settled from their recent move, Jessica could only pray Trey's stress level would drop, and things at home become more peaceful. Losing the house, and living in another, was a small price to pay if their marriage improved. But things only grew worse, and she soon felt the pressure of more volatile responses.

Trey's appetite to climb the church conference ladder and make a bigger name for himself only enhanced his aggravated status. More callas than before, his behavior escalated to new levels of rage, but always came at another's expense.

***

In a rare moment he decided to watch the children while at play. But a loud cry from the sandbox brought new panic to Jessica's heart, and she quickly raced to the porch.

Alarmed, she tried to brush past, but he reached his arm out, and stopped her. "I'll go," he said, a mock smile on his face. He stood from his chair, sauntered to the sandbox, and lifted Josh from the sand. Kayla and Ayden, oblivious to the baby's cries, continued to play nearby.

"His diaper's wet, and he's rubbing his eyes," Trey said.

"I'll take him," Jessica said, reaching out as memories of past roughness surfaced in her mind.

"No, I can handle it," Trey said. He sat down, still holding Josh, who continued to cry.

"Shut up—shut up," he said in response, then forced the baby down on the cement porch, where more squalls erupted.

"Please, let me take him," Jessica said, heart in throat.

"I said I'd handle it," Trey said, and swatted at the sand in the baby's eyes. Josh only wailed louder.

"Get me a wet washcloth," Trey said.

"That will make it worse."

"I said, get me a wet cloth."

The tone in Trey's voice was strong, emphasizing his demand, and Jessica was instantly terrified. Feeling defenseless, she returned with the cloth, but cringed on the inside. Unable to watch, she turned away, knowing one doesn't apply anything wet to dry sand without expecting a disaster.

And instantly Josh's screams ripped her heart to shreds. "Anything wet makes it worse," she said, then stepped back, still cautious. She dreaded the worst.

"Shut up you ugly Bitch," Trey said. He grabbed Josh, turned him over, and spanked him with hands of steel.

Please God—please help Josh.

In blind faith, and a prayer on her lips, Jessica reached for the baby.

Trey then stood, and shoved Josh into her arms. "Here," he said. "You take him." He turned on his heel and headed to the car.

"I'm leaving now," he growled. "I don't like stupid kids." The door slammed, tires squealed, and he was gone.

Jessica, thankful for the respite, ran inside for a dry cloth. Minutes later, and dry from top to bottom, Josh's cries smoldered to sniffles.

Forever grateful, she thanked God for wisdom on how to remove wet sand from a child's eyes.

Chapter Twelve

Merciless Driver

"Get in. We're late." Trey's undisciplined bark was enough to send Jessica into a tailspin.

It was her responsibility, as expected, to help the children into their car seats before climbing in. As she was getting secured, all but one leg remained when a gust of wind blew past, the door vibrated, and the car squealed from the curb.

"You're making me late," Trey said after the door slammed shut, with Jessica barely inside.

"Couldn't you find anything better to wear than that?" he asked, pointing at her dress. "You look like an old hag."

"It's the best I have," she said, still winded. Trying to hide her embarrassment, she smoothed the top of her outdated dress while recalling his recently purchased suit and tie.

"Well, wear something better next time," he said. "You make me look bad." And he jerked the steering wheel to emphasize his words. "Better yet, do something with that ugly hair."

Fire instantly blazed across her face.

I'm doing the best I can. You're the only one who gets new things in this family.

He accelerated his way through town, and she grabbed the arm rest for support. Still frenzied, he raced through two red lights before the road widened into the main drag. His rage was out of control.

The car began its incline, and Jessica methodically analyzed the sharp curves ahead. Every bump and pothole seemed to accentuate the narrowness of the road as they rushed headlong up the mountain.

Loud profanity and vulgar insinuations flowed from Trey's lips as easily as did his sermons. But why couldn't others see him as she did?

The next instant he turned the car toward a ravine, all the while sneering and cursing. "We'll never make it by seven," he said. His words, spit through pursed lips, destroyed all confidence as the unsteady car slid from the edge of a precipice, and just in the nick of time.

"Please, please be careful," Jessica said, fear in her voice. Could he get any angrier? Dread in the form of a knot was slowly creeping up her throat. Meanwhile, the kids randomly cried out in fear and pain as they methodically slammed into each other.

Shifting in the seat, Jessica positioned herself for another hard slam against the door. Bruises forming beneath her skin throbbed from a crushing jolt just seconds before. The car continued its trek, blazing through a wide curve, and sliding toward the edge of a deep gorge.

Please help us, Lord.

Her heart raced as Trey jerked the car back. It continued to swerve, weaving, and swaying back and forth under the duress of speed. She prayed they would make it to church.

Tires screeched a reminder of unknown horrors as they whiplashed back and forth in the veering car. Spiteful out-of-control maneuvers and vicious language rattled her brain. She cringed at his innuendos.

Terrified, she reached behind the seat and steadied the baby's lopsided car seat. What else could she do? She feared for all of them.

The crazed auto swiped past a border of prickly brambles close to the gorge, and she gasped. "Please slow down. Please," she said, heart in throat.

"Shut up, you mother-fucking bitch," Trey said. His words were cold. The car then raced upward. When they reached the pinnacle, huge boulders and massive crevices rose from below—as if to defy them.

His out-of-control rage spurred them downward—

the car weaving and swaying relentlessly on a dangerous trek toward church. Hateful, menacing words shred her heart, as his actions held them captive. Then, as if divinely orchestrated, the brakes slammed, and they had arrived.

With a shove of the hand, Trey yanked the shaft into park, jerked the door open, and stepped outside. "Good to see you this evening, Brother Jim," he said, extending his hand to a seasoned church member.

But for Jessica—well she was just happy to place shaky feet on solid ground again; even more thankful Trey's haste and recklessness hadn't landed them all at the bottom of a ravine.

***

The following week seemed to fly by, and it was again Sunday. After church that same morning Trey insisted they accept a church member's invitation and spend the day with them. Although Jessica dreaded caring for small children away from home, it was easier to comply than to argue.

At long last the day ended, and she could breathe easier. Parental responsibility had all been hers, and she was exhausted. "God is our refuge and strength, a very present help in trouble." Powerful words repeated again and again helped to calm her spirit and refresh her mind.

Once home, she plopped into bed, and pulled the blankets over her worn out body. Just the thought of sleeping children eased her mind, and she released a long sigh of relief. It was time for some much-needed rest.

She sank deep into the comforter, resigned to the solace of fatigue. Could she do another thing? Well, probably not. The next instant a door slammed, and heavy footsteps roused her. Trey was in the room.

He tossed his shirt and jacket on the foot of the bed and cleared his throat. "Why don't you get up and make me something to eat?" he asked.

"I'm really tired," she said, and her eyelids drooped after a fleeting glance through slanted lids. "We've been gone all day."

"Well, I'm hungry," he said, and stood in the doorway, hands on hips.

"Can't you make your own sandwich this time?" she asked.

"You know I don't know where anything is," he shot back. "Besides, I'm tired too, you damn bitch. I preached twice today, remember?"

"Can I skip it this time?" she asked, and her lids sagged. "I watched the kids all day by myself."

"Wasn't my fault."

Heavy footsteps tromped to the door, a switch clicked, and the room instantly illuminated. The next instant she squeezed her eyes tight, trying to block the light as unexpected brightness gave her migraines. But an aura of fog surrounded her, and ever-gnawing ache of head pain began to slowly settle in.

Trey's voice now echoed from down the hallway; and she struggled to sit up. "Wake up, kids," he said. "Time to get up and play with your toys."

The haze around Jessica swirled and mocked as she crawled from bed, and stumbled down the hallway, rubbing her head. "What are you doing?" she asked.

"Time to get up," Trey said, shaking Ayden by the shoulder. "Wake up, little buddy. Get up and play."

"Please don't," she said, and blinked as Trey lifted a toy truck, and waved it in the air.

"Look Josh. See what Daddy's got? Don't you want to play?"

Josh stretched and opened his eyes.

"Hey, Mama wants to play with you," Trey said.

"Please stop," Jessica said. "They need their sleep."

He flung her hand away. "Get up," he said, again shaking Ayden's shoulder. "Don't you want to play? It's time to play."

"Please don't wake them," Jessica said. "Please."

Her head continued to swim so she closed her eyes, only to open them again when Trey's laughter resounded from Kayla's room.

"Wake up, Kayla," he said. "It's time to play."

"Please stop," Jessica said, stepping through the bedroom door. She reached out, and grabbed Trey's arm, but quickly dropped it when he pinched her.

"Look Kayla," he said. "Mama wants to play with you."

Kayla sat up, yawned, and rubbed her eyes.

"Get up, Kayla—time to play. Don't you want to play?" Trey's tainted words seemed to echo through the house. His look was taunting, and Jessica winced at his demeanor. But when the boy's cries again caught her attention, and she turned away.

But Trey grabbed her by the hair, stopping her dead in her tracks. "Where do you think you're going?" he asked.

"The boys are crying."

"So what?"

"I don't like them crying."

"Do they need their mommy?" he asked in a tone that both mocked and heckled.

She jerked free of his grasp and hobbled away. Still the snickering continued.

In the boy's room she lifted Josh from the crib. Then she turned to Ayden. "It's okay," she said in a soothing tone. "Shhhh."

She patted him on the head. "Lay back down," she whispered. "It's alright. Go back to sleep."

Ayden stared up from the pillow, eyes brimming. And then her own eyes filled.

Oh, God. Please help me. My head is pounding, and I can't see through this migraine. What am I going to do? Oh, God, please help me know what to do?

In the background Trey's car keys jangled against each other. The next instant the outside door slammed, and Jessica breathed a deep sigh of relief.

Thank God he's gone. But here I am again, calming everyone down. Will it always be this way?

She needed help—but where could she find it? Trey's family would never accept the fact that he was mean to his family. Neither would hers. And, heaven forbid, she tell anyone at church. Besides, they wouldn't believe her. Trey was too charismatic to discredit.

She sighed again, closed her eyes, and squeezed back swollen tears.

Where does he go anyway when he leaves the house? And do I really care?

Resigned, she held her bursting head, and allowed the tears to flow at will.

Chapter Thirteen

Life on the Edge

Trey's car sputtered and stopped, and the car door slammed. Half afraid, Jessica scurried to the living room; and prepared to greet him. "You're home early," she said as he stepped through the door.

Ignoring her comment, he flung his jacket at the sofa, turned, and glared at her.

"Dinner's ready if you're hungry," she said, backing away.

He grimaced, reached back, and slammed the door shut. "What is it?" he grumbled before throwing his car keys on a table near the door. He kicked the cat to the wall and sauntered toward the kitchen. Abrasive grinding advised he was scraping his chair across the tiles toward the table.

A silent prayer was lifted as she hung his jacket on a hook, took a gulp of air, and hurried to the kitchen. "Today I made spaghetti," she said, but her gut was choking on fear. With heart pounding, and a quick glance at the floor, she heaped a large spoonful of noodles and sweet-smelling sauce onto a clean plate.

The earsplitting sound of metal scraping wood sent shivers up and down her spine. The next instant he bolted from the table, grabbed his plate and, in one quick jerk, hurled the contents to the ceiling.

Out of instinct she recoiled as meat and noodles crashed to the floor in a tangled heap. Her well-planned meal was now peeling off the splattered ceiling—leaving a sticky trail on its way down to the floor.

"Clean it up," he said. His teeth were gritted, and his fist clinched. "Clean it up now." He shook his fist, and more words erupted—all laced with profanity.

Frightened, she grabbed a soft cloth, stooped down, and began to wipe the oozing mess off the now greasy floor. In the background his eerie laughter kept her on edge.

The next instant a chair scraped the floor, and Trey began pacing the small kitchen, corner to corner. An avalanche of insults and profanity rolled from his lips as he mythically beat his fists together.

"You'd better get this mess cleaned up before I get back," he said. His words struck a new chord of terror in Jessica's heart and demanded instant obedience.

Glancing up, she noted a triumphant smirk on his face. When he caught her eye, his flashed. "I'm going to Hardee's and get some real food," he said, then turned on his heel and tramped to the next room.

"Where's my keys?" he asked. His words, spoken through gritted teeth, were explosive.

Terrorized, Jessica stood from her crouched position on the floor. "Right there on the table where you left them," she said. Her words were weak as the disaster around her was more than unsettling.

Heavy footsteps and the rattle of metal jarred her thoughts. A loud crash followed. "Keep this stuff out of my way," he said. His words were spat and seemed to reverberate through the house.

Her flight to the next room was swift.

Seventeen-month-old Josh was huddled near his new wheelie. The handlebar was bent, and the wheels dislocated. A gust of air blew past when a tightened fist swatted her face. "You'd better not buy him another one," Trey said, hands clinched.

Another prayer was lifted after he stomped to the door. He jerked it open, still uttering vulgarity, and stepped outside.

Josh's lips puckered as Jessica lifted him in her arms. With a gentle hand she rubbed his head followed by a kiss. Holding him close, she carried him to the bedroom.

"Where are my other two?" she asked, searching with her eyes. But she already knew and reached behind the bed for Ayden.

"You can come out now," she said. "Everything's going to be all right. I promise."

This is becoming more and more frequent," she whispered under her breath. The sound of running feet then caught her attention, and she turned as Kayla sprinted into the room, a questioning look on her face.

"Don't worry, Kayla. Daddy's gone now," Jessica said, and wrapped her arms around her daughter. "Always remember. God will take care of us."

Words recently read in the Bible popped into her mind. "The righteous cry out, and the LORD hears them; He delivers them from all their troubles" (Psalms 34:17) and "...be strong in the LORD and in his mighty power" (Ephesians 6:10). And she was comforted.

***

The following afternoon Trey's car rolled to the curb in front of the house and stopped. A huge lump formed in Jessica's throat, and she took a staggered breath.

"Please God," she whispered. "Help him be in a good mood. This love-hate scenario is getting harder and harder to understand."

She knew better than to ask where he had been all night. Deep breaths kept her calm as she recalled the difficulties of scrubbing spattered spaghetti from furniture, cabinets, and tiny crevices in the kitchen. "He may still be mad. I don't know—"

Loud thumping footsteps outside the kitchen door accelerated her need to seek cover. The next instant she slipped between the door and refrigerator, her place of refuge when Trey came home in a foul mood, which was more and more frequent as time revealed.

The children also reserved a place to hide. Ayden would scoot behind his bed, and Kayla would slip to her room, close the door, and play in silence. The baby just toddled around, often in harm's way. But that's just the way it was.

The next instant the door flung open, and a burst of

hot air gushed inside. Trey reached for Jessica and pulled her out. "What are you doing in that corner?" he asked.

"Looking out the window, I guess," she said. The corner of her shirt dangled after it dropped—twisted out of shape by nervous fingers as his mood was analyzed.

"Let's go downtown and get some ice cream," he said. He grabbed Kayla and swung her around. "What do you guys think?"

"Swing me too, Daddy. Swing me." And the younger ones lifted their arms, for once unafraid.

All Jessica could do was swallow her pride and brush her worries aside. "I guess we could," flowed from her lips as she pulled her skirt straight and pressed the wrinkles flat with her hands.

"Well, come on," Trey said. "Let's go." He hoisted Kayla to his shoulders and headed to the car. Ayden followed close behind.

A silent prayer was lifted as Jessica shifted Josh to her hip and locked the door. "Please God. Please help Trey not get mad at me, or the kids," she prayed. "And please, please keep us safe."

"I guess I'll put on my happy face," she whispered in Josh's tiny ear. "Who knows? Maybe things will get better after all."

Chapter Fourteen

Syrup of Ipecac

Jessica stood in the doorway, coat in hand, and waited for Trey to glance her way, realizing his attention span was as limited as his ability to respond. "Can you watch the kids a few minutes?" she asked. "We need milk and bread at the store."

"Noooo—don't throw the ball," he said, snapping his fingers as if to hurry the football players on the television screen. His muscles flexed in agitated response.

"Please. I'll be quick. It's too cold to drag them along."

"What?" He glanced up, but quickly refocused on the action at hand.

"I need to run to the store. I'll only be gone a few minutes," she said. "It's too cold to take the kids out in the snow."

"Okay, okay," he said, and waved his hand.

"They're playing in the bedroom," she said, and watched for a facial response. There was none.

"Are you listening?"

"Huh? Yeah."

"Are you sure? I'll take them with me if you don't want to watch them."

"Go on. They'll be fine."

"I'll hurry," she said. She ran to the car, jumped in, and sped to the store.

Working fast, she grabbed the needed items, and accelerated back home. But when she opened the kitchen door, her heart instantly leaped to her throat. "What are you eating," she asked, as waves of terror rippled through her torso.

Instead of waiting for an answer, she dropped her grocery bag on the counter, and grabbed the vitamin bottle Josh was holding. It was empty. A dark purple residue swathed the slobbery mouths of both boys—an instant indicator of possible drug overdose. She was instantly horrified.

In a panic she turned the bottle over and scanned a black label on the bottom warning consumers of iron poisoning if more than one vitamin was ingested each day. "Quick, call Poison Control," she said.

"I'm glad you're back," Trey said, meandering to the kitchen.

"You don't know?" she asked, hands on hips. "You didn't watch them, did you?"

"You were gone too long."

"I wasn't gone long at all," she said. She dropped her coat on a chair, turned, and grabbed the phone. "I can't believe you let them eat vitamins. Why didn't you give them a cookie, or something?"

"Why didn't you take them with you?"

"You promised to watch them."

"You had them. They're your problem, not mine," he said. He turned and left the room. Seconds later he returned with his coat.

"I just called Poison Control," she said, in measured tone. "They told me to give them both Syrup of Ipecac and make them throw up."

"What?"

"I hope it's not too late," she said, her voice trembling.

"What do you mean?"

"This syrup is for people who swallow poisons and need to throw them up."

Trey pulled his coat on, turned, and swung the kitchen door open. "Well, I'm not helping with that," he said. Cold air swept past when the door slammed shut.

Why won't he ever help me? Why is it always just me? But she didn't have time to worry. *What can I do? What can I do?*

Panicked, she ran to the bathroom and jerked the medicine cabinet open. Inside was a recently purchased bottle of Syrup of Ipecac.

Thank God. But how can I do this by myself?

"I'll call my sister-in-law," she said out loud. "Maybe she'll come over and help me."

Minutes later the bathroom sported a stained array of cotton towels covered in sticky fragments of purple residue. Exhausted, but triumphant, two tired women plopped down on separate kitchen chairs as two messy boys, shirts more stained than before, gobbled down bowls of cold cereal with their sister.

"At least they're okay," Jessica said, at last relieved.

"I'm glad I was home, and could help," Emily said, and smiled. Then she stood, and straightened the top button on her coat.

"Are you leaving?"

"I need to run," Emily said. "It's getting late."

"Thanks for helping," Jessica said, and a smile broke through. "Trey didn't want to."

"Well, it's over now," Emily said, "and everything is back to normal."

"Yes, I guess it is," Jessica said. She slid her chair back and stepped to the door—arms extended.

"Thanks, again, sister-in-law," she said, and gave Emily a quick hug. "I knew I could count on you. You're the best."

Chapter Fifteen

Skating to Disaster

Kayla and Ayden had been invited for an evening at the local skating rink. In fact, everyone at church able to don a pair of skates and tackle the challenges of wheel balancing, were going.

Designated for local churches, this event had been meticulously planned as Christian music would highlight the evening for skaters doing their rounds on the floor. Jessica, at Kayla's insistence, donned a pair of skates, ready to test her endurance with the other skaters.

Ayden, somewhat hesitant, edged out on the floor. Kayla, more exuberant than he, rolled ahead with the older kids. Josh, too young to skate, was spending time with Mrs. Williams, whom he called Granny.

But for Jessica, trying to stay balanced was a disaster in the making after the floor filled with skaters. As she ventured out on the floor, a caravan rushed past at break-neck speed. A strong arm struck her from behind, and she was instantly facing the floor. Her attempt to look steady on wheels had failed.

Splintering throbs from elbow to hand exploded through her left limb, and she cringed in pain. Leaving the floor was impossible as untold agony was sending her adrift with each beat of the heart. The torture only increased, and she began to slip in and out of consciousness. Oblivious to those around her, she was dragged from the floor.

"I'm going to faint," she whispered. "Somebody please help me. I'm going to faint."

"You need to go to the hospital," a voice said. "I think your arm is broken."

Realizing it was Ashley, Jessica opened her eyes. "What about the kids?" she asked. To herself she sounded muffled, and distant.

"We'll take them to the hospital with us," Ashley said.

Jessica watched through blurry eyes as Ashley grabbed several coats from a nearby chair and tossed them at a small group huddled near the door. After that her eyes refused to focus, and she drifted in and out of consciousness.

Minutes later Ashley grabbed her by the arm, helped her to stand, and pushed her to the car. Holding Ashley's arm, Jessica staggered through the hospital entrance, overcome with pain. The children followed close behind.

At the hospital she was helped into the emergency room. "Your left wrist is broken, and your elbow's fractured," the doctor said, pointing to X-rays pictured on the screen. But Jessica barely heard his words as darkness folded in around her.

Doctor and nurse, working together, pulled the bone sitting atop her hand back down into the wrist fragment, allowing the ridges of both arm and hand to meet.

Lamaze—Lamaze breaths. Oh God, it hurts.

"I'll seal the cast on your arm and elbow," the doctor said, when Jessica again opened her eyes.

Confused, she stared back.

"You'll need to wear this cast at least six weeks," he said.

Six weeks? How can I possibly live in a cast for six weeks?

"How do you feel?"

"Much better after you put my arm back together," she said, still winching in pain.

"Well, that's good," he said, a smile of sympathy on his face. "Take some aspirin for the pain, and I'll see you again in two weeks."

A long sigh escaped. But, somehow, she would manage. Everyone depended on her.

Once home she staggered through the door and

flopped down on a chair. Trey, consumed with the television, only grunted in response to her appearance.

"I broke my arm tonight," she said, and new tears formed.

He glanced up, but his eyes quickly returned to the television screen. "Well, you shouldn't have gone skating," he said. His voice lacked emotion.

"But it was church night, and the kids wanted to go. Besides, I didn't know I'd break my arm."

"Well, you're on your own," he said. He stood, face immobile, as Kayla and Ayden rushed through the door.

"Mama broke her arm," Kayla said, gasping for air as she pealed her coat off and threw it on the sofa.

"Pick it up and go to bed," Trey said. The sternness in his voice, and the look on his face, sent both children scampering to the back of the house.

"Where's the baby?" he asked.

Ashley's keeping him tonight," Jessica said. "She'll bring him by in the morning."

"So, what happened?"

"I was knocked down at the skating rink. When I fell, I broke my wrist, and fractured my elbow."

"Well, too bad for you," he said, and his head moved back and forth in a mocking way.

"It hurts," she said, holding the cast close. "The doctor told me to take aspirin for the pain. But I don't think it helps much."

"Well, get them yourself," he said.

His lack of emotion was hurtful; and she desired more concern. Still, she wasn't surprised at his disdain, although she dreaded the struggle as it was obvious, he truly didn't care. His next words jerked her back to reality.

"As for the kids," he said. "You had them." And he lunged at her. "You can take care of them." The next instant he and his keys were out the door. The engine roared, and he was gone—at least for a time.

"Thank God he's gone," she said under her breath as she stumbled to the kitchen gripping the cast. "Hey, kids anybody hungry?" And immediately they ran to the kitchen, bumping into each other on the way.

Ayden, with a nervous eye, glanced around the room. "Where's Daddy?" he asked.

"Gone somewhere," Jessica said, trying to smile. But it was impossible. The pain was just too great.

Responsibility was important, so she pressed on. "How about a quick snack before bedtime?"

Struggling for strength and composure, she ripped open a new bag of loaf bread with her free hand. With that same hand she slapped peanut butter and jelly on one slice and placed the other on top.

"I'm sorry it's sloppy," she said as she handed half to each child after it was haphazardly sliced. "I'll read one short story each, and then its bedtime, for real." Could she survive the pain? Six weeks was a very long time.

Her body sagged as elbow and wrist continued to throb. Having only one hand to work with was an early indication of what lay ahead.

***

It was impossible to lay flat. Jessica's arm and wrist throbbed incessantly—the pain so severe that the doctor's suggestion of sleeping in an upright position sounded realistic.

With wrist and arm still throbbing, she glanced around the room. Her eyes landed on Trey's recliner. It looked inviting enough. Besides, he wouldn't care if she slept in his bed, or not. With only one functioning hand, everything would be a challenge. Cast or no cast, life would continue—with or without assistance.

Taking care of the kids would be a real test. His family couldn't. It would be the same with church members. Again, it was just her—stuck between a rock and a hard place.

As expected, Trey didn't bat an eye at her struggles, or her pain. He didn't flinch even once at her hardship. His rhetorical laughter often resounded to the rooftops at her disposition. But his disdain for her temporary disability was noted and tucked away for future reference.

When she stepped outside the doctor's office following her six-week check-up, she allowed the tears to flow once more. She would be wearing the cast at least two more weeks. Her wrist wasn't healing fast enough to please the doctor.

Two weeks later and the doctor was all smiles. "I didn't want to tell you eight weeks ago," he said, "but I was afraid your wrist wouldn't heal properly. But it did. You're one lucky lady."

Chapter Sixteen

A Real Princess

Trey's actions brought Jessica on a run—this time to the back porch. "What are you doing?" she asked. But her words were more of a gasp. In his hand was a pistol.

"I don't want that dog anymore," he said, and his face was set. "Now get out of my way." He shoved her toward the wall and strode outside.

Princess, a beautiful blue-eyed Husky, began wagging her tail as he walked toward her but remained in her place as the attached chain was tangled. The dog, a gift to Trey from Rick, Emily's husband, only added to Jessica's workload. But a dog in chains was one thing. Killing her was another.

"Please don't kill her," Jessica said, catching up, and moving closer. She reached out, and gingerly touched his shoulder. "Princess didn't do anything wrong. She's a good dog."

"I said I don't want that dog anymore," he said, and his teeth gritted. He aimed the pistol, and a shot rang out. And instantly the dog let out a yelp.

Jessica's heart was now in her throat. How could he do such a thing?

"Please, stop," she said, and squeezed her eyes tight, trying to stop the flow of tears. "Please don't shoot again— please."

Sweat moistened her upper lip as the dog whimpered and pulled against the chains. She feared for the dog's life. "Please stop—don't kill her," she begged. "Please."

"Get out of my way," Trey said, and his eyes blazed. "Just get out of my way."

"Princess can be fixed," Jessica whispered. "I know she can. I'll take her to a vet. He'll remove the bullet. She'll be okay." But when another shot rang out, she grabbed her heart.

The dog thrashed about as blood gushed from her shattered thigh and drizzled to the ground. Jessica's heart was ripped to shreds. Yet before she could move, another bullet whirred past. This time it splintered a dogwood tree.

"Please stop," she said. "Please." And she leaned against the porch rail, still pleading. But the sound of death again whirled past, and a third bullet hit Princess square in the jaw.

"I'm out of bullets," Trey said, a cruel smirk on his face. He turned, shot Jessica a look of disdain, and hurried inside.

Jessica followed close behind and continued to beg for the dog's life. "What about Princess?" she asked. "She needs a doctor." She needed to stay calm—for the dog.

"I'm not doing anything for that dog," he said, and his lip curled. "I'll call Rick. He can finish her off."

"Please," Jessica said, and tears cascaded down her cheeks. She leaned against the wall for support. "Please."

"Don't do anything for that dog," he said. His tone demanded obedience. "I mean it. Leave her alone."

"What about the kids?"

"Don't tell the kids."

***

That evening, after everyone was in bed, Jessica's eyes refused to close. Princess, outside the bedroom window, whimpered and cried out through the night; and her heart was broken for her. Trey's actions were cruel, and she continued to struggle with the consequences.

What can I do without him turning on me? If I take Princess to the vet, I'll get in trouble. But if I do nothing, she'll die. What if he turns the gun on me?

The next day Rick dragged the dog to his truck and drove away. As the truck rambled past Jessica's heart broke in two. At least Princess would soon be out of her misery.

Words from the Bible filtered through her head. "A righteous man cares for the needs of his animal, but the kindest acts of the wicked are cruel" (Proverbs 12:10)

At that moment Jessica had yet to realize those canine eyes of blue would haunt her for years to come.

***

"I'm putting the big television on the boy's bureau," Trey said several days later as he strode down the hallway. In his arms was the oversized set.

"At least he's in a good mood for a change," Jessica whispered as she followed close behind. Then she glanced up at the tall furniture, and gasped.

"Don't you think this bureau is too high?" she asked. "The boys might pull it over when reaching up."

"Well, that's where it's going," Trey said. He lifted the set to the top before scooting it to the middle of the bureau. "I'm only doing this once. It had better stay put."

"I still think it's too tall for that television set."

"Don't worry about it," he said.

Minutes later a deafening crash echoed from down the hallway. Jessica dropped the laundry basket and raced back to the bedroom as she mentally prepared for the worst.

In the room she found Josh crawling out from beneath the bureau. A large gash on his forehead gushed blood, and he was crying incessantly. Ayden, mouth gaping wide, stood to the side.

The set itself lay in two pieces on the floor, tubes exposed, and the glass front cracked in several places. Assorted piles of clothing from lopsided, half-opened drawers haphazardly spilled to the floor in colorful piles of cotton.

Panicked, she grabbed a tee from an open drawer, and quickly dabbed the cut on Josh's head. "Trey. Where are you?" she asked, her voice rising. "Come here. Quick."

What is taking him so long?

Kayla was crying as Trey strolled in.

"Well, now they won't have a TV anymore, will

they?" he asked when he finally arrived.

Jessica chose to ignore his comment and pressed on. "I think Josh needs stitches," she said.

"You shouldn't have left them alone," Trey said, a sneer on his face. He turned and kicked the broken set a couple of times before stomping from the room.

"We need to take Josh to the emergency room," Jessica yelled. There was no answer.

"Aren't you going to help?"

"You take care of it," he yelled back. The door slammed, the car revved, and he was gone.

Josh continued to whimper as the cloth on his wound turned crimson red. Jessica took a deep breath, re-wrapped the cut, and lifted him in her arms.

"Ayden, hurry up and get in the car. Kayla, grab my purse, and hold the door open. I need to take your brother to the hospital."

"What happened to the love Trey and I once had?" she whispered. "Unforgettable moments contemplating new rendezvous together? Lips pursed, and ready to always kiss? Faithful and unified while serving God—anticipating our lives together with nothing but love to steer us forward. Where did it all go? Exactly when did it end?"

Overcome with emotion, Jessica cried bitter tears.

Chapter Seventeen

Obsessed

"Come in here," Trey said, his voice tense, his words demanding.

Dreading what was ahead, Jessica cautiously entered the living room. "I don't think this is going to be a good thing," she whispered.

Trey glanced up and motioned her over. "I rented a movie for tonight," he said.

"What movie?" she asked, and then looked down. The letters XXX leaped out from the cover of a black and white case, now opened, and positioned on the table. "Is this a porno movie?"

"Sit down," he said. "You need to watch it with me."

"I don't want to watch it," she said, and took two steps back. "I don't think you should either."

"I'm watching it, and so are you."

"No, I'm not."

"I said you are," he said. "Now get over here."

"I don't want to watch," she said, and edged toward the hallway.

"This will make our marriage better," he said. His eyes were glazed, and she noted a wine cooler in his hand.

He never drinks this stuff. What is he doing?

"What if the kids wake up?" she asked and glanced down the hall while her brain scrambled for more excuses.

"They won't."

"I really don't want to watch that movie," she said. "I'm tired." She tried to cover a yawn, but it went unnoticed. At this point, all she could do was pray he would leave her alone.

"Sit down," he said. His words were raw and

unfeeling, demanded compliance; and he waved a pre-made fist in the air.

"Please," she said, looking down in shame. "I don't like stuff like this."

"I said get over here," he said. "Now."

There wasn't any way around his demand. He meant exactly what he said, so she gingerly sat down on the edge of the sofa and dropped her head. When she glanced up, several pretty girls in the nude were masquerading across the screen. A man holding leather whips was chasing them through a large field.

Embarrassed, she turned away. Vulgarity was nothing she cared for. In fact, her shame was more for Trey who had recently become obsessed with pornography.

Words from the Bible filtered through her mind. "If I regard iniquity in her heart, the Lord will not hear" (Psalms 66:18)

Minutes later she was able to slip quietly from the room, unseen. At last glance Trey's eyes were still glued to the television screen.

***

"You're home early," Jessica said, dropping her keys on the counter. Josh climbed from her arms, grabbed a toy, and ran to the next room to play.

"Make me a sandwich," Trey said, coming closer.

"We just stepped in the door," Jessica said. "Ayden and Kayla are right behind me."

"I'm in a hurry," he said.

She slipped her jacket off and tossed it on a chair. "I need a quick bathroom break, and I'll be right back," she said.

"I said, make me a sandwich," he said, his words overriding hers."

"Just give me a minute."

"I don't have a minute," he said, but his voice was more of a growl. "I'm playing golf with that new minister this afternoon." And his fist pounded the table.

"I'm in a hurry," he said again. "Where's my clubs?"

The scowl on his face was disturbing, so Jessica pushed the children down the hall, and into a bedroom. "Where you left them," she said, upon her return. Trembling in fear, she lifted a loaf of bread.

"I said, fix me a sandwich," he yelled. He reached down and grabbed a large piece of splintered firewood from a metal container adjacent to the wood stove. The next instant the projectile grazed past Jessica's head as it jetted through the air.

Her hair fluttered in the draft when a colossal thud exploded in the room. Kayla rounded the corner just seconds before a second piece propelled toward Jessica. She bolted when he reached for another.

A third plunged through the air, grazing Jessica's head, and shattering the attached clock on the cook stove.

She touched her head, expecting blood. "Thank God he missed," she whispered.

A Bible verse instantly popped into her head. "You intended to harm me, but God intended it for good to accomplish what is now being done, the saving of many lives" (Genesis 50:20)

Days later Kayla returned home with a stack of school papers tucked away in her satchel. Thumbing · through the pile later that evening, Jessica noticed one circled in red. Kayla's account of the firewood incident had been noted by her first-grade teacher.

***

After things had somewhat settled, it was again time to fall in line with Trey's guidelines. Coats were donned, the door opened, and three hesitant children ambled past.

Minutes earlier, severe pain had flooded Jessica's head, as cluster migraines overtook her senses. Without success she tried to ease the throbs and reduce the maze of assorted geometric designs light sensitivity seemed to create. She was also nauseous.

Still, it didn't matter. Barely able to see one step in front of the other, she realized compliance to Trey's demand was her only recourse. An hour of driving lay ahead. Could she make it?

The children were headed to the car when she stumbled and missed a step on her descent from the porch. Her arm caught the rail just before she would have tumbled to the ground, and she was able to steady herself. "Thank God, I'm okay," she whispered.

Cold rain, now a steady downpour, pelted the ground as she staggered to the car. Once inside she turned the wipers on, slid the seatbelt over her chest, and felt around for the switch. "Kayla, make sure your brothers are strapped in," she said.

"Okay, Mama," Kayla said.

Barely able to see for herself, Jessica would need her assistance during the trip. Blinded by the migraine, she could only pray God would steer the car for them.

"Kayla, please close the car door."

"Do we have to go, Mama," Ayden asked.

"Your father insisted we drive up for the church picnic," Jessica said. "He said we had to be there."

"It takes forever to get to church anyway," Kayla said. She pulled out a game as was her habit, opened it, and passed out player pieces to her siblings.

The key was inserted, the car sputtered, and quietly purred from the curb. Seeing through the window was impossible, so Jessica twisted around, trying to find a more comfortable way to drive. "If I didn't know better, I'd say this picnic has been cancelled," she said.

The next instant Ayden smacked his sister on the back on the arm. "Mama, make Ayden stop," Kayla whined.

"Hey guys," Jessica said, rubbing her head, and squinting. "I'm having a hard time driving through this rain. I've got a terrible headache, and I need some peace and quiet on this trip. Please, work with me now."

Holding her head with one hand, she turned the car onto the main road, all the while praying for God's mercy, but realizing that Trey's wallops would be applied if they didn't show up.

"Oh, God. My head hurts too much. It's killing me," she said under her breath. "But why do I have these migraines?" The next instant a squirrel scooted across the lane, and the brakes slammed.

"Oh, God, please help me—help us," Jessica said. "I've probably been hit in the head too many times. I should be home, and in bed."

Often, when a migraine hit, she would stagger when walking. *But what if this is caused by another medical issue? Trey says I'm fine, even when my head throbs.*

"I hope it stops raining," Kayla said, interrupting her thoughts. "This picnic won't be any fun if it keeps raining."

"I know, honey. But it doesn't matter. We still have to be there."

"Why does Daddy make you go when you have a headache?" Ayden asked. "I get to stay home when I'm sick."

"I don't know," Jessica said, and a long sigh escaped. "But all of you need to stay as quiet as you can. I need to concentrate on the road. Between the rain and my blurry eyes, I can barely see a thing."

She continued to drive, squinting through the headache daze as the slickened roadway raced around her eyes.

If I don't drive faster, we'll lose time. But if I drive slower, we'll be late."

The car light coming toward them was blinding, and she instinctively swerved to keep from hitting the driver. After that, as a precaution, her acceleration slowed dramatically.

Oh, God—help us. Please be with us. Please keep us safe. But why is it necessary to always do exactly what Trey says? Well, I know. He'll beat me up if I don't.

***

After several harrowing episodes, the car rolled into the church parking lot, unscathed. Blinking tears away, Jessica stumbled from the car, thanking God for their safety.

I don't know how we made it on our own. God must have been watching over us, or we wouldn't be here now.

69

Chapter Eighteen

Weathering the Storm

Years of assaults and untold battery had Jessica worn down to the point she no longer cared for herself. Only the children kept her focused on what was truly important. Bruises and black eyes were normal for her on any given day.

But if Trey's family didn't care, and the church didn't notice, life would continue without recourse. Still, she realized this type of mistreatment couldn't be right. Although he sometimes apologized, on the inside she felt unimportant, and wasted.

Everyday conflicts were getting harder to understand. When Trey's actions fell short her accountability soared—finding his lost keys, accepting blame for his running late, to even what he wore. His wants and desires always overrode her needs. Compliance, however, was essential for maintaining the peace.

How she longed for someone to talk to that would understand her situation and tell her what to do. But no one seemed interested. After many prayers and untold deliberation, she decided to record Trey's rants. One day she might need proof.

The following evening, after he came through the door, she grabbed the recorder, switched it on, and quickly shoved it behind a towel.

"What do you think you're doing?" he asked, and strode toward her, hands clinched.

He saw me. What do I do now?

The next instant he jerked the machine from its hiding place and hurled it against the wall. Shattered pieces of plastic and metal littered the floor as he stepped closer.

"Just what are you trying to record?" he asked and lunged at her. "Now clean this mess up, and don't ever record me again." A fist plunged her shoulder, lifted, and came at her face.

Dodging his arm was futile, and she landed hard against the door where a foot roughly kicked her in the shins.

"You'd better not buy another recorder," he said. "If you do, I'll kill you."

Cold tiles reached up to meet her when a fist slammed her face. Blood dripped from her mouth, and her eye began to swell. He only laughed, stepped over her legs, and walked away.

Shaken and in pain, Jessica decided to report this assault to the police as soon as she had a chance. Calling them felt safe this time as Trey was at Emily's home, two doors down. Minutes later, after the call, action outside the window began to hold her attention. Police cars were parking at Emily's house, and she drew an instant sigh of relief.

"They're here," she whispered out loud. "At least this time they've responded."

Her heart began to pound, so she took a deep breath, grabbed her jacket, and rushed outside. Two policemen in blue uniforms stared at her from the steps of Emily's porch as she hurried down the street.

"At least they responded," she whispered again, then prepared to join the group. "Maybe they'll do something this time."

When she stepped closer, she noticed Mark, Ashley's husband, sitting on a wide porch swing, lazily swaying back and forth in the gentle breeze. His curly brown hair wafted in the breeze, and the look on his face was as unconcerned as the smile on his face. She could only speculate why he was at Emily's house, and not at work.

Coming closer, she glanced at Trey, who was calmly leaning against a porch rail quite relaxed, and unafraid. Emily stood silently in the doorway and stared at her. When she reached the group, Mark turned and pointed his finger directly at her. "She's the crazy one," he said.

Startled, she stopped midway up the steps. This wasn't what she had expected. Fear gripped her by the throat as she recalled the last time the police were alerted. No one responded. Later, when asked, the officer's response had been chilling. "We know your husband," he said. "He would never assault anyone."

The next instant she jolted back. One of the officers was speaking. "You need psychiatric help, lady," he said. "Can you justify your report?" And instantly her legs grew weak.

She glanced at Trey, who had a smirk on his face. "He punched me in the face and shoulders," she said, and fidgeted with her finger while waiting for a response.

"You look fine to me." The officer was scoffing. "I don't see any evidence of violence."

Trey's face revealed a look of achievement, as if taunting her. And since there was no recourse, Jessica turned away, and stumbled back down the road.

"The police didn't believe me after all," she whispered. "What else could I do but leave?"

Her face flamed as the truth of her reality was again swept under the rug. She was still on her own. Did she know even one person who would stand with her?

Her heart continued to pound as both frustration and disbelief flooded her mind. "So do not be afraid of them. There is nothing concealed that will not be disclosed or hidden that will not be made known" (Matthew 10:26)

There wasn't any doubt another beating was in her future.

***

The following week Mrs. Williams stopped by, prepared to watch the children for the afternoon. "The kids will be fine while you're gone," she said after sitting down on a porch chair. She dropped her purse on a concrete step, waved at the Kayla and Ayden in the sand box, and then asked, "Who's cutting your hair?"

"That new place in town," Jessica said. "I forgot the

name."

"The one Emily told you about?"

"Yes, that's the one."

"Will you stop and pick me up a loaf of bread on the way home?"

"I'll be glad to," Jessica said, and handed a toy to the baby.

"We're not going anywhere," Mrs. Williams said as she tousled her grandson's hair. "We'll be just fine playing in the sand, won't we honey?"

"I promise I won't be gone long," Jessica said. She grabbed her purse, kissed Josh again, and waved at the other two in the sandbox.

"Take your time," Mrs. Williams said.

"Thanks for helping me out."

"We'll wash my car in a little bit," Mrs. Williams said. "We'll stay busy."

"Bye for now," Jessica said, then hurried to the car. It was nice having a little time to herself.

"Your last name sounds familiar," the stylist said. "Are you related to that preacher who works at that furniture store in town?"

"You mean Trey?" And Jessica sucked in her breath. "Yes," she said. "That's the one."

Uneasy with the questions, Jessica shifted in the chair. "He's my husband," she said in response.

This is so embarrassing. I didn't know she knew him.

"Really?" the stylist asked, then stopped the trim, swirled the chair, and pumped it higher.

"Yes, really," Jessica said, but tried to conceal her red face.

"You know, I've heard so many good things about him," the stylist said.

How I wish I was somewhere else. I want to run away. If I could, I would.

"He's very good looking," she said, continuing her banter. "Dresses fine. Nice man—friendly too."

"Thanks."

"You don't know how lucky you are having him for a husband," she said.

Jessica glanced up but she said nothing. It was obvious this lady didn't have a clue.

Chapter Nineteen

Threats

Once home Jessica grabbed her grocery bag and scrambled from the car. But she stopped after noting several heads bobbing through the bay window. She slowed her pace to a crawl, opened the back door, and squeezed inside. She could only pray no one would see her.

Stealth was a recent technique she now used to gather information as her own advocate. Playing detective was serious business after she'd learned a cheating husband was the reason her life was more brutal than before. But why were members of Trey's family at her house? And why was he home? Was this a private family meeting she wasn't invited to? Or, perhaps, they were here to rally for her.

Using caution, she stepped into hearing distance. But she stopped dead in her tracks. Trey's voice was blasting from a few feet away. "If she doesn't stay out of my business," he said, "I swear I'll blow her brains out."

His words were revealing. Was he talking about her? Well, probably. Recent actions indicated his hatred was growing. She could only imagine his intent.

Joe, another brother-in-law, piped up. "You don't want to do that," he said.

What was he doing here?

Emily's voice cut in. "Now calm down, Trey," she said. "No need to even think about killing her. If you can't work things out, there's always the option of getting a divorce."

"She's been nosing around," Trey said. "She just needs to stay out of my life."

"What about the children?" Mrs. Williams asked.

"You don't want to repeat your father."

"I don't want to hear it," Trey said.

"Then don't be like him."

"You don't understand," he said, and his voice was harsh. The next instant a loud thud penetrated the wall. *That's probably him hitting something with his fist.*

"If she gets in my way, I promise I'll blow her brains out."

"That's crazy," Rick said. "You don't know what you're saying, man."

But Jessica knew exactly why Trey was angry. When driving past his work earlier that week she saw a woman she didn't know having what appeared to be an intimate conversation. And the way he responded every time the phone rang had also been noted. After the call he would take off in his car like a mad man. Probably meeting someone, and probably pre-planned.

It was impossible to count the times he'd left the house after the phone rang. When asked, he would threaten to kill her. Not to mention the time she stopped by a convenience store with the children, and he was there. No problem cursing her out—and in front of the children too.

"I'll blow your brains out," were Trey's favored words. Jessica had never taken him seriously. Maybe now she would. And what about that earring she'd found? Who did that belong to?

A blue, diamond shaped earring had been found in the floorboard of the car after the door was opened. When questioned, Trey had become angry, and insolent. "Are you having an affair?" her words were scripted.

"What do you think?" His words were acid, and his eyelid twitched.

"I think you are," she said.

"That's none of your business," he said.

"Then you are having an affair," she said, and her heartbeat accelerated.

"No, I'm not. Are you?" His words were insulting.

"I'm not the one with a strange earring."

"I don't know where it came from," he said. And, as

if dismissing her, he turned, and walked to the door.

"Well, you know it isn't mine. I don't wear earrings."

Reeling around, he gaited back, grabbed the earring, and shoved it in his pocket.

"Why did you—?"

"None of your business."

"I think it is."

"Shut up, Bitch," he said. "Just leave me alone." With a smirk he turned, grabbed his keys, and slammed the door on his way out. Seconds later the car cranked, and he was gone—again.

What about the time he was parked on the side of the road? Was he waiting to meet someone?

"What are you doing here?" she asked, after she stopped. But he waved her away—words of profanity streaming profusely from his mouth.

Terror had grabbed Jessica by the throat. His look was more than frightening, and she dreaded even the thought of later going home. But clues of his rendezvous kept showing up—and right in her face. All she had to do was watch for them. There was no way she could trust him now. And he wanted to blow her brains out?

She didn't have time to worry. Between him and three kids she was busy twenty-four seven. Still, she wanted him to know she was aware of his misdeeds. But was he? And would his family believe, after hearing his threats in person?

How many times had she mentioned her plight, and they simply blew it off? "Maybe he'll change." Everyone said it. Were those words of concern, or simply denial?

"Words are all I'll ever get from Trey's family," Jessica whispered softly.

She couldn't understand Trey's hatred. What had she ever done to deserve such contempt? And did he really intend to kill her? What about the kids? Didn't he care about them? Her mind was playing tricks, and forcing hurtful thoughts to overwhelm her sanity, and her mind.

That same evening Mrs. Williams decided to stay the night, and sleep on the sofa. Her plan—to see if her son acted out, or so she said. But nothing unusual happened until Trey went to the bedroom. Seconds later a thunderous clatter erupted, and Jessica dashed to the room. He was dumping her personal items in a trash can.

"Please don't throw my perfume away," she said, her hand on her heart. Her favorite outfit was also in pieces. An opened pair of scissors lay on the bed beside the clothing. The next instant a raw fist belted her in the face, then came at her shoulder. Writhing in pain, she dropped to the floor in a fetal position.

"You're such a bitch," he said.

When she tried to stand, he again shoved her down.

"Don't move," he said. "Don't you dare move."

She cringed, and drew even deeper into herself, not knowing what he would do next, but praying her mother-in-law would come in the room.

Minutes later, when Trey sat down on the bed, Jessica was able to stand. She leaned against the wall for support, praying he wouldn't notice. Her eye was swelling so she reached up and touched the puffy lid. She knew it was also turning black.

Her legs felt wobbly. In fact, her entire body was weak. But he didn't care. He just flopped on the bed and howled with laughter.

Internally she struggled with what to do, still hoping Mrs. Williams would soon come to her rescue. After realizing she wasn't, she cautiously edged from the room. Coarse hilarity followed as she stumbled back down the hall.

When she reached the living room, Mrs. Williams glanced up from where she sat on the edge of the sofa, as if waiting. "He just hit me," Jessica said, holding her shattered jaw, and limping.

"I don't know that he hit you," Mrs. Williams said.

"But he did."

"I don't know that he did," she said. "I didn't see him do it."

Chapter Twenty

Tennis Partner

"I'm taking the day off," Trey said. He jerked the closet door open and removed a colorful sports shirt. He tucked it into a new pair of white shorts, grabbed a thin tennis sweater from the opening, and casually slung it over his shoulder.

Jessica couldn't help but giggle as he strutted through the house, admiring his new attire. Still, he wasn't easily forthcoming, and she couldn't help but wonder what he was up to. But she had her suspicions.

"I'll be gone all morning," he said, as if in a hurry. He grabbed his keys off the counter and swiveled to the door. He glanced at her, then glanced around for another glimpse of his back side.

"Where are you going?" she asked.

"None of your business," he shot back.

"It is my business," she said, following close behind.

"Not really," he said, but continued his stride to the car. "I'm playing tennis, if you must know."

"What tennis court?" she asked, stepping closer.

"You know which one," he said, then rolled the window half-way down after slamming the door. "You'd better not follow me either, if you know what's good for you."

"What do you mean?"

"I said you'd better not follow me if you know what's good for you."

"What—"

"If you come where I'm playing tennis," he said, and his jaw was set. "If you do, I'll kill you."

She knew he meant business, but shook off her

79

apprehension, and hurried back to the house. The sound of his revved-up engine roared in her ear as she opened the door. She turned her head just in time to glimpse the tail end of his red sedan as it rounded the corner, only to disappear in a puff of smoke.

In the past she would say a prayer for her husband's safety. But now, after all she'd been through, she couldn't honestly pray those words. She no longer wanted him back.

On the other hand, her curiosity was getting the best of her. Maybe she would play detective once more and take the kids for a short ride. It was time to learn what Trey was up to.

A few minutes later Jessica and the children were in the car, and on their way to the designated tennis court.

In the distance a much younger woman flagged a racket back and forth as she swiveled toward a yellow tennis ball. Her skirt bared slim legs to the hip and whipped about in the gentle breeze. Jessica wasn't surprised. In fact, she had expected as much.

She parked the car, cut the engine, and stared out the car window, arms crossed. Minutes later Trey glanced in their direction, turned, and quickly barged toward the car. His already reddened cheeks flamed, and he wiped a sweaty residue from his brow.

Fear instantly consumed Jessica, and she took a ragged breath—preparing for the onslaught coming at her. Her boldness would certainly cost her. Still, she didn't regret seeing Trey's tennis partner for herself. At least she deserved that much.

"You piece of shit," he said, and continued to spit more vulgar, derogating words—all through clinched teeth. "I warned you not to come here."

She drew a staggered breath but remained silent, trying to stay calm.

"Get these kids out of here," he said, and pointed at their three gazing out the car window. His next words were barked. "Don't ever come back here, Bitch. I'll kill you if you do."

Killing her must certainly be on his mind. He had

been tormenting her for days with those words.

She sighed as he spun on his heel, turned, and marched back to the tennis court. Seconds later he and his partner were again twisting and swaying to the beat of tennis rackets.

On the way home Jessica's head began to droop as the reality of her investigation started to sink in, and she wiped a tear away. Trey was openly betraying their marriage vows without a second thought.

That evening Trey's foul mouth and arrogant mood only excelled. "You're just a piece of trash," he shouted after his return home. He strode forward, and from his lips jetted a stream of spit that splashed Jessica in the face. The next instant she was sprawled on the floor.

"Who gave you permission to come by the tennis court?" he asked.

"No—no one."

"Don't you ever follow me again," he barked.

Jessica licked her lips, reached up and touched her face. Splotches of sticky red remained on the tips of her fingers.

"You know what else?" he asked, his breath hot on her neck. "I've been with lots of women, and they're all better than you."

How can he say that to me? More women than his tennis partner?

He stood, arms folded, and stared down. "Got a problem?"

Still cowering, she pulled herself up, but remained frightened.

"I can treat you any way I want, and you can't do one thing about it" he said, and his torso whipped back and forth as if mocking her. "So, what do you have to say about that?"

"I don't know," she said, still cowering.

His hand formed another fist, ready to pelt her again.

"Please don't," she said, glancing up, and then down again.

"You know why I'm not worried?" he asked. His words purred as they mocked.

The word "No," quietly slipped from her lips.

"Because we're married, and we'll always be married."

She remained silent. His look was toxic, and she instinctively recoiled.

All I wanted was a loving husband. And now, what do I have?

"I can treat you any way I want," he said again, and his lips curled. "You'll never leave me."

It was best if she remained silent. His anger could easily leave her in a heap of disfigurement. He was in his blame game again. She would just ride it out until he calmed down.

After years of practice, she understood that staying quiet worked best when he played his mind games. So, she clamped her lips tight, and wrapped her arms around her chest—just in case.

***

"Someone at work cashed in their retirement," Trey said two days later. "I think I'll do the same thing."

For a moment Jessica stopped washing the dishes—somewhat interested, but not much. "Why?" she asked. Her words were guarded.

"So we can get out of debt," he said. And, for the first time in a long time, he sounded pleased.

"How much money?" she asked.

"A few thousand."

The thought of being debt-free whirred through her mind. Since his resignation as church pastor, Trey was employed full-time at a furniture store nearby. But money was still hard come by, and an added stress for her.

She was thankful his masquerade as church pastor had ended some time before. Perhaps after things were paid off, she could leave the marriage debt free. By now she was more than ready. Deceived, betrayed, and battered, yet the claws of abuse still held her deep within its guttural clutch. Perhaps—and a flicker of hope stirred within her shattered heart.

"We'll pay everything off, and split what's left—fifty-fifty," he said. He picked up a pencil and began tapping the tabletop. "Get me some paper."

Jessica grabbed a notepad and handed it to him.

"What all do we owe?" he asked, and the tapping stopped. "Let's make a list."

Thinking fast, she quoted their debt from memory. After jotting down some numbers, he began to rummage through a kitchen drawer. "Where's the calculator?" he asked.

"In the desk—over here," she said, and handed it to him. The sound of fingers tapping keys was encouraging, and she almost smiled.

"This should be enough to pay off our credit cards, one car, and the appliances," he said.

"Are you sure cashing in your retirement is what you want to do?"

"Everybody's doing it," he said, and the tapping stopped. "Besides, it's an easy way out of debt."

"I'm not so sure," she said. But it was his money. He should be the one to decide how it was spent. When decisions were questioned, he would become angry. For now, trusting his opinion would be best.

Keeping things in perspective would also keep alive the suspicion he might change his mind. Since he was openly fooling around, what were his true intentions?

He stood, then abruptly sat back down. "It only takes a couple of weeks to get the money," he said.

"Really?" But Jessica refused to get excited. Trey's ideas kept her way too stressed to think beyond the moment. Already a lifetime of hopes had been crushed.

It was hard seeing beyond a crisis, so she clutched at the thought of a brighter day, and tried to believe a better future could exist, but far in the distance. Trey's subdued manner was also confusing, so she decided to simply stay out of his way. Had he had a change of heart? Was he repentant? She could only pray it was so.

Chapter Twenty-One

Christmas Fiasco

Christmas was just around the corner, but Jessica dreaded the season. Over the years she'd learned to squelch her feelings, realizing it was best to remain complacent, and detached. Even the thought of a holiday was challenging.

Nothing ever changed in the scheme of things although, after several battering episodes, her physical appearance was somewhat questionable. Not only was she exhausted, but also depressed. For her, the joy of the season was dead. Looking the part of a happy wife was tiring as her heart was more than broken.

What did her marriage offer that was worth preserving? She had husband who no longer strove to be a Christian, much less a minister of the gospel. His roving eye easily captured the attention of women, and he gleefully flaunted his excursions in her face without batting an eye. His attempt to disguise the deception hadn't mislead Jessica. It had been easy, after a few investigative measures, to uncover his secrets.

She dressed in silence for Trey's company party, overcome with the pressure of the unknown. Nervous reservations had surfaced. The invitation, a personal request from his female employer, had been insulting.

But he was excited over the upcoming festivity, and insisted Jessica attend with him. She dreaded the ruse, and desired to stay at home. He was adamant, however, so she prepared for the party, and prayed she could endure the evening.

Would anyone at the party be aware that Trey and the hostess had been seen together at a local motel? What if the gossip was true? If so, how should she react? Secretly she wondered how the charade would play out. Maybe she could catch him in his own lies.

The children would be staying with Granny—one less worry on her mind.

***

Jessica and Trey climbed the short steps of a nice brick home, and he rang the doorbell. Her heart suddenly skipped a beat, and she drew a deep breath. Was she dressed well enough? It was doubtful as her wardrobe was limited. But when a sparkling lady in evening attire opened the door, she instantly she felt out of place. And who wouldn't be swayed by someone this dazzling?

As the evening progressed, she found herself sitting on a sofa with the woman's husband, whose breath reeked of alcohol. He was non-talkative, and consumed glass after glass of liquor without batting an eye.

His initial beverage offer had been declined. Instead, she sipped a wine glass full of sprite, and remained a silent observer.

What was the man trying to cover up? And why would anyone drink so heavily?

Later she noticed Trey and the hostess together, sitting in a cozy nook. As she watched they leaned into each other, deep in conversation. How easily this had happened. She couldn't keep her eyes off the two. His glass had been re-filled several times. Was he also getting plastered?

Boredom, disgust, and disappointment held her bound. Would this evening never end? She would rather be home than a partner to this weird fiasco.

***

After midnight Trey staggered off the front steps, and into the yard. Jessica followed close behind. But when his silly, high-pitched laughter echoed through the courtyard, she turned red, and sighed with embarrassment. The next instant he reeled around and faced the hostess. "It's been funny," he said. "Thanks for the inanition."

Was he drunk? Never had ever she seen Trey in this

way, so she stood in her place, both embarrassed and overwhelmed. Then, as if on cue, he began to throw up in the yard. His face turned pale, and he stank of alcohol and vomit.

How much more disgusting could he get? How much more degrading can this be?

She reached inside her purse and searched for a set of car keys. "I'm driving," she said, and waved them in the air.

Trey complied without hesitation, although he staggered on his way to the passenger side of the car. "I knew I'd need a driver," he said, a giggle in his throat. "That's the only reason I brought you along." His words were slurred.

God help me.

Once home Jessica parked the car, helped Trey inside, and into bed, thankful the evening was finally over. For once his true character as liar, cheat, and drunkard had been exposed. This wasn't the preacher man she had married. This was a complete stranger.

***

Three days later Trey sauntered into the kitchen holding Kayla by the hand. "I'm leaving for a while," he said looking straight at Jessica, "and I'm taking her with me."

Trey never took the kids anywhere. Where was he going this time? She reached for Kayla but ducked when he took a swat at her. Then she bristled as deep fear overwhelmed her mind. "No, please don't take her," she said, hands outstretched.

"Shut up," he said, and his eyebrows lifted in a menacing way. The sound of his voice was strong, and she cowered in uncertainty and dread. With a smirk he shoved her aside and stepped outside.

After hoisting Kayla to his shoulders, he walked to the car, and they both climbed in. And immediately they were gone.

Where was he taking her this late in the afternoon?

Jessica's hands shook uncontrollably as fear overcame her senses.

***

The face on the clock registered ten-thirty-eight as darkness immersed the outside—just as fear immersed Jessica's heart. The next instant the door opened, and she leaped from the sofa. She sprinted to the kitchen as Trey stepped inside. Kayla was asleep in his arms.

Overcome with emotion, Jessica released a huge sigh of relief. But she shook herself free of restless anxieties and followed Trey into Kayla's bedroom.

She stood in silence as he placed Kayla on the bed, using more care than ever before seen from him. Then, without saying one word, he headed to the living room. Television voices instantly flooded the air and filled the room with noise.

Jessica tucked Kayla under the cover, grateful she was again safe at home.

The following day Kayla provided details of visiting a pretty lady's house where she was given candy and ice-cream. A red balloon drifting through the living-room was another gift from the same woman.

Jessica could only speculate who the mystery lady was, but supposed it was Trey's female boss. Yet she dared not say a word. Fear of the unknown flooded her mind as she realized her life could be in more danger than ever before.

***

Days following the party and Trey again threatened to kill her. But by this time, she was afraid of her own shadow, and feared retaliation if she tried defending herself. When will it end? And did she dare learn more about the darker side of her husband's life? Although abused, lied to, and cheated on, she still desired the missing elements of a concrete marriage—love, respect, and trust.

Growing up she never once saw a man hit a woman.

But in her own marriage, the necessity of hiding secrets while masquerading under the guise of happiness was essential.

Had she been too sheltered as a child to understand that a bad marriage could exist? She had lived a secluded life on a farm, protected from the world outside by hard labor, few necessities, and even fewer friends.

Lacking a social network she could trust was a huge disadvantage as her only associates were Trey's family, and the people she attended church with. But they remained uninterested, or unaware that she was a battered woman. So, she withdrew even further into herself, and continued to live in silence.

Chapter Twenty-Two

Stolen Sanity

The sun dipped behind the horizon as Jessica sat alone, perched on an outside porch step, head bent over. The children were asleep, allowing time to think of ways to escape her broken marriage. Whatever it took, she was now game. Life was getting more dangerous with each passing day. But most of all the children needed a more peaceful home life.

"He causes His sun to rise on the evil and the good and sends rain on the righteous and the unrighteous" (Matthew 5:45)

"Thank you, Jesus, for reminding me of this verse."

She pulled her coat close, and an inner strength seemed to surge. She realized this was the perfect time to seriously plan her getaway. But when should she leave? And how? No, she couldn't just leave. She would need to escape.

God, please help me. I need your help.

"Where are you?"

Her body twitched in response to Trey's insistent tone, and a weathered flowerpot tilted and spilled sending dry dirt and a dead geranium tumbling down the porch steps.

An overwhelming fear gripped her by the throat. Last evening's assault was still fresh in her mind, and she was instantly conflicted on how to respond.

He flopped down on a nearby chair as disgraceful terms demeaning her very existence tumbled nonstop from his lips. She instinctively cowered beneath his gaze.

What will he now do?

He wasn't drunk as most would expect from

someone so verbal. For the most part he didn't drink. Admired and respected all over town as a minister of the gospel, he maintained a solid and irreproachable label. No one dared think less of him than who he portrayed himself to be.

He's called me these same names many times. Later he'll say he's sorry, and that would be the end of it—as far as he's concerned. Was this what my dad meant when he said, "You've made your bed, now sleep in it?"

The evening shadows seemed indifferent to Trey's arrogant laugh as they sifted in the gentle breeze. But for Jessica, the sound was just pure evil.

"If you're thinking about leaving me, well—don't even think about it," he said. His words, spoken through gritted teeth, pierced her heart; and she bristled.

How could he possibly know I was planning to leave him?

The crickets chirped an evening croon as the day's lingering warmth closed in around them. His next words jerked her back to reality. "If you leave, I'm keeping the kids."

Her hands began to quiver, and she sucked in her breath. Dread then summoned a nightmare of emotions. What more could he say?

"Don't even think about taking them away from me," he said. His words were laced with profanity.

I'm not a lying whore.

"You'll never take my kids from me."

You don't care about your kids.

"If you do, I'll kidnap them back, and you'll never see them again."

His words were strong, and slapped Jessica in the face. Out of habit she recoiled and withdrew even further into herself. The next instant waves of terror ripped through her torso, and her heart pulsated wildly as it exploded into her extremities.

Could he really keep the kids if I left him? And would he?

The twilight's fading tranquility failed to ignite a

sense of harmony inside her despairing soul.

"You won't get anything in the house either, you ugly bitch. Don't even try." His teeth were still gritted.

Was he serious, or just playing another mind game? And would a judge let him to keep the kids if they went to court?

Jessica's twisted hands were now drenched, and her forehead furrowed, in response to Trey's temperament. But instead of responding she became a coward—afraid to speak, or even defend herself.

"I'll kill you before I let you have my kids," he said. His words cut like a knife.

Afraid to move, or even speak, she remained rigid on the step as dreams of a blissful life began to slowly dissolve—dreams of escaping her abuser—dreams of keeping the children safe from harm.

Her cold hands oozed a sweaty residue, and she gripped them tight. Her nails dug deep into her palms creating trickles of blood mingled with sweat. An adage then came to mind. Hold your hands and you will remain calm, and relaxed. She squeezed them again, but tighter this time, and prayed those words were true.

"Besides, everybody thinks you're the one with the problem," he said.

His words jarred her thoughts. But he was right. No one believed he was a wife beater. Although every member in his family, at one time or another, heard him say he was going to kill her, they chose to ignore his threat. Others believed he was a wonderful husband, and father.

New words, raw and twisted, slammed her thoughts. Vile threats, mixed with vulgar oaths, rolled from his lips nonstop, and his fists beat together as if anticipating a brawl. From experience Jessica knew Trey intended to do exactly what he said. His words stung far worse than a fist.

What does a snaggle-toothed whore look like anyway?

Tears instantly formed and trickled down her cheek. But she quickly wiped them away. She dared not allow him the pleasure of her concern. What would he then do? If she showed fear, she was weak.

"He's never cared about the kids," she whispered. "Why now? And does he really intend to do everything he said? Or is he just saying those things to scare me?"

From instinct she stiffened, recalling many graphic injuries from the night before.

Would tonight be the same? Could she endure more cruelty? And dare she risk his threats for her freedom?

He stood, his silhouette tall and menacing in the moonlight. "Go ahead. Pack your bags and leave," he said. "But the kids aren't going with you."

No matter the circumstance, she would never leave without them. All she had, at this point, was God's word to keep her steady.

"...but those who hope in the LORD will renew their strength. They will soar on wings like eagles; they will run and not grow weary, they will walk and not be faint" (Isaiah 40:31)

If she didn't leave Trey, she was doomed. He would one day kill her, and the children wouldn't have a mother. He would go to jail, and they would be raised by someone else. Her refusal to give up would be a challenge. Yet in her heart of hearts, she felt that God would, somehow, see her through.

Fear spurred her forward as words from the Bible filled her heart with hope. "Weeping may endure for a night, but joy comes in the morning" (Psalms 30:5)

Her insides churned as Trey pelted her with more chilling profanity. Did he have no respect? Did he have no remorse?

"God, strike me dead." Blasphemous words, spoken in anger, struck a new chord of horror in her heart.

How could he say such things in front of God and man, and then preach in a church somewhere on Sunday?

She would never understand his logic. In fact, she had long ago stopped trying.

Chapter Twenty-Three

The Final Straw

Living on the edge, for Jessica, had been a pattern of accepted brutality, rage, and assault. Trey's insensitivity made life a torturous nightmare. Routine battering and spiteful comments were the norm on any given day. But the children remained oblivious to undercurrent problems in the home. They scooted about early Christmas morning playing with new toys and an array of assorted gift

Thank God.

Minutes later Trey sauntered into the room carrying an unwrapped attaché case. He leaned over and handed it Jessica. But his arrogance brought tears to her eyes. Why would he give her a gift that someone, most likely, had purchased for him? She didn't need the case. What would she do with it?

Nothing was expected, or desired, from him. Recent assaults were too raw—too painful—too unforgettable. His nature disallowed gift giving so his generosity was an undesired novelty. Her surprise was an inadequate term for this unexpected bombshell. Instead, preparation for what was ahead kept her cautious, and focused.

Her recently obtained job was part of a plan to leave the marriage. The emergency room was first on her agenda after returning to work. Injuries from the weekend needed treatment, and documentation—also essential for the plan to work. But as far as Trey was concerned, her injuries were non-existent. His attitude illustrated he simply wanted them to disappear.

Jessica, on the other hand, was determined to obtain documentation. She was confident Trey's infidelity, assaults, and hatred would only increase if given the opportunity. Her one desire was to get her life back.

Later that afternoon, as she and Kayla sat on the floor dressing Barbie's, Trey meandered over to their corner, and stopped in front of them. "Hey, you," he said, looking down. In his hand was the attaché. "I think I'll just keep this for myself." And he tapped the case with his fingers. "You don't deserve it."

***

A few days after Christmas Trey sat in his car racing the engine again and again as if a teenager. The engine sputtered, tires squealed, and he was out of range.

His cashed-in retirement had finally arrived in the mail. In a flurry he scooped it up, promising to put the entire amount in the bank. Jessica could only pray he would.

Should she trust him, or ignore his actions? Every muscle in her body tensed as, once again, fear overtook her senses. What if he left town without giving her a dime?

In the back of her mind, plans to leave the marriage were escalating. Once school was out for the summer she would go. Less disruption for the children would make the transition easier to accomplish. Already, part of her paycheck had been stashed away.

With head bowed, and eyes closed, she prayed Trey would allow them to leave when the time came.

***

That evening, as darkness closed in around them, harsh blows began to pound Jessica from all directions. The children, asleep in their beds, were hopefully immune to the brutality that was occurring. But why was Trey mad? It was impossible to determine the reason.

Her body shook and quivered as she ducked, trying to avoid the worst of the pummels. More than frightened, she dropped to the floor in a fetal position, and covered herself as best she could. What else could she do? Should she run for help? Could she?

But why was Trey angry? The minute he'd entered

the room she felt his rage. And there was nothing she could do to dodge the hostility. Simply said, she was trapped.

When a booted foot kicked her in the side she instinctively recoiled. Still on the floor, she ducked her head, and wrapped already swollen arms around her torso. Amid the chaos, she realized she was in for the beating of a lifetime.

Oh, God, help me. Am I going to die this time?

An agonizing onslaught of kicks and punches, followed by harsh oaths, pelted her from all directions.

Who can help me? It's the middle of the night. All the neighbors are asleep.

Again, and again Trey's heavy boot hammered Jessica's stomach and thighs. Fresh blood oozed from swollen lips when a rigid fist crushed her face. His actions simply spoke his heart.

Oh God. Help me! Will I die right here on the floor? Will anybody know—or care?

After a short respite Trey turned and walked to the next room.

Jessica stood on wobbly legs, staggered to the side door, and slipped through the opening. She stumbled down the steps, and into the yard, not looking back. Adrenalin propelled her forward, as new strength ruptured her emotions. "Help! Help! Somebody, help me!"

A streetlight nearby cast eerie shadows on several cars parked out front, but the houses remained dark, and hushed. No one came to the door. No light illuminated. No one responded to her cry. The only sound in the obscure darkness was a dog barking in the distance. All was quiet—too quiet for a Friday night.

Her body quivered when Trey grabbed her from behind. An onslaught of profanity then rolled from his guarded lips, making his toned-down words even more sinister.

Should I struggle, or give in?

As hair was jerked, and teeth cracked, she released a labored scream. His breath, hot on her neck, indicated an out-of-control rage.

Strands of blooded curls floated to the ground as the burn of roughened asphalt ripped her feet to shreds. Her body, no longer hers, throbbed and blazed in the transit moonlight. "Help! Help! Somebody, help me!"

Her voice was instantly stifled. Still, she continued to struggle, realizing this could be her last chance to survive.

"Shut up. Shut up," he said through gritted teeth as raw nails clawed soft flesh, digging new abrasions into already inflamed limbs.

Her breath, once heavy and labored, became shallow as she fought for her very life. Breaking free was impossible.

As exposed legs scraped uneven cement steps, she cried out in agony. Once in the house, the tepid floor beneath her rose to meet her when Trey dumped her from his arms. Her escape had failed.

Fresh profanity rolled from his lips as another punch caught her off guard. His feet were engaged once more and hammered her body again and again with brute force. But the curses spewing from his mouth were words she would never utter, and certainly not who she was on the inside. His vulgarity was as crude and degrading as a discarded piece of trash.

Well, that's what he calls me—Trash.

"But I'm not."

***

No longer could Jessica deny Trey's aggressive assaults coming against her. Her very existence had been based on restrictions and damaging outcomes. Could she, somehow, change the result?

Neglected and abused as a child, immaturity and ignorance reigned. Finding her place in society was also dwarfed as manipulation from emotional demons created tremendous fear and confusion.

Ignorance and wrongful trust had forced blind mistakes. ow her children were growing up in an unhealthy and dysfunctional environment. Already they had witnessed more mistreatment, manipulation, and exploitation than most.

Training received as a child restrained verbal or physical retaliation for Jessica. Emotional support from church and family had delayed her escape and reinforced the notion that deflecting Trey's assaults was futile. Still, she believed God's word would keep her grounded.

He would be her solid rock, her shield, and her deliverer. His divine guidance would provide the inner strength needed to hold firm her decision to leave her wasted marriage and strike out on her own.

A perfect breakaway would fall into place when she ultimately stepped away. Of this she firmly believed because "The LORD makes firm the steps of the one who delights in him; though he may stumble, he will not fall, for the LORD upholds him with His hand" (Psalms 37:23,24)

"The LORD is my light and my salvation; whom shall I fear? The LORD is the strength of my life; of whom shall I be afraid?" (Psalms 27:1)

Chapter Twenty-Four

End of the Beginning

The following day Trey pulled out his wallet completely ignoring the ramifications of his assault on Jessica the previous night. "It's time to divide the retirement money I cashed in," he said.

He must be feeling guilty, or maybe—for once—he's keeping his word.

"Our outstanding debt has been paid" he said. In a gesture of compliance, he reached out and handed Jessica a handful of cash. "I promised we'd split what's left. You get two thousand, and I get two."

"Thanks," she said, and a sliver of a smile formed on swollen lips. Her words were grateful as she shoved the loose bills into her purse.

Thank you, God.

***

"Come in," Jessica said. Her smile crooked as the ravages of abuse took center stage.

"How did you get all those scrapes and black eyes?" Emily asked, after stepping through the door. "What happened?"

Jessica shrugged her shoulders. Trey was in the room.

"Well, you need a doctor," Emily said. "I'll take you."

"She doesn't need a doctor," Trey said, standing solid in the hallway.

"I think she does."

"Well, she's not going to see one," he said, and turned away.

"Why not?"

"She deserves what she gets," he said in dry undertones.

Emily stepped forward and followed Trey down the hall. "What did you just say?" she asked.

"Nothing—nothing you need to know."

"Did you hit her?"

"Leave us alone," he said, turning around.

"She really needs a doctor," Emily said, and pointed at Jessica. "Just look at her."

"Don't you dare take her to the doctor," he said. "Leave her alone. She's fine."

"I'll take you to the doctor," she said, again glancing at Jessica. "Just say the word."

"Trey doesn't want you to," Jessica said, and her eyes darted away. "I'm okay, really. I only have a few bruises."

"Did he hit you?"

"Well—"

"You can go home now," Trey said, and waved his sister away. "She's fine."

She glanced at Jessica's bandages, and blackened eyes. "You need a doctor," she said.

Jessica twisted the hem of her shirt. "I'll be okay," she managed to say.

Trey turned, looked directly at Jessica, then raised an eyebrow. In response she lowered her head.

"She's not going to any doctor," he said, frowning at his sister. "Just go on home."

Emily glanced at Jessica once more. "If you change your mind," she said, "let me know."

All Jessica could do was shrug and turn away.

Emily glanced at Trey. Then she walked out the door.

Jessica stumbled to the refrigerator. It was time to get lunch.

I can barely walk. I can hardly move. Oh, God, everything hurts—everything.

She tried to suck up the pain, but it was impossible.

"I've never hurt so much after a beating," she

whispered. "He could have killed me. At least I'm still alive."

Trey refused to leave her alone. He kept stepping in her way as if afraid she would try to leave. But she ignored his actions as she shuffled around re-heating a pot of the kid's favorite soup. She wanted to stay clear of him. She feared for her life.

Her keys had been stolen, her mobility removed, and her spirit crushed. What more could he do?

I'll just pretend everything's fine and take care of the kids as normal. Nothing stops just because I'm injured.

***

"Why don't you move in with me until Trey settles down?" Mrs. Williams asked after stopping by the house later that evening.

More than eager to get away, Jessica accepted her offer without a second thought.

"Jessica's going home with me for a couple of days," Mrs. Williams said, "and the kids." Then she patted Trey on the shoulder.

Clothes were packed, under Trey's direction. Minutes later, Jessica and the children were walking out the door. For once he agreed they needed time apart.

***

Monday arrived, and not soon enough, as far as Jessica was concerned. "Time to get dressed," she said, again glancing at the clock. 'Hurry up, kids. You have school today."

As she dressed, she tried to visualize her day. A loose-fitting skirt would look best for hiding limps. Flat shoes would benefit if she stumbled while climbing stairs. And thank God for make-up. Her secret stash always seemed to come in handy. When applied, she turned and stared hard in the mirror. Staring back was a drained, battered, and scared looking woman.

Three-year-old Josh suddenly ran past, and instant joy flooded her injured soul. "What are you and Granny doing today?" she asked, giving him a squeeze.

"Watching 'toons," he said, and blew her a kiss before racing to the next room.

Minutes later she was driving Kayla and Ayden to school.

***

Hoping no one would notice, Jessica slipped into her office, and closed the door. She propped her leg on a stool beneath the desk and prayed her unkempt appearance would remain hidden. And so began the day. When the clock struck noon, she slipped down the stairs, praying no one would notice. However, a couple of salesmen saw her, and broke the silence.

"What's going on?" one asked. "You look like you've been knocked around the block."

At first, she started to cover for Trey, as usual. Then she decided it was best to reveal the ruse. "My husband beat me up this past week-end," she said, and lowered her head.

"What a jerk. Anything I can do?"

"If Trey comes around, please—please don't let him come upstairs to my office."

"Don't worry," he said, and smiled. "He won't come anywhere near you. I promise."

"Thank you," she said. She turned away and limped her way to the parking lot. In the background, endearing words floated back to her ears.

"She's too nice to be treated that way."

"I'll whip his ass if he shows up around here again," the other man said.

Although course, their words brought a warming sensation to Jessica's troubled mind. Maybe someone was watching over her after all.

***

Subdued, but committed, Jessica drove to the hospital, and parked the car. Then she stumbled out.

At the entrance, two revolving doors opened into a

wide expanse of waiting rooms. Steadfast in her commitment, she hobbled through doors, and staggered to the receptionist's desk.

"May I help you?" a lady asked as Jessica moved closer.

"My husband beat me up this past week-end," Jessica said, and rubbed sweaty palms together. "Actually, twice in eight days."

"Do you need a doctor?"

"Yes, please."

"Wait here," the receptionist said.

Minutes later a male nurse was escorting Jessica into an enclosed examining room. The curtains were drawn, and she was left alone to re-think her decision of why she was sitting on a cold gurney in the middle of the day. In what seemed like hours, a doctor was examining her injuries. X-rays followed.

"You have several fractured ribs," he said. "Here. Look at this." And he pointed at several bone fractures highlighted on the screen.

"We use large elastic bands for injuries like this," he said. "It helps to ease the pain while the ribs are healing. You'll know when they've re-bounded."

"How long?" Jessica asked, realizing her workload at home wouldn't stop just because she was injured.

"Several weeks," he said. "We'll make that determination at your next appointment."

"It feels better already," Jessica said after the band was adjusted, and in place.

"When did your husband assault you?"

"The last time was Friday night."

Without missing a beat, he continued. "Let's have a look at those eyes," he said, and scooted his stool closer. "I see several abrasions and rips in the corner of your left eye. There's also some swelling and bruising. The right one isn't so bad." He touched her eyelid with the tip of a gloved finger and she grimaced,

"That hurts." she said, reaching up.

"Takes time to heal," he said. "But your lips are

already showing signs of healing. The bruising has faded some, which is good. All the swelling should go down in a couple of days."

Jessica tried to smile but was more concerned with the throbbing in her broken ribs.

"Here's some salve for the bruising and abrasions," he said. "Apply twice daily," and he patted her lightly on the hand. "Just make sure you wear that elastic brace until released from my care."

"I will," she said, and forced a smile. "Thanks."

"I'll need to see you again, in my office, in two weeks," he said. "Now wait here. I'll be right back."

The alcove where Jessica sat was cold and unfeeling. In silence she stared at the wall, realizing the load she now carried was more than overwhelming.

Trey will be so mad that I went to the doctor. But I need documentation. I needed proof of this assault.

Her only goal, from this time forward, was getting away from her husband.

The curtain in the alcove again swung wide, and a deputy sheriff, dressed from top to bottom in uniformed attire, stepped inside. A leather holder by his side revealed the tip of a gun, and his jacket sported several buttons of achievement. Although his demeanor was intimidating, Jessica could only pray he was there to help her.

"I understand you were assaulted Friday night," he said.

"Yes—by my husband."

"Can you tell me about it?"

Unrestrained tears slid down Jessica's face as she re-told the happenings of Friday past.

"How many times have you been assaulted?"

"A lot," she said, as tears continued to flow.

"How long have you been married?"

"Almost twelve years," she said, again twisting her hands. Her fingers, now red, were also raw from gripping them.

"You realize it's against the law for a husband to beat his wife?"

"I didn't know," she said, again lowering her eyes.

"Well, it is," he said, then took a step forward, still fingering his gun holster. "My advice to you is get away from your husband. Move out. Find someone who will help you get away from this man. Whatever it takes."

"I'm planning to leave when the kids get out of school this summer," she said, glancing up.

"You need to get away now. Right now."

A jolt of fear raced through her body.

"You can go to a woman's shelter," he said. "I'll give you an address if you'll take it."

"I don't know—"

Trey will feel betrayed. But maybe, for once, I need to think about myself, and the kids.

"Is there someone in the family who can take you in?"

"Maybe—maybe my mother-in-law. Actually, I'm staying at her house right now."

"That may not be a good idea," he said. "Is there anyone else?"

"No, not really. My parents don't live close."

"That's okay," he said, biting his lip. "But once you get a restraining order, you can move back to your own place. Then your husband can't touch you."

"Are you sure?" she asked but squirmed as he again fingered his holster.

"Yes," he said. "I'm sure."

His words were holding her attention. But her lips were again dry, so she ran her tongue over them to moisten them. Feeling vulnerable, she shifted in her seat, and tried to find a more comfortable position as explosions of fractured pain rippled through her rib cage.

"You'll need an attorney to file a restraining order," he said, stepping closer.

"How?"

"I'll give you an attorney's card. Call him today and make an appointment. In the meantime, stay away from your house, and your husband. My advice is to not say anything to anyone until you get papers for protection."

"I—I'll try," she said.

"If you want to stay alive, you will."

That instant Jessica decided to make it work—at least until the restraining order was signed. Already she knew how keep a secret. When papers were served, everyone would be surprised.

She grabbed her side and looked deeply into the man's eyes. "Thanks," she said, and a hint of a smile formed on split lips. "I think you are an answer to prayer."

Black eyes, broken bones, and swollen lips can be treated. But fractured emotions need healing too. After all, make-up can't hide everything.

Chapter Twenty-Five

Rubber Meets the Road

Parked in front of Jessica's house were two cars, and new adrenalin raced through her veins. She took a deep breath, cut the ignition to her car, removed the key, and stumbled out. Her hands were crimson red—more from her grip than the cold. Climbing the porch steps was Trey. On his heels was a deputy sheriff.

In an instant she realized this scene wasn't designed to unfold in her presence. The timing of her arrival home had been misjudged, but she remained glued to the asphalt, unable to move.

Her weakened legs began to buckle, as fear, anxiety, and panic surrounded her; leaving her anchored to the moment. Tears of both frustration and anger were blinked away as she leaned hard against the car for support.

What should I do? I should leave. But I can't move.

Twelve years. Abused for twelve years.

Alone and frightened, but her resolution was solid. Her mind was made up. The decision to force separation on her husband was a must, or she would face certain death.

The sheriff's department had been more sympathetic than local police, who never once believed her reports. But why would they? The chief of police, as later learned, was related to Trey.

Her heart ached for her mother-in-law who must surely know by now that her son was a wife beater. But did it matter?

At this point her self-esteem was so low she wanted to die. But death was not the legacy she desired to leave her children. For them alone she would stand and refuse to again accept weak promises and undeserved threats.

***

It was over—finally. For once the legal system had worked. After hiring an attorney, a restraining order was obtained, and Trey ordered from the house. Only then could Jessica safely return with the children.

Rick, somewhat concerned, pulled the pens on Trey's guns, rendering them unusable. But fear would remain to paralyze her emotions as Jessica's separation only triggered more terrorization through stalking.

TEMPORARY ORDER
FOR EMERGENCY RELIEF
UNDER CHAPTER 50 OF THE
GENERAL STATUTES OF NORTH CAROLINA

This cause coming on to be heard and being heard before the undersigned District Court Judge Presiding, and being heard upon plaintiff's motion for emergency relief, as provided by Chapter 50 of the General Statutes.

And it having been made to appear to the Court and the Court finding as a fact from the plaintiff's verified Complaint the following:

1.

That the Plaintiff and Defendant are citizens and residents of North Carolina

2.

That the Plaintiff and Defendant are husband and wife

3.

That the Plaintiff reasonably figures she is in danger of imminent serious bodily injury as a consequence of the Defendant's history of violent acts towards her.

4.

That the Defendant has assaulted the Plaintiff and caused serious bodily injury in that the defendant has beaten the Plaintiff on several occasions during the course of the marriage; the latest being on December 31; that the Defendant has a violent temper and has threatened the kill the Plaintiff on a number of occasions.

5.

That the Plaintiff has an immediate need of shelter and security and support, to be provided for by the marital residence, and the furnishings therein, and also the Honda automobile, free from the interference and harassment of the Defendant.

6

.

That the demonstrated behavior of the Defendant is such as to constitute good cause of the belief that the plaintiff is in immediate and present danger of domestic violence at the hands of the defendant

CONCLUSIONS OF LAW

That the Court has jurisdiction of the subject matter and of the parties to this cause

2.

That the Plaintiff is entitled to an immediate temporary order for emergency relief to protect her and minor children from the interference, harassment, and violence of the defendant, and to provide a secure residence for her free from the interference and harassment of the Defendant pending further hearing of this cause; that this cause should be calendared for hearing within 10 days from the filing of the Complaint and Motion for Emergency Relief, and the execution of this order.

IT IS THEREFORE ORDERED,

ADJUDGED, AND DECREED:

1.

The Defendant be and is hereby ordered to henceforth refrain from all acts of violence and threats of violence towards the Plaintiff and the minor children, and all direct and indirect acts of interference with or harassment of the Plaintiff and minor children;

2.

That the Plaintiff be and is hereby awarded immediate and exclusive temporary possession of the marital residence, and the furnishings located therein, and of the Honda automobile titled in both names all free of interference from and harassment by the Defendant;

3.

That the Defendant be and is hereby ordered to appear before the Honorable Judge Presiding of the District Court at 9:30 o'clock a.m. on Friday, January 17, or as soon thereafter as the Defendant might be heard, for a hearing on the Plaintiff's motion for emergency relief.

4.

That a copy of this order is served upon the Defendant, and a copy of the order to be delivered to the appropriate law enforcement agencies as provided by Chapter 50B of the North Carolina General Statutes.

IN THE GENERAL COURT OF JUSTICE
DISTRICT COURT DIVISION

COMPLAINT

The Plaintiff, complaining of the Defendant, alleges and says:

1.

That the Plaintiff and the Defendant are citizens and residents of North Carolina

2.

That the Plaintiff and Defendant were married to each other on April 17

3.

That there are three children of the marriage, to wit: Kayla, born October 18, Ayden, born February 20, and Josh, born May 10.

4.

That the Plaintiff is a faithful and dutiful wife and has done nothing to provoke the behavior of the Defendant as herein alleged.

5.

That the Plaintiff is a dependent spouse within the meaning of Chapter 50 of the General Statues of North Carolina

6.

That the Defendant is a supporting spouse within the meaning of Chapter 50 of the General Statutes of North Carolina.

7.

That the Plaintiff is a fit and proper person to have the care, custody, and control of the minor children, and it is in the best interest of the minor children that she has care, custody, and control of said minor children.

8.

That the Defendant has committed such indignities to the person of the Plaintiff as to render her life burdensome and her condition intolerable by engaging in the following course and pattern of conduct:

(a)   That the Defendant has assaulted and beaten the Plaintiff on a number of occasions, the latest being December 31, said beatings being of such severity that the Plaintiff has had to seek medical treatment, and is still under the care of a physician as a result of the beatings inflicted upon her by the Defendant;

(b)   That the Defendant has verbally abused the Plaintiff, both within and outside the presence of the minor children, and has used vulgar and indecent language directed towards the Plaintiff on numbers of occasions;

(c)   That the Defendant has threatened to kill the Plaintiff, and has threatened to kidnap the children of the parties;

(d)   That the Defendant has advised the Plaintiff that he has slept with several other women, and that he did not love the Plaintiff anymore;

(e)   That the Defendant has, on several occasions, thrown projectiles towards the Plaintiff, including pieces of wood, and has damaged articles of property in the house, in fits of rage;

(f) That the Defendant has kept the Plaintiff and the children awake into the wee hours of the morning on numbers of occasions, with his cursing's and carrying on;

(g) That the Defendant has generally put the Plaintiff in fear for her life and the lives of her children by his actions.

9.

The Defendant constructively abandoned the Plaintiff, forcing her out of the marital home, in fear for her life, and for the safety of her children.

10.

That the Plaintiff and the Defendant are co-owners of a marital residence, and the Plaintiff is in need of an order permitting her to reside therein, along with possession of all the furniture located therein.

11.

That the Plaintiff and Defendant are joint owners of a Honda automobile, which has been driven primarily by the Plaintiff; that the Plaintiff is in need of an immediate order allowing her continued possession of said Honda

12.

That the Defendant is capable of providing support for the Plaintiff and the minor children, both on a temporary and permanent basis, and the Plaintiff is in need of substantial support for herself, and the minor children

13.

That the acts of the Defendant, in intentionally causing bodily injury to the Plaintiff, and placing the Plaintiff in fear of imminent serious bodily injury by the threat of killing her, or such acts, under G.S. 50B et. seq., that entitles the Plaintiff to temporary emergency relief.

WHEREFORE, the Plaintiff prays:

1.

That she be granted a divorce from bed and board from the Defendant.

2.

That she be granted an order of reasonable alimony, both on a temporary and permanent basis.

3.

That she be granted the general care, custody, and control of the minor children of the marriage, with the Defendant being required to pay an adequate amount of support for said children, both on a temporary and permanent basis;

4.

That she be granted the sole and exclusive use and possession of the former marital residence of the parties, along with the furnishings located therein, along with the Honda automobile which is titled in both names;

5.

That a temporary order for emergency relief be issued pursuant to Chapter 50B of the General Statutes of North Carolina.

6.

That this verified complaint be treated as an affidavit within this cause and in support of her motion for temporary and emergency relief.

7.

For such other relief as the Court deems just and proper.

Trey neither denied nor appealed his court ordered separation as his true character had been revealed.

The money he shared from his cashed-in retirement paid for an attorney and bought Jessica's freedom. The money he kept for himself purchased a brand-new car.

Chapter Twenty-Six

Discarded Memories

An unexpected knock at the door caused an insatiable panic to surface. Standing behind the door, Jessica grabbed her heart, and began to tremble. Was it Trey? If so, she couldn't let him in.

Terrified, she cautiously pulled a corner of the closed curtain aside and peeked through the window. Her mother and her Aunt Rose had never looked so good. "Am I ever glad to see you two," she said, and promptly swung into action. Her joy resonated beyond a smile as she reached through the door, grabbed them both, and pulled them inside.

In Jessica's mind they were simply angels sent to guard her. Now she wouldn't face her demons alone. Trey could no longer disregard his restraining order, and she could leave the children at home while at work. For the first time in a long time, she felt safe under her own roof. Reinforcements had arrived.

***

She peeled her coat off, laid it across her arm, and walked across the kitchen tiles. The sound of her own footsteps echoed back as she continued her stride. "I'm home from work," she said, as Josh scampered across the floor to greet her.

A voice spoke from the next room. "Guess who came by today?"

"Don't know," Jessica said and gave the baby a hug. But when she glanced up, her mother was in the room.

"It was one of your sisters-in-law," her mother said.

"What did she want?" Jessica asked, as feelings of

apprehension crept up her spine.

"She said her brother needed some clothes. He didn't get them all when the police picked him up."

Jessica began to shake as unrestrained fear whipped into action. She scanned the room, hoping nothing more than clothes. Her bond with Trey's family was fast fading, and she knew it. Not one word from any one of them since her court-ordered separation.

"What else did she take?" she asked, as her eyes roamed the room.

"I don't know what she took," her mother said. "Some clothes, I guess."

"Why didn't you stay with her?" Jessica asked.

Out of nervousness she picked up a sock and tossed it in the laundry basket. Then she jerked the closet door open. It was bare. Only a few dresses remained but were shoved in a corner. She turned and opened the bureau drawers.

"Mama, why didn't you watch her?" she asked, and squeezed back hot tears. "She took my pictures. They're all gone."

"I didn't see what she took," her mother said. "I guess I trusted her."

"You can't always trust people," Jessica said, as frustration again took center stage. An escaped tear was wiped away. "Especially now."

"Maybe you can get them back."

"I doubt it," Jessica said. "I'll probably never get them back."

Her mother's uninterested attitude was irritating, so she cleared her throat, and took a deep breath. Out of frustration she began pacing the floor, creating an uneven path between wooden blocks and colorful Lego's. It was hard to believe her sister-in-law had taken her pictures—stolen them was more like it.

I can't believe this is happening. What next?

"I think I'll call Ashley," she said, thinking out loud. She picked up the phone and punched in the number. Minutes later the piece dropped.

"What did she say?" Aunt Rose asked.

"She gave them to Trey," Jessica said, and angry tears were brushed away. "He has them now."

"Why would she take those, of all things?" her mother asked.

"I have no idea," Jessica said. But her words were automatic, and she continued pacing the floor.

"The only thing men are good for is giving us babies," Aunt Rose quipped.

"I guess, " Jessica said. But tears continued to flow and gather on her blouse as intense hurt and deep frustration were unleashed.

"I'll never see those pictures again," she said. "I just know it." And she wiped more tears away. "Those were my memories—pictures of my children as babies, and Christmases, and birthdays."

In frustration she sat down and held her head in her hand. "Will this pain ever end?" she whispered. "How could Ashley do this to me—a sister-in-law who is more like a sister?"

Deep in her heart, Jessica knew those pictures were forever gone—just like her marriage. And they were.

Chapter Twenty-Seven

On Notice

Monday came, and Jessica mentally readied herself to turn in a two-week notice. She was also preparing to move back home with her parents. Although reluctant, they finally agreed to her request.

Only three-months employed at Health Aid Medical, yet she dreaded giving it up. But could she survive two weeks while working a notice? She feared Trey's harassment in public—even worse, his threat to kill her.

Nights were now more than nightmares. Trey's disregard for his restraining order brought new bouts of fear to her already disrupted life. Adding insult to injury, he would appear at gas stations, supermarkets, and convenience stores when she was there. It was doubtful local police would uphold the order so she decided not to contact them. Disbelief had jilted her before.

She was also terrorized he would kidnap the children from school—another reason for panic. A copy of her separation agreement was now in the hands of school personnel and provided some comfort. But not enough. Although warned, could they be trusted to keep her children away from Trey?

A lack of faith in others had again surfaced, as loss of sleep and fear of the unknown claimed her sanity. Stressed to the max, Jessica sagged beneath the emotional load she carried. Her body, still healing from Trey's last assault, resisted food despite a desire to keep her strength up. Although the first step in her plan was behind her, she remained frightened, tense, and nervous.

Running on fumes of fear, anxiety, and dread allowed what energy she had to quickly fade once home from work each day. "Trey's removal from the house didn't stop everything," she said under her breath while climbing the stairs to her office.

"He's downstairs," a gruff voice said, from below. "What do you want me to do?"

"Please don't let him come up," she said. Her legs were now shaking.

"Done," he said.

She leaned against the office door but felt instant paralysis. The sound of running footsteps then caught her attention. The next instant the salesman burst into view. "He's gone," he said, quite out of breath.

Somehow her legs regained enough strength to carry her to a chair in the office. But then her knees buckled, and her body began to shake. "What happened?" she asked, and nervously rubbed the brace on her ribs.

"We ran him off," he said. "Told him to never come here again, and to leave you alone." Then he grinned.

"Thanks a million," was all she could manage as nerves rattled beneath her skin. Her legs remained as pulp beneath her.

***

A couple of hours later the receptionist placed a vase full of aromatic flowers on Jessica's desk. "Look what the florist just delivered," she said, and a smile covered her face. "Aren't these roses gorgeous?"

"For me?" Jessica asked, and her heart began to pound in disbelief.

Did Trey just send me flowers?

"Wow! A dozen red roses," the receptionist said. "You must be special to someone."

"Who sent them?" Jessica asked.

"Look at the card," the receptionist said.

Jessica's hands trembled as she pulled the insert from a tiny envelope. "They're from my husband," she said, and walked through the door to the trash can, ready to dump the arrangement.

"What are you doing?" the receptionist asked, and

quickly grabbed her heart. "Don't throw them away."

Jessica turned and pushed the vase into the receptionist's hands. "Here," she said. "You take them."

"Don't you want them?"

"No. No, I don't."

The receptionist's eyebrows lifted. "Are you sure?" she asked.

"Yes. I'm sure."

"Then I'll put them in the front office for everyone to enjoy," she said.

"As long as I don't have to look at them," Jessica said.

"You must really be mad at your husband."

Jessica turned away. "He won't be my husband for long," she whispered. Rubber legs carried her back to her office where she tried to gather her thoughts.

"Whew," she said, grabbing her sore ribs and slowly releasing new air. "Thank God for adrenalin, and a rib brace."

Chapter Twenty-Eight

Moving On

Snow in the forecast did not deter Jessica's plans. As intended, and still on target, Friday would be her last day at Health Aid Medical. Somehow, she was managing a two-week notice.

Rick insisted she rent a large truck. He and Emily would be her driving team. They felt it best if she and Trey separated and were assisting in the move.

***

Jessica handed the key to Rick for truck pick-up. With that action she was also surrendering to emotions of jubilation. Already packed boxes were then shoved into the trailer along with household items, boxes of clothing, and toys. Furniture placed against other pieces in the van filled the remaining gaps.

Everything would be needed for the children, so Jessica was cleaning house. Well, almost. Trey's request for the large screen television, and their bedroom set, would be honored.

A recliner, ministry materials, books, and several snapshots of the kids would remain for his return to their home. A large writing desk, given as a gift, would also remain. Reminders of the life she once had were best left behind.

***

Saturday morning, after the final box was loaded, Jessica and her caravan began winding its way through town. From behind the wheel of the U-Haul, Rick grinned and waved. Her car, packed, to the max, followed close behind. Emily, at the rear, ended the motorcade.

Although smiling to show elation, on the inside Jessica remained demur. And when her car rolled from the curb, tender tears were blinked away. Three children were staying behind with Granny, and a non-caring husband—if only for the weekend. Words of praise and uplifting prayer would remain on her lips as her venture began to unfold.

Her new life was falling into place as if divinely orchestrated. Success was beckoning her forward, allowing happiness to surface despite a serious lack of resources at destination's end. She had survived the worst of times, and things could only get better. Now was not a time of worry. Now was a time of rejoicing.

Sunday afternoon Trey returned the children to Jessica at her parent's home, as previously planned. And so began a new era in Jessica's life.

***

Due to an overly restrictive background Jessica was anchored to a marriage that should have ended long before it began. The dictators in her life had been overbearing, demanding, and restraining, making her a recipient of their misguidance.

The judgments of others had been unrealistic, but she was now ready to move forward.

With limited human intervention she had escaped a cruel and violent marriage. Her husband, tamed with legal restraints, had been removed from her life. And the children were content, and happy. What more could she ask?

After the dust had settled, Jessica realized that God was still on her side. Her escape had been swift, and uneventful. And, for the first time in years, she was content and happier than ever before.

Because "...the steps of a good man (or woman) are ordered by the LORD, and He delights in his way" (Psalms 37:23)

Chapter Twenty-Nine

Miracles

The home where Jessica's parents lived was now a haven of retreat. It was also a place of new beginnings.

"Come on kids," Jessica said. "It's time to go." Still stressed, her brow wrinkled as she hustled Kayla and Ayden out the door.

Before she left, she gave Josh a quick kiss, and squeezed him tight. "Be good for Grandmother," she said. "I'm taking your brother and sister to sign up for school. We won't be gone long."

As her car rolled down the frozen hill, she glanced back at the house. Josh was staring through the picture window looking sad and forlorn. His demeanor brought new tears to her eyes. But she must proceed.

Crusty snow covered the ground and glistened in the brisk sunlight as the car headed out. Several scraped piles, laden with dirt and debris, remained on the side of already scraped roads, and hinted at the temperature outside. The car was icy to the touch as it bounced over frozen bumps and sunken potholes as her small family trucked along.

Registering Kayla and Ayden in school was yet another step in the plan. Enrolling them would seal her destiny and hold her to the plan. The next hurdle would be finding a job. She was ready to ditch her scars and move forward in a new direction.

***

The office at Randolph Primary looked daunting. Still Jessica pressed forward, trusting an inner instinct to retain a positive attitude. She was desperate for friends. Reaching out to everyone along the way would be a start.

Her new endeavor would be embraced with a prayer on her lips, and hope in her heart.

"Do you want to enroll your children in school?" the receptionist asked after they stepped inside the main office.

Jessica nodded, then reached in her pocket and pulled out a tattered envelope. In her haste to retreat she had somehow remembered to get the children's school records before their move.

"This is Kayla, and Ayden," she said, and pointed.

"Are you employed?" the lady asked.

"No, no not yet" Jessica said, coming back to reality. "I'm recently separated." And instantly the chair beneath her felt stiff. But she took a deep breath, realizing new patterns of descriptive responses were being created.

"I get child support," she said, lips trembling.

"How much?"

Four hundred a month," she said, embarrassed at the amount.

"Then your kids qualify for the free lunch program."

A lopsided smile swathed Jessica's face. "That's great," she said. "I didn't know you had a free lunch program."

At least her children would have good food to eat. Worry over their hunger had now been eased. "Thank you, Lord," she whispered softly.

After another deep breath she pressed forward. "I'm looking for a job," she said. Her voice quavered. On the inside she wanted to vomit.

"As a matter of fact," the lady said, "a bookkeeper is needed at Gray Optional School."

"Gray Optional School? I thought it closed years ago."

"It did," the receptionist said. "But the county re-opened the school, this time as a non-traditional optional primary—for kindergarten through fifth."

"How do I apply?" Words of confidence came from nowhere. Where they hers?

"Go to the Board of Education and fill out an application," the lady said. "You'll need two references. I'll write down the address and telephone number on this card."

"Thanks," Jessica said. "You've been more than helpful."

"The principal will need to interview you too."

"Oh—okay. Thanks."

"I hope everything works out," the lady said.

"So do I."

"It's been two weeks since that job was first listed," she said. "It hasn't yet been filled." Her smile was warming, and Jessica's heart filled with new hope.

"It's unusual that a job opening in the school system doesn't immediately fill," the lady said.

"Thanks again," Jessica said. On the inside she was jubilant, causing her words to gush.

"Since there's snow on the ground, make sure to watch the news for school attendance," the lady said.

"Just like when I attended this same school years ago," Jessica said.

"Exactly the same."

"Thanks," Jessica said, and her smile was instant. "Thanks for the information."

The lady turned and grinned at Kayla and Ayden. "I guess you're excited about going to a new school," she said. And immediately their heads bobbed up and down, a sure sign that change was good.

"This is a great school—one of the best. Alex Jordan is a wonderful principal. You'll enjoy coming every day."

Jessica smiled her biggest, then turned, and reached for the children's coats. And instantly the pressure in her head seemed to ease. "Put these on," she said. "It's cold outside."

"Good luck on your job hunt," the lady said.

"Thanks again, Jessica said. "I've been filling out applications all week, but no luck."

"Maybe this is the job for you," the lady said. In her heart Jessica prayed it would be.

But who could she use for job references? Twelve years had passed since living in her hometown, and her list of old friends had dwindled to none. Then she recalled a former church member she had used as a reference years before. He wouldn't mind if she did again. Who else could she use? She prayed God would provide.

***

The words *County Board of Education* inscribed on the dark brick of an old school building indicated the administrative offices were inside. As Jessica stared at the old building, prayers again rolled from her lips that all would go well with her quest. Then, with bold determination, she climbed the wide cement steps that lead to multiple entry doors.

The heaviness of aged wood released a musty smell as she swung the doors open. Inside, the hallways echoed their emptiness around her as a reminder of school days as a child. Footsteps coming toward her clacked on the old, planked floor, and she quickly refocused. A man was striding toward her.

It was a former teacher, Mr. Adams, who taught co-operative office practice when she was in high school. From him she had learned office machine operations, as well as secretarial skills.

"Hello, Mr. Adams."

"Jessica, how are you?"

"You remember me," she said, and grinned—both inside and out. Things might be looking up after all.

"Of course, I do,' he said. "I never forget my students."

From down the hallway the muffled drone of keyboards, muted voices, and spurts of laughter echoed through closed doors. Jessica, overcome with her new life, wanted to pinch herself.

"What brings you here?" he asked.

"To fill out an application for the job at Gray Optional School," she said, all the while praying he wouldn't notice her nervousness. "Could I use you for a reference?"

"Of course, you can," he said, then pointed to the

second door on the right. "Just go in that room, and someone will give you an application."

He reached out his hand for a quick shake. "Good luck," he said, then turned on his heel and walked away.

Jessica now had two references and she did a little two-step. Mr. Adams was a good one. Maybe she had a shot at this job after all.

A couple of hours later she stepped inside Gray Optional School. The voices echoing around her were pleasant, and she glowed from their exuberance. Chatter from classrooms down the hallway made the environment an exciting place to be.

A pretty lady with short, dark hair and hints of gray greeted her. "Hello," she said. "I'm Mrs. Dorsett, the school principal. Can I help you?"

"I'm looking for a job," Jessica said. "I was told you needed a bookkeeper."

"Come in my office, and have a seat," the lady said, "and tell me a little bit about yourself."

Minutes later she asked the question Jessica longed to hear. "When can you come to work?"

"When do you need me?"

"How about tomorrow morning at 7:30?"

"I'll be here," Jessica said.

"I've been waiting two weeks to fill this position," Mrs. Dorsett said. "I knew the minute you walked in the door you were the one for the job." With a smile and a firm handshake, the deal was sealed.

"See you first thing in the morning," she said. Jessica was elated.

"The sun is shining all over the world," Jessica sang in soft undertones as she stepped back outside.

Two weeks. The exact amount of time I was working my two-week notice before moving God was holding this job for me.

"Pack your bags and leave." Trey's spoken words had shattered her trusting heart. After hearing them again and again she had finally taken the initiative. After all, wasn't obey one of her marriage vows? Her only regret was not leaving the union earlier.

Everyone trusts a preacher. If he couldn't be trusted, then who could? And who would think the pastor of a church could also be an abuser? It just wasn't believed.

Scripture in the Bible became Jessica's consolation. As more revelations of truth were revealed, she realized that her once silenced cries had truly heard.

"For such people are false apostles, deceitful workers, masquerading as apostles of Christ. And no wonder, for Satan himself masquerades as an angel of light. It is not surprising, then, if his servants also masquerade as servants of righteousness" (2 Corinthians 11:13-15)

At last, she was free—free from the man who lashed out with a vengeance and terrorized her life.

"...He said to me, "My grace is sufficient for you, for my power is made perfect in weakness" (2 Corinthians 12:9)

More words from the Bible lifted Jessica's spirit, and her joy manifested in song and praise.

Chapter Thirty

A Place of Her Own

The home of Jessica's parents was too small for all of them under the same roof. Her intent was to move out as soon as possible, and never sponge off them. She also realized that finding her own place would cut the umbilical cord once more, and provide the confidence needed to stand on her own two feet.

"Who is it?" she mouthed after her mother answered the phone. Three rings were enough to send her into a tailspin. Was it Trey? She prayed it wasn't. His calls were callous, and he continued pounding her with threats. Promises to kidnap the children was a constant obstacle of dread.

After a huge gulp of air, she tried to calm herself. Her stomach was tied in knots and began to rumble and churn. How she dreaded the jarring ring of the phone—fearing yet another threat. Would she ever feel normal again? Living on the edge was an everyday occurrence.

"It's Bonnie, your childhood friend," her mother said, and handed Jessica the phone.

"Hi, Bonnie," Jessica said, and her voice cracked. "I'm glad it's you and not my Ex."

"How's the job hunt going?" Bonnie asked.

"Oh, I found one," Jessica said, and her excitement spilled over as this bit of news was relayed. "At Gray Optional School—today." She couldn't help but smile out loud. The joy in her heart was simply therapeutic.

"I love that little school," Bonnie said. "What's your job title?"

"Bookkeeper, secretary, office lady, receptionist, Band-Aid applier" Jessica said, and a small giggle rapped around her tongue. "I guess I'll have many titles—Bookkeeper being the first. It's a small school, you know."

"You'll enjoy working there," Bonnie said. "I have friends who put their children in that school a couple of years ago."

"By the way," Jessica said, "I've been looking for an apartment to rent."

"Have you called Cottage Hill Apartments?" Bonnie was prodding her along.

"Never heard of it," Jessica said. After a sigh of relief, she plopped down on the sofa for a long chat.

"You can probably afford this one," Bonnie said. "It's near Hendersonville."

Jessica shifted positions. "How much is the rent?"

"Its government subsidized. The rent depends on your salary."

"Sounds good—really good," Jessica said. "Is it listed in the phone book?" As a calming peace settled in her heart, she absentmindedly leafed through the phone book as she talked.

"My friend Linda lived there," Bonnie said.

"Did she like it?"

"She said it was nice, with a playground." Bonnie said, but then paused. "There's usually a long waiting list. It took Linda a long time to get an apartment."

Jessica's jaw dropped. *A waiting list?* Still, it was worth checking out. Maybe, just maybe...

***

Several days later, after the Cottage Hill Apartments manager handed Jessica a set of keys to a three-bedroom apartment on the first floor, she almost exploded with excitement.

"There's usually a long waiting list before an apartment comes available," the manager said. "But you got lucky. The key to this one was turned in this morning. It takes two days to have it cleaned. You can move in this week-end."

Jessica tried not to dance a jig.

131

"You also qualify for a government discount in your monthly rent," the manager said after opening the door. "Just make sure your part is paid on time.

"I will," Jessica said.

It was difficult for her to restrain her excitement. Only thirty days living with her parents, and she now had her own place. She could hardly wait to share the news with her children. At that moment she was both joyful and ecstatic, and the happiest she had been in years.

Refrains of melody filled her heart with rapture as the shattered pieces of her existence fell into place. Whitney Houston's song *The Greatest Love of All* spoke to her heart, as love for her own self began to surface.

As horrific as life had been, nothing compared to knowing that God was still on her side. His provision surrounded her, and the children, as together they embarked on their new lives with enthusiasm, and unwavering peace.

***

Cottage Hill Apartments provided the perfect place for a battered woman to begin again. After the dust had settled, Jessica's family of four soared into peaceful routines of daily living. A permanent reprieve from violence was simply heaven on earth.

Even more noticeable were the calming effects of waking up and going to sleep in peace. She and her family could come and go at will without fear of sabotage. The happiest days of her life were before her. Her imprisoned existence was finally over, and she was at last free from the bondage of hostility.

As the Holy Spirit wrapped His arms around her, confidence in her own self opened the door to pure bliss. Soon a church was found where songs of consolation could minister to her weary, and fractured heart.

Downpours of new rain were eagerly embraced as huge droplets splattered the ground around her. She soaked in the sunshine as countless rays of glamour streamed upon her. She reveled in newfound friendships as her new beginnings were embraced. And, for once, her fear seemed to subside. Life's darkest storm had passed, the sky was again blue, and the world a brighter place to be.

Chapter Thirty-One

Too Close for Comfort

Trey's visits with the children following Jessica's recent court ordered separation had been pre-arranged. He would pick them up Friday afternoon at her childhood home, thus reducing any risk of altercation. Her parents promised to oversee the operation, leaving her free to disappear when needed.

Friday afternoon, after her move to the apartment, Jessica's little ones were dropped off at their home, and she quickly drove away. Her plan—not to be anywhere Trey was.

As she meandered back down the road toward the apartment, she lazily glanced in the rear-view mirror. Horror then collided with terror. Trey's car was advancing, and memories of former threats instantly held her hostage. Her heart leaped to her throat. She was in full panic mode. But why was he following her?

Seconds later his car slid up beside hers, and he motioned her over. Her strength instantly dissolved. *What can I do? Do I even have a choice?*

God, please help me.

Her body began to tremble—so violently the car began to wobble. She realized the risk was great. The freedom she had worked so hard to achieve—liberty from her assailant—was crumbling at her feet.

With strong reservation she steered the car into a gas station and applied the break, allowing the engine to run. Her body sagged as shock from the drama unfolding before her was intense. With heart in throat, she uttered a quick prayer for safety, and prepared to see Trey—face to face.

The next instant he jumped from his car and strode to hers. When he stepped closer, she reached over and locked the door. As a precaution, she rolled the window only half-way down. She was more than cautious, fearing for her life. Not only was her body dripping with sweat, but her hands continued to tremble.

"Why are you following me?" she asked and gripped the steering wheel tight. Reaching deep inside, she prayed for calmness and more strength. "I thought you were getting the kids."

Trey moved closer to the window. "I'll still get them," he said, "but I wanted to see you first."

"You don't need to see me," she said. Horrified, her knees began to knock together in bone-chilling rhythm. She prayed he wouldn't notice.

"I want you back, Jess."

"No." Petrified, her voice came across as harsh, and decisive. She shifted in the seat, still uncomfortable and vulnerable.

"You never talk to me on the phone," he said. "I want you back."

She remained silent but gripped her hands together.

"If you come back, I'll give you everything you what."

"No." Bracing gulps of air were inhaled as she tied to stay composed.

"How about some new clothes."

"No." Still holding her ground, Jessica slid away from the window.

"You can have my new car. Anything you want."

"It's over." Her lips pulled into a thin line. "Our marriage is over."

"I want you back."

The tone in his voice, and the look on his face, brought new bouts of dread to her already dwindling courage, and she shivered in fear.

"The children need me."

Panic delayed a response, but she gripped the wheel even tighter.

"We'll take a trip together," he said. "I've got tickets to the Bahamas from being best salesman this month." And his lips curved. "I won't ever hit you again—I promise. We can start over."

How many times has he said that?

"No." Her words were bold. On the inside, she was proud.

"Then I'll—I'll move here with you."

Conflicting dread instantly arose in Jessica's throat. His words stirred insurmountable fear. Would she ever get beyond this terror?

"Please, don't." Her words were tempered.

He put his hand out as if to stop her. "Just think about it," he said. Stepping closer, he rotated his hand in a circular motion. "Roll the window all the way down."

She cowered in her seat. "No. Just leave me alone."

"I want to kiss you."

"I don't think so," she said, and reached for the window control.

"Don't close the window yet," he said.

"We have nothing more to discuss," she said, her voice quivering. "Please, just go away." Her words were strangely cold, even to herself.

"You know I still love you," he said. But his tallness was intimidating as he flashed his famous smile.

"Yeah, right," she wanted to say. "Still lying?" Instead, she bit her tongue.

Unwavering in her commitment to never return to her old life, she refused submission. She didn't want him. And it really was over. She couldn't help but smile. On the inside she was jubilant.

"Why are you smiling?" He looked confused.

"Huh? Oh—nothing."

"Where do you live? I want to come by and see you, and the kids"

Fear jerked Jessica into action. "No," she said. The sternness in her own voice kept her grounded. "You have the kids every other week-end," she said. "You don't get me."

"Why won't you give me another chance?" His words were agitated.

How she hated his begging—his pleading. "No. It's over. Just go away and leave me alone."

She slapped the control, and the window shot up. On the inside she was more than proud.

Thank God, he didn't assault me in the parking lot.

She knew of women who ended up dead in violent relationships, so she remained fearful of his next move. But maybe, just maybe, their separation would hold up after all. She prayed it would.

Sweat rolled down her back as her car jetted back across the highway. She peeked in the rear-view mirror and saw his car was going in the opposite direction, and she breathed a long sigh of relief. "Thank you, Lord," she said out loud. Still, she needed miles of distance between them.

Her heart was beating at a fast pace, so she took deep breaths, trying to calm herself. Somehow, she resisted the urge to push the gas petal to the floor; but only because she wanted to stay alive for the children.

The light ahead rotated to orange, and she slowed the car to a stop. As she waited, she rolled the window half-way down, and breathed in the fresh mountain air. In the distance the tranquility of snow-covered mountain peaks, and the chill of winter, helped to clear her head.

As a mother, Jessica always expected the worst when Trey drove away with the children. "Please protect them and bring them back safe and sound," she prayed, realizing they would see their dad in the next few minutes.

"I'll just leave everything in God's hands," she whispered. "Mine are way too limp."

Chapter Thirty-Two

Protected

A few weeks on the new job and Jessica was more than jubilant. Internal happiness filled her life with joy. Things were going well, work was easy to learn, and she enjoyed the environment of school staff and students—often thinking of the little learners as her own.

The heels on her shoes clacked loudly on the hardened tile in the hallway and made her smile as she went about her duties. Her thoughts then meandered from shoes to kids. She would enroll Kayla and Ayden in Gray Optional School next year—pull them out of Randolph Primary.

As she walked, she glanced up, and noted several pieces of student artwork haphazardly plastered on the wall. She stopped one moment to examine the mix. In her head she pretended the work belonged to her own children.

How they would love this small school with all its pomp and variety. Students sharing common interests, close friendships, and camaraderie would be perfect for her small family.

Still smiling, she continued her trek. The next instant her feet started sliding on the hard surface. Her two-inch heels were slick from wear, and she instinctively grabbed the wall to keep from falling. This was something she would need to remember to take each step with caution. Her shoes were worn out. Cheap five-and-dime types purchased years ago, used for church, but now her only work shoes.

Mrs. Dorsett had mentioned earlier how much her shoes needed re-heeling at a shoe cobbler's. She was a great mentor for sure. Jessica thought she would do the

138

same. Or, somehow, manage to buy some new ones for her tired, aching feet. But since the worn-out heels were the only dress shoes she owned, she breathed a quick prayer for safety, and continued her errand.

Later, as she sat in the office typing, Mrs. Dorsett stepped to the door. "I have a doctor's appointment at eleven," she said, rubbing her shoulder and neck. "Can you handle the office by yourself?"

"Oh, sure," Jessica said. "Don't worry about a thing."

"I'll be back as soon as I can," she said, and shifted her handbag to the other arm. Then she glanced at her watch. "I shouldn't be longer than a couple of hours."

"Are you okay?"

"Just stressed," she said. "New job as school principal, I guess. The last time I saw the doctor, he said stress often generates shoulder and neck pain."

"I hope this time he can help," Jessica said.

Mrs. Dorsett frowned, then fingered her watch band. "I've had quite a bit of pain lately," she said. "I'm going for a re-check, and some stronger medicine."

Jessica's own neck and shoulders ached, and long before the day she had launched out on her own. But she couldn't afford a doctor like Mrs. Dorsett, so she would just tough it out. At least, for now, she understood what was causing her own pain—anxiety and stress.

***

The muffled drone of children's voices wafted back from down the hall as Jessica swung the back entry door open. She stepped outside and bounded up mature steps to the top of the landing. Sitting atop a weathered post for mail collection was the box. Handling mail was one of her many duties, but she embraced them all with joy in her heart.

She glanced around and noticed several songbirds perched atop the handrail crooning the joyful songs of spring. A small planting bed full of yellow jonquils and red tulips adjoining the entrance drew her in. In the distance, several pink and white dogwoods spread their budding blooms for all to see.

The fragrance of spring filtered through Jessica's nose, and the morning sun reminded her of a loving God, as if a warm blanket of protection covered her. For a moment, the weight of fear seemed to lift from her shoulders. Life was again worth living. God was her protector, provider, and confidant. At last she was content, and happy.

After moments of joyous rapture were embraced, she meandered back down the steps, and into the building. The emotional load she carried seemed lighter than before. Her day was off to a great start.

***

The following day, and just before the school bell rang the dismissal of sixty students, Trey's face appeared in an outside window—and Jessica instantly froze.

His suit jacket swung in the breeze as he sauntered to the entrance of the small building. Dread overwhelmed Jessica's senses. In a daze she stumbled from her desk and scrambled to Mrs. Dorsett's office—her designated safety net.

"He's here," Jessica said, still shaking. She grabbed the back of a chair to steady her wobbling legs.

"Your Ex?"

"Yes." Each labored breath was inhaled and exhaled at an uncalculated speed.

"He's walking down the sidewalk," Jessica said, panting. The next instant her energy level dropped, and she collapsed on a chair.

"I'll take care of him," Mrs. Dorsett said. "You wait here." She strode through the office door and closed it behind her.

Jessica hated relying on others for protection. But, what else could she do? At least someone was willing to step up in her place. "Thank you, God," she whispered. "Thank you, thank you—thank you."

Trey was stalking her again. Would she ever feel safe again?

What was going on outside the office door? Why was he here? What about the kids?

By the time Mrs. Dorsett again opened the door, Jessica's breathing was labored.

"He's gone," Mrs. Dorsett said. "I don't think he'll be back."

"What happened?" Jessica asked, fear filtering through her voice.

"I told him if he ever comes here again, for any reason, I'd have him arrested."

"Thank you," Jessica said, and rubbed her hands together. Her ankles had strangely regained strength, and her heart felt renewed.

"Calm down, and get a drink of water," Mrs. Dorsett said. "I'm sure he won't be back."

***

After work Jessica glanced around the school—her refuge from the outside world. She squeezed herself, making sure she was truly okay. In her mind, she felt validated. Someone in authority had stood up to Trey, and he had caved without a whimper.

There wasn't any doubt in her mind as to why he had come. He would use the excuse of wanting to see the kids, but his true motivation was intimidation.

Still shaken, Jessica left work, ready to pick the children up. Kayla and Ayden should be at her parents by now, as time for bus drop-off had long before passed. It was just a matter of time before she would learn why Trey had been at Gray Optional School.

At the house she watched for even a hint of expression from her mother as she asked the pointed question, "Do you know who came by the school today?"

"Was it Trey?" her mother asked.

Jessica's knees began to buckle, and she grabbed the door for support. "How did you know?"

"Well, he came by here earlier."

"What?" Jessica was now shaking from head to toe.

"He came to the door and wanted to know where

you worked."

"And you told him?"

"Well, he asked."

"Why?" Jessica's legs buckled. "Why did you tell him?"

"Because he said he needed to know."

"What else did you tell him?"

Her mother paused, then said, "Well maybe how to get there." Her voice was guilt ridden—her face ashen.

Jessica crumpled in a heap on the sofa. "How could you do that?" she asked. "I thought you understood that I'm in danger."

"I—I'm sorry."

"He still calls on the phone and threatens to kill me."

"I'm sorry," her mother said again. "But I can't do anything about that now." She threw her hands in the air and sat down on a rocking chair.

"Mama, I told you before. Never tell him anything."

"I didn't know what to say."

Jessica's rage was now over the top, but she tried to restrain it. "You didn't have to answer the door," she said.

"He kept knocking," her mother said, and picked up her knitting.

All trust shattered Jessica stood on shaky legs. "Come on kids," she said. "Let's go."

Her mother glanced up. "See you tomorrow," she said, and waved at Josh. Kayla and Ayden had long since retreated.

"Thanks for watching the kids," Jessica said, realizing the need to come across as meek and humble. Her mother was the only childcare she had—and only because it was free.

"I'm blessed to still be alive," she whispered, "no thanks to my mother."

At least her sweetest treasures were safe, and she drew in a satisfied breath of pride.

"Let's go home," she said out loud.

"Home," Josh said, repeating her. His three-year-old voice was music to her ears.

Chapter Thirty-Three

Compromised

"Can you at least meet me half-way?" Trey was begging. "It's a long drive—three hours each way. That's six hours for me."

Jessica's teeth clenched in annoyance. "I—I don't know," she said. She took a deep breath and slowly exhaled. How she regretted answering the phone. Although her response had been swift, her words were still shaky.

"Oh, come on," he said. "Just this once. Give me a break."

Six hours was a long time to be on the road, three to pick them up and three back to his house. "I—I'll need to think about it," she said.

She wasn't happy about this call, much less changing the kid's visitation schedule. In fact, she didn't want anything to do with Trey's visitation. She preferred he not be with the children at all. She feared for their safety. But court documents clearly stated he was responsible for his time with them. This arrangement, although not the best, was somewhat suitable.

"I don't have a penny to spare for gas," she said.

"Oh, come on," he said. "Work with me, won't you?" He was begging again. "The kids need to see me."

Why does he do this to me? Besides, he didn't spent time with them before. Why now?

Jessica took another ragged breath and tried to stay calm.

"Tell you what," he said. "I'm a little strapped for time. It's my week-end with the kids, but I have a meeting Friday after work."

"And..."

"If you'll meet me half-way, that's half the time for both of us. That will make things a lot easier."

"I don't know."

"Come on—for the kids."

"No."

"Give me a break."

She preferred to say, "Stop hounding me," instead "Okay, maybe," slipped from her tongue.

"I won't ask you again. I promise."

Yeah, I know all about your promises.

"You remember that gas station we used to stop at?"

"The big one?"

He cleared his throat. "Meet me there with the kids at 7:00 on Friday."

"What about my gas?"

"I'll give you twenty to help you out."

"I'm not doing this again," she said, lips drawn. "I mean it."

"I just need your help this time."

She dropped the phone and her anger exploded for being so gullible. He was playing her again. He knew she wouldn't say no. Then grabbed her head with both hands. *What if he brings a gun?*

"I'd better stick to my own guns next time," she said under her breath. She realized her ability to hold her ground was important for survival. She thought she was good at refusing Trey. But today she had failed her own test.

"What if he kidnaps me? No one will know where I'm at."

In a panic she picked up the phone and quickly punched in her mother's number. "Can you give me Wade's phone number? Yes, Wade my cousin."

A nice-looking man with her on the trip could be a good thing—especially if Trey got out of line.

***

Wade and Jessica settled in for the return trip home. The transition had gone well. Trey looked jealous until he learned that the man was only a cousin. The kids then hopped in his car, and away they went. But Jessica was dead tired. Mental fatigue was worse than physical. More than ready to go home, she relaxed and closed her eyes. The return ride should be less stressful. At least she was home free.

Conversation with Wade was easy as most related to their growing up years. But as the road leveled out, a hand lightly touched her leg. What was he doing? She didn't move. His touch may have been accidental, so she remained silent, eyes closed.

The bantering continued a moment longer but stopped when he squeezed her leg. This was no accident. As a hand of velvet moved up her skirt she instinctively recoiled. "Stop," she said. "What are you doing?"

"You know you want it."

"Want what?"

How did I get in this predicament?

The car moved off the highway, joined a dirt road, and Jessica grabbed her throat. A lump of fear was constricting it. "Where are we going?" she asked.

"Just up the road a little way, so we can talk," he said. The car stopped, the ignition was cut, and he slid over beside her.

"Just trying to help you out a little bit," he said.

"What—what do you mean?" she asked and brushed his hand off her leg. She didn't want to make him mad. He was her ride home. But what did he think he was doing?

"Let's get in the back seat."

"Why?" She was stalling.

"So we can be together."

"No."

"All divorced women want it," he said. His words sounded effortless but brought a new round of panic to Jessica's mind.

He lifted her hand and placed it on his expanding crouch. "You know you want it," he said.

"Not me," she said, and removed his hand. "I'm not like that."

His arm tightened. "You know you want it," he said again. "You've been doing without. You know you need it."

"No, I don't." But she was stumped. What could she do?

"You know you want it," he said again, forcing his lips on hers. "We're kissing cousins, you know."

Would he rape her? What was he going to do?

"I'll—I'll tell your wife."

Immediately he dropped his hold and bolted upright. "No. Please don't," he said. "Please don't tell her."

"I will if you don't stop."

Where did that idea come from? Jessica had to give God the credit.

The engine started, and the car was again on the road.

Jessica took a gulp of air, straightened her skirt, and stared out the window. Her hands, still gripped, held the shaking at bay; but her heart continued to pound. She couldn't trust anyone. Not even her own flesh and blood.

Chapter Thirty-Four

Untrustworthy

"It's time for church," Jessica said, and marched three mismatched youngsters to the car. The drive would take approximately thirty minutes. Thirty minutes? Could she tolerate the bickering that long? Of course, she could.

Their new church was a respite from the world outside—a haven in the middle of life's storm. Jessica believed this church to be the safest place on earth for her family.

Playing the piano for an absentee pianist landed her a new position, and she was ecstatic. She loved every minute of church attendance. Devotion to God could be spoken through music, and another way of worshiping Him—the God who had delivered her from certain death.

Christian music was healing and therapeutic, giving purpose beyond parenting, and work. Perhaps the drive was a bit long, but the rewards were immeasurable. The children could enjoy new friends outside of school and their neighborhood.

On many occasions new friends squeezed in the car with them to attend VBS and other church activities. Yes, this was the life.

***

One Sunday, after the service began, a couple of visitors sitting in the corner of a church pew caught Jessica's eye, and a small gasp escaped her lips. The man and his wife were former pastor friends of Trey. Should she go and speak with them, or ignore them? They must know she and Trey were getting divorced.

Following the benediction Jessica made her way to

the visitors. "How are you?" she asked and extended a hand of welcome. "Do you remember me?"

"Yes, I remember you," the man said. "And I'll tell you this. You need to go back to your husband."

Aghast, and without a second thought, unrehearsed words fell from Jessica's lips. "What do you mean?" she asked. "He was abusive to me."

"I know he did some terrible things in the past, but you were wrong to leave him," he said. His wife nodded in agreement.

Jessica was stunned. Could this woman also be a battered wife? And who are they to judge her? At that moment she decided to never again subject herself to such nonsense. Still stunned, she turned, and walked away.

Her mother was adamant that she seek counsel and set up an appointment with her own church pastor.

"Once married, the Bible says you have to stay married—no matter what," the minister. "You need to go back to your husband, and pray he forgives you for leaving him."

"What is wrong with these people?" Jessica said out loud, once in the car. "Do they want me dead?"

It was then she decided to trust no one, but her own instinct, and guidance from above. This alone would dictate what was true.

***

Later that week as Jessica sat on the edge of the bed a floodgate of memories began to release. Snippets of horror from the past flooded her mind and refused to go away.

"Ayden needs a dentist," she once said to Trey after tucking their son in bed.

"Kids don't need dentists," he said, stepping into the bathroom.

"He has cavities," Jessica said, following close, and twisting a strand of hair.

Dear God, please help Trey listen with his heart.

"Baby teeth don't matter," he said, then reached for

a toothbrush, and stroked his own pearly whites.

"Can't we at least find out from a dentist?"

"No." His words were cold.

"I really think he needs a dentist," she said. Shaking in fear, but determined, she plunged ahead; cringing all the while as she risked being pelted. "His baby teeth probably hurt."

"Kids don't need dentists until they get permanent teeth," he said, and slammed his own toothbrush in the holder for emphasis. "Why don't you shut up—you nagging bitch?"

"Please." She stepped closer. "He has cavities.

"I don't care," he said. "Now get out of my way." He shoved her through the door, and she folded. Her hands were tied.

Now, after their recent move, the children's new dentist reiterated the importance of having baby teeth repaired long before permanent ones were damaged. She shuttered at the pain Ayden had endured. If only he had been to a dentist earlier. But that was just water under the bridge.

Chapter Thirty-Five

Ramshackle

The phone rang, Jessica stiffened, and her heartbeat instantly accelerated.

Why do I always do that? Had something happened to the kids?

She had been on pins and needles from the moment they left with Trey for the weekend. Were they hurt? Her lips went instantly dry as she grabbed the phone. "Hello," she said, but her voice squeaked.

The voice on the other end was quiet, and smooth. She'd heard that voice before. Who was it? Her forehead wrinkled in annoyance as she scanned her brain. Nobody outside of work, except her parents and best friend, had her phone number. Who was calling? "Hello." Her voice was a bit stronger.

"Just thought I'd see what you were up to."

It was him. It was Trey.

"How did you get my number?" she asked, her voice cracking.

"Don't worry about it," he said. His voice was smooth and mellow, and flowed through the connection with ease.

"How?" she asked, as hot air bubbled through her lips. "I need to know."

"I just wanted to talk to you—to hear your voice again."

"But I—I don't want to talk to you." Her words, although measured, were unfeeling.

"Please don't hang up." He was begging.

"How did you get my number?"

"I have my ways."

No longer able to stand, Jessica flopped down on the nearest chair, and hugged herself. "Where are the kids?"

"They're fine," he said, and his throat cleared. "I just wanted to talk to you—."

"Let me speak to Kayla."

"The kids are fine. They're with Mom right now."

"Then this conversation is over," she said. She tried to stand, but her legs refused to budge.

"Come on, Jess."

"Don't call me again," she said, and tapped her nails on the phone in annoyance. "I don't want to talk to you."

"Come on, now. You know I want you back."

Her anger was rising. "Don't call me again," she said.

His words were causing her knees to buckle. Unsteady but determined, she stood to her feet, dropped the phone, and stumbled to the bathroom. Throwing up was on her mind.

How did he get my number? It was a secret. Did Mama give it to him? Did one of the kids tell him? How did he get it?

Her head was twirling in a crazy spin. Trey didn't want the kids this weekend. He wasn't even taking care of them. His mother was.

She dropped her head again and embraced it. At least I know they're safe with Granny. Him I don't trust. She lifted her head but sighed. I'll be glad when the kids get home.

Her head was now throbbing, so she stumbled to the kitchen, opened a bottle of Excedrin, and popped several tablets. Then she began to pace the floor—back and forth and back again.

"How did he find me?" she said out loud. "I didn't tell him. I didn't want him to have my recently changed phone number or find out where we live. It's none of his business. He can pick the kids up at my parents like he already does."

As more panic surfaced, her heart continued to pound. As a precaution, she stumbled to the door and checked the latch, making sure it was locked.

"He doesn't need to know anything about me—just when the kids are going to visit," she said out loud, and volunteered a half-laugh.

"Here I am, talking to myself again," she said.

Why did I answer that phone? What was I thinking? It's going to voicemail next time. I'm not talking to him unless it's about the kids per my attorney's advice.

"Yes, that's exactly what I'll do from this time forward."

Chapter Thirty-Six

How Can I?

"Mama, I'm hungry." Three starving innocents looked to Jessica for relief, and she didn't want to disappoint them. But her heart was in shreds. What could she feed them? The cabinets were almost bare, her paycheck wasn't due until the end of the month, and child support, as expected, was again late.

Untold trials and tribulations were starting to pile up as she sat in the fetal position, head bent over. Frustration, lack of sleep, and constant worry was eating her alive. She was certainly feeling the pressure of single parenting, with no relief in sight.

How would she pay the electric bill? What would she feed the kids without money? And how could she drive to work on an empty tank?

Her cries for mercy seemed to go unheard. Wet eyes, draining energy, despair, and desperation held her bound. And, to keep hunger growls under control, she would massage her stomach.

She was tired of being hungry. Money was always tight, her paycheck was spent long before it was received, and child support was usually late. Her car was also falling apart, and the children needed clothes. Sometimes their tummies were empty too.

"Help me, Lord. Please help me. I'm desperate."

"What's the matter, Mama?"

Jessica lifted her head, not wanting her distress to show. The urge to give up was stifled, and she forged ahead. "Let's play a new game," she said, and a smile was forced with emotions no longer felt. "Want to?"

"Okay, Mama."

"Go, and empty your piggy banks," she said.

Three enraptured youngsters scurried to separate containers, and returned with tiny assortments of nickels, dimes, and pennies.

"Ayden, can I borrow seventy-five cents? I'll pay you back Friday when I get paid."

"Kayla, have any birthday money I can borrow?"

"Josh, got any pennies I can have?"

Small change, pieced together, bought milk and a few much-needed items; and seemed to fill the refrigerator.

"What do we say when we pray?" Jessica asked.

"Thank God for piggy banks," Josh said.

Giggles and belly-laughs instantly erupted in the room.

***

"And thank God for store-brand flour and Crisco," Jessica whispered hours later. "Add a little water to the mix, and a dinner of biscuits and gravy is served."

How many times had she prepared this same meal for the children? "Fit for a king," she would say. And they believed her.

What amazing food staples these two ingredients were for a meal. God was taking care of her family in ways seemingly impossible to others.

She couldn't help but recall a story in the Bible about a widow, and a prophet. All the widow had was a little oil and some meal. As she prepared her last rations, she knew the next step for herself, and her son was death.

With no one to provide, they were helpless, and hopeless. But God sent a prophet to visit. Afterward her provisions stabilized, and they were able to eat during a time of great famine.

Exactly how many times had Jessica been like this widow woman? The times were too numerous to count.

Chapter Thirty-Seven

Christmas Basket

"Consider the ravens: they do not sow or reap; they have no storeroom or barn; yet God feeds them. And how much more valuable you are than birds" (Luke 12:24)

Jessica placed the school's accounting ledger in the bottom of her desk, shut the drawer, and locked it. Next, she straightened some paperwork scattered across the top, refilled the stapler with staples, and slid three ink pens into a plastic holder. "I'll be glad when today is over," she said in a whisper. "I'm ready for some off time."

The day was Thursday before Christmas, and she was anxious to spend some quality time with her children. Her new job as Bookkeeper in an optional school had been enriching as well as enjoyable. But exhaustion following the stress of her recent separation was a constant issue. The responsibilities of single parenting were tiring, and overwhelming.

She flicked the light switch in the off position and meandered down the short hall toward the side exit door on her way outside. The head custodian, patching a square tile in the floor, glanced up.

"Bye, Clarence," she said "Hope you have a good Christmas. You're not working late, are you?"

He wiped the back of an ebony hand across a wrinkled brow. "As soon as I'm done with this floor," he said, "I'm out of here." Then he smiled. "Have a good one."

"Thanks, Clarence," she said. "You too." With a smile and a quick wave, she turned, and continued walking toward the exit door.

She stopped one short moment to examine several new pieces of artwork created by the first graders, and neatly taped on the exit side of the door.

The festive creations of little students had captured the Christmas season in an assortment of color and design and made her smile. But memories of past holidays brought instant tears, and she quickly turned away. She glanced around one last time, then opened the door, and stepped outside.

Cold wind hit her squarely in the face as she sprinted through the parking lot. She glanced at her watch and realized it was getting late. After pulling her jacket close, she breathed in the cold, frosty air. At each excelled breath puffs of velvety clouds floated above her head and wafted away through the frigid air.

The tips of her fingers were now numb. All day bitter cold had thrust freezing tentacles into everything around her, and everything was now capped with ice. She shivered again, thrust her car key into the frozen door, and climbed inside.

The rusty car ground and groaned in resistance. The corroded door hinges scraped together, and then the door was slammed. With a stiff hand she plunged an icy key into the ignition, praying the car would start.

Black smoke with a charred odor escaped through the hood, and she relaxed as it swirled into the wintery chill. "At least the car started," she said to herself. "I'm sick and tired of this old engine huffing and puffing every time I turn the key."

Feelings of guilt then flooded her mind. "Please forgive me, Lord," she said. "I really am thankful I have a car—and I'm glad it still runs."

But as embarrassing smoke continued to spout through the hood, she ducked, hoping no one would notice. She knew the smell of burning oil would remain long after she drove through the small parking lot. And yet, despite everything, she was glad to be on her own, free from the ravages of abuse, and a volatile man. In fact, she was happy to still be alive.

"Thank God the school bus has a route to my parent's house," she said out loud as the dated auto rambled down the road.

Once home Jessica placed a small basket filled to the brim with various goodies on the kitchen table and tried to stifle a giggle. "Look what my boss gave us for Christmas," she said, grinning from ear to ear.

"Let me see, Mom," Ayden said. He threw his kindergarten reading book on the sofa and sprinted to the table.

"Let me too," Josh said, rolling into a summersault on his way, and squealing with excitement.

Kayla shoved a second-grade workbook into a worn red satchel and ambled to the table. "I didn't see that basket in the car," she said. "Where was it?"

"In the trunk so you wouldn't, until we got home," Jessica said, laughing. But her lips curved, revealing her excitement. "I wanted it to be a surprise."

Ayden reached up and spun the basket around. "Let's see what's in it," he said.

"Looks like candy and cookies and some canned beans and stuff," Kayla said, and her eyes lit up.

"I want some candy—I want some candy," Josh said, jumping up and down, and smacking his lips.

"Me too," Ayden said, but glanced at Jessica for permission.

Kayla eyed her mother again before lifting a small bag of red and green M&M's. "Can we have some?" she asked. "Please."

"Let's wait until after supper," Jessica said. "Then you can each have a hand full before bedtime."

"Thanks, Mama," Kayla said, and her face lit up.

"Oh, goody, goody," Josh said, still bouncing up and down. "Let's hurry up and eat. I get all the red ones."

"Look," Kayla said as her eyes scanned deeper inside the basket. "There's a canned ham in the bottom."

"I guess we'll save that for Christmas dinner," Jessica said, pleased with the notion that, at least on that day, their bellies would be full. She then placed three mismatched plates on the table.

"Aren't you eating, Mama?" Ayden asked.

"I'm not hungry," she said. But her scripted words were automatic as she held her stomach tight, praying the growls would stop.

Christmas Day would be special. For once her family would have a good meal to eat together.

Chapter Thirty-Eight

No Condemnation

"Please, just leave me alone." More than annoyed, Jessica twirled a strand of already twisted hair, and took a deep breath. "If you want to speak to the kids, say so. If not, I'm hanging up." It was him again. How she hated for Trey to call.

"Please don't," he said. "I'm begging you."

"Is this all you have to say?"

"I'm having it hard without you," Trey said.

"I'm hanging up now," Jessica said, and dropped the phone.

"Here I am—shaking again," she said out loud. "He makes me so mad. Why doesn't he just leave me alone?"

"Mom," Ayden said. "It's ringing again."

"And I'm not picking it up," she said. "Let it ring all night. I'm not answering."

Ayden just stood, as if waiting.

"He just says the same old things over and over again," she said. "I'm sick of his begging. I'm sick of his intimidation. I'm sick of him."

"Was that Daddy?"

"Yes, and I'm not talking to him. Do you want to talk to him?"

"No, not really," Ayden said, looking sheepish.

"Okay then."

He went back to his toy cars, and she put the phone on vibrate. Tons of messages would remain to erase, but at that moment she didn't care. Vile cursing and violent threats she could do without. Trey's pattern had been in place way too long for her to think otherwise.

After listening to many demeaning messages over

the past several months, she was learning to steer clear of his negativity. Humiliating words were hard to forget and filled her mind with undeserved guilt.

In the past his words of hate had been pushed deep inside her heart. If she could just erase them all—

Chapter Thirty-Nine

A Good Samaritan

Jessica washed the supper dishes in slow motion, her mind overburdened with the adversities of life. All she could do was pray for strength to persevere.

Her groceries had dwindled down to half a pack of saltines, and a few scrapings of peanut butter in a jar. With that in mind, she turned and stared at the cabinets. What would she feed her hungry children the next few days?

Her paycheck wasn't due for three more days. Already her stomach growled from lack of nourishment. Still, doing without was worth the effort to live without harassment, and fear of retaliation from a sadistic husband.

A knock at the front door instantly jolted her back to reality. Although the sound usually brought the children running, for some reason they remained in their rooms, and continued to play. But crash-night Friday was their night to stay up late, and they weren't in any hurry to give it up.

She peeked through the living room window and noted an overcast sky and the hazy silhouette of a lady about her age.

"Hi Ann," she said, recognizing a new friend who also lived in the apartment complex. "Why are you out so late? Come on in."

Held tightly in her friend's hand was a brown paper bag. "No, I can't," Ann said, a tired look on her face. "I just came from the store. I brought you some food." And she handed the sack to Jessica

Tears filled Jessica's eyes, but she blinked them away. "I can't take your food," she said, and tried to return the bag. But Ann refused the offer.

"God told me to bring you this food," she said. Her words were firm.

"No, Ann," Jessica said. "I can't take it. You don't have much either. Your family has needs too." And the bag was thrust back.

Ann stepped aside and folded her arms. "You're not taking my blessing away just because you won't take my food," she said.

Stunned, Jessica began to shake, and the contents of the bag started to settle. "I don't know what to say," she said.

"You don't have to say anything," Ann said, and smiled.

"How did you know we were out of food?"

"God told me."

Squeezing her tears away, Jessica reached out, and grabbed her friend for a quick hug. "You don't know what this means to me—to us."

"You would do the same for me," Ann said. "That's what friends are for." She smiled a tired smile, turned, and walked back to her car. As the vehicle pulled away, hope filled Jessica's heart.

"Are not all ministering spirits, sent forth to minister for them who shall be heirs of salvation?" (Hebrews 1:14)

"Kids, come quick," Jessica said, "and see what God just did for us."

***

Several weeks later, after a long day at work, Jessica held up what looked like a book of stamps for her children to see. "Guess what I got today," she said, and waved the small packet back and forth.

"Let me see. Let me," Josh said, and reached for her hand. He grabbed the booklet, shoving his sister's arm away at the same time.

"Mom, that's not fair," Kayla said. "Make Josh stop." As oldest sibling, she wasn't about to let him beat her to the punch.

Ayden, at the far end of the room, glanced up from his homework, a smile of interest creeping out from behind closed lips.

"It's two books of Ronald MacDonald coupons," Jessica said. Her words were gushed. "Twenty dollars' worth."

She twirled around and did a little two-step. The kids joined in, and together they bounced around in excitement.

They never ate out—no money for extras, not even a candy bar or a Happy Meal to split between the three. They would use these coupons several times—stretch them as far as they would go. Jessica wouldn't eat—just pretended she wasn't hungry.

"How did you get the coupons, Mom?" Ayden asked, showing more interest.

"A representative from the fire department came to Gray Optional School today, gave a presentation, and passed out coupon books to all the students. They gave me a couple of books too—just because I work there."

"Can I hold them?" Josh asked.

"Only one minute," Jessica said, before handing the coupons over. "Don't get them dirty."

Kayla hovered near the doorway. "Mom, can we go to MacDonald's right now?"

Jessica stared down at the floor, stalling. It was so quiet they could have heard a penny drop—if there was one. "In or out, sprout," she said. "Last one to the car is a rotten egg."

Jessica's heart did summersaults as the joys of her life rushed past, bubbling with excitement. The car door opened, and all three scrambled to their seats faster than ever before, even buckling up without a reminder.

At least, for now, they could eat out like their friends, and not feel embarrassed, or out of place. God was still taking care of them—this time with coupons.

Chapter Forty

Undeserving

"How I wish I could find us a house," Jessica said as she and her mother sat in the living room following work one afternoon. "We're tired of living in the apartment." Another sigh, and she continued. "Having our own yard would be so nice."

"Why don't you try and find one?" her mother asked.

"I've been looking, but there's no way I can afford one," Jessica said, and raked tired fingers through frazzled hair. "House rent is too high. Or the house isn't in a good location. Besides, I'll never get a loan by myself."

"Why do you want to move?"

"Because, every time I get a raise at work, my apartment rent goes up. Somehow the government knows I'm making more money, and they take it."

"That's too bad," her mother said, rocking back and forth in her chair.

"What about the house Aunt Rachael owns?" Jessica asked. "When she passes, you're in line to inherit."

"The lawyer says it's tied up right now."

"But it's empty," Jessica said, and clinched her hands together. "I thought you might let me live in the house so the kids would have a good neighborhood to play in, and I could get ahead on my bills."

"It may need be sold to pay her nursing home expenses."

"That may never happen," Jessica said. "Besides, the house is just sitting there—empty."

"Well, you can't have it."

Jessica's legs stiffened. "But couldn't I just move

there for now?" she asked.

"No. If I inherit the house, I'm giving it to James."

"James? My cousin?"

"Yes, your cousin."

"Why him, and not me?" Air bubbles shot through Jessica's mouth, and she blinked away new tears.

"He's the only person who helped your Aunt Rachael. He fixed her heater and did all her plumbing. If anyone gets the house, it should be him."

"But James already has a house," Jessica said, and new tears were wiped away. "He's established, and all his kids are grown."

"I don't care," her mother said, and drew her lips into a firm line. "Like I said before, he deserves it."

Turning away, Jessica tried to swallow her pride. Without God's help she would never survive her nightmare of struggle.

Chapter Forty-One

Telephone Call

A pale pink envelope covered in a floral design was the only piece of mail in the box, and Jessica let out a long sigh. No child support today. Disappointed, she slowly turned the envelope over, and noted Emily's return address in the left-hand corner.

She never writes. I wonder why this time.

With a flick of the wrist, she ripped the envelope open, and a newspaper clipping dropped to the ground. After picking it up, she released a gasp. A man had been arrested for killing his wife, cutting her body into separate parts, and leaving them in the trunk of her own car.

"Why would Emily send this to me?" she said out loud. "Well, I guess she realized this could easily have been me."

She breathed a quick prayer of thanksgiving that it wasn't, then turned, and walked back to the apartment. Once inside, the phone began to ring, and she inhaled quick gulps of air. How she hated that ringtone.

"That's probably Trey," she said out loud. But as far as she was concerned, their conversations were wasted. Although her attorney cautioned that she needed to talk to Trey when he called, she dreaded the sound of his voice. Intimidation was the game he would play.

Past threats continued to haunt Jessica. Trey's promise to blow her brains out before their split kept her focused, and frightened. The answering machine retained many angry, menacing messages. Her life was still at risk. Only faith in God could keep her safe—and sane.

Although months of time had passed without incident following Jessica's separation from Trey, sounding relaxed on the phone was imperative when he called. It was detrimental if he realized his ability to terrorize remained.

Her voice waivered, then began to stabilize. "Hello?" To herself she sounded strong.

It was him.

"Hold on a sec," Trey said. Loud noises in the background filtered through her ear after he placed his phone on a solid surface.

"I'm back," he said. "The delivery boy from Burger King was at the door."

"Okay," she said, blowing out some air. "What did you need to talk about?"

"Nothing really."

"If it's not about the kids, then I'm hanging up."

"Hold on a minute, will you?" he said. "I just wanted to talk to you."

"Well, make it quick. I'm busy."

"You don't have to be so impatient," he said.

The sound of munching grew louder, causing Jessica to grab her stomach. "What's that noise?" she asked.

"Oh, just extra-large fries and a good old hamburger with all the fixings," he said. "Hold on a sec." Again, the phone dropped.

He's making me hungry.

The next instant he was back. "Cheese was oozing out on the table, and I needed a napkin to wipe it up."

We're nearly starving here. Saltines and water for lunch today, and he can afford a meal—plus delivery?

"Hold on."

Again?

"He's wasting my time," she said under her breath. Why am I even talking to him?"

His next words brought her back with a jolt. "I just wondered if you'd thought anything about us getting back together," he said.

"No," she said. "Never going to happen."

"I promise. If we do, things will be different."

He's trying to ease his conscience.

167

"No," she said. "I need to go."

"Just think about it."

"Bye."

A sigh of relief filtered through Jessica's mouth. Doing without was an easy price to pay for freedom. Even so, she wondered what the kids could eat that wouldn't clear the cabinets.

***

The next day Trey's words leaped out from the answering machine, and Jessica didn't even hear the phone ring.

"It's your fault we're not together, your ugly mother-fucking-whore. You took everything important to me, and now I'm going to pay you back. You'll come out of work one day and I'll blow your brains out. I'll be in the bushes hiding, and you won't even know what hit you, you ugly Bitch. You'll never make it on your own. You'll see you need me."

Silence.

"Come on—talk to me. Please."

The answering machine was full of recorded messages from Trey that crushed and mocked. Threats and coercion still sent chills up and down Jessica's spine each time she listened to his new messages.

"When he stops ranting through the phone, I'll lift the receiver to my ear," she whispered.

Seconds later she lifted the phone. Despite the respite, she twisted the hem of her shirt in fear and annoyance.

"Just leave me alone," she said. "If you want to speak to the kids, say so. If not, I'm hanging up."

"Please don't," he said. "I'm begging."

"Is that all you have to say?"

"I'm having a hard time without you."

"Doesn't sound like that to me."

"No-no. I only wanted to talk to you."

"Sounds like you're trying to kill me."

"No. You don't understand."

"Do you have anything good to say—anything about the kids?"

"No. I only wanted to talk about us."

"There is no us," she said. "I'm hanging up now." And she dropped the phone, turned, and walked away.

"Here I am shaking again," she said out loud. "He makes me so mad. Why doesn't he just leave me alone?"

"Mom," Kayla said. "I need new shoes. These are falling apart."

The cheap pair Jessica recently purchased for her at the dime store was now in shreds, and her eyes instantly filled with tears. But she brushed them away. She was doing the best she could. Money was always tight. Pinching pennies was essential for survival.

"I know, honey," Jessica said. "I need to buy new shoes for you, and Ayden.

I can't afford new shoes. But I don't have a choice. I'll have to charge them on my credit card. But I can't afford another bill. Oh God, please help me.

Chapter Forty-Two

Insurance Failure

The mailbox was full to overflowing. Jessica stood and stared long and hard at the box before letting out an aggravated sigh. She slowly lifted the conglomerate and meandered back to the apartment, half afraid to examine the mix.

In fact, she wasn't in any hurry to rearrange the bills just to pay the most important ones. Without looking, she tossed the mail on a table and decided to tackle the pile later—after the kids were asleep.

Later that evening she shuffled through the dreaded stack, placing the most recent bills on the bottom. She breathed a prayer for enough money to pay what was due, plus food and gas. Thus began the tedious task of paying the monthly debt.

Each month, after her paycheck hit the bank, it was painstakingly doled out again. Utility vendors, apartment rent, car payment, and creditors were all hounding her for money. Ten dollars in quarters would cover laundry expense, and fifty would remain to buy groceries and gas for the month. Child support would fill in the gap—if and when it arrived.

A strange looking envelope in the stack caught her attention, and she paused. She studied the return address, then ripped the envelope open. An invoice from Ayden's last doctor's visit fell out, and a letter stating he was no longer covered under Trey's insurance plan. She was now responsible for the balance.

"What? Trey canceled the kid's insurance. Well, I'm not surprised." Ballistic anger then erupted, and she quickly put her hand over her mouth to mute her verbal rage. Her face flamed. Her anger was to the roof. Without thinking, she picked up the phone and punched in Trey's number. There was no answer. But she wasn't surprised.

She slammed the re-dial button.

"Hello."

"Why did you cancel the insurance on Ayden?" Her anger was coming through loud and clear—so strong she was shaking. "Did you cancel the other kids too?"

"Now, hold on a minute." The voice on the other end was calm and collected, and she shivered in annoyance.

I think he enjoyed my outburst.

"What are you talking about?"

Her next words were spoken with bated breath. "I got a letter in the mail today stating that Ayden isn't covered under your insurance. You're supposed to keep insurance on the kids. It's in our separation agreement."

"Well, now, don't get excited."

"Do they have insurance, or not?"

"Well, I dropped the family plan because you were on it."

"I don't need your insurance," she said. "I have my own insurance through my job." She took a deep breath, and slowly released.

"Well, I didn't want to get stuck with your bills, so I dropped the family plan."

"You're not being fair to the kids," she said. "They need insurance."

"Not my problem."

Slamming the phone down brought some relief.

"Our court-ordered separation requires Trey provide health insurance for our children," she said out loud. "I guess this call puts all into perspective."

But how can I pay the children's medical bills from an empty pocket?

It was time to add her children to her own insurance plan. Despite the cost, the added premium would be money well spent.

Every day Jessica was learning to trust only in herself, as most around her were proving untrustworthy.

And forget court orders. As far as she was concerned, they didn't exist. Right here and now was what mattered.

After taking matters into her own hands, she could breathe a little easier. The children's health care was now in her hands, and not in Trey's.

What other choice do I have?

"Absolutely none," she said out loud.

Chapter Forty-Three

The Price of Freedom

The sun was still shinning when Jessica re-visited her afternoon strategy. Starting today, the entire weekend was hers. And she had plans. The children also had plans. They were on their way to visit Trey three hours away. Their Aunt Emily had volunteered to pick them up.

All were smiles as small arms waved and voices piped their good-byes. Suppressed tears then flowed, and usually long after they were out of sight. It was difficult letting them go. The vigor's of apartment life stopped the moment they walked out the door. But, for once, Jessica didn't have time to dwell on being lonely.

Spring was in the air, and the aroma of roses, mixed with gardenia, gently filtered past her nose. A neighbor's freshly potted plants caught her attention, and she wanted to see them up close.

She locked the apartment door, anxious to be on her way. She stopped a moment to flavor the display. But she needed to hurry. The Blood Plasma Center would close soon, and she needed to get there before it did.

A newspaper clipping carefully guarded in a zippered compartment of her purse was now in her hands. The ad filled her heart with hope. Donate Plasma for Money it read.

The ad—bold and provocative—the address—simple and direct. Extra money in her pocket would mean more gas in the car—perhaps enough to defray some upcoming summer expenses. The process sounded simple, and not too painful. "Short breaths," she coached herself. "Take short breaths."

As her car sputtered up a rounded roadway, and into

an oversized parking lot, she breathed a sigh of relief. A brick building, once seen at a distance, loomed tall in front of her. She glanced at her watch, and noted the time registered at a quarter 'til five. She would need to hurry.

Once inside, a nurse took her pulse and other vitals, and her finger was pricked. Minutes later the nurse returned. "Honey, I'm sorry," she said, "but the iron level in your blood registers zero. We can't use it. The test says you're malnourished."

"Malnourished?" Jessica took a quick breath, but quickly rebounded. "Please," she said. "Test me again." And she wiped a tear away. "I—I really need that money."

"I'm sorry, but we can't use your blood this time."

Jessica's jaw dropped, and instant weakness swayed her legs. All hopes were crushed.

The nurse stopped one moment, as if concerned. "Eat plenty of green vegetables such as collard greens and broccoli," she said. "Build your iron. Come back in a few months, and we'll test you again.

Blinking to hide her disappointment, Jessica hurried outside, wiping her face to mask the flow of tears. No iron? No wonder her hair was falling out by the handfuls, and her nails peeling, not to mention always being hungry.

"Well, I guess eating right really does matter," she said out loud.

Her ration of food was limited, but she always made sure the children ate first. If nothing was left, she got nothing. Only one paycheck a month, plus child support, and both needed to last until the end of the month. Doing without was the only way her small family could survive.

A recent trip to Social Services was also a disaster in the making. But she was desperate. Summer was coming. As a ten-month employee she was more than worried.

How would she pay her bills during the summer months without a paycheck? She couldn't ask her parents. They had limited cash flow. Pride kept her from asking the church. She was on her own, in more ways than one.

After several sleepless nights she recalled several apartment friends who received government assistance.

Maybe she should visit Social Services. After all, she did receive a discount on rent each month due to low income.

At the Social Services office she fidgeted with her purse, trying to stay calm. The children were tired and driving her crazy from boredom. Not to mention chasing Josh around the room, trying to keep him out of trouble.

She hated taking the children with her every time she went for an appointment. But she had no choice. They were her responsibility, and she took it seriously. Forty minutes later she was called to the desk.

"Stay right here," she said, giving instructions to her brood. "Kayla, make sure you watch your brothers."

Jessica's heart pounded with anxiety. Leaving the children by themselves in a waiting room was always scary.

Once in privacy room she gingerly sat down on the edge of a chair, folded her hands, and tried to remain calm. As she waited, a hefty woman of color, quite rude in the scheme of things, shuffled through a stack of papers before giving her full attention.

"I need to apply for some sort of financial aid," Jessica said, when at last noticed.

"What kind of aid?" the woman asked in a voice that was both crusty, and harsh.

"I'll be out of work this summer," Jessica said, rubbing her hands together. "I work for the school system."

"Do you have any other income?"

"Child support."

"In what amount?

"Four hundred. I have three children."

"How much money do you make from work?" the woman asked.

Jessica handed her a pay stub.

The sound of fingers thumping stiff calculator keys made her nervous, and she stiffened.

"You don't qualify," the woman said. Her words sent chills up and down Jessica's spine.

"Even if I'm out of work two months?"

"Your child support disqualifies you," the woman said.

"That doesn't make sense," Jessica said.

Silence.

She slid deeper into the chair and swallowed her pride. "I won't have enough money to pay rent and bills this summer," she said.

Still no response.

Perhaps standing would have more impact, but her legs refused to cooperate. "How is it possible that I—I don't qualify?" she asked.

"We add all income together and divide by twelve."

"But I won't be working two months in the summer," Jessica said, and her knees began to knock into each other. "Can we at least get food stamps those two months I'm not working?"

"You don't qualify," the woman said.

Cold chills ran up and down Jessica's spine.

Why can't this hard-headed woman understand I'll have no money during the summer?

Pangs of abandonment were again slapping her in the face. Should she take one more chance, and be bolder this time? She found her legs and stood. "Please. I really need help."

The woman only frowned.

"Please."

"Next?"

The woman was dismissing her, so Jessica turned, and stumbled to the door. Her shoulders sagged, as did her spirit. Defeat was written all over her face.

How could she survive the summer with nothing but child support? It wouldn't be enough. But she squared her shoulders and stepped back into the waiting room where three rowdy kids were waiting.

Would this strangle-hold go on forever? And what just happened in there? Why did she even mention child support?

"Well, because I'm an honest person."

Still, she found it hard understanding how Kathy, one of her neighbors, and her two children qualified for food stamps, and she couldn't. Steak, potato chips, and colas were staples in their house, and purchased with food stamps. Would this insanity never end? Food stamps in her hands would purchase cheap meat, vegetables, and fruit.

Turning away, she verbalized her thoughts. "I can't understand government logic," she said out loud. "I just don't understand."

And now, as she left the blood plasma center, her heart was again fractured. Severe weakness was attacking her limbs, and her legs went numb beneath her. Overcome with weakness, she dragged herself the rest of the way to the car. Once inside, she rubbed her head in frustration, trying to soothe the pain of hopelessness.

She was tired of the effort and tied of the insanity. She was tired of working hard for little pay. She was tired of doing without just to survive. She was tired of pretending she was happy when the struggle was overwhelming. She was tired of everything—tired of it all. Surviving as a single mom was harder than she thought it would be.

"Maybe I'll just end it all—right here and now," she said out loud. "Nobody cares. The kids will be okay—Granny will take care of them. They love her. But how should I do it? Make the car go faster? Jump off a bridge? Take some pills?"

Ideas were coming fast and hard, making her head swim. No one cared if she died. Besides, she was tired of begging for scraps of food—tired of people looking down on her poverty—tired of struggling month to month. Simply said, she was just tired. What was the point?

Physically exhausted, and emotionally drained, she sucked in her breath; and closed her eyes. She now realized freedom had a price.

Chapter Forty-Four

Where's the Money?

The past few days Jessica was more than worried. As a ten-month employee her salary would end two weeks after the students were released for the summer. However, Mrs. Dorsett, noting her despair, put in a word for her at the school's Central Office. At her recommendation she would be the summertime switchboard operator. At least cleaning toilets wasn't on the agenda, although any job would have been accepted with a smile on her face.

Her parents promised to watch the children as daycare camps weren't an option. But the cost was harsh as punishment for even minor misdeeds wasn't optional, as far as her mother was concerned. She often directed Jessica to re-punish if she felt the necessity. But that notion was a constant noose around Jessica's neck, and she refused to deliver.

***

The following year Jessica was promoted to Bookkeeper at a local high school. Now a twelve-month employee, she could truly relax, and enjoy her work. Not only did full-time employment mean more benefits, but more time on the job. Still, there was never enough money.

The children, now older, challenged the budget even more than before. Making ends meet was still a struggle, and often fell short. There was little money for extras. Pinching pennies was essential for survival, but she was determined her children would have a good summer.

In the afternoons, and on weekends, she learned that swings and slides at local parks were free. The public pool was a great place to cool down, and reasonable if enough cash could be scraped together, plus gas for the car.

The library, another option, provided free books, free movies, and other free programs.

Signing the kids up for baseball and soccer was worth scrounging for the fee. All three were worthy of at least that much. They deserved a happy childhood, even if it cost everything she owned in the process. Besides, there wasn't anyone but God to depend on.

"God will provide," she often said.

The outdoor playground at Hendersonville Library East became their favorite pastime. After work she could rest on a bench while her restless brood exhausted themselves at play. The recreational area at Cottage Hill Apartments provided a turn-about glider. Great escapes didn't always require money. Yes, Jessica could be creative if she had to.

***

The mailbox was empty again and Jessica wrung her hands in disbelief. "It's late as usual," she said out loud. "Eleven days past due, and still no child support. What am I going to do?"

Her shoulders drooped as she returned to the apartment. Once inside she felt the heaviness of despair drop on her shoulders.

What could she fix for dinner tonight? The cabinets were bare—two days now. But just in case she was wrong, she opened a cabinet door, and peered inside. An empty jar of peanut butter, already scraped and ready to toss, was the only item inside. "We're out of everything," she said out loud.

The children, hearing her in the kitchen, ran up with the words "I'm hungry" on their lips.

"We're almost out of food," she said, wiping her eyes. "Child support's late—again." And, she wanted to add, "as usual," but instead bit her tongue. But bad-mouthing Trey was getting easier with each passing month.

She didn't want to sound harsh when speaking to the children about their dad. But was it wrong to say those things when they were true? Maybe the truth would be easier for the children to understand than half-truths. Besides, biting her tongue was making it raw.

From now on, she would speak the truth. Whatever the circumstance, they needed to know just why there wasn't food in the house. Her mind then shifted to her last conversation with Trey. "I haven't seen child support yet," she said.

"Well, it's coming," he said. His words were spit. "I don't know why you're complaining. I need that money more than you do."

"How can you say such a thing?"

"You have a good job," he said. "You make good money. You know you do."

His words slapped her in the face, and she cringed under his sarcasm. "Not really," she said. "We're barely scraping by."

"Well, that's your fault," he said. "You left me, remember?"

Her face flamed as he continued his banter. But his words no longer moved her, as anger had long ago replaced that fear. "I'm hanging the phone up now," she said, and walked to the center of the room, ready to drop the phone. But then she changed her mind. "I need to know when I'll have child support."

"With all that money I send, you're probably buying new clothes for yourself—new shoes, new outfits, and things like that."

Trying to stay composed, Jessica shifted the phone to the other ear, and then her thoughts were verbalized. "That money is for the kids—to help pay rent and buy food—for them—not me. I can live under a bridge. They can't."

"Yeah—right. You know you're spending all that money on yourself."

What a jerk.

"This call is a waste of time," she said. "Good-bye." And, as a way of venting, she dropped the phone and walked away.

School was scheduled to begin again in one week, and Jessica was concerned. She glanced at her feet and drew a sharp breath. The kids needed new shoes—all three of them.

Her thoughts continued as she walked through the school parking lot to the car. Seconds later her vehicle rolled from the lot and headed up the road. It was time to pick her children up at their grandparents.

As for shoes, she had learned the hard way that cheap ones didn't last. Maybe a good pair of sneakers would be worth the price. Yes, it would cost more up front. But shoes should last longer than six weeks—longer than the cheap stuff Trey once purchased for the kids. After the first wash Ayden's clothes were handed down to Josh. Because everything shrunk, he and Kayla both ended up with nothing.

Jessica allowed a long sigh to escape. "What can I say to the kids?" she said out loud. "It will break my budget if I buy shoes. I don't have money for shoes. And if I buy three pair, I'll never get my credit card paid off."

Another sigh. "Oh well," she said. "The kids need shoes."

Seconds later the Honda rounded a curve, spun up the driveway, and stopped. Jessica glanced out the window as the prides of her life, three bright-eyed youngsters, rushed out to greet her. "Let's go, and buy new shoes," she said.

Squeals, shiny eyes, and glistening cheeks was all she needed to realize she had made the right decision.

Chapter Forty-Five

Holiday Pause

"Hurry up," Jessica said, and jiggled the car keys. "It's time to go." When they ran past, she closed the door, and stepped outside into the blustery wind.

Chilled to the bone, she drew in a sharp breath. Kayla, now twelve, and Ayden, nine, climbed into the car; noses freezing. A seatbelt strap was found for Josh, and he was secured.

"I hope the car doesn't conk out," Jessica said under her breath as she sprinted to the driver's side. The engine was thrusting billows of smoke from the hood each time it cranked. But the Honda was all she owned, so she breathed a quick prayer, and closed the door. Her prayer was answered. The car started.

The vehicle, now using a vast amount of oil, was a serious concern. Cans of oil in the trunk were used daily to keep the engine from blowing up.

Despite the financial struggle Jessica promised herself the children would have a good Christmas—at least as much as was possible. So, she drew a cold breath and plunged ahead with inner fortitude and blind faith in God.

A co-worker had invited them to an indoor drama titled *Back to Jerusalem* at the Episcopal Church downtown. With a serious lack of funds, Jessica was thankful the admission was free. If not, the invitation would have been declined. All she could afford these days were necessities.

The children were excited this particular Saturday, two weeks before Christmas. Bundled in undersized coats and assorted caps, they seemed oblivious to the harsh winter wind.

The cold more than accentuated the season as

freezing air swept through the parking lot of the church and nuzzled at their ears. Inside, cold tiles on both floor and wall enhanced the temperature as puffy breaths were exhaled, and hands squeezed for warmth. But the excitement of the holiday was embraced and made the wait tolerable.

After a small intermit, Jessica and her three followed a guide down the stairs of the church, and into a huge basement redesigned as Jerusalem—all the way back to the time of Jesus' birth.

Drama shop keepers selling wares on the street huddled in tents scattered throughout the city. A town crier warned residents and visitors alike to register for a census in the town square. Priests, dressed in traditional robes of the time, were selling doves for sacrificial offerings as chaos reigned.

Other locals traveled on foot through straw-covered streets on their way to the center of town. Joseph, a weary looking man with a leather strap in his hand, walked beside an exhausted donkey.

A pregnant woman with the man was hunched over the animal, and was tearful, as the man asked again and again for a place to stay. Mary, his wife, was about to give birth. The words, "No room—No room," were repeated over and over—some rudely, and some compassionate.

At long last an inn keeper offered the couple a place to stay, in his humble stable. Mary and Joseph would share a stall with the few farm animals he owned.

Straw was arranged in the manger for a place to lay the new baby. A bed of hay heaped in the corner would give Mary support during delivery. The animals could eat their fodder elsewhere in the barn.

Reverence and calm serenity captured the essence of the season as Mary and Joseph, surrounded by shepherds and angels, presented the newborn babe amid chaotic Jerusalem life. Christ, the Redeemer had been born.

After the display, and beyond the manger scene, Jessica stepped outside into the windblown sunshine. The children followed close behind. A snowflake or two cascaded through the squall as renewal beckoned them forward.

Jessica's small family, with a group of others, meandered to a camel staked near a tree. A beggar, part of the drama team began asking for alms. Digging deep in the bottom of her purse, she prayed, through some miracle, each child would have a gift for the vagabond. But coins could never replace the love this drama had instilled in their hearts.

***

Five days before Christmas Kayla, Ayden, and Josh acted out their own rendition of the birth of Christ with other youth in the church, and the joy of the season seemed to explode.

Still, Jessica was concerned. How could she possibly scrape together enough money from her meager earnings to make the final payments on her children's lay-away gifts?

Following their performance, presents under the church tree were shared. Fear and despair were soon forgotten as her name was called again and again. Although she felt underserving, God's arms were still holding her close with reminders that His promise to never leave, nor forsake her, was solid.

Each child received a coat for the winter, and assorted toys. A brown paper bag full of goodies and fruit handed to each attendee was also embraced, and greatly appreciated. But money given to spend only on herself is a legacy she still holds dear to her heart.

With gifts in hand and a renewed faith in God, Jessica's family made their way home while singing the joyful carols of Christmas.

A brilliant array of colorful lights displayed on homes throughout the neighborhood evoked a new sense of wellbeing in all of them. Even a smoking car, with dents and peeling paint, couldn't destroy the thrill of the season. This would certainly be a Christmas to remember.

"For unto us a child is born, unto us a son is given:

and the government shall be upon his shoulder: and his name shall be called Wonderful, Counselor, The mighty God, The everlasting Father, the Prince of Peace" (Isaiah 9:6)

Chapter Forty-Six

The Debate

Dating? Are you kidding? I don't think so.

Another man in Jessica's life was not a consideration. She had almost been destroyed by one. But Pansy, an older lady in Jessica's church, was passionate about a newspaper dating service she had found. As a retired widow, she loved companionship, and often dated. She also lived at Cottage Hill Apartments and was one of Jessica's neighbors.

A couple of months in a row she doggedly insisted that Jessica try the service, assuring her the organization was authentic—a real Christian organization that truly desired perfect matches for their clients. It was an original dating service for Christian singles.

When November's ads arrived in her mailbox, she eagerly shared them with friends. But for some odd reason, Jessica was first on her list.

"Hi Pansy," Jessica said, after answering the door. "Come on in."

"You remember that dating service I told you about?" Pansy asked, after taking a seat. "I've decided to give you a couple of listings. Maybe you can find a young man to suit you."

"Thanks, Pansy," Jessica said, and tried to stifle a laugh. "But I don't think I'm interested."

Pansy smiled back—as if defying her. "Take it anyway," she said, "and look it over. You just never know."

That evening, after the kids were in bed, Jessica sat down on the sofa and flipped through several pages of available men—first names only—listed on thin sheets of paper. But the notion of another husband was quickly brushed aside. A few dates after her divorce only proved she wasn't interested in long term relationships. And yes, she was afraid.

***

The following month Pansy returned with a new list of bachelors from her mail-order list. Jessica, still dubious, scanned the names of available men looking for Christian companionship. The name Daniel kept leaping off the page.

Daniel. Why do I like that name so much?

But she laid the list aside for more pressing matters. The children needed her, and the list was forgotten. But when another weekend rolled around, she again scanned the list.

"Daniel" she said out loud. "A man named Daniel. Maybe I'll write him a short letter and see what happens."

The following Monday when Jessica stepped inside the apartment the telephone rang. The kids, scrambling to be first inside, almost pushed her over, but she managed to grab the phone just before it stopped ringing.

After catching her breath, she pushed her heels off and kicked them to the side. "Hello," she said, inhaling deeply.

"Is this Ms. Williams," a male voice asked.

Multiplied butterflies swarmed in Jessica's stomach. "Yes?" she asked. Her words were winded.

"I received your letter in the mail, and thought I'd give you a call."

"Who is this?"

"It's Daniel."

"Oh," she said, as multiplied butterflies again swarmed. But a hint of a smile shadowed her face.

"Your letter said you might be interested in getting to know me."

"You realize I have three kids, right?"

"Yes," he said, and cleared his throat. "I'm okay with kids."

And so began a new chapter in Jessica's life.

A week into January, following the Christmas

holidays and Daniel said it was time for them to meet. A visit was planned—a blind date as it were—and the day marked in red on Jessica's calendar.

Chapter Forty-Seven

A Taste of Redemption

"I'll keep my date with Daniel a secret," Jessica promised herself. "After all, this date is nothing more than a reason to get out of the apartment." But she couldn't help but smile.

"This week-end I wish Trey was keeping his visitation schedule with the kids," she said out loud. "At least they have a birthday party to attend, and I can still go on this date."

The timing couldn't be more perfect. Her date with Daniel would be at a Mexican restaurant close to the apartments. The children wouldn't even know she was away.

"Will he recognize me when we meet?" she whispered. "How will I know him after only a few phone conversations, and a picture?"

Her thoughts scattered as the phone's jarring ring set center stage. On the other end Daniel's explosive laugher was energizing, and catchy. "It's a good thing I looked at a map last night," he said, "or I wouldn't be driving to Hendersonville today."

"Are you still coming?" she asked.

"I'm on the road right now," he said. "I thought you lived in Henderson. But when I looked at the map again, I knew I'd be leaving earlier. Hendersonville is quite a bit farther than Henderson. Remember, I live in Rocky Mount."

"Are you sure you want to drive that far?" she asked, and held her breath, waiting for the answer.

"Sure, I do," he said. "It's a long drive, but I want to meet you. Something keeps telling me I'll be glad I did."

He was coming after all, and Jessica danced around the table on her way to the closet. Her mind was exploding with the possibilities of a new friendship as she stared inside her closet. Dressing for a blind date was electrifying, even though her nature was more tranquil than not.

After an uplifting prayer, her favorite perfume, used only for special occasions, was sprit-zed on arms and neck; making her feel glamorous. Or, perhaps she was just happy getting out of the apartment, for once, without the kids. Whatever it is, everything just felt good.

And when Daniel walked into the restaurant, shortly after her arrival, she knew exactly who he was. "I'm over here," she said, waving from a bench nearby.

***

The evening went better than planned. Still, Jessica was cautious, and somewhat anxious to check on her children.

After dinner, as she and Daniel walked through the parking lot, the frigid January air hit them both squarely in the face. She shivered a couple of times, then moved closer to him. She linked her arm into his, not only for warmth, but to convey her happiness they had met.

He smiled, reached over, and patted her on the same arm. She smiled back. But on the inside, she was giggling.

"Why don't you come by later after I put the kids in bed?" she asked. "Maybe we can talk more then."

Now, that was a bold thing to say.

In her heart of hearts, a gentle stirring of desire was beginning to surface. Was this more than just a chance meeting? Could this be a perfect match?

***

He reached out, and quietly wrapped his arms around Jessica. "Driving to see you every week-end is getting harder and harder to do," Daniel said. "I'm on the road all the time now."

"You can stop any time you want," Jessica said, and grinned.

"But what if I don't want to?" he asked.

Laughter followed and was sweet to her ears, and the excitement of youthful anticipation exploded in her heart.

"Maybe—maybe we should start making plans for our future," he said.

"Our future?"

He reached inside his pocket, pulled out a velvet box, and opened it. Bending down, he lifted a diamond ring in one hand while balancing from his knee. "Will you be my bride?" he asked. "Will you marry me?"

Overcome with both humor and excitement, Jessica reached for the ring, and slid it on her finger. "Is this a Valentine's Day present?" she asked.

"Well, it could be. What do you say?"

Tears formed beneath closed lids. On the outside, she was smiling, but on the inside she was ecstatic. "Yes, I'll marry you," she said.

"I didn't think you would ever answer," he said, again standing. He was grinning from ear to ear.

"I didn't think you'd ever ask," she said.

He laughed, then drew her close. "Well, we've only been dating a couple of months."

She smiled back and pursed her lips for an invited kiss.

"Don't you really think it's too early to get engaged?" he asked, moments later.

"You're the one who brought the ring."

"I knew you wanted it."

"When should we get married?" Jessica asked. "We're not getting any younger, you know."

"When do you want to?"

"I think we're ready," he said, and placed another kiss on her lips.

"I want a real wedding this time," she said, and drew a deep breath. "I eloped the first time—had a bad marriage afterwards. But you already know that."

He smiled, and his eyes melted her heart.

"Will you move to Rocky Mount with me, or should I

find a job here?"

Jessica didn't need to think twice about the answer. "I don't want to up-root the kids from school, and their friends," she said. "Besides, I love my job."

"I don't have a problem moving," Daniel said. "But I need to find work before I do."

"Let's start praying," she said. "God can find the perfect job for you, right here in Hendersonville—or a town nearby."

"Make a list of companies nearby," he said, "and I'll send out blind resumes."

"We need to pray over each one before you send them out," she said, and patted him on the knee.

"Agreed," he said. "That way, if I get a job here, we'll know our plans are in God's will."

***

"Let's go ahead and plan the wedding," Jessica said.

"A long week-end will work best for me," Daniel said.

"I want my kids in the wedding too," she said. "And a pretty dress—a new one."

"I know you can't afford a new dress by yourself," he said. "Pick one out, and I'll pay for it."

"Really?" she asked, then jumped off from the sofa, and into his arms. "I haven't purchased a new dress in a very long time."

"Whatever you want," he said.

"No one ever said that to me, and meant it," she whispered. "Dare I believe?"

"I'll need to pick out some colors for the wedding," she said. "There's a lot to plan."

"I think you need to pick out a day first," he said.

"I think you're right," she said, and giggled again.

Daniel reached over and pulled a calendar off the table. "Here," he said. "Let's have a look."

"When is your next long weekend?" she asked, staring at the calendar. "We could plan our wedding for that same week-end."

"Maybe you're right," he said, then paused and pointed at the calendar. "I have a week's vacation coming. It's the week of April fifteenth."

"Tax week?" Jessica couldn't help but laugh. "How about Tax Day?"

His smile was unforgettable.

"That way we'll never forget our wedding anniversary," she said, and they both laughed.

***

The week of the wedding Jessica's telephone rang. It was Daniel. "I just picked up the mail," he said. "A letter came in response to one of the blind resumes I mailed out. Gerber Baby Foods offered me a job, sight unseen. I have an interview with them in two days. They want to meet me and verify my skills."

Her phone dropped, and she did a little Hallelujah dance around the table. When she lifted the phone, he was laughing.

"This job begins two weeks after the wedding," he said.

"It's a miracle," she said, and tears began to run down her cheeks. "Nothing more than a miracle."

"You're the one who found the job."

"But you're the one that landed it."

"Our prayers worked," she said.

"This is a God-thing," he said.

"We're really happy together, aren't we?" she asked. As more tears dropped on her cheeks, she dabbed them with her fingertips.

"Don't cry," he said. "You're the light of her life. There's nobody like my Jessica."

Chapter Forty-Eight

A Fairy Tale Comes True

Jessica felt like a princess in her new wedding gown. Well, not a gown exactly, but certainly a dress fit for nuptials—faded lilac lace with a fluffy white veil. A gorgeous pink, lilac, and white floral bouquet draped her arm, and finished the ensemble.

Kayla, dressed in flowing pink chiffon, was the flower girl. Ayden and Josh were dressed in white slacks and pastel shirts. They were the groomsmen.

The small mountain church where Jessica retained membership was full on the big day. Well-wishers, friends from work, and local church members were also in attendance. Her parents even came. Everyone seemed delighted she'd found someone to care for her, and the children. Already Daniel was accepted into the fold, no questions asked.

At the bottom of the stairs Jessica and Daniel linked hands, and together strolled to the front of the church. A smile would remain on her face the entire day.

"I've never seen you so happy," Daniel whispered softly.

"It's the best day of my life, except when my kids were born," she whispered back.

The minister interrupted their undertones. "We gather together here in the sight of God, and in the presence of these witnesses, to join together Jessica and Daniel in holy matrimony. At this union they desire to enter into a sacred covenant with each other..."

With hands entwined, Daniel and Jessica made their commitment. Following the ceremony, their guests headed downstairs to the fellowship area where balloons, ribbons, and pastel decorations had been draped from ceiling to floor in springtime array. A three-layer white chiffon cake with eatable pink and lilac roses also awaited the couple's arrival.

As friends gathered near, the sweetness of their union was embraced, and celebrated.

Later, and still holding hands, Daniel and Jessica slipped outside, ready to embark on their honeymoon as husband and wife. His white sports car had been decorated, and overflowed with streamers, confetti, and old tin cans.

Several guests followed them to the parking lot where everyone else had gathered to celebrate the nuptials. Loud clapping, whistling, and cat calling, stopped them dead in their tracks. Bird seed from every direction cascaded over clothing and hair, covering both from head to toe.

Together they waved their good-byes through an opened window as they huddled close in the front seat. Kayla, Ayden, and Josh, arms bursting with streamers and silly string, urged them on their way. Their upcoming week was also a planned event. They would be the guests of a close church member, and their family of five.

When Daniel's car rolled from the celebration, several vehicles followed close behind. Horns blasted, voices yelled, and tires screeched noisy congratulations as the couple drove from the parking lot.

A conglomerate of old shoes, tin cans, and various trinkets jumbled, slapped, and clanged against their coupe in the warm April breeze as they headed to the beach for their honeymoon retreat.

Their wedding, as later learned, was the talk of the day.

Chapter Forty-Nine

Residual

Jessica managed to crawl to a chair before intense pain in her left side overcame her. Writhing in pain, she resigned to her fate.

"Jessica, honey, where are you?" Daniel asked after coming through the door later that afternoon.

"In here," she said. Unable to drag herself to bed, she had remained in the chair.

"What happened?" he asked, running to her side.

"I don't know,' she said. "I left work because I was in too much pain. I'm still in pain. My left side is killing me."

She tried to stand, but the pain was overwhelming, and she fell back in the chair.

"I'm taking you to the ER right now," Daniel said. "Where are the kids?"

"They came home from school," she said. "I guess they're downstairs in the family room." She squeezed her eyes tight, still in pain. "I told them to stay close."

"Why didn't someone call me?"

"I tried, but the line was busy. I didn't try again. I was in too much pain."

"Kids," Daniel said, his words resounding from the top of the stairs. Kayla came running with the boys close behind.

"I'm taking your mom to the hospital," Daniel said. "She's sick. But why didn't one of you call me?"

Kayla looked dazed.

"It's okay," Daniel said, not waiting for an answer. "Doesn't matter anyway."

He paused, then said, "You guys stay inside. I'll give you a call when I find out what's wrong with your mom."

"Will she be okay?" Ayden asked.

"Say a prayer for her," Daniel said. "That's all we can do right now."

He lifted Jessica from the chair and helped her to the car. Her arms, although weak, clung to him.

"Lock the door behind me," he told the kids. "I'll be home as soon as I can."

"At least they're old enough to stay by themselves," Jessica said. "That's one less worry on my mind."

***

Daniel prepared Jessica's pain medication after their return home.

"The doctor put your mom on pain pills after running some tests," he said when the kids came running. "If she doesn't get better in a couple of days, she goes back for exploratory surgery."

"I knew something was wrong when she wasn't in her office," Kayla said. "The principal told me she got sick, and he sent her home."

"I tried to be quiet like she asked," Ayden said.

"We just left her alone," Josh said, bouncing around. "But I got my homework done."

"Will she get better by Christmas?" Kayla asked. "Remember, it's next week. We're out of school for two weeks."

"I hope so," Daniel said, then tousled Josh's head. "Now get your baths, and your homework done. Tomorrow's another day."

***

The children were out of school for the holidays. But the pain in Jessica's side only increased throughout the week, and she failed to enjoy the expressions of the season.

Early Christmas Eve morning she awoke in severe pain. Stabbing intervals of excessive throbs encased her side, and she cried out in pain. "Oh, God—it hurts too much," she said. "I can't wait any longer. My left side is killing me."

"What?"

"Daniel. Call the doctor."

"But it's the middle of the night. Can it wait 'til morning?"

"No. It's killing me," she said. "Those pain pills aren't working. I think I'm dying."

Daniel jumped from bed, grabbed his pants and shirt, and hurried to the bathroom. "What about the kids?" he asked through the opened door.

"Call Mrs. Revis next door. She won't mind checking on them."

Minutes later, and leaning on Daniel's arm, Jessica was guided into the emergency room, where an attendant helped her into a wheelchair. The doctor was called, and she was assigned a hospital bed. A gown for surgery was donned, with Daniel's help, and intravenous drugs started.

"I'm so ready for get this over with," she said. "This pain is horrible. It's killing me."

Daniel's face looked worn, and his lips silently moved in prayer.

"I'll have my surgery today," Jessica said. "Christmas will have to wait. When I wake up, this pain will all be gone."

After the attendant rolled the gurney into the surgical arena, her thoughts rested.

***

In recovery, Jessica's eyes blinked open, but felt weighted. Dozing on a chair beside her was Daniel. "I don't know why they always put Vaseline on a person's eyes during surgery," she whispered. "Maybe I'll ask."

At the sound of her voice Daniel's eyes popped open, and he bolted upright. "You're awake," he said. "How do you feel?"

"Okay," she said. "I guess." Her words slurred.

"You sound like you're still asleep," he said, and reached over to brush a few scraggly bangs from her brow.

"I'm only half awake," she said, trying to laugh.

"I'm glad you're awake," he said.

"What did the doctor say?" she asked, still blinking.

"You had the surgery. You're going to be okay."

"What did he take out?"

"Here's the doctor now," Daniel said, and stepped aside.

The doctor moved closer. "How do you feel?" he asked.

"Drowsy," Jessica said. "I don't know. Better, I guess." Her words were still slurred and to herself sounded distant.

"I spoke with your husband earlier," he said. "Did he tell you about your surgery?"

"No, not yet. This medication makes me sound funny."

"Actually, you're doing quite well considering the surgery you've just come through."

"What was wrong?"

"We removed your left ovary and residual scarring from Endometriosis. We cleaned the surrounding organs and tissue as much as possible. Your right ovary is perfect. No endometriosis found on that side. Only the left side of your organs were affected. Actually, your left ovary has been damaged for quite some time."

"Will I be okay?"

"Once you heal, you should be fine."

"Thanks for everything," she said.

"You'll have a scar from the surgery," he continued. "But as far as hormones are concerned, your right ovary will take over, and supply enough to keep you from taking replacements."

"That's good, right?"

"That's very good," he said, then stepped back, and reached for her chart. "Your incision was stapled. We'll remove the staples in about ten days."

"Okay," she said.

He stepped back to the bed and closed the chart. "We can talk about that later," he said. "Any questions?"

"Why did I need this surgery?" she asked.

He paused, then looked directly at her, his pointer finger resting against his chin. "Let me ask you this," he said. "Is there any reason you can think of that would have caused your left ovary to burst open? I'm surprised there haven't been problems before now."

She grimaced and grabbed her heart. Her eyes, still heavy, opened wide. "Oh—no...," she said, emphasizing the word 'no'. It was Trey."

Shocked by her own revelation, she blew dry air through already parched lips, and squeezed her eyes tight. Ruptured tears were now flowing.

"That last beating, when Trey tried to beat me to death," she said. "He kicked me in my left side over and over again with his right foot."

After a staggered breath, she continued. "My ovary may not have burst right then, but that's exactly what caused all this pain, and why I needed surgery. I think I would have died without it."

Chapter Fifty

Hospital Protocol

That afternoon while recovering in the hospital, Jessica eyes opened. "Is it Christmas yet?" she asked.

Daniel smoothed her pillow. "Honey, tomorrow is Christmas day."

She glanced at the doctor as he wrote in her chart. "Can I go home today?" she asked.

"I wouldn't recommend it," he said.

"Please. My kids want me home for Christmas."

"Well—"

"My husband will take good care of me," she said, and looked at Daniel. "I promise."

The doctor glanced at Daniel, then looked back at Jessica. "I don't know," he said. "The hospital may be the best place for you right now. You just came through major surgery."

"Please. I'll do everything you say," she said, and glanced at Daniel again, who looked concerned.

"You know what's best, Doc," he said.

"Please—"

The doctor frowned.

"Please."

"Well—," he said, then hesitated.

"I'll be good," she said, and her smile curved. "I promise."

"Well, if you insist," he said. "Tomorrow is Christmas Day." He closed the chart and hooked it on the foot of the bed.

"You'll need to continue your pain medication," he said, glancing up. Then he turned to Daniel. "Get her prescription filled today. It may be difficult finding a drug store that's open tomorrow."

"Then I can go home for Christmas?"

He placed his pen in a top pocket. "Only if I see you again—in my office—in five days," he said.

"I'll be there," she said, and smiled.

He turned to Daniel, reached out, and they shook hands. "I'll have my nurse give you an appointment card," he said.

"Thanks for everything," Daniel said.

"See you Thursday," he said, looking at Jessica. After a quick smile, he turned, and headed toward the nurse's station at the far end of the hall.

***

Is it Christmas yet?" Jessica asked from a makeshift bed on the sofa two days later.

"Honey, yesterday was Christmas day," Daniel said.

Shocked, she tried to sit up, but the pain was overbearing, and she cried out. She touched her side and rubbed it gently. The staples felt rough to the touch. "I should've stayed in the hospital longer," she said, wiping tears of pain from her eyes. "My incision hurts."

"We tried to warn you," Daniel said, "but you wouldn't listen."

"I wanted to be home for Christmas," she said.

"Well, you were."

"And the kids?" she asked, pulling the throw closer.

"Playing downstairs with their new toys," he said. He reached down and kissed her on the lips. "Where else would they be?"

She glanced at the corner where colorful lights from the Christmas tree bounced off shiny ornaments, casting beams of random color on the wall nearby; and her eyes drew more tears. "I can't believe I missed Christmas," she said. "I just can't believe it."

"Well, you did," Daniel said, and grinned.

"Did I even wake up once after coming home?" she asked. "I hardly even remember doing that."

He smiled, reached over, and touched her gently on

the arm. "You were asleep most of the time," he said. "You ate some food a couple of times. Drank sips of water now and then. Other than that, you were out like a light."

"How did the Santa thing go?" she asked.

"The kids had a blast. Santa Claus was a very good man," he said, and nodded his head up and down.

"Did they open all their presents?"

"What do you think?" he asked and laughed.

"All of them?"

"You know they did."

"And I missed it," she said. "I missed everything."

"I took pictures and videos for you to watch," he said. "When you feel better, that is."

"I still can't believe I missed Christmas," she said, and wiped another tear away. "I've never missed even one."

She sighed, then tried to pull up, but more pain erupted, and she cried out again.

Daniel rushed over and gently lifted her into a sitting position. "It's time to rest now," he said. "Doctor Daniel at your service." He grinned and kissed her on the forehead.

"I saved all your presents," he said, and massaged her neck. "Don't rush, though. You've got all the time in the world to have your own little Christmas."

"At least I can watch Kayla and Ayden and Josh's expressions when they watch me open them. That is, the gifts they gave me." And a giggle erupted. "I can't even talk straight. Must be the meds—making me sound crazy."

"You sound just fine."

She winced. "I'm still in lots of pain," she said. "I guess more from the stitches than the surgery. Well, it all hurts. What else can I say?"

Daniel shook his head in a comical way, then glanced at his watch. "It's time for more medicine," he said. He gaited back to the kitchen, and returned with a bottle of pills, and a cup of water.

"You'll get better," he said, and handed her a couple of pills. "Just take one day at a time. Listen to Doctor Daniel. He knows."

Jessica snickered but grabbed her side to ease the pain. "Wearing one of your many hats again, huh? Lumberjack Daniel, Plummer Daniel, Mechanic Daniel, Electrician Daniel, Builder Daniel, Daniel the Toy Fixer. Who else?" She laughed again but held her side. "It hurts. Even when I laugh it hurts."

"Then don't laugh," he said. "Just listen to Doctor Daniel."

"You're the best doctor I've ever had," she said, and a smile flickered.

"I'm glad," he said. His face then contorted and twisted into a grimace.

Still laughing, she held her side until the pain was unbearable.

"I've had lots of Christmases to remember," she said minutes later, glancing at the tree. "But I think this is the one I'll always remember."

"And why is that?"

"Because I missed it."

Chapter Fifty-One

Unknown Visitor

A knock at the front door went unnoticed as commotion inside the ranch-style house was deafening. Ayden's fourteenth birthday was in full swing, and party attendees were busy bursting helium-filled balloons as fast as they could be blown up.

"Get the door," Jessica said, accentuating the word door, but continued to slice a huge ice-cream cake. But the racket in the next room grew louder as the pounding continued.

"Somebody, get the door," she yelled.

"I'll get it," Josh said. He slid off a wooden stool in the kitchen, licked his fork one last time, and dropped it in a dish. Then he sprinted to the door.

Jessica watched as he stared through the peep hole. He turned back around—a funny expression on his face. He then sprinted to the kitchen, knocking a chair over in the process. "Hey, Mom," he said, panting. "There's some dude at the door."

Without opening the door, he sprinted back to the helium-inspired group looking for his brother. "Hey, Ayden," he said. "There's some dude at the door. Go and see if you know who it is."

Jessica glanced through the kitchen door as Ayden gazed through the living room window. "You know, I met that guy once," he said. "I didn't like him."

"Who is it?" she asked, stepping closer. But when no one answered, she glanced through the window herself. The next instant her heart began to pound, as revolts of terror played havoc with her senses.

Why is Trey here? And when was the last time we

saw him—much less heard from him?

Her hands shook with each beat of the heart as she opened the door. "I—I don't know what to say," she said, staring at Trey. Her words were forced. "Why didn't you call first? The kids haven't heard from you in—forever."

"I was driving through and wanted to wish Ayden a happy birthday," he said. "Where is he?"

"Over there," she said and pointed, then inhaled a mouth full of air.

"I'm such a coward," she whispered. I shouldn't be afraid, but I am..."

"Hey, Ayden—it's your dad," Trey said, and tossed him a ten-dollar bill. "Don't you know who I am?"

Ayden turned red. "Uh—no," he said. "Not really."

Jessica straightened her shoulders and took another deep breath. "Things certainly haven't changed," she whispered. But when she glanced back, tears filled her eyes. Trey still knew how to wreck a perfectly good day.

Later that evening, after the remains of an active party disbanded, Jessica fell into Daniel's arms, seeking comfort.

"It's okay," he said, holding her close. "Remember, I'll always be here to protect you. And I'll always love you, no matter what."

Chapter Fifty-Two

Journaling

Jessica picked up a pen, said a quick prayer, and reached for her journal. "It's been a long time since I've taken time to write," she said, talking to herself. "But if I jot things down, perhaps I can figure out exactly why Trey was able to control me the way he did all those years."

In the Beginning

Red, yellow, splotched, and crunchy brown leaves slithered silently to the ground in the gentle breeze. But more leaves remained on huge oaks and lofty maples in the woods behind the house.

"I hate this time of year," she said. Her words were whispered. Then she took a deep, agitated breath. "I'll be raking leaves 'til June."

Her seven-year-old eyes squeezed tight, trying to stop the flow of tears. "But, if I don't keep raking, I'll be very, very, very sorry."

Recent whelps on her legs and arms were still stinging, and she groaned. Punishment was always harsh even though she always did what she was told. She aimed to please. It was just her way.

But nothing ever changed. Everything she did seemed to make her mother angry. Would it always be this way?

Broken Song

She meandered down a well-worn walking pathway toward the chicken house, a yellow basket held tightly in her hand. This was never fun, but gathering eggs was one of the many chores assigned to her. It was an everyday requirement. Six hundred or more chickens could lay dozens of eggs in one day.

The eggs, now collected, were on their way to the basement for processing. But she tripped and landed on the hardened ground, and the eggs scattered around her. Panicked, she grabbed the basket and started picking the eggs up, one at a time. Several were cracked, and oozed a sticky, yellow gob on the ground. Then she saw her father coming toward her.

"Look at all these broken eggs," her father said. "Why did you break them?"

"I—I tripped and fell," was all she could say. She winced as her scraped knee was bleeding and screamed for attention. Instead, she wiped her tears away, and sucked in the pain.

"Pick these eggs up," he said. "You'll pay for every single one that's broken. I can't afford broken eggs."

"I didn't mean to fall," she said, and wiped a tear away. But her bloodied knee continued to throb, so she reached down and touched it.

"I don't know why I tripped," she said, and looked up.

"It costs me money when you break an egg," he said. The tone in his voice, and the look on his face, made her shudder; and she cowered in fear.

"Count all these broken eggs," he said. "You'll pay for every single one that's broken."

She didn't have money. Well, her birthday money, but it wasn't much.

She prayed it would be enough.

The Unspoken

"Now, you listen here," her mother would say. "Get me a switch."

Was forgetting to wash a couple of cooking pots so terrible? The stove, counter, and tabletop had been full of dirty dishes. How did she miss those pots? All the scrubbed dishes had been stacked in the cabinet. Only a couple of greasy pots remained. Dried food plastered over every inch of porcelain had been difficult to scrub.

She glanced at her mother, then scrambled to the tree used for switches. The branch needed to be long enough, and thick enough. Even better were nubby sprigs growing on the stick. It had to please her mother, or she would be lashed twice as long. This wasn't the first time she had been in trouble. It surely wouldn't be the last.

She visualized many throbbing stings that would last a few minutes, and probably bring blood. Scars would remain for weeks, yet her teachers never asked about the scratches and scabs on her legs. But they must surely notice.

The tree branch, now pre-tested, was selected but she slowed her pace down to a crawl. She didn't want another beating. She just wanted to finish the dishes so she could read her new library book.

Oh, how she loved to read. But what else was there to do when a spare minute surfaced? No television, no radio, no phone—didn't go anywhere but school, and church.

Reading was a fantasy world for her, as household duties, and work on the farm, took most of her time when not at school, or at church. But responsibilities at home often stretched her energy. She was, after all, just a child.

Her mother stood, hands on hips as she handed the stick over, and cowered; preparing for what was ahead—a good whipping. But the sternness on her mother's face, no matter the reason, was enough to push the panic button.

"You stand right there while I whip you" her mother said. Her words brought instant compliance.

The arm lifted, and the branch came down on her legs. As the switch descended again and again, she tried not to cry out. The strokes were merciless and harsh. But that's just the way it was.

"Oh, God. Please help me. How can I continue to write? Memories from childhood are tearing me apart. Why have I not realized the role my parents played in the decisions I've made over the years. And now—"

But revelation is truth. And truth is revelation. So, pen in hand, the journaling continued.

Responsibility

Her father took a final sip from his coffee mug, then looked at her. "It's time to go," he said. "You ready?"

She nodded, and he pushed his chair back under the table, and stepped away. "Make sure you keep a record of your rides," he said." You can pay me when you get paid."

"Does this mean per day, or per trip?" she asked.

"Every trip. That's two a day."

"Like a taxicab?"

"Yes—like a cab."

Her eyelids drooped, and she squinted in the pale moonlight. Her internal clock was screaming for more sleep. It was 5:00 a.m. But she needed to wake up. If she didn't, she would surely be in trouble.

Her eyelids stretched, and she choked back a yawn. I don't know how to be a waitress. But I hope someone will teach me.

Again, another yawn.

"Why did Mama get me this job?" she whispered. "Well, she said I could buy the clothes I needed. And shoes. Maybe she'll let me buy some shampoo too."

The truck rolled through a rock gate, and she pulled her thin sweater close.

What if nobody likes me? And what if I'm the only

kid who works there?

The truck rolled up to the cafeteria entrance, the break was applied, and the engine stopped running. "Remember, I get off at two," she said, and waited for a response.

"I'll be here when I get here," her father said. "Did you tell your mother what time?"

"She'll remind you."

After the truck drove out of sight, she panicked. She had never worked in a public place before. At least for now, she could buy some new shoes. Her old ones were scruffy. New shoes would be nice.

She opened the cafeteria door, a worker's permit in hand, and stepped inside. Trembling with dread, she broke out in a sweat. "Where is Mrs. Bramlett, my new boss?" she asked.

Getting a worker's permit as a thirteen-year-old, her mother by her side, was easier than going inside a century-old building alone.

Blue Shoes

She pulled a thin gray cardigan—one size too small—over her head and headed out the door. In her hand was a small purse where a few dollars had been tucked. Martin's, a local shoe store in her hometown, was the destination

Her heart pounded with excitement. Today she would replace her scruffy worn-out shoes with a brand-new pair. Her scrunched-up toes were screaming to escape their cramped confinement. Today they would be released.

The dated truck rattled in the wind as they bounced along. The outside air was chilly. But air in the compacted cab was also nippy as the heater had long before stopped working.

She rubbed her hands together, trying to stimulate some warmth. Accelerated breaths of warmth collided with the cold, creating tiny cloud puffs that gently wafted away in the frigid air. Winter was sometimes harsh in their small mountain town.

At Martins, the designated shoe store, she stared long and hard at a polished array of new shoes sparkling in the window display. Once inside she stopped for a moment and glanced out the window. Far in the distance her father's truck meandered back down the road. He needed a couple of tools from the hardware, so she would be shopping alone.

She turned and skipped to the center isle where the warmth of vented air enveloped her. Muted blue brogans with elastic slits on the side caught her attention. They looked sturdy, and quite stylish. Besides, she loved blue. The shoes were a perfect fit.

With tote in hand, she stepped back outside to wait for her father. The blustery wind caught the hem of her sweater and flapped it hard against her face. But she brushed it away, and hunched over, trying to stay warm— her box of shoes tightly encased in her arms.

The truck rattled to the curb, and she climbed inside. "I need to run by the Johnston's on the way home," her father said as they pulled away.

As they bounced along, she stared at the hood over the truck engine, and tried to entertain herself. Peeling paint of different levels left the impression of maps in her head and made her smile. Meanwhile her father's whistling echoed through the cab. When the song ended, they rode along in silence.

Her new purchase was calling her name, so she looked down, and stared long and hard at the package in her lap. She drew a heart-felt breath, peeled the box open, and stared down at the contents. What beautiful shoes they were—muted blue resting on a crumpled bed of white tissue. "I love my new shoes," she said. "I can't wait to wear them to school."

Minutes later the truck rolled into the Johnston's drive, and her father climbed out. "You can play with those kids over there," he said, pointing. "That is, if you want to."

The direction of his finger revealed a group of children playing with a yellow ball.

"Stay close," he warned. "I'll only be a few."

She covered her new brogans with tissue, closed the box, and shoved it in the glove compartment. Confident her shoes were safe, she jumped down from the step bar to the ground. The door slammed, and she looked across the way at a short girl in a pink jacket. The girl was waving for her to come over.

When motioned back, she sprinted to the truck, and climbed in. Hot, sweaty, and out of breath from her run, she took several quick breaths as the door swung closed behind her.

***

"Where are your new shoes?" her mother asked, a smile on her face.

"They're still in the truck," she said, and raced back to get them. She jerked the glove box open and let out a gasp. Her new shoes were gone.

A knot of dread began to creep up her throat as she reached under the seat, scrambling in her haste to find the lost box. Each side of the seat was then explored. Every nook and cranny were searched until her fingers were stiff and numb. Her new shoes were gone without a trace.

"I can't find my new shoes," she said. "They're gone." And tears streamed down her face.

Seeking comfort, she raced back to the house.

Her mother's face instantly fell. "What happened?" she asked.

More tears slid down her cheeks. "I left them in the glove compartment of the truck—like Daddy said."

Another staggered breath.

"Some kids wanted me to play when he stopped at the Johnston's."

"Was the truck locked?"

"I don't know. I think so."

"You know we can't buy you another pair," her father said as he walked across the floor. "You should have

213

taken better care of those shoes."

"I didn't know they would get gone," she said, and new tears formed.

He only turned and walked away.

That same afternoon, as she sat on the porch step alone, she scrunched up her eyes, and tried to understand what had happened to her new shoes.

"There's always a reason why things happen," she said, nodding her head up and down. But her heart was broken, and she lifted the hem of her dress to dry her eyes.

She glanced down at her scruffy browns. "I'll polish them one more time," she said, "and hope they don't look too ratty."

Another sigh escaped.

"I didn't see anyone near the truck at the Johnsons," she said to herself. "But I was busy chasing that old yellow ball." How did my shoes disappear?"

Her shoulders slumped as she resigned to her fate. "It's not my fault those shoes got gone," she said in low tones, "so I shouldn't be upset."

In gesture of surrender, she turned both hands up. "After all, they're just shoes. Someone must have needed them more than I did."

A Cry for Help

She dreaded making this call, but there was no choice.

"Mama, my car broke down," she said. "Can you get Daddy to come and get me?"

"Where are you?"

"About an hour away."

"Hold on."

Noises in the background increased after her mother dropped the phone. Minutes later it lifted. "He said it's too far, and he needs his rest."

She wasn't surprised. Still, she felt uneasy. Being

alone was scary, even as a young adult.

"It's getting dark, and the station will close in a couple of hours," she said, glancing around the small enclosure. A group of strange men huddled together on the outside caught her attention, and fear gripped her by the throat.

Braving a three-hour trip alone had been overwhelming. But the need to get away from Trey for a breather was essential. Visiting her parents provided the excuse.

"I'll see if your cousin can drive down and get you," her mother said.

"Okay. Let me know if he can. In the meantime, I'll see when the car can be fixed."

She didn't have much to depend on—certainly not Trey, or her own father. Neither cared if she was stranded. The truth stung.

***

When the weekend was almost over, she was glad. Spending time with her parents had revealed several serious drawbacks. Boredom and inactivity were to blame.

She sighed, placed the phone on the table, and rubbed her head. "That was my mother-in-law," she said. "She and Trey's brother are driving down to get me. We'll pick my car up on the way back."

"How nice of them to drive all that way," her mother said but continued rocking in her chair. "When are they coming?"

"Tomorrow morning. They should be here before noon."

"What did the station say about your car?"

"The starter's been replaced and tested. It's good to go."

"Well, that's good," her mother said, then reached for a knitting basket beside the chair.

"What are you making?"

"Slippers," her mother said, still rocking. "I'm knitting all my friends at Sunday school a pair for

Christmas."

"That's nice. Pretty color too."

"I hope they like them," her mother said.

Jessica's return smile was forced. "I think I'll go and pack my things. Tomorrow will be here before I know it."

Living with Trey, as bad as it was, was better than visiting her parents.

***

Jessica closed the journal and wiped swollen eyes. The box of tissues beside her was now empty.

"What good is it now to realize that the people in my life, who should have cared the most, didn't?" she whispered. "Their lack of support has all but stifled the life out of me and caused me to accept what was unacceptable."

She winced, blinked her eyes, and took a deep cleansing breath as new wisdom took center stage.

Chapter Fifty-Three

Resignation

Jessica handed her ticket to the flight attendant, stepped aboard the jet, and found her seat. Flying to Hendersonville for a previously scheduled court appearance with Trey was on the agenda.

Daniel was now employed at Conagra, a prominent Manufacturing company located in Savannah, Georgia. Ayden, sixteen, and Josh, fourteen, were part of their moving entourage. Kayla, recently graduated, had launched out on her own; and would remain in the mountains of Western North Carolina.

For Jessica, the rigors of chasing an ex-husband for child support over the years had been exhausting. His support, over time, had dwindled to nothing. Daniel's provision, however, far outweighed what would have been Trey's supplement.

Still, she wanted Trey to feel the pressure of compliance once again, and decided to try and collect back child support, while requesting the court's approval for future funding. The appointment was in place before their move, and she was determined to keep it.

An hour later, after the plane landed, she swallowed her fear, and climbed down narrow metal steps onto the tarmac. Once disengaged, the effects of mountain breezes and cooler temperatures seemed to quiet her inner turmoil. She was now ready for the challenge.

The following morning, as she climbed the marble courthouse steps, she mentally prepared to see Trey. Less than an hour later, she was back down the stairs. He was a no-show.

She was surprised, but not really. At that moment

she decided to never again pursue Trey for child support. As far as she was concerned, he had won the battle.

Child support was nice, and once desperately needed. But a faithful, loving husband was much better. Daniel's role as father-figure would continue with or without child support from Trey.

It came as no surprise how easy Trey had fallen in line with other delinquent dads. His true character was still shining through.

The following day Jessica boarded a return flight to Savannah. Although short in duration, this trip had resulted in understanding, resignation, and acceptance. The next year she and her family were living in Dallas. Daniel's employer had relocated them to the big state of Texas.

Chapter Fifty-Four

Covenant of Peace

Divorced many years from Trey, yet Jessica still faced severe difficulties in relinquishing past hurts.

One morning, after opening the Bible, words of consolation found in the book of Isaiah leaped off the page, and into her heart. This portion of scripture was, without a doubt, a direct word from God to her.

"Do not fear, for you will not be ashamed; neither be disgraced, for you will not be put to shame. For you will forget the shame of your youth and will not remember the reproach of your widowhood (separation, divorce) anymore.

For your Maker is your husband, The LORD of hosts is his name; and your Redeemer is the Holy One of Israel; He is called the God of the whole earth.

For the LORD has called you like a woman forsaken and grieved in spirit; like a youthful wife when you were refused," says your God.

"For a mere moment I have forsaken you, but with great mercies I will gather you. With a little wrath I hid my face from you for a moment; but with everlasting kindness I will have mercy on you," says the Lord your Redeemer.

Oh, you afflicted one, tossed with tempest, and not comforted. Behold, I will lay your stones with colorful gems, and lay your foundations with sapphires.

I will make your pinnacles of rubies, your gates of crystal, and all your walls of precious stones.

All your children shall be taught by the LORD, and great shall be the peace of your children. In righteousness you shall be established.

You shall be far from oppression, for you shall not

fear; and from terror, for it shall not come near you. Indeed, they shall surely assemble, but not because of Me. Whoever assembles against you shall fall for your sake...

No weapon formed against you shall prosper and every tongue which rises against you in judgment you shall condemn"

This is the heritage of the servants of the LORD, and their righteousness is from me," says the LORD" (Isaiah 54:4-17)

In an instant, years of anguish were let go as tears of release splattered the open page. Revelations of Jessica's dark past were now revealed, and she could heal from the pain of the past.

Chapter Fifty-Five

Deathbed

Texas summers are brutal—the heat often unbearable for those on the outside. "Thank God for air conditioners," Jessica said, after the phone disconnected. Still, Kayla's shared information was somewhat unnerving.

"Ayden—Josh," Jessica said, urging her sons, then nineteen and seventeen, into the family room. "It's time for a family conference."

When the two gathered near, she spoke in soft undertones. "Hey guys—listen," she said, moving closer. "I just talked with your sister. Your real dad isn't doing so well." She pulled out a chair and sat down. "Actually, he's on his deathbed."

"What?" Their startled response echoed through the room.

"You knew he was diagnosed with cancer. Three cancers to be exact."

"Yeah, I knew," Josh said. "So what?"

"Well, he's dying," Jessica said, then twisted around and looked closer at them.

"When?" Ayden asked, standing in silence, but taking it all in.

"Nobody knows, really," she said. "Probably soon."

Josh grinned, then plopped down on a chair beside her, and fingered a cushion. "So, why did you call us in here?" he asked.

"Daniel and I think you two, and Kayla, need to see him before he passes," she said. "What do you think?"

Josh reached for a loose CD and twirled in though his fingers. "When?" he asked.

"We thought we'd get tickets and fly from DFW

Airport to Hendersonville. Kayla said she could drive everyone in her car to see your dad."

Josh sat in silence, still twirling his disc.

"Ayden, you and Josh can ride with her."

"Huh? Oh, okay," Josh said, then stopped his twirling, and glanced up. "When?"

"Next Wednesday," Jessica said. "We'll stay until Saturday. You're out of school a couple of days, so you won't have any make-up work. Ayden, you need to tell your boss you can't work those days, and your teachers at college."

"Aren't you going with us?" Ayden asked, looking concerned.

"Only to Hendersonville," she said. "Since Kayla lives there, the transition will be easy."

She tried to stand, but quickly sat back down. Her knees were buckling.

"Why should we go?" Josh asked.

"Because—I think you need to see him. He's dying. I know he's never been much to you, but—he is your natural father."

Ayden glanced away, inhaled some air, and slowly released. "Okay—I guess," he said.

"At least we get to fly most of the way," Josh said. Still twirling the disc, he left the room.

***

"How did it go?" Jessica asked, as beads of sweat popped out on her forehead.

"Dad was glad to see us," Kayla said, smiling. "He hugged us all."

Josh grinned, then plopped down on the sofa beside Jessica. "He was in bed the whole time," he said, before throwing a pillow at his brother.

"He looked really skinny," Ayden said, and ran his hand through his own thick mane. "All his hair was gone, and everything."

"Aren't you glad you went to see him?"

"Yeah, I guess so," he said.

"How did his new wife treat you?" Jessica asked.

"She wasn't too friendly," Kayla said. "I don't think she liked us being there."

"He never got out of bed," Josh said. "Not even once. I didn't really remember him from before."

"Did he give you anything?" Jessica couldn't help but ask.

"Uh, well, not really," Josh, said, but looked evasive.

"What does that mean?"

"Uh, nothing," he said, but turned his head, and glanced away.

"Ayden?"

"Uh, not really." His look was sheepish.

"Kayla?"

"I'm not going to talk about it," she said, then turned, and left the room.

"It would be nice if he had given you something," Jessica said. "After all, he's never done much for any of you. Anything to remember him by, or something to make up for everything he didn't give you in the past."

"I wanted his Bible," Kayla said, coming back in the room. "I asked, but his wife wouldn't let me have it."

"We weren't supposed to tell you anything," Ayden said.

"Why not?" Jessica asked.

"Dad told us not to," Josh said.

"Oh, come on," Jessica said, and rubbed her hands together, trying to stay calm. "What's the big secret?"

"He said—"

Kayla interrupted. "Dad said not to say anything," she said.

"But— "

Kayla glared at her brothers. "Remember, Dad said not to tell Mom." And she put her finger on her lips.

"What's the big secret?" Jessica asked again.

Picking the kids for answers was irresistible, but she was determined to find out, one way or the other.

Later, when she cornered Josh, a whiff of the truth was revealed. As the story unfolded, she realized Trey was still using lies to cover himself.

"Dad said your attorney sent him a letter saying not to give us anything," Kayla said.

"I don't have an attorney," Jessica said, and looked surprised.

Kayla looked her straight in the eye. "He showed us the letter," she said.

'What?" Jessica couldn't help but laugh. "What did it say? After your dad quit paying child support years ago, I gave up on the legal system. Every time I went to court trying to collect what he owed, he always lied to the judge about not having a job. Why would I hire an attorney now? That makes no sense."

"Well, Dad said you'd take legal action if he gave us anything." Josh was standing his ground.

"I've always wanted him to give you things," Jessica said. "But he stopped years ago. When was the last time you got a present from him?"

The unease in the room was rising.

"I'll bet you can't even remember the last time."

Ayden stood to his feet. "But Dad said—"

"Your dad pulled the wool over your eyes," Jessica said. "He lied to all of you."

"But what about the letter?" Kayla asked, and began to pace the floor, holding her head in her hands. "What about that letter?"

"Listen," Jessica said. "I didn't hire an attorney to write a letter to your dad. As I said before, I've always wanted him to give you things. It would have helped a lot if he had. Instead, my money paid for everything—what you wore—the toys you played with. School supplies too. Band instruments—field trips. He never paid for any of it."

She paused, then said, "What about us paying for this trip so you could see him before he died? What about that?" A long sigh escaped. "Why would you even think I would do such a thing—hire an attorney so he wouldn't give you anything?"

"Maybe his wife hired the attorney," Josh said, then laughed at his own innuendo.

"Maybe she's the one who typed the letter," Ayden said.

This suggestion sounded more like truth than not.

"His wife is a businesswoman," Jessica said. "Her family owns a workshop business, where your dad worked. She would certainly know how to deal with legal issues."

Her words were starting to take root.

"You know," Kayla said, "she kept coming in to see how things were going when we were talking to Dad."

"She probably wrote that letter to make sure you kids didn't get anything after he passed."

He's still telling lies to hide the truth—nothing's changed at all.

"He did give us something," Ayden said. He reached for his suitcase, pulled out a wallet, and opened it. Inside was a crisp fifty-dollar bill.

"Here's mine," Josh said, and reached for his new wallet.

"He gave me fifty dollars too," Kayla said, "except mine wasn't in a wallet."

"At least he gave you something," Jessica said, and sighed.

"Was it worth the trouble, keeping them from getting something after he died?" she whispered. "I'll never collect the thousands he owes in back child support. So, what's the difference?"

Memories of Trey's deception, created by this trip, would remain in her head a very long time.

Chapter Fifty-Six

Point of View

The events in Jessica's life had been a huge hurdle of conflict and survival. But now was the time for heart and mind to examine the struggle, the what-ifs, and the why's of life's journey. So began an intensive time of study, research, and renewal.

Informative material allowed memories of childhood and first-marriage devastation to collide with Biblical truth and medical knowledge. Over time, understanding and confidence became hers as she learned to appreciate the new life God had blessed her with.

Due to religious beliefs, she was anchored to a marriage that should have ended shortly after it began. But ignorance and pressure from family and church made her a prisoner of her own commitment.

Isolated and uninformed, yet the desire to provide a safe environment for her children became her only focus.

She began to understand that submission in a marriage does now mean accepting abuse.

As leader in the home, the husband bares the responsibility of love by example. But many refuse to accept their authority in the way it was intended.

Often used as an excuse, an evil man will bully, and literally antagonize, threaten, and attack those placed under his protection and provision—making the scripture, "Wives, submit yourselves to your own husbands as you do to the Lord" (Ephesians 5:22) a stumbling block for those who abuse their authority in ways never intended by God. Control is the deciding factor.

Another truth. Salvage what remains of material goods and be thankful for what's left. Reclaim what you can and let go of the rest. Understand that some things will never be recoverable.

Although difficult to grasp, forgive the one who stole from you. Nothing more can be done, at this point, if the damage is beyond repair. Accept what cannot be changed and move forward with your life.

Jessica's anchor was the Bible—the word of God. Without God on her side, hope for survival, and a better future, would never have been realized.

Although Trey retained a fierce passion for preaching the gospel, he also reserved a dark side that manifested in cruelty to animals, as well as family. It was years following their divorce before Jessica was able to piece together the truth as it was.

In a Nutshell

To the world Jessica was known as the wife of a church pastor. To family she was daughter, daughter-in-law, sister-in-law, wife, and mother. Although memories of her first marriage have faded, the residual of cruel and malicious assaults remain.

But why didn't Jessica leave the marriage when Trey began to abuse?

Church teachings, parental guidance, and in-laws who disapproved of divorce were the directing factor—not to mention that her husband was the pastor of two churches.

It may sound simple to leave an abusive partner, but often it's not. Only after miracles, and years of time, could Jessica again feel safe.

Following their separation, Trey continued to stalk, threaten, and terrorize. He often attested that his threat of death was imminent. For years, Jessica believed his words.

Symptoms of Multiple Sclerosis surfaced as did post-traumatic stress disorder, often referred to as PTSD.

Depression and severe panic attacks enhanced many un-manageable migraines. But her escape from abuse has proven every hardship worth the struggle.

"I have been young, and now am old; yet have I not seen the righteous forsaken, nor his seed begging for bread" (Psalms 37:25).

Daniel, a profound miracle, has more than enhanced Jessica's life. Today their love is strong. In the process, her children inherited a new father. Other miracles are also part of the equation.

But the biggest miracle of all is Daniel's unending love.

Till Death Do Us Part—Not

Jessica's parents let her down. The church let her down. The police let her down. Her first marriage let her down. Her in-laws let her down. Society let her down. But God never left her down. He restored with delight what Satan meant for evil.

"For I know the plans I have for you," declares the LORD, "plans to prosper you and not to harm you, plans to give you hope and a future" (Jeremiah 29:11)

Tribute to a Perfect Husband

Passionate, compassionate, concerned, loving, and gentle, a constant lover in word and deed; a man of his word, integrity his motto, trustworthy, a maintenance man literally and emotionally, a caretaker of both wife and home, loving with every emotion possible from the breadth, depth, and height his soul can reach; a gentleman in every respect of the word, a friend who would lay down his very life if asked; handsome, good-looking, and striking in both tone and stance; and a man who desires his companion at all times. What more could any woman possibly want?

Chapter Fifty-Seven

Matters of the Heart

Trey and Jessica were married twelve years. Following their divorce he suffered three separate cancers, one after the other. He was forty-three years old when he died— twelve years after their divorce.

Her marriage to Daniel has lasted over twenty-four years.

Many scripture passages in the Bible have proven true, including this one. "I will repay you for the years the locusts have eaten" (Job 2:25)

Trey suffered three cancers before his death.

Breast Cancer—Over the Heart

"The heart is deceitful above all things and beyond cure. Who can understand it?" (Jeremiah 17:9)

Brain Tumor—Head of House

"The trouble he causes recoils on himself; their violence comes down on their own heads." (Psalms 7:16)

Bone Cancer—Strength

"Because of your (God's) wrath there is no health in his body; there is no soundness in his bones because of his sin" (Psalms 38:3)

Breast cancer—issues of the heart

Brain cancer—head of home and church

Bone cancer in leg—trampled wife under his feet

"Woe unto the wicked! It shall be ill with him: for the reward of his hands shall be given him" (Isaiah 3:11) (KJV)

"Do not be deceived: God cannot be mocked. A man reaps what he sows" (Galatians 6:7)

"Though hand join in hand, the wicked shall not be unpunished: but the seed of the righteous shall be delivered" (Proverbs 11:21)

"Dearly beloved, avenge not yourselves, but rather give place unto wrath: for it is written, Vengeance is mine; I will repay, saith the Lord," Romans 12: 19) (KJV)

Chapter Fifty-Eight

An Honorable Love Affair

Jessica snuggled deeper into Daniel's arms, reached up and gently massaged his labored brow. His hair, now white with age, was soft and yielding to the touch. In return he wrapped his arms around her—an invitation to slide deeper into his warm embrace.

"Tell me again exactly why you married me years ago," she said.

"Because I needed someone to take care of, and you needed someone to care for you—and the kids."

"And—" he smiled and squeezed her hand. "And that's why God put us together."

***

"Therefore hath the Lord recompensed me according to his righteousness, according to the cleanness of his hands in his eyesight" (Psalms 18:24)

"O Lord my God, in thee do I put my trust: save me from all them that persecute me, and deliver me" (Psalms 7:1)

"...To him that overcometh will I give to eat of the hidden manna, and will give him a white stone, and in the stone a new name written, which no man knoweth saving he that receiveth it" (Revelations 2:17)

"Therefore hath the Lord recompensed me according to his righteousness, according to the cleanness of his hands in his eyesight" (Psalms 18:24)

"O Lord my God, in thee do I put my trust: save me from all them that persecute me, and deliver me" (Psalms 7:1)

"...To him that overcometh will I give to eat of the

hidden manna, and will give him a white stone, and in the stone a new name written, which no man knoweth saving he that receiveth it" (Revelations 2:17)

Focused View

I've been lots of places
I thought I'd never go
I've lived a lot of years
Yet life was never slow

I've done a lot of things
I thought I'd never do
I've met many people
But not all have been true

I've given all I've had
To some along the way
The forces of this world
At times led me astray

But as the curve ahead
Comes into focused view
I'll leave it all behind
Save memories of you

© *Phoebe Leggett*

Part Two

Vows & Lies Survival Guide

Survival Guide is a follow-up to *Vows & Lies*. In both narratives, names and locations have been changed at the author's discretion.

If things have gone this far it's time to get help or get out.

235

Chapter Fifty-Nine

Battered Wife Syndrome

The battered woman syndrome
n. A pattern of signs and symptoms, such as fear and a perceived inability to escape, appearing in women who are physical and mental abused over an extended period by a husband or other dominant individual.

ᵃssault

noun \ə-ˈsȯlt\
1
a: a violent physical or verbal attack *b*: a concerted effort (as to reach a goal or defeat an adversary)
2
a: a threat or attempt to inflict offensive physical contact or bodily harm on a person (as by lifting a fist in a threatening manner) that puts the person in immediate danger of or in apprehension of such harm or contact — compare battery 1b *b*: rape

Synonyms: <u>rape</u>, <u>ravishment</u>, <u>sexual assault</u>, <u>violation</u>

What is a Battered Woman?

To better understand battered wife syndrome, one must first understand how a woman becomes "battered." Dr. Lenore E. Walker, the nation's most well-known expert on battered women, reports that a woman must experience at least two complete battering cycles before being labeled a "battered woman. Within this period of time, three obvious phases will occur.

1. tension-building phase
2. explosion or acute battering incident
3. calm and loving phase—often called the honeymoon stage

Repeated physical and verbal assaults directed at the wife by a husband, or partner, will result in serious physical and psychological damage to the woman. This violence tends to follow a predictable pattern beginning with verbal abuse, then escalates into dangerous assaults and cruel violence. Most episodes follow an accusation that I call the 'blame game'.

At times the severity and frequency of assaults may result in death of the female. The longer she remains under the batter's control, the more difficult it will be to make a more permanent escape from her abuser.

Often the woman is blamed for the assault. What remains are emotional and physical scars of abandonment. She feels useless, helpless, and hopeless. Most physical scars will heal. But serious emotional baggage remains to haunt the victim for decades following an assault, or series of assaults.

Reasons to Leave an Abusive Partner

If your companion displays a combination of the behaviors listed below, you may have a potential batterer on your hands. Be aware, and don't gloss over the truth. Study statistics, research the internet, and learn from others so you aren't caught up in a never-ending saga of abusive behaviors from your companion.

Don't be fooled into believing your relationship is different. Knowledge could be your salvation.

Use caution or reconsider your commitment.

- **He pushes for quick evolvement**. He comes on strong and claims he's never loved anyone like this before. He will pressure you for an exclusive commitment almost immediately. Over time he isolates you from all other relationships.

- **Jealous:** He becomes possessive and calls often to check on you. He will make unexpected visits, or prevent you from going places you normally go, such as shopping, or even to work, because you "might meet someone else."

- **Controlling:** He interrogates you about who you've talked to and where you have gone. He insists you get permission before going anywhere or doing anything.

- **He has strange expectations:** You are expected to be the perfect woman and meet all his needs and desires.

- **Isolates:** He tries to keep you away from your family and friends, and often accuses those close to you of causing problems between the two of you.

- **Condemns:** He blames others for his own personal problems and mistakes, and never accepts responsibility for himself. It's always the fault of someone else.

- **Is Hypersensitive:** He complains about things that are just part of everyday life.

- **Cruel to animals and children:** He kills or irritates animals in sadistic and brutal ways. Sixty-five percent of abusers who beat their partner will also abuse their children.

- **Uses force during sex:** He enjoys throwing you down or holding you against your will during sex. He also introduces strange methods that make you feel uncomfortable, initiate pain, or requires others to participate in the activity with you.

- **Assaults verbally:** He criticizes, using blatantly cruel or hurtful things while degrading you with cursing and raw language. This is called verbal abuse.

- **Strict and rigid sex roles:** He expects you to obey, and do everything he says without question, or hesitation.

- **Mood Swings:** He switches from sweet and loving to explosively violent behavior. His mood swings are unpredictable.

- **History of former battering:** He admits to hitting a woman in the past but blames her for making him do it.

- **Uses threats:** He says, "I'll kill you" then dismisses those threats with "I didn't mean it," or "That's the way everybody talks."

- **Is in Denial:** He tells you no one will ever believe you're being abused. In this way, he controls your every move. He threatens you not to tell. In this way he keeps you under his control.

Why Women Stay

Women who remain in an abusive relationship often feel tied by family pressure, religious dogma, or the desire to raise her children in a complete family unit which includes both parents. Lacking self-esteem, group support, or finances will keep her under the same roof as her abuser. Her concern for adequate provision for her children holds her in a less-than-adequate position.

As keeper of the peace, the woman feels responsible for maintaining the marriage. While in the honeymoon phase of the relationship, she is reinforced, and feels everything in her life is positive. Once she discovers the tenderness was a ruse, she cowers and remains under the man's domination.

Other women stay in the relationship as it feels safer to stay than to leave.

Feelings of hopelessness and psychological paralysis will keep her in dangerous situations. Because the woman fears for her life, she remains connected to the abuser. His control causes her to feel he sees, and knows, her every move. Therefore, she is caught between a desire to leave, and the fear of leaving. In her mind, survival on her own remains a gamble—and perhaps isn't worth the challenge.

Note: There are men who are also victims of domestic violence and abuse at the hands of dominate and aggressive women. If this is the case, the same rules apply.

**The only relative you will ever choose is a spouse.
Seek God's wisdom before you do.**

Chapter Sixty

Domestic Violence

Many aspects of abuse have been documented, but three are specifically associated with domestic violence.

"Call to me and I will answer you and tell you great and unsearchable things you do not know. Nevertheless, I will bring health and healing to it; I will heal my people and will let them enjoy abundant peace and security. Give thanks to the LORD Almighty, for the LORD is good; His love endures forever" (Jeremiah 33:2, 6, 11)

Verbal Abuse

Abuse is never a justifiable behavior. Seek counsel if you are verbally mistreated. If harsh words hurled at you become a pattern, set boundaries to keep yourself from hearing them. Create a support system so others are aware of how you feel and can provide consolation and assistance if needed. Over time, negative words will have negative effects on your self-esteem.

If verbal abuse has escalated to physical, perhaps it's time to leave the relationship. Don't engage in verbal or bodily conflict with your abuser. If he becomes angry, try to remain calm, and walk away. Don't allow him to see your reaction to his words. If you react, your abuser is being rewarded for his vulgarity and threats. Don't allow him the pleasure of knowing how you really feel.

Leave the marriage, or relationship, if he refuses to seek counsel. Don't allow his words, and actions, to control your life.

Use caution as verbal abuse will most certainly transform into physical abuse. It may be necessary to break all ties with your abuser, even if that also means his family, and friends.

It's wise to prepare for what may be ahead with information easily available in every corner of your world. The Internet offers multiplied varieties of venues on the computer. Counselors are easy to find through a family doctor. Or find a good attorney who understands domestic violence laws. There's always someone who can help you decide what's best for you, your family, and your situation.

Verbal abuse is easy to hide. Men will abuse a wife using words of shame simply to degrade her to a lower level. Mocking, cursing, or yelling will make the abuser feel superior, but has far-reaching implications for the abused. Hearing critical words again and again causes shame and degradation for the woman.

Physical Abuse

Physical abuse is easy to identify because the scars are visible, and easy to see. When a man is violent in a relationship, his one desire is to have complete control over the woman. When he gets physical, he feels strong and domineering. He will then allow his anger to rule his emotions. To lead in this way makes him feel important.

To retain his stance, he will manipulate the woman with physical force. Being in control makes him feel powerful, but the result is a woman who is controlled, manipulated, and reduced to a useless state of mind.

Once the battering is over the abuser often apologizes. He expects his victim to forgive and forget. The woman, however, will retain her emotions long after the assault has ended.

Some remain in a battered state of mind long after the assault is over.

Physical Abuse Includes:

- Pushing or shoving

- Slapping or hitting

- Beatings

- Being punched with a fist

- Biting

- Choking

- Holding the victim down

- Refusing the victim medical treatment

- Throwing items and projectiles at the victim

- Locking the victim outside, in a closet, or separate room

- Threatening the victim

- Trying to make the victim have an accident while driving

- Aggravated battery

- Physical or verbal assault

"Call to me and I will answer you and tell you great and unsearchable things you do not know. Nevertheless, I will bring health and healing to it; I will heal my people and will let them enjoy abundant peace and security. Give thanks to the LORD Almighty, for the LORD is good; His love endures forever" (Jeremiah 33:2, 6, 11)

Events that Lead to Violence

- Tension builds

- Verbal attacks increase

- A violent outburst occurs

- Abuser blames victim

- Promises to never again batter

- Believes everything is now okay

Over time the woman will retain physical and psychological scars that may never heal. This is a vicious cycle that plays out again and again on women who feel they don't have a choice in the matter.

Damage created by long term abuse will have emotional, economic, spiritual, and social repercussions; and is a serious concern for society.

Once a beater, always a beater.
Once a batterer, always a batterer.
—Judge Judy Sheilan

Chapter Sixty-One

Forms of Abuse

Abuse presents in various forms and degrees. Although some aren't fully understood, all are part of the process of being battered.

Emotionally Battered Woman

- She is isolated from family and friends

- He threatens to take the children away if she doesn't agree with his wishes

- She is accused of being unfaithful, or friends are told she is cheating

- He doesn't want her to be involved with any outside activity such as work, or spending time with friends

- She is criticized about her weight, clothing, or friends

- He expects her to meet his every need without question and makes her feel guilty if she doesn't comply. If she says no, she is harassed, beaten, or otherwise punished, making her feel used, useless, and cast- off.

- He doesn't allow her to make decisions without his approval

- She is degraded to the point she feels damaged and useless

Cathy Meyer, a certified divorce coach, marriage educator, and legal investigator, reports that emotional abuse in a marriage is such a covert form of domestic violence that many were unable to recognize themselves as a victim. The woman believes that something is wrong with her.

She may feel stressed, harbor a sense of depression and anxiety, or be unable to identify the reasoning to clarify her feelings. Emotional abuse is used to control, degrade, humiliate, or punish a spouse, or partner. Although emotional abuse differs from physical abuse, the result is the same.

After many abusive actions, a spouse will become fearful of her partner, and changes her behavior to keep him happy. The more satisfied a partner becomes, the less violence the victim will suffer.

But by the time a wife, or partner, identifies her true problem, she feels as if she has gone crazy. She will even doubt her own sense of reality. Emotions of abuse will make her question every thought, and behavior.

Mental Abuse

Mental abuse is an emotional or psychological abuse that occurs in close relationships such as marriage. The damage caused by this abuse allows the woman to believe she is worthless, and at fault. It also lowers her self-esteem until she feels useless, and unwanted.

Mental abuse is a consistent and chronic pattern of

mistreatment that causes significant distress in the abuse. It will interfere with her ability to develop stable patterns of friendship with others. The abuser intimidates with name calling, blaming, or rejection, thus gaining complete control over his victim.

Sexual Exploitation and Rape

Marital rape of a spouse is non-consensual sex where the perpetrator is the victim's husband, or partner. This exploitation is also labeled as domestic violence.

In the past it was condoned and ignored by the law. Currently it is considered a criminal assault, and includes divorced or separated ex-spouses, and co-habituating partners. This action is legally equivalent to stranger rape, or date rape. In other countries, spousal rape is accepted as part of the marriage agreement.

Rape is all about anger and control, and not about intimacy. Sex is used by the male to exploit his aggressive behavior, as he wants to control the victim for various reasons. He could be angry at his mother, or another female, or in retaliation to another abnormal situation. The rapist may resent women in general and feel the need to dominate just to gain his own self-respect.

There are times when a perpetrator uses a child, or a woman, for his own sexual gratification. But this goes against God and nature and is an abomination with horrific ramifications.

Victims will carry toxic amounts of shame to the grave unless God is allowed to heal their emotional wounds. Abusers, on the other hand, will shift blame from themselves to others, exhibit harsh judgments, and are deceptive in word and deed. Victims tend to accept what they have been told as truth. The concept is to believe the victim deserves what has happened to them.

Shamed into consent is another ploy used to engage

a victim into compliance. There is nothing that justifies the sadistic mistreatment of a female. The pain inflicted is more than just physical. The emotional aspects of this assault will be far reaching. Some women will never get beyond this form of aggression. Even worse is the victimization of a child. The Bible itself speaks against sexual assault.

"...a man...rapes her, only the man who has done this shall die. Do nothing to the woman; she has committed no sin deserving death" (Deuteronomy 22:25, 26)

"He who digs a hole and scoops it out falls into the pit he has made. The trouble he causes recoils on himself; his violence comes down on his own head" (Psalms 7:15, 16)

Breach of the marriage vow with repeated bouts of infidelity is another type of abuse. Mind games that keep one wondering what is true, and what is not, are serious indicators, and will damage a relationship. The inability to trust one's partner is the ultimate violation.

The United States of America has a Declaration of Independence document that declares every citizen has the right to life, liberty, and the pursuit of happiness. But that right can easily be removed by someone who wants complete control over your life. If allowed, they will destroy every ounce of freedom you once had.

How unfair for a woman, married many years to the same man, learn that her husband is having an illicit love affair. The marriage then crumbles, and the wife has no choice but to change her lifestyle. Coupled with menopause, grown children leaving the nest, and loneliness, a disaster is waiting to happen.

Add a younger woman with flowing hormones to the equation, and enough ammo is available to make any woman go insane. How can anyone justify forcing a faithful wife into such a position?

Only selfish, uncaring, and self-centered men would be so callous, or stoop so low.

Spiritual Abuse

Churches labeled as abusive are characterized as having strong control-oriented leadership. Tactics such as guilt, intimidation, and fear that manipulates members while trying to keep them in line are used. Associates of these churches believe there is no other religious organization that qualifies by belief, or standard.

They also believe God has singled them out for special purposes higher than traditional churches. Their stance is accentuated in rebuking others. Dissent is discouraged while subjective experience is emphasized.

Members are subject to scrutiny, rebuke, and embarrassment when rules, legalism, and church dogma abound. Persons and members who rebel are ceremonially excommunicated.

Using intimidation as a tool, pastors and spiritual leaders who have this mindset will manipulate their position to create self-preservation, or for their own gratification. Husbands, as leaders in the home, can also become manipulative toward their wives, and offspring.

Presenting themselves as knowledgeable and qualified, they will use their status to gain access to a victim's sense of dignity, well-being, and self-respect. The stage is then set for the abusive side to move in, and gain access without regard to a victim's sense of purpose. Strict, severe, and spiritual laws have caused some to doubt their own ability to live within the realms of holiness.

Generations of family are raised in Christian environments. But religion itself keeps members under scrutiny as guidelines are often overbearing, strict, and relentless when one goes astray.

Members of these churches are persecuted by outsiders who don't understand the rules of the church. This causes insiders to rebel and stray from the church altogether.

For example: the basic teachings of Pentecostalism follow the Biblical layout of salvation but also include the Baptism of the Holy Spirit as relevant to living a spirit-filled life.

A downside from Jessica's past was a rigid list of parental guidelines as well as church rules that restricted her, and other church members, from attending, or participating, in recreation such as ballgames, dances, or attending movies. The wearing of shorts and swim attire was also prohibited, as were beachgoers, and men who went shirtless.

Women were expected to be chaste in both look and deed. Clothing must depict those beliefs by long below-the-knee dresses, with a disallowance of pants and shorts. Also not allowed was sleeveless clothing as too much of the arm was shown. Make-up and jewelry, including the wedding band, was also prohibited.

The dictates of the church required female members grow their hair long, and never visit a beauty shop. The hair requirement for men was short, with an accepted length only to the tip of a shirt collar. Today those beliefs have been dropped as a more modern approach to Christian living has surfaced. But for some it's too late as the damage has already been done.

Restraining dominance in religious arenas has caused many to rebel against God, and the church in general. By diminishing one's values, controlling entities place themselves higher in position and knowledge. The victim is at risk for a future of misery, heartache, and low self-esteem as their feelings and convictions have been demeaned.

Oppressive rules and regulations have kept many from the church as they have witnessed domination of stringent supremacy ruin the lives of those entrenched by their methods.

**Big religion may talk the talk,
but do they walk the walk?**

Shame

The implications of this emotion are strong and repetitive, leaving powerful feelings of insecurity that come and go. But a victim of domestic violence and abuse struggles even more with these concepts than do others. An inability to overcome their circumstance will become a stronghold in their life. Only God can take away these perceptions and bring peace to their storm.

- Low self-esteem

- Feeling as if one doesn't belong

- Jealousy

- Insecurity

- Has a need to compete with others

- Low-grade depression

- Addicted to a substance, or action

- Wants to blame others

- A tendency to sabotage intimacy in relationships

- An inability to accept criticism

- Hypercritical of self, and others

Allow God to be your strength as you erase the effects of an abusive past

Chapter Sixty-Two

Infidelity

A man who maintains a highly respected position in life isn't excuse enough to justify his lust for women. Many from every walk and stance in life download pornography from the Internet, purchase vulgar and explicit materials, or engage with prostitutes or swinging couples to enhance their marriage, or relationship.

"You will have these tassels to look at and so you will remember all the commands of the LORD, that you may obey them and not prostitute yourselves by chasing after the lusts of your own hearts and eyes" (Numbers 15:39)

"Do not lust in your heart after her beauty or let her captivate you with her eyes" (Proverbs 6:25)

"But I tell you that anyone who looks at a woman lustfully has already committed adultery with her in his heart" (Josh 5:28)

"For everything in the world—the lust of the flesh, the lust of the eyes, and the pride of life—comes not from the Father but from the world" (1 John 2:16)

Signs He May be Cheating

- He picks fights with you

- He leaves earlier for work, or comes home later than usual

- He acts unappreciated

- He finds fault with everything you do and criticizes you openly

- He becomes distant and uncommunicative

- He changes his behavior when it comes to money issues

- He buys unexpected gifts or does good deeds such as helping clean up

- He changes his style by purchasing different clothing, or loses weight to change his appearance

- He has absences he can't explain

- He tells you there is something wrong with you, and encourages you to get professional help

- He changes his sexual behavior including positions, frequency, or patterns

- There are hang-ups on the phone when you answer his

The Ultimate Betrayal

A cheating man blames the wife for his adultery. In his mind, he is drawing attention away from himself, and believes to have disguised his sin. Most likely the woman has never cheated on her husband, and is appalled when she learns of his unfaithfulness.

In his rants he uses foul language concerning her alleged infidelity, trying to justify himself. He desires she feel unworthy of him. But the fact remains, a traitor in the marriage will continue their sinful ways, and most likely, should never again be trusted.

"Not by might nor by power, but by my Spirit,' says the LORD Almighty" (Zechariah 4:6)

I am confident. Fear cannot conquer me.

Prayer of Unfaithfulness

A biblical prayer for those who have sinned.

"Have mercy on me, O God, according to your unfailing love; according to your great compassion blot out my transgressions.

Wash away all my iniquity and cleanse me from my sin. For I know my transgressions; and my sin is always before me. Against you, you only, have I sinned and done what is evil in your sight; so you are right in your verdict and justified when you judge.

Surely I was sinful at birth, sinful from the time my mother conceived me. Yet you desired faithfulness even in the womb; you taught me wisdom in that secret place.

Cleanse me with hyssop, and I will be clean; wash me, and I will be whiter than snow. Let me hear joy and gladness; let the bones you have created rejoice. Hide your face from my sins and blot out all my iniquity.

"Create in me a pure heart, O God, and renew a steadfast spirit within me. Do not cast me from your presence or take your Holy Spirit from me. Restore to me the joy of your salvation and grant me a willing spirit, to sustain me" (Psalms 51: 1-10)

"Do not be misled: Bad company corrupts good character" (1 Corinthians 15:33)

"The Lord knows those who are His..." (2 Timothy 2:19)

Emotional wounds will remain as a reminder of outrageous trauma.

Chapter Sixty-Three

Domestic Violence and Children

Children who view domestic violence in the home will most certainly be affected in negative ways. Research shows that keeping children with an abuser is not in their best interest.

Children who see nothing more than parental violence, but aren't hit themselves, are still affected. Somatic and emotional problems will surface and are like children who have been assaulted. Most will suffer Post-Traumatic Stress Disorder later in life.

A child who learns this type of behavior stays reinforced with a tendency to repeat those same patterns of abuse later in life, as learned at home.

Boys, when they get older, tend to identify with the aggressive parent, lose respect for their mother, or feel guilt over their inability to protect her.

It's never a good idea for a child to live with an abusive parent. The demonstration of dominance an authoritarian figure shows will cause a child to become a perpetrator of domestic violence.

Studies found in *The Judges Journal* reveal that spousal abuse typically doesn't stem from relational problems, but instead arises from the man's emotional insecurities, low self-esteem, or a history of abusive behavior seen in his own childhood.

Placing a child with an abusive parent long term has proven harmful, if not damaging for a child. It would be wise if the custodial parent also be the one who offers the most productive love, training, and attention for the child.

Reasons to be Cautious

- Placing a child with an abuser perpetuates a cycle of violence by exposing them to an environment where exploitation is acceptable

- A wife-beater's violence damages the emotional health of the couple's children

- The mother normally has better parenting skills because she has, most likely, been the children's primary caregiver

"Now choose life, so that you and your children may live" (Deuteronomy 30:1)

Casualties of Divorce

Children will remain casualties of divorce following their parent's separation. Even if escape from an abusive situation was for their own good, the ramifications could still be devastating.

The financial aspect of the split will have consequences that are far-reaching. Many times, as a single parent, Jessica had difficulty scraping together enough money to buy just a loaf of bread, or a gallon of milk. Although food was scarce at times, God always came through for her.

There were times, however, when all she had were pennies from piggy banks to purchase life-saving sustenance. It was during those times of struggle she learned to trust in God.

"The LORD is my shepherd, I lack nothing" (Psalms 23:1)

258

"I was young and now I am old, yet I have never seen the righteous forsaken or their children begging bread" (Psalms 37:25)

"Have I not commanded you? Be strong and courageous. Do not be afraid; do not be discouraged, for the LORD your God will be with you wherever you go" (Joshua 1:9)

Other casualties of divorce are more difficult to swallow. A child's divorce, children searching for identity—even the death of a child isn't unexpected following this type of invasion.

"I waited patiently for the LORD; He turned to me and heard my cry. He lifted me out of the slimy pit, out of the mud and mire; He set my feet on a rock and gave me a firm place to stand. He put a new song in my mouth, a hymn of praise to our God. Many will see and fear and put their trust in the LORD" (Psalms 40: 1-3)

Violence and Children after Divorce

An APA study suggests the after-affects for children following their parent's divorce is relevant to violence in the marriage. Preschool children who were traumatized while observing their mothers being battered also demonstrated negatively in their development.

PTSD and other stress related disorders are predictable in children who are exposed to parental violence again and again, especially when combined with poverty, or their own neglect and mistreatment. Mental illness of one or both parents is also a risk factor. Even sibling violence is relational to marital violence in the home, with higher ratings than non-violent homes.

Another study signifies that the occurrence rate of childhood abuse in homes where the mother is battered at forty percent. Other results estimate between forty and sixty percent of children raised in violent marriages will become easy targets for both parents.

Violence in the home is also related to a lack of satisfaction in life which includes low self-esteem and violence among one's own peers, psychological distress, or a lack of closeness with their mother as a young adult.

Children raised in abusive homes are more likely to experience academic and behavioral problems at school. Aggression, delinquency, anti-social behavior, depression, and disobedience toward parents and teachers is not uncommon.

Jeers and insults toward other children in an aggressive environment will cause a high-impact child to withdraw into themselves. Buffers to protect the child is having a good relationship with at least one parent, a sibling, or a friend.

A father's violence presents in a lack of closeness to their child, or children. Results may vary, but often remain negative, even years following childhood trauma suffered in the home.

Men need to take their role as husband and father seriously. There are severe consequences to ignoring one's responsibility. How easy it is to destroy the lives of those they love by disregarding their God-given position as head of the household.

To raise godly children, one must put God before themselves. Character matters. Lay aside dishonesty, laziness, and lust; and replace with honesty, truth, and reliability. Step up the plate and be the man you claim to be.

Which is it? Doesn't know how to give love or doesn't have love to give?

Absentee Parent

An absentee parent who isn't involved in his or her own child's life doesn't excuse or make them unaccountable to God, and the child, for their lack of parenting. It's easier to use the excuse of being unavailable because of work, or other activities than to be accountable to your child.

There is no excuse for a parent to neglect any child brought into this world. Even if the relationship with the other parent doesn't work out, a personal responsibility to nurture and provide for their child is essential, and is not excused.

Children aren't blind and understand better than most what is going on in the home. They also recognize why their parents are divorcing as too many times they witnessed their mother being assaulted.

Many fathers are slack in involvement with their children following a divorce. In the end, his children will pay a bitter price for his lack of parenting.

I can't fix anything, but God can.

Raising Your Child

Who is raising your child?
Do you want to know who?
Are you really so clueless
That you thought it was you?

What you don't understand
And don't care to see
Is that he's being raised
By his grandpa and me

Who is raising your child?
So, you still don't know who?
Well, get a grip on the truth
Because it sure isn't you

© *Phoebe Leggett*

Chapter Sixty-Four

Scars of Abuse

Physical scars often heal. But the residual of abuse will linger for a lifetime.

Depression

Depression is the father of neurosis, or self-hate. This phobia can overwhelm as one who is possessed with an obsession of loathing, or despondency. When depressed, one will become lethargic, and lose interest in activities, work, or life in general as emotions are sorted through.

Depression often follows a recipient of domestic violence in the home, as dealing with an abuser daily is confining, and disheartening.

It may be difficult to forgive yourself for various and undefined reasons. Sudden bouts of crying, a serious lack of interest, or withdraw from others can also occur, but is a normal reaction.

Feeling out of control, and unable to change your circumstance also causes depression.

Many victims suppress emotions too complicated to control. But if conflicts remain overwhelmingly brutal, now is the time to consult a physician—or an attorney.

Depression - de·pres·sion

noun \ the size of an angle of depression an act of depressing or a state of being depressed: as *a*: a pressing down : lowering *b (1)*: a state of feeling sad : dejection *(2)*: a psychoneurotic or psychotic disorder marked especially by sadness, inactivity, difficulty in thinking and concentration, a significant increase or decrease in appetite and time spent sleeping, feelings of dejection and hopelessness, and sometimes suicidal tendencies.

Languish

So here I sit
Day after day
As I slowly
Languish away

Sadly afloat
In waves of woe
Wasting away
And feeling low

Don't let me drift
In masked disguise
Please rescue me
Before my demise

© *Phoebe Leggett*

Depression has been described as living in a black hole while sifting through sensations of sadness, insecurity, and impending dread.

But depression is more than an emotion of sorrow. Feeling listless, hopeless, or abnormal numbness associated with any normal emotion is an instant indicator. Intense feelings of worthlessness, sadness, or anger that interfere with one's ability to eat, sleep, work, or enjoy life in general is another indicator.

There's little relief if overtaken by what is known as clinical depression.

Symptoms of Clinical Depression

- Lack of concentration making it difficult to perform normally

- Feelings of hopelessness and helplessness

- Over-sleeping, or an inability to sleep in a normal way

- Huge consumption of alcohol, drugs, or food is another indicator

- Loss of appetite, reckless behavior, or a lack of concern in preserving one's own life

- Presenting as short-tempered, irritable, or more aggressive than normal

- Constant overeating

- Out-of-control negative thoughts and feelings

- Suicidal thoughts

- Unexplained aches and pains

- Self-loathing

- Thoughts of self-injury or manipulation

- Feeling trapped

- An inability to see one's way out of an abusive situation

I Say
(From an abuser's perspective)

I say I can
But then I don't
I say I will
But then I won't

Call me clever
Or call me a fool
Call me incompetent
But I'm going to rule

I say what I say
I am what I am
I do what I do
And it's not a scam

What can I say
To make things right?
What can I do
So we won't fight?

It's not going happen
I'm not going change
I know I am right
And I'm taking no blame

© *Phoebe Leggett*

Grades of Depression

Categories of depression have separate and unique symptoms, causes, and effects. Understanding what type or category you have will help the doctor provide the most effective treatment available for your depression.

Listed below are three types of depression a victim of domestic violence will suffer.

- **Atypical Depression** will cause weight gain, excessive sleep, an increase in appetite with feelings of heaviness in legs and arms, or rejection sensitivity. If the abuse was short in endurance, this depression should last only a short amount of time.

- **Mild depression** has low-grade symptoms of depression, which may have gone untreated for years. The victim who has suffered domestic violence short in duration over a long period of time may have symptoms not associated with the abuse. Suppressed feelings of rage caused by violence will have consequences. Ignoring them only makes it more difficult to understand why feelings of hopelessness surface when least expected.

- **Major Depression** is an inability to enjoy life, or experience pleasure. Seek treatment if this decline lasts longer than six months.

Allowing God to be your guide is the only way to move beyond the pain of abuse

Chapter Sixty-Five

Don't Surrender

Depression varies from person to person, but there are common signs and symptoms that indicate a loss of joyfulness. These same symptoms can also be part of life's normal ups and downs. But if the list continues to grow, take note as depression can quickly overtake a person's emotions. Thoughts of suicide may develop, and could become a major risk factor, or mental disorder.

Despair and hopelessness go hand in hand with domestic violence and abuse. These same emotions can make one believe suicide is the only way to escape the pain of being violated.

Thoughts of death are serious symptoms of depression. When someone discusses suicide, it's simply a cry for help. Seek assistance if the symptoms listed below are cause for concern.

Suicidal Frame of Mind

- Talks about killing or harming themselves

- Expresses strong emotions about feeling trapped

- Pre-occupation with death

- Acts reckless such as speeding in a car

- Tells people goodbye

- Gives away personal possessions

- Says things like "Nobody loves me," or "I'm useless"

- Mood changes from happy to sad

"I have set before you life and death...Now choose life..." (Deuteronomy 30:19 "...hard pressed on every side, but not crushed; perplexed, but not in despair; persecuted, but not abandoned; struck down, but not destroyed" (2 Corinthians 4:8, 9)

Are you capable of surviving beyond an abused, broken, or damaged life? Only God can provide what's needed to overcome depression and live to tell others about it.

Living in the darkness of repression restrains the light of freedom.

Chapter Sixty-Six

Recovering From Abuse

Pain and bitterness following a relationship gone bad, the desire to get even, or a belief that one is worthless describes a woman who has been battered and beaten beyond comprehension by her lover.

To begin the healing process, refuse to keep the pain locked inside. Learn to share with others who have also survived similar situations.

Realize emotions left unchecked will later become more damaging than when first created.

Understand that depression abounds for those who have escaped an abusive relationship. Even though the circumstance of one's situation has changed, justification doesn't always provide emotional freedom.

It may be time-consuming to work through all the damage caused by an abusive relationship—not only physically, but emotionally. Your willingness to accept psychological or medical treatment and overcome inflicted injuries could be your salvation.

Depression often surfaces during and following victimization. The damage may be short lived or remain for an extended amount of time. However, this is normal, and has been documented.

In the aftermath it's best to take responsibility for your own recovery. The refusal of some to believe they really were victimized will only increase in anxiety if not nipped in the bud.

But use caution when seeking someone to support your account of the abuse. If they can't be trusted with what you have to say, expecting them to be an advocate is simply a waste of time.

If one expects justice from the legal system, don't be surprised if expectations fall short. From judges to local police, corrupt policies are in place that often deny protection for those who need it most. The fact remains, you may be on your own, and not yet realize it.

An overwhelming amount of Judges side with the assailant and deny assistance for the victim.

One judge recommended that a battered woman and her abuser remain under the same roof but divide the living quarters. A common area would be used for both. The result was a dead wife, beaten to death with a baseball bat in that same area.

Many legal authorities actually assist the perpetrator by withholding needed assistance. The victim is then rendered helpless in the most dangerous of situations. In society today it may be necessary to protect yourself. Keep mace or alternative protection close at hand, and preferably on your person. The purchase of a firearm is not an unreasonable option.

There will be times when your actions may be embarrassing for others as you react in unusual ways under duress and change of routine. Panic and fear following a separation could be non-stop, and quite severe.

Apprehension of what could happen next may cause a victim to cower in expectation of an abusive episode. At this point, it's best to seek medical or psychological assistance to completely recover from related feelings of dread due to a terrorized existence.

Information and treatment, if accepted, will provide an immediate benefit, as well as support for years to come. Medication is often helpful in easing stress caused by a change in lifestyle.

As a casualty of cruelty, you will remain afraid of unplanned encounters with your abuser, even years following your separation. Dread of mistreatment is a continual concern, as it creates noticeable apprehension and undue nervousness.

Fear will even dictate a victim's very existence. Threats of impending death before and after a separation will keep one scared out of their wits. Symptoms of a dread disease may later surface when anxiety has hit its limit.

Abuse and Disease

Stress following a sadistic relationship may cause sickness, serious infections, or disease.

Take note as depression is common among people diagnosed with different diseases. This does not indicate weak character and should never be considered shameful enough to remain hidden.

Significant emotional stress often triggers symptoms of sickness. Many studies show the functioning of the immune system to be remarkably altered by emotional stress. Sufferers of a diagnosed disease could have profound emotional consequences as well.

Stress *noun* \
Definition of: constraining force or influence: as a physical, chemical, or emotional factor that causes bodily or mental tension and may be a factor in disease causation: a state resulting from a stress; *especially*: one of bodily or mental tension resulting from factors that tend to alter an existent equilibrium

Anxiety **anx·i·ety**
noun
plural **anx·i·eties**

Definition of: a painful or apprehensive uneasiness of mind usually over an impending or anticipated ill *b*: fearful concern or interest *c*: a cause of anxiety; an abnormal and overwhelming sense of apprehension and fear often marked by physiological signs (such as sweating, tension, and an increased pulse rate), by doubt concerning the reality and nature of the threat, and by self-doubt concerning one's capacity to cope with it.

Loneliness **lone·ly**
adj \

*Definition of: being without company : **lone** cut off from others: **solitary** not frequented by human beings: **desolate** sad from being alone: **lonesome***
: producing a feeling of bleakness or desolation
— **lone·li·ness** *noun*

Accusation *ac·cu·sa·tion*

noun \

Definition of
1: the act of <u>accusing</u>: the state or fact of being <u>accused</u>
2: a charge of wrongdoing

Self-Esteem *self–es·teem*
Definition of: *noun*

1: *a confidence and satisfaction in oneself: **self-respect***
2: <u>self-conceit</u>

Depression depression ***noun*** \

1: the angular distance of a celestial object below the horizon *b*: the size of an angle of depression

2: an act of <u>depressing</u> or a state of being <u>depressed</u>

Hope verb \
Hoped hop·ing
Definition of: intransitive verb
1: to cherish a desire with anticipation <*hopes* for a promotion>

2 *archaic*:
transitive verb
1: to desire with expectation of obtainment
2: to expect with confidence: trust

— **hop·er** *noun*
 — **hope against hope:** to hope without any basis for
  expecting fulfillment

 — **Restoration**
  res·to·ra·tion
  Definition of: *noun* \

1: an act of <u>restoring</u> or the condition of being <u>restored</u>: as
a: a bringing back to a former position or condition :
<u>reinstatement</u> <the *restoration* of peace> *b*: <u>restitution</u> *c*: a
restoring to an unimpaired or improved condition <the
restoration of a painting> *d*: the replacing of missing teeth
or crowns
2: something that is restored; *especially*: a representation
or reconstruction of the original form (as of a fossil or a
building)

 "...for thou shalt surely overtake them, and without
fail recover all" (1 Samuel 30:8) (KJV)
 Reach out to others and allow their support to
provide the assistance you need, and desire. Or find a care
group for abused survivors and learn from others how to
survive and thrive.
 Sharing information and stories of abuse will be
healing, and therapeutic. New friendships often form that
continue to be encouraging, and helpful. In this way, you
will understand that you are not alone.

Chapter Sixty-Seven

Understand Yourself

If one has an inability to understand, perhaps a therapist, or trusted church leader, could be of assistance.

Realize You Have a Problem

Abuse in any form is never acceptable. Advise a friend or relative if you've been mistreated. If they refuse to believe, or provide needed help, find someone who *will* listen, such as the police, or clergy. If those around you aren't helpful, keep looking. Unless someone is on your side, it will be difficult, if not impossible, to survive the trauma of abuse.

Keep a journal and record the happenings of violence and abuse after they occur. Journaling will help ease feelings of isolation and loneliness or assist in gaining a better prospective of the situation at hand. If needed, this information could provide proof of the battering when you speak with an attorney.

Victimization allows one to remain trapped in an abusive situation for years—even decades. For some it's difficult to understand that battering doesn't occur in normal relationships.

It's also possible that the injured party has never observed a good relationship, and simply became a victim without realizing the role they played in their own choices.

If they abuse you once, shame on them
If they abuse you twice, shame on you

Examine the Abuse

- It's not your fault. You didn't cause your partner to mistreat you.

- You should be respected, and not battered.

- Everyone, including children, deserves to live in a safe environment, free from the fear of assault

- Don't accept blame for your mistreatment

- You're not alone. There is someone somewhere who understands and will provide aid and assistance if asked.

It's difficult for some to understand why an abused woman doesn't leave the marriage, or relationship. But for the one who's being abused, it's never as simple as just leaving. She has been isolated from her family and personal friends for some time and is afraid to stand alone. But when children are involved, the situation could become more volatile—even dangerous.

Psychologically beaten down, emotionally drained, financially dependent, and physically threatened daily makes it difficult for a victim to see a clear way of escape. Feelings of guilt over breaking up the family, or the realization that you will be blamed for what is not your fault, can be overwhelming.

Confusion, desperation, and feelings of entrapment will make one feel it's safer to remain in an abusive household than to strike out on your own.

Many blame themselves. Because of a weakened emotional status, they remain afraid to confront, or seek help.

Understand that your safety, and the well-being of your children, truly does matter. Decide at that point to never again allow the intimidation of others to rule over your decision to leave an unhealthy, violent, or restrictive relationship.

Inform Yourself

Read about others who have been abused and survived. Find resources that will provide help with your situation. Or locate a counseling group of peers who have also survived a similar violence. Understand that knowledge is power. Appreciate the ability to share with others. There's always comfort in knowing you're not alone.

When facing a decision to salvage your abusive relationship, or to leave, keep in mind that your abuser will continue to abuse if you remain. It will be difficult, if not impossible, to reverse those traits simply because he has a dominant personality.

To make an informed decision, research the statistics of domestic abuse relationships, and realize that the signs aren't pretty.

Domestic violence has long been a threatening entity with devastating results and irreversible consequences. Abusers develop deep emotional and psychological problems, sometimes filtering back to their own abused childhood.

Change is never easy, and often unachievable for the abuser. Only his willingness to change will delegate his ability to reverse his actions.

He may never fully accept responsibility for his behavior, seek professional treatment, or recognize his role as an abuser. But he cannot blame others for his unhappy childhood, work related circumstances, drug or alcohol habits, or his temper. He alone is solely responsible for the choices he makes in his own life.

It's natural to desire helping your partner. After all, you did promise to love, honor, and cherish '*till death do us part.* You also believe it's your responsibility to fix his problems because you alone understand everything about him. Staying in the relationship, and accepting the abuse dumped on you, is only reinforcing the problem, and keeping the action alive.

Remember. It's *not* your responsibility to fix his problems.

Most abusers make empty promises to stop the battering if threatened with exposure. He will plead forgiveness with a guarantee to change. Instead, he continues to control while resuming verbal and physical assaults. He now believes he's home free as you have never followed through on any one threat to leave the relationship. Once forgiven, he quickly forgets his promise to stop the abuse as he now realizes you're not going anywhere.

Most abusers will continue their pattern of control, violence, and abusive actions even after the completion of many counseling sessions. Getting help does not guarantee a partner will change.

At this point it may be time to make a more permanent decision. Do you want to continue living in an explosive situation, or is it time to get out?

The key is to understand that violence does affect children. It's inappropriate to risk your life and their future just to save your marriage. If abuse is rampant, even more essential is the need for safety. Don't allow fear of the unknown to keep you, and your children, in harm's way.

Proof He Hasn't Changed

- If he continues to deny his role as abuser, and minimizes the damage done by his battering

- If he refuses to acknowledge his rage

- If he continues to blame you, or others, for his actions

- If he promises to go to counseling but doesn't.

- If he refuses to attend the sessions unless forced

- If he begs for another chance

- If he tells you he can't change without your help

- If he wants everyone, including children, family, and friends to feel sorry for him

- If he expects something from you in exchange for getting help or treatment

- If he pressures you into making decisions about the relationship, and then blames you when things don't go his way, then he hasn't changed.

Accept the facts and resolve to get help.

Keep your friends close—your enemies even closer

Chapter Sixty-Eight

Help for the Abused

Until you are ready to leave your abuser, there are things you can do to protect yourself. The safety tips listed below can make all the difference between injury or death when trying to escape with your life, and your children.

Prepare for Emergencies

- Be alert to your abuser's red flags. Use caution when he is upset or shows signs of rage that result in explosive battering.

- Memorize unbelievable reasons to use as an excuse for leaving the house (day or night) when a violent episode is about to occur.

- Discover safe places in the home to go when your abuser becomes violent, or when an argument gets volatile.

- Avoid small spaces or enclosed areas without exits such as bathrooms or closets. Only use rooms that have windows or a door in case the need to escape arises.

- If possible, have a portable phone available. Cellphone technology has changed the scope of our world and is a wonderful tool in finding someone to assist.

- Use a secret code with your children, friends, or neighbors so they can be alerted if you're in danger and need police assistance.

Have a Plan

Be prepared to leave the home at any unexpected moment. As a precaution, keep the car full of gas, and parked in a way that makes it easy to get inside and drive away.

- Hide a spare key—just in case.

- Alert the children of your escape plan. But use caution. Children often tell what they know without realizing the consequences.

- Keep a list of trustworthy places to go. Memorize numbers for emergency contacts such as police, shelters, or domestic violence hotlines.

- Use caution so your partner doesn't discover your plan. Cover your tracks. Be careful when using the computer or phone, and don't leave a trail of information behind.

- Use a friend's or public telephone. Most public phones allow a 911 call for free. Or use a prepaid card so there isn't a trail left to follow.

- Use caution while using a computer, as with the phone. Change e-mail usernames and passwords frequently.

Map Your Escape

Learn what will be needed to survive before leaving your abuser. Hire an attorney to handle the legal applications of obtaining a restraining order, separation agreement, or other legal documentation related to domestic violence issues.

Realize you are now the one in control and allow that motivation to give you the confidence needed to move forward.

Trust only those who understand your pain and are willing to provide a safe place for you. Your in-laws and friends may not be the ones to count on at this time.

Don't be afraid to find other advocates if someone you've confided in falls short. There is hope and security somewhere so keep looking. Remember to use caution when revealing your concerns to others. Not everyone can be trusted.

Shelters

Locate a women's shelter in your area if the need for protection becomes essential for survival. Once you've taken the first step to flee your abuser, it's important to maintain your safety if you plan to survive long-term.

Make sure the information you share is only with people you trust. Again, use caution, as not everyone who acts responsible, is. It may be necessary to move long distances just to remain safe. Changing schools for the children could be essential for survival.

Remember to keep all personal information private. Be vigilant when sharing phone numbers, addresses, and other important information. Not everyone can be trusted.

Realize restraining orders may not be enforced if the abuser is known as a good old boy by local police, and others. Some will never believe someone they know is an abuser.

It's important to stay focused while fleeing. Until everything has been settled, use every precaution possible for your safety, and the children's.

Find a safe place to hide until all conflicts have been resolved in a legal and secure manner.

"I lift up her eyes to the mountains where does my help come from? My help comes from the LORD, the Maker of heaven and earth" (Psalms 121:1, 2)

With God's help, a leap through your darkened tunnel into the light is achievable.

Chapter Sixty-Nine

Phases of Battering

The best way to understand Battered Wife Syndrome is to talk with someone who has survived it. Dr. Lenore E. Walker writes that a woman will experience at least two battering cycles before she is labeled a battered woman. This cycle is broken down into three phases.

The first phase begins with tension-building moments followed by an explosion of battering episodes. A time of calm follows which allows the episode to subside.

The second phase of battering is an explosion or encounter when the woman is battered and could be seriously injured.

The third phase includes remorse with petitions of forgiveness from the batterer. Promises to never again repeat the episode allows a loving relationship to rekindle. This is referred to as the honeymoon phase.

The abuser's promise to refrain from the beatings will quickly become a lie if the battering is allowed to continue. To ignore the violence only produces future episodes of abuse.

Because women have been programmed to keep the peace in the relationship, she is inclined to carry the responsibility of holding the marriage together. But this only creates more reasons to stay in the union despite the battering.

Over time the abused will retain low self-esteem, and fear of an inability to provide for themselves, and their children. A lack of psychological energy to leave the marriage then surfaces, and the victim feels helpless to change her situation.

Depression will follow and often demonstrates as

hopelessness at her inability to find someone who understands her situation. This may trigger self-inflicted obsessions, or suicide as well.

Battered Wife Syndrome describes a pattern of behavioral and psychological symptoms found in women living in abusive relationships. The dominance their partner creates will overwhelm as it restricts her ability to think with a clear mind.

Characteristics of a Battered Woman

- She believes the violence is all her fault.

- She is unable to place the responsibility of the battering on anyone else.

- She fears for her life and the lives of her children.

- She believes her abuser knows everything she does and hears everything she says.

How Domestic Violence Affects Children

Documentation supports the recommendation that, in most states, custody decisions in the courts won't be made without taking domestic violence into consideration. A non-violent parent will be recommended as there is a presumption against awarding custody of children to an abuser.

Children who witness violence in the home, but aren't hit themselves, demonstrate evidence of emotional and behavioral problems that are similar to those experienced by children who are physically abused.

Children who witness violence will suffer PTSD at some point in their life. It has been noted that children who witness aggression from their fathers often become sadistic and brutal toward other children. They may be abusive as an adult.

The older boy will identify with his aggressive father and lose respect for his mother—usually because of his inability to provide protection for her when she is assaulted in front of him.

A more consistent predictor of future aggression is children who witness violence between their parents on a regular basis. They will learn to accept this behavior as normal, and acceptable. Since they see compliance by the victim, they learn to use those same alternatives in their own relationships.

This becomes a vicious cycle that is played out again and again in the lives of those who come from a family where abuse is a normal part of daily living. It's been proven that a wife-beater's violence damages the emotional health of his children.

Deliverance

"...hard pressed on every side, but not crushed; perplexed, but not in despair; persecuted, but not abandoned; struck down, but not destroyed" (2 Corinthians 4:8, 9)

The connections in your life will either make you or break you.

Chapter Seventy

Begin to Heal

First and foremost, forgive yourself for allowing the abuse to happen in the first place. Then pray for the ability to forgive your abuser. As you gain control of your life, release anger and hatred toward your assailant as well as those who protected him or failed to believe you were in danger. Lastly, be thankful that you can now live free from cruelty, manipulation, and the control of a volatile man.

Continue to journal your thoughts and feelings as you move forward into your new lifestyle. Keep a list of resources close at hand for future reference. As your confidence soars, replace old friends and ex-family with new acquaintances and new friends. You're now in charge of your life, and happiness is just around the bend.

During the process don't become isolated or withdraw from society. Seek others with whom you can interact. Look for professional guidance if needed. But most of all, allow God to be your source of strength and healing. Don't blame him for what others have done to you.

"...forgive one another if any of you has a grievance against someone. Forgive as the LORD forgave you" (Colossians 3:13)

"The LORD is my strength and my defense; He has become my salvation" (Exodus 15:2)

A minister's wife, known for her cute phrases and silly clichés, was happy to share one with Jessica, a newlywed.

"Where he leads me, I will foller," she said. "And when he hits me, I will holler."

Although Southern in dialect, her lack of perception

or relational experience disallowed knowledge of Jessica's situation. Her declaration instantly pierced Jessica's heart. Unknown to most, she was living her words.

Scars

Scars from domestic abuse and violence run deep. The trauma you've experienced will remain long after you've escaped an abusive situation. Counseling, therapy, and support groups for domestic abuse survivors should help process what you've been through as you learn to build new and healthy relationships.

Upsetting scenarios, scary memories, or constant fear of danger ahead will follow the trauma you've just escaped, if only for a short time. Numbness, an inability to trust, or feeling disconnected from the world will also be emotional.

To embrace a speedy recovery, allow friends and family—the ones you trust—to be your support. Your ability to heal and move forward in life is an attainable goal.

Building New Friendships

Use caution when choosing new relationships to replace old ones, especially when searching for intimacy and the support you need. Refrain from making quick decisions about your future. Take time, and don't rush into a situation you may later regret.

Victims of abuse often repeat their mistakes by selecting relationships that fit the pattern of the assailant they've just separated from.

Decisions concerning romantic relationships should only be made after a complete recovery from former traumas. New situations that provide a safe environment for you, and the children, doesn't necessarily mean you are home free.

Continue to seek professional care to overcome any abuse-related difficulties that may later develop. If memories of past abuse continue to surface, the difficulties of coping with them could be more than you can handle.

Substance abuse, alcohol, and eating disorders can become ways of surviving the emotions of cruelty. It's best not to allow these crutches to take over your life as more problems will surely develop if allowed. Memories of past abuse have a way of controlling the future, if permitted.

Everyone who experiences mistreatment does so in different ways. Recovery will also be in stages, depending on the type of abuse you have suffered. A victim has little control over the violence imposed on them. But it's important, not to accept blame for what you did not initiate.

What *can* be controlled is how you recover your self-respect, and your future. No one deserves to be assaulted, either physically, emotionally, or sexually—whether child or adult. Remember, you did not cause the abuse. Also understand that your assailant was never your friend.

Those who use the Bible as a weapon to judge, exclude, or condemn is the same as abandoning the Holy Spirit and Jesus as their example.

Once a victim escapes her abuser, liberation from captivity brings freedom to heart and soul. A prisoner of manipulation and violence has been released. But use caution and restrain from impulsive behavior. Newfound freedom isn't cause for reckless actions. Wrong choices will affect your future in negative ways.

Independent at last, a comeback into the real world will be exciting and spontaneous but may cause irresponsible behavior. Some will act out their freedom in outrageous ways, even going against their own better judgment.

Conduct yourself in a safe and responsible way. Realize it will take huge amounts of time to re-adjust, free from the battering that once held you captive.

It's best not to rush into new love relationships, as the impact of freedom hasn't yet settled in your mind. Don't bond with another man just because you're alone or believe he will be your salvation.

It may take months, even years, to overcome the damage caused by your assailant. Take baby steps until sound decisions can be made concerning your future.

"...greater is He that is in you, than he that is in the world" (1 John 4:4)

Characterization

"For there is nothing hidden that will not be disclosed, and nothing concealed that will not be known or brought out into the open" (Luke 8:17)

Everyone on the outside believed Jessica's marriage was perfect as it appeared that way. Beneath the façade, however, her relationship with Trey was falling apart. Support from family and friends wasn't enough to hold the union together. Commitment and integrity were the missing elements.

Trey's abusive actions surfaced shortly after their marriage began. A few years later he wanted out. Destructive actions demonstrated the truth of his spirit. He felt trapped. Unknown to most, his lustful, roving eye had changed his heart.

Spiteful retaliation emerged with a vengeance and assaulted those in the home with hatred. When his wrath erupted, he became a monster. The aftermath of his rebellion revealed a battered spouse, and three frightened children. But he did not care.

Biblical knowledge wasn't enough to keep him on the straight and narrow. Even his status as church pastor became irrelevant, causing him to exploit his position. Failing to deter his resolve, family values were ignored, and carelessly tossed to the wind.

His words and actions indicated a petition for divorce. But his refusal to accept responsibility for that acquisition left Jessica in the lurch. Yet the truth remained. He wanted her gone. Perhaps if he intensified the battering she would leave. Then everyone would know she was the one who left the marriage, and he would come out smelling like a rose.

And it was so—for a time.

"Then you will know the truth, and the truth will set you free" (John 8:32)

Chapter Seventy-One

Marriage, Abuse, and Divorce

"Hope deferred makes the heart sick, but a longing fulfilled is a tree of life" (Proverbs 13:12)

Deceiver of my Heart

According to Cathy Meyer from About.com, a victim of domestic violence should obtain a Restraining Order for protection by the law. Any person who has been subjected to domestic abuse by a spouse, a person who is a present, a former household member, or the victim is eighteen years of age or older, or an emancipated minor, is able to obtain this order.

A victim of any age who has been subjected to domestic violence by a person who she/he says will be the father/mother of the child when the pregnancy is carried to term is also covered under this law.

Also included is any person who has been subjected to domestic violence by a person with whom the victim has had a dating relationship. The occurrence of one or more assaults committed against a victim by an adult or an emancipated minor, is considered domestic violence.

Categories of criminal domestic violence.

- Assault

- Burglary

- Criminal mischief

- Criminal restraint

Healer of my Soul

"May your fountain be blessed, and may you rejoice in the wife of your youth" (Proverbs 5:180)

"You may ask, 'Why?' It's because the LORD is the witness between you and the wife of your youth. You have been unfaithful to her, though she is your partner, the wife of your marriage covenant" (Malachi 2:14)

"Has not the one God made you? You belong to him in body and spirit. And what does the one God seek? Godly offspring. So be on your guard, and do not be unfaithful to the wife of your youth" (Malachi 2:14-16)

There were times when Jessica was venerable, and destitute as a victim of abuse. But God knew exactly where she was.

"My dove in the clefts of the rock, in the hiding places on the mountainside, show me your face, let me hear your voice; for your voice is sweet, and your face is lovely" (Song of Solomon 2:14)

"Enduring is your dwelling place, and your nest is set in the rock" (Numbers 24:21) (ESV)

"I will put you in a cleft of the rock, and I will cover

you with my hand..." (Exodus 33:2)

"The pride of your heart has deceived you, you who live in the clefts of the rocks..." (Obadiah 1:3)

God Grace

It's not what others have done to us, but what Jesus did for us, that matters. The key is forgiveness and essential for healing. With God's help, and the passing of time, the pain of the past can be eliminated.

Although memories remain, peace and tranquility will come with forgiveness.

"...weeping may endure for a night, but joy cometh in the morning" (Psalm 30:5)

The Key

I've lost some needed friendships
Along life's rough highway
Relationships thought endless
Have strangely gone away

I've lost faith in some colleagues
I thought would always care
Like waves and ocean breezes
No longer here, nor there

But with my disappointment
In seasons of great pain
One thing has never wavered
And one thing never changed

I've never lost my praise
And never lost my hope
I've never lost my faith
But cling to heaven's rope

For joy comes in the morning
With love that's pure and free
It conquers pain and hurt
Forgiveness is the key

© *Phoebe Leggett*

Chapter Seventy-Two

Initiation

As the recipient of overbearing, restrictive, and reclusive parents, Jessica soon learned that obedience was essential. But their parenting process was missing an important element—a serious lack of affection. Forced submission was on the agenda, but created whelps, blood, and inner turmoil. Legalism, tempered with conditional love, was the accepted protocol.

Shunned and ignored as a child, Jessica felt unloved, unwanted, and a burden on family resources. Her father was happy only when she worked hard on the farm, stayed out of his way, and restrained from making noise.

On the flip side, her mother's love presented by inflicting punishment in the form of beatings almost daily for simple and undeserved infractions. The strength of her arm ruled, as the harshness of her gaze and the tone of her voice intimidated.

Her idea of parenting was to *spare the rod and spoil the child*. Although both parents were quick to impose stringent rules, their restrictions made life impossible to enjoy. A distorted perception of relational association created residual indecisiveness that has carried over into the present time.

"Children, obey your parents in the LORD, for this is right" (Ephesians 6:1)

School was a disappointment as classmates bullied Jessica for her odd name, weather-inappropriate clothing, and restrictive beliefs learned at home and at church that she then upheld.

Instigation began with shaming the moment she

stepped aboard the school bus as a first grader. Days at school were tempered with remarks, both demeaning and spiteful. Even after high school, the residual burden of tormentors' evil innuendos continued.

A lack of self-esteem, and overt shyness, made it easy to accept bullying as her lot in life.

At the age of fifteen she became a Christian, and life at church began to fill a gigantic void. Boyfriends in the Christian arena became outlets as she was driven to find the love that was missing in her home through other venues. A permanent relationship was never the goal.

Restrictions from fornication were essential as her desire for love broke many hearts. When she married at the age of nineteen, she was still a virgin. But a chaste lifestyle was never appreciated by Trey, her new husband.

Abuse is a secret one doesn't tell. It's just the way life is on any given day.

Both parents ignored the fact that Jessica was mistreated while married. They also refused to support the idea of separation, or divorce. In their eyes, abuse wasn't reason enough to compromise the marriage juncture.

Twelve years later, after the battering accelerated, they relented, and opened their home to her, and their grandchildren. One month later, Jessica and her children were living in their own place.

There are two sides to a batterer—the polished, public figure that surfaces in public settings, and the person who shows up in private. -Unknown

Family Tree

My grandma gave our family
A lovely orange flowering tree
As many years shaped history
That tree become a legacy

So often Mother would send me
Outside to that family tree
For switches used to thrash my knee
That she would call my whipping tree

Next generation's kids would see
Their grandma sent them on same spree
But I've removed that legacy
For I cut down the family tree

© *Phoebe Leggett*

Jessica's father was a quiet man by nature, but always meant exactly what he said, and was always obeyed. To her knowledge he never once struck her mother. But when she reached adulthood, she learned that spousal abuse did exist in a marriage.

A father should be a concerned supporter of the family. A mother is nurturer and protector. Jessica's parents were neither and quenched her spirit with overly zealous guidance and limitless restrictions.

"When my father and my mother forsake me, then the LORD will take me up" (Psalms 27:10)

A Father Who Cares

"Cast all your anxiety on Him because He cares for you"
(I Peter 5:7)

On Father's Day the pastor spoke of the importance of having an honorable dad. As he spoke tears slid down her face.

Embarrassed, she quickly brushed them away. Although sensitive to the pain of an un-fulfilled relationship, she was hesitant to acknowledge the hurt. She was afraid.

Over time she saw many women happily relate to their fathers—the warmth of his love spilling over their lives like a bubbling waterfall. But, for her, that part of the puzzle was missing.

While growing up her mother often said her father didn't want her. Although she needed him, he didn't need her. But this lack in her life only made love difficult to understand.

She was obsessed in her search for someone to fill that void. "So, why did I come to church on Father's Day?" she whispered under her breath. "Why am I here?"

I wish there was someone who could make everything right. I need a father.

It was then the Holy Spirit whispered in her ear. "You have a father," he said. "God is your father, and He will make everything right for you."

A calm, peaceful feeling settled over her spirit as those words were whispered in her heart. This was going to be a good day after all.

Now, when she's overwhelmed with the issues of life and in need of someone to lean on, she can rest in the arms of her heavenly Father. He is the father she always wanted and needed.

**God is faithful and provides in ways
unexplainable to man**

299

Oh, Be Careful Little Eyes

Oh, be careful little eyes what you see
Oh, be careful little ears what you hear
Oh, be careful little hands what you do
For the Father up above
Is looking down in love
So, be careful little hands what you do

Unknown

**Bliss, happiness, elation, and ecstasy that comes
from God above, that's all I need**

Chapter Seventy-Three

Roots of Abuse

There is a huge difference between disciplinary spanking and abusive hitting. Exactly when is it appropriate to tell a daughter it's okay when you hit her, but not okay for a husband to do the same?

Currently physical punishment is legal in the United States, although banned in at least twenty-four other countries. At least nineteen states allow corporal punishment in their schools.

It's not just a swat on the bottom, study author Tracie Afifi, PhD. University of Manitoba in Winnipeg, reported. Its about physical punishment used regularly to discipline a child.

This analysis excluded individuals using more severe maltreatment such as sexual, physical, and emotional abuse as well as neglect; both emotional and physical. It also indicated that parents should be aware of a link between physical punishment and mental disorders in children, reaching into adulthood, and beyond.

According to this same report, researchers examined data from more than 34,000 adults and found that being spanked significantly increased the risk of developing mental health issues as an adult. The result of corporal punishment is often associated with mood disorders including depression and anxiety, as well as personality disorders where alcohol and drug abuse are used as a crutch.

In the past, battering in a marriage was ignored. If a girl told her mother the husband was mistreating her, she was cautioned to keep quiet, and not talk about it. The abuse was swept under the rug and forgotten by everyone but the one being battered. If exploitation of a minor occurred, this too was denied, and remained a secret.

Violence, foul language, indecent verbal abuse, insults, cruelty, physical and emotional injuries, exploitation, and threats are all part of the equation. If experienced, difficulties of catastrophic proportions will remain a quandary in the everyday life of a victim. Even today, violence in the home is a serious concern.

**Every eighteen seconds
a woman is beaten somewhere in the United States
of America**

Changing the Rules

After years of late and sporadic child support, Trey, with the help of his new wife, learned to weasel out of paying at all—making it difficult for Jessica to support their children on her own.

The last presiding judge was also nonchalant, and believed Trey's lies of unemployment, albeit he *was* working, but paid under the table so wages weren't unaccountable.

His visitation with the children became infrequent as time moved forward. The first visit following their separation was timely and expected. Their court-ordered agreement set visitation at every other weekend.

After a few months he transferred that responsibility to his family, who took turns driving the distance to pick the children up for visitation. In the months that followed, this arrangement dropped to once every six weeks until completely non-existent.

Although visits were never refused, neither were they encouraged. Fear for the children's safety was constant; and quite unsettling each time they left for a visit.

Horror stories concerning fast driving and

irresponsible parenting often followed their return home.

Their last visitation with Trey was just before he remarried. During this visit, the children were left with perfect strangers—his future in-laws. They were never again invited for a visit. But this was a blessing in disguise.

T-ball, baseball, and soccer kept the children busy. Over time they appeared oblivious to their missing father. Extra-curricular activities through church and school kept them busy through the week, and weekends. Piano lessons required practice, and easily accomplished since trips away no longer remained a quandary.

For the most part Trey remained absent from his children's lives. It became natural to carry on without his influence.

Later, as teens, they did need him but mostly for emotional reasons. Yet he remained non-existent. Birthdays and Christmases passed with the regularity of time, but without recognition from him.

"I call on the LORD in my distress, and He answers me. Save me, O LORD, from lying lips and from deceitful tongues. Those who devise wicked schemes are near, but they are far from your law" (Psalms 120:1, 2, 150)

A Deserved Thank-You

It's amazing when one hears a father complain about not being thanked for paying his court-ordered child-support.

A return remark could be, "When have you thanked me, the mother of your children, for everything I've done for them?"

How would he respond? Would he not care, or would he say?

1. Thank you for teaching my children right from wrong, respect for others, and honesty.

2. Thank you for being the responsible parent twenty-four-seven. I was too busy golfing, playing basketball, or spending time with friends, or watching sports on television.

3. Thank you for all you've sacrificed so the kids could take expensive field trips, play their favorite instrument in the school band, and wear a name brand pair of shoes like everyone else.

4. Thank you for taking them to the doctor when they were sick, the dentist for care and braces, and the church for their spiritual needs. I was too busy with my career, or taking another elaborate vacation, to care.

5. Thank you for staying with my son night and day when he was hospitalized, and for sitting by my daughter's bedside when she was having nightmares.

6. Thank you for soothing the children's broken hearts when I didn't show up for visitation.

7. Thank you for being both mother and father to them—for the shopping, cooking, bill paying, nursing, counseling, the laughter and tears, and the worry over their safety all by yourself.

8. Thank you for soothing their pain when I forgot Christmases, birthdays, graduations, concerts, weddings, and everything else because I was too busy to attend.

9. Thank you for being there because I never was.

10. But most of all, thank you for my children. When I look at them, I realize they bare my name, but not my heart.

Compared to the gigantic task of raising a child, how significant is paying child support in a timely manner?

"And when you thank me for all I've done, I'll thank you for making sure your support is paid on time."

Where Was He?

- When his children proudly performed in band concerts at school?

- When they played in various sports while needing approval or assistance?

- When his children graduated from high school?

- When his daughter walked down the aisle to be married?

- When important events involving the children came and went without even a phone call to cheer them on?

- When his youngest needed affirmation and direction as a teen?

- When his children needed a firm hand, or a kind shoulder to lean on?

- When they wanted a father.

- Where was he?

He was busy with his own life

"A good man brings good things out of the good stored up in him, and an evil man brings evil things out of the evil stored up in him" (Josh 12:35)

If you bungle raising your children, I don't think whatever else you do well matters very much.
Jacqueline Kennedy Onassis

Chapter Seventy-Four

Opposites Attract

When a couple first meet their attraction may be instantaneous. However, becoming romantically involved too fast often evolves into disappointment, and regret. The couple may truly be incompatible due to dissimilar backgrounds, different goals, and opposite desires. Good relationships take time to develop.

An opposite may be the one to look for when searching for a short, passionate relationship. Most will search for someone comparable to themselves instead of someone totally opposite.

Finding someone for a long-term relationship, or someone to marry, takes time, and understanding. Learn more about yourself so you can choose a companion who is truly compatible.

A House that's Not a Home

"...Has anyone built a new house and not dedicated it? Let him go home, or he may die in battle and someone else may dedicate it" (Deuteronomy 20:5)

When is a house not a home?

Where un-forgiveness abounds, or restrictions overwhelm—when dictatorship rules, or impatience complains. When children are ignored, abused, or hated. And when a man's true love isn't his wife, but himself.

"If a house is divided against itself, that house cannot stand" (Mark 3:25)

Forgiveness

"Why should I be the one to forgive? I didn't ask to be abused. He should be the one to ask me for forgiveness. After all, I'm the one who's hurting, not him. Besides, he doesn't deserve my forgiveness."

Forgiving your abuser doesn't excuse what has been done to you. It doesn't matter if the relationship was long lasting, or short lived—desired, or despised. It only signifies that to move on with your life it's essential to absolve your abuser. Forgiveness is crucial to overcoming the hurdle of mistreatment. This does not mean we forget or agree to continue accepting the abuse.

Forgiveness is free. Trust must be earned.

Withdrawing from society is pointless. It's best to confront your reality and choose to forgive so the past doesn't dominate the future. When forgiveness is relinquished, freedom is paid for.

Reconciliation isn't required to forgive someone. It only means your abuser no longer has control over your life.

Vengeance

"Bless those who persecute you; bless and do not curse.

Rejoice with those who rejoice; mourn with those who mourn. Live in harmony with one another. Do not be proud but be willing to associate with people of low position. Do not be conceited.

Do not repay anyone evil for evil. Be careful to do what is right in the eyes of everyone.

If it's possible, as far as it depends on you, live at peace with everyone. Do not take revenge, my dear friends, but leave room for God's wrath, for it is written: "It is mine to avenge; I will repay, says the Lord."

On the contrary: "If your enemy is hungry, feed him; if he is thirsty, give him something to drink. In doing this, you will heap burning coals on his head.

Do not be overcome by evil, but overcome evil with good" (Romans 12:14-21)

Chapter Seventy-Five

Generational Abuse

If someone in the home is being abused, children in that environment will play out those same cycles of abuse on playmates, family members, and friends. This behavior, learned in the home, most likely has been kept hidden.

What a child sees when small will remain a leaned behavior as an adult. If abuse is observed as an adolescent, the battering of others is not unexpected. Parental secrets are often exposed after the child becomes older, and repeats behavior learned while in the home.

Battering could become a natural occurrence if not blocked by interceptive measures. Psychological treatment may be needed to control a desire to violate.

Cycles of generational abuse are passed down by example and exposure—from parent to child. Episodic abuse occurs in patterns of repetition within the context of at least two individuals within a family system. It may involve child abuse, spousal abuse, or elder abuse.

A son who was verbally or physically abused by his father will most likely mistreat his own children in the same way. A daughter who hears her mother tear down, criticize, or belittle her father often adapts to this same behavior which involves verbal control.

A child who sees parents engage in abusive behavior toward each other will violate his or her own spouse in similar ways. These are all examples of generational abuse.

Most families have a member they secretly call the Black Sheep. Although most accept them as one of their own, many cringe when they do.

Most Black Sheep are shunned by outsiders due to the embarrassment they tend to cause.

Odd family members are rebels by nature and respond in eccentric ways that society won't accept as a rule. The strange way they dress, or weird habits they portray, are cause for rejection.

The title Black Sheep is bestowed because one member comes across as too bold, or not conspicuous enough, therefore making them abnormal.

A Black Sheep may simply be the one who goes against family tradition by disregarding the unit's reputation, customs, or convictions, therefore rendering themselves an outcast in their own lineage.

Like Father—Like Son

Trey's father was a prime example of the Black Sheep anomaly. Although generations in his family were Christian, he himself denounced church teachings and Biblical truth for another woman. During his rebellion he divorced his first wife and married another, leaving four children fatherless in the home.

Informing family, friends, and an entire church congregation that his first wife had committed adultery was lie number one. He then portrayed himself as the model of marriage and family, even serving in respectable church positions.

His second marriage was based on lies, deceit, and hypocrisy. But his lack of integrity was apparent as the children from his first marriage grew up without a father's love and attention.

The first wife did not believe in divorce. After their break-up she never remarried but considered herself a widowed woman until her death. In the aftermath, both daughters chose their own bitter paths to take. The first conceived a child out of wedlock.

The second, while married, conceived a child with another man she later married after divorcing her first husband. In the process she broke up the man's family. All is not fair in love and war.

His sons also had demons to chase. Trey, the oldest, and Jessica's first husband, had affairs on the side, and was brutal and abusive to her—his first wife. He then chose to be non-existent concerning his own children following their divorce. He was named for his father, and was, without a doubt, his father's son.

Another son, although married, never fathered children. The last child conceived with the second wife was the *only* child in action and deed.

"...For I the LORD your God am a jealous God, visiting the iniquity of the fathers upon the children unto the third and fourth generation of them that hate me" (Exodus 20:5)

Devastation following this family is now in its fifth generation. If one retraces their own family line, God's truth will speak volumes concerning generations of family in relation to Exodus 20:5. Many families have similar backgrounds, but few are willing to talk about them.

The offspring from the first generation (Jessica's father-in-law's first marriage) suffered further humiliation at his funeral. Not only were they excluded from participating in the interment, or eulogies, but none were invited to speak on behalf of their siblings. Instead, an outside member was the appointed spokesman.

The funeral itself must certainly have been offensive to the first offspring as the deceased was described as a wonderful, loving man. However, they never experienced that love as children, and remain devastated their father chose a woman over them.

The ceremony was traditional military with all the required pomp and circumstance. But the committal was less than soothing as the original family was somewhat shunned by their father's friends, and members of his church. In the past the first wife recalled many difficulties raising children without a husband. Not only was she shunned as a divorcée, but also blamed for lies she had no control over.

Trey followed in his father's footsteps, making Jessica a recipient of his father's sin. He died at the age of forty-three after suffering three separate cancers following his divorce from Jessica. The first was breast cancer, for which he was treated, and declared cancer free. The disease then migrated to his leg bones. After treatment he was again declared cancer free. But the cancer resurfaced—this time in the brain.

Surgery allowed a short respite before his death. After his death, his second wife and their child, (who was not his biological child) became the only recipients of his inheritance—repeating his father before him who left his entire estate to his second wife and fifth child. The children from his first marriage were, expectedly, disinherited.

It must also be mentioned that Trey lost his capacity to father more children after a performed vasectomy while his third child was still in the womb. Six weeks following surgery and the urologist declared him incapable of ever again reproducing.

Possessions and Inheritance

"I have seen another evil under the sun, and it weighs heavily on mankind: God gives some people wealth, possessions and honor, so that they lack nothing their hearts desire, but God does not grant them the ability to enjoy them, and strangers enjoy them instead"

"A man may have a hundred children and live many years; yet no matter how long he lives, he cannot enjoy his prosperity...I say that a stillborn child is better off than he.

It comes without meaning, it departs in darkness, and in darkness its name is shrouded. Though it never saw the sun or knew anything, it has more rest than does that man—even if he lives a thousand years twice over but fails to enjoy his prosperity..." (Ecclesiastes 6:1-6)

"I have seen a grievous evil under the sun: wealth

hoarded to the harm of its owners, or wealth lost through some misfortune, so that when they have children there is nothing left for them to inherit" (Ecclesiastes 5:13-14)

First to Fourth Generations

While growing up Trey and his siblings for the most part was ignored by their father. Years later, after their mother passed, they again reunited. Only then could they accept his current wife and their half-sibling or be considered part of the man's family.

Situations in Trey's childhood scarred him for life. For this reason, Jessica became his punching bag. He was also second generation as referenced in the Bible.

Following their divorce, he married a woman who convinced him a baby she had while they were married was biologically his even though she wasn't. (A previous surgery prevented that possibility.)

Several grandchildren (of Jessica's father-in-law) as third generation have surrendered to infidelity and divorce as recipients of the family curse, as referenced in the Bible. Time will tell if the fifth generation—the great-grandchildren—are affected by this same curse.

Most family histories include a Back Sheep. It may be rare, or generational.

Some families will never conceive of such an occurrence within their own family unit. But if members search closely, an odd one may surface.

Daniel, Jessica's husband for over twenty-four years, raised her children as his own. However, the natural disposition of a child is to follow in their biological father's footsteps. Although complicated, this often renders good advice and Christian training from mother and stepfather as null, and void.

Her children, now in their thirties, have their own demons to conquer as they reap the residual damage created by those before them. In 2004 Josh, the youngest, died in a car crash at the age of twenty-two. As a teen he used drugs and alcohol to deaden his emotional controversies. He was a special needs child—his disabilities most likely stemming from intentional stress caused by his father Trey while in the womb.

However, and to whomever it concerns, the blood line stops here.

"Oh, that their hearts would be inclined to fear me and keep all my commands always, so that it might go well with them and their children forever!" (Deuteronomy 5:29)

Actions are easily justifiable if one becomes a chronic liar.

Strongholds

The hold an abusive man has over a partner doesn't always end with divorce. There are instances when it continues for years and years. Fear, anxiety, and terror can reign long after a relationship has ended.

It's difficult to rid oneself of mind manipulation. The reality of truth—that he really is out of your life—may be hard to grasp as former exploitations have psychologically strangled the mind.

It may take years of time to release the emotional clutch a perpetrator's mistreatment generated during time spent together, or while married. Because your self-respect has been smothered, your motivation to enjoy life has been choked from existence.

It may be difficult to move beyond the strongholds that long held you captive. But be encouraged. God will be your advocate as you regain your independence as a survivor of domestic abuse, and violence.

Outside scars eventually heal. Emotional pain—it lingers still.

Chapter Seventy-Six

Death of a Marriage

Divorce, no matter the reason, can be as painful as physical death as it slices through the very core of a valued promise—vows to love, honor, and cherish until the day of natural death.

Those who suffer the effects of a dying marriage can certify there's nothing worse than a bad marriage. And those who've found a loving, faithful partner can confirm there's nothing better than a good one.

When divorce is inevitable, trust and honor will be replaced with dishonor and mistrust. Hopes, desires, and plans will be dumped, recycled, or cast-off to create a landscape of remorse, anger, and pain. These feelings are like stages of grief that follow the death of a loved one.

Divorce can be illustrated as a demonstration of split firewood. Your very existence has been devalued, and your worth scattered as litter on the ground. This exploitation leaves emotions as open and exposed as piles of raw sewage. A natural death is often easier to tolerate than the death of a marriage.

Residual scarring from an abusive marital demise will remain following a divorce. Recovery from rejection and victimization can be painful, and vicious. Fears of loneliness and legitimate questions concerning the ability to survive on your own will be terrorizing. The struggle ahead may be intimidating as regret and worry overwhelm the senses.

Anger at your former spouse is normal but should abate over time. A sense of gloom and despair, no matter the circumstance, is also common. It's advisable to seek professional counseling if exceptional feelings of doom persist.

Another avenue is to share your experience with others in similar situations. Care groups are springing up everywhere in churches, and other organizations. If controversy is unending after a marital split, find a meet-up that will embrace your hurt with reinforcements of understanding and assistance. There is hope through the support of others.

It will take time to work through your loss as marriage was meant to be a lasting commitment. As with all heartache, allow God's word to bring you comfort as you struggle through this period in your life. This stage will eventually pass, and a brighter day should surface.

Realize you are not alone. Neither are you an unlabeled statistic, as divorce is more common in this generation than before. It may be hard to release your desire for a perfect marriage. There are times, however, when your very existence will insist on the reversal of such an obligation.

"Therefore, what God has joined together, let man not separate" (Mark 10:9)

Nuptials should carry one through the thick and thin of life. But all too often those dreams become shambles if promises in the marriage dissolve. Divorce strips plans into shreds, and way too many lives are destroyed by it.

All separations aren't justifiable as divorce wasn't God's original plan for his people. But when children are involved, the emotional pain will be doubled. There are times, however, when divorce is justifiable.

God did not intend for a woman to be a man's punching bag. Abuse in any form is never acceptable, and a reasonable incentive for divorcing. Infidelity is also legitimate, and a Biblical justification for divorce.

Unfaithfulness creates insurmountable problems for the future, and someone will always be the grieving partner following this deception.

It isn't sinful to divorce a partner who is unfaithful (adultery) if this is the road you choose to take. But sharing guilt for another's sin should never be accepted. Shed that responsibility and continue your life in peace.

"My people will live in peaceful dwelling places, in secure homes, in undisturbed places of rest" (Isaiah 32:18)

"But if the unbeliever leaves, let it be so. The brother (or sister) is not bound in such circumstances; God has called them to live in peace" (2 Corinthians 7:15)

"Make every effort to live in peace with everyone and to be holy; without holiness no one will see the Lord" (Hebrews 12:14)

***

"For such people are false apostles, deceitful workers, masquerading as apostles of Christ. And no wonder, for Satan himself masquerades as an angel of light. It's not surprising, then, if his servants also masquerade as servants of righteousness" (2 Corinthians 11:13-15)

Their end will be what their actions deserve.

Chapter Seventy-Seven

Bible on Divorce

"Another thing you do: You flood the Lord's altar with tears. You weep and wail because He no longer pays attention to your offerings or accepts them with pleasure from your hands. You ask, "Why?"

"It is because the LORD is acting as the witness between you and the wife of your youth, because you have broken faith with her, though she is your partner, the wife of your marriage covenant. Has not the LORD made them one? In flesh and Spirit, they are His. And why one? Because He was seeking godly offspring. So, guard yourself in your spirit, and do not break faith with the wife of your youth."

"I hate divorce," says the LORD God of Israel, "and I hate a man's covering himself with violence (himself meaning his wife also as they are considered as one) as well as with his garment," says the LORD Almighty. So, guard yourself in your spirit, and do not break faith" (Malachi 2:13-16)

"Why then," they asked, "did Moses command that a man give his wife a certificate of divorce and send her away?

Jesus replied, "Moses permitted you to divorce your wives because your hearts were hard. But it was not this way from the beginning.

I tell you that anyone who divorces his wife, except for marital unfaithfulness, and marries another woman commits adultery.

The disciples said to him, "If this is the situation between a husband and wife, it is better not to marry" (Matthew 19: 7-10)

"But if the unbeliever leaves, let him do so. A believing man or woman is not bound in such circumstances; God has called them to live in peace" (1 Corinthians 7:15)

"Now for the matters you wrote about: It is good for a man not to marry. But since there is so much immorality, each man should have his own wife and each woman her own husband. The husband should fulfill his marital duty to his wife, and likewise the wife to her husband. The wife's body does not belong to her alone but also to her husband. In the same way, the husband's body does not belong to him alone but also to his wife.

Do not deprive each other except by mutual consent and for a time, so that you may devote yourselves to prayer. Then come together again so that Satan will not tempt you because of your lack of self-control. I say this as a concession, not as a command. I wish that all men were as I am. But each man has his own gift from God; one has this gift, another has that.

Now to the unmarried and the widows I say: It is good for them to stay unmarried, as I am. But if they cannot control themselves, they should marry, for it is better to marry than to burn with passion.

To the married I give this command (not I, but the LORD): A wife must not separate from her husband. But if she does, she must remain unmarried or else be reconciled to her husband. And a husband must not divorce his wife.

To the rest I say this (I, not the LORD): If any brother has a wife who is not a believer and she is willing to live with him, he must not divorce her.

And if a woman has a husband who is not a believer and he is willing to live with her, she must not divorce him. For the unbelieving husband has been sanctified through his wife, and the unbelieving wife has been sanctified through her believing husband. Otherwise, your children would be unclean, but as it is, they are holy.

But if the unbeliever leaves, let him do so. A believing man or woman is not bound in such circumstances; God has called them to live in peace. How do you know, wife, whether you will save your husband? Or, how do you know, husband, whether you will save your wife?" (I Corinthians 7:1-16)

***

You may have been the faithful partner that rejected divorce. Perhaps you were the one who initiated it, and now feelings of regret are forming. But if counseling hasn't worked, and reconciliation isn't possible, moving forward may be your best strategy.

Allow God's word to be your guide, and never underestimate the fact that miracles do happen. Although it's easier to blame others for their mistakes, forgiveness is best in any situation.

"Who can discern his errors? Forgive my hidden faults" (Psalms 19:12)

If compromise isn't an option, don't be discouraged.

"Have I not commanded you? Be strong and courageous. Do not be terrified; do not be discouraged, for the LORD your God will be with you wherever you go" (Joshua 1:9)

Strive to keep anger and resentment from demolishing your dreams, and your future.

Realize that time doesn't heal all wounds. It will take a great deal of it just to feel normal again. Your heart needs to heal from the pain of being mistreated, rejected, or replaced. Allow yourself the time that's needed to recover from all former relationships.

Chapter Seventy-Eight

Certificate of Divorce

God allowed Moses, a great leader in Bible history, to give documents of divorce to his people, the Jews, to keep peace in the home. Tranquility was to be maintained at all costs.

This document provided an escape for the Jews who had issues too great to maintain harmony in the home. But this reasoning has been ignored by modern church leadership for years, making the act of divorce unjustifiable —even for an abused spouse.

In the past the church was quick to discontinue membership with anyone who divorced. At this point, family respect was forever lost.

"...Moses permitted a man to write a certificate of divorce and send her (his wife) away" (Mark 10:4)

"It has been said, "Anyone who divorces his wife must give her a certificate of divorce" (Josh 5:31)

"Make every effort to live in peace with all men..." (Hebrews 12:14)

God hates divorce; but for reasons most have yet to realize. Divorce divides families and scars, wounds, and shatters everyone involved. Peace in the home is disrupted when family units are destroyed, and emotionally uprooted. Children from divorced parents will remain emotionally disabled, or permanently damaged the rest of their lives.

"Like arrows in the hands of a warrior are children born in one's youth" (Psalms 127:4)

Betrayal

Every victim has a story to tell. Abuse, divorce, and dysfunctional relationships are common issues that need to be addressed in most families. Honesty in sharing will help alleviate many painful memories and assist in establishing a more stable outcome for a marriage on the rocks. But could infidelity be the greatest of all betrayals?

Scars of Life

The scars of life
Within—without
But deep within
Leaves not a doubt

To be the scar
That makes me mad
That causes grief
And makes life sad

A scratch, a burn
A cut, a scrape
Takes time to heal
Not time to make

The scars of life
Have left me broken
Have never mended
Yet are not spoken

© *Phoebe Leggett*

**There's nothing worse than a bad marriage,
and nothing better than a good one**

Chapter Seventy-Nine

When Truth Hurts

When the abuser is a father, his actions prove a serious lack of concern for his children.

Claws of Abuse

By Cindy Sproles

Who defines what abuse really is, and who saves them? Those are questions I still ask twenty-seven years past. It was a shameful thing, and not something I even realized was happening until I ended up eight months pregnant, and in the hospital ER alone.

"Are you and your husband having issues?" The ER doctor pressed the stethoscope against my bulging stomach.

"What? No. My husband is a preacher. Things are fine between us."

The doctor peered across his glasses.

This was the first time I'd heard those words—or even thought them. I wasn't abused. How ridiculous. I was a minister's wife. I loved my husband. It was a fall down the steps. I wasn't pushed.

But the doctor didn't believe me. My husband would never push me or hit me. And it was true. He never once laid a finger on me. I'd truly missed my footing on the staircase and fell. What didn't occur to me were words from his mouth when I lay face-first down on the steps. "I can't believe you're that clumsy."

My husband sat in his recliner across the room. He

324

never stood, never offered to pick up our fourteen-month-old son. He just shook his head. But when I regained my wits, I drove myself to the ER fifty-seven miles away—at night, along a desolate two-lane road.

Throughout the seven-year duration of our marriage, my husband never tried to hit me; but I can't count the times I wish he had. In fact, I stood toe-to-toe with him and asked, "Why don't you just hit me?" The pain would have at least stung and died away.

However, words never die. They continue to dig into our souls, steal away our identity, and drive us into the pits of despair. Words can be brutal.

It had taken seven years for me to realize my husband, no longer a practicing minister, wasn't only an alcoholic, but one who would drink alone downing a fifth of Vodka and a two liter of Sprite in one sitting.

I stood in the kitchen window and watched him pour and sip, and all the while dread the words that would fall from his mouth hours later. I was stupid—a mountain girl who was dumb because of her moral values; lazy, a bad mother, and a worse wife, irresponsible, unreliable and, here's the clincher—insignificant.

I'd much rather be slapped across the jaw than to hear those damming words repeated over and over again.

I had been raised in a middle class, southern home, in the church—defined by my values, and naïve. Abuse was something I'd hardly heard about, much less experienced as a child. Now, as a grown woman with two children under the age of three, my husband, a minister of the gospel, and a marriage counselor, was uttering those horrible words.

"This is abuse. Do you understand? This is abuse. And if you can wait thirty-days, I'll force him to make a decision to divorce. Otherwise, you'll die."

Abuse comes about in mélange ways. It's not all physical but much is mental. It happens to men, and women, to children and teens. In fact, no one is exempt from its clutches when they are placed in the right situation. The claws of abuse begin with small things, and then escalate to monsters that wail out of control, destroying anything and everything in its path. Mix that with drugs and alcohol, and you will find it can become a deadly mixture

It's easy for those on the outside of abuse to utter the words, "Why doesn't she just leave?" That, in and of itself, is part of the bond that chains the abused. But more times than not, a victim will never realize what happened. They've been torn, beaten down, and told how lucky they are to have what they have because no one else would give it to them.

There is an indebtedness that tightens the grip of the abuser. There is fear, and the inability to see enough self-worth for a victim to care for herself. It's rarely as easy as, 'just walking away.'

But I did walk away. On our seventh anniversary my husband took me out to a nice dinner, gave me a pretty shirt and a sweet card, then handed me a paper and said, "Tomorrow you need to go and sign the divorce papers.

I sat, stunned. The slap to my heart was worse than being hit in the face.

I stared at the paper—words blurred with tears. I then stood, leaned close to my husband and said, "I will take our boys and go home. I will raise them as gentlemen, and in a godly fashion. I will never say a bad word about you. However, a day will come when you'll be forced to face your children man-to-man. And for you I say, 'God rest your soul.'"

I signed the papers, took my children and what little I could afford to move, and went home. The torturous words he had driven into me every day formed scars. From that I've become a stronger person because of the God I cried out to; "Lord save me. Please save them." Rarely a day passes that I don't read the saving scripture I clung to in Isaiah (53:5) "...and by His wounds we are healed."

I'm blessed. God introduced me to a man who values me fully, who raised my boys with the same godly values and Christian beliefs I have. He loved them despite their wounds and helped them heal. Our marriage has passed the twenty-fourth year mark, and our love is as fresh as it was the day we married.

I'm sure my story is less the painful and tragic than others, but within it lays mercy, and peace. The details only serve to breed bitterness, but forgiveness of those details preserves life.

So, I ask again: Who defines abuse, and who saves them from it? The answer lies in Isaiah 53. "But He was pierced for our transgressions, He was bruised for our iniquities; the punishment that brought them peace was on Him.

Who saves them? ... and by His wounds we are healed."

The Burley Bully

By Cathy Baker

"Get out of my way," the burly bully shouted while shoving his young son into the endcap at Target. I paused to pay the clerk until I was certain he'd caught a glimpse of the righteous anger welling up within me. He had been seen, and I wanted him to know it.

The little boy regained his balance and cowered behind his mother, who looked to be as terrified as he was, if not more. If this man abuses his family in public, what must he do behind closed doors?

While pushing her buggy back into place, a woman approached me. "I know exactly how you feel," she said. Her head lowered as she sauntered slowly back to her minivan.

Should I call the police? Did I even have the right to do so?

I didn't know, but this brief encounter with domestic abuse jolted the rosy-colored glasses clean off her head.

The incident was very unfortunate, but no coincidence. That terrified woman now has at least one person standing in the gap for her. I sense it may be an expansive gap in need of prayer warriors—especially on behalf of the burly bully.

"Jesus looked at them and said, "With man this is impossible, but with God all things are possible" (Matthew 19:26)

Chapter Eighty

Where Am I?

"O LORD, you have searched me and known me. You know my sitting down and my rising up; you understand my thought afar off. You comprehend my path and my lying down and are acquainted with all my ways. For there is not a word on my tongue, but behold, O LORD, You know it altogether.

You have hedged me behind and before and laid your hand upon me. Such knowledge is too wonderful for me; it is high, I cannot attain it.

Where can I go from your Spirit? Or where can I flee from your presence? If I ascend into heaven, you are there; If I make my bed in hell, behold, you are there. If I take the wings of the morning, and dwell in the uttermost parts of the sea, even there your hand shall lead me, and your right hand shall hold me.

If I say, "Surely the darkness shall fall on me, even the night shall be light about me; indeed, the darkness shall not hide from you. But the night shines as the day; the darkness and the light are both alike to you.

For you formed my inward parts; you covered me in my mother's womb. I will praise you, for I am fearfully and wonderfully made. Marvelous are your works, and *that* my soul knows very well. My frame was not hidden from you, when I was made in secret, and skillfully wrought in the lowest parts of the earth.

Your eyes saw my substance, being yet unformed. And in your book they all were written, the days fashioned for me, when as yet there were none of them.

How precious also are your thoughts to me, O God! How great is the sum of them! If I should count them, they would be more in number than the sand; when I awake, I am still with you.

Oh, that you would slay the wicked, O God!

Depart from me, therefore, you bloodthirsty men for they speak against you wickedly; your enemies take your name in vain. Do I not hate them, O LORD, who hate you? And do I not loathe those who rise up against you? I hate them with perfect hatred. I count them my enemies.

Search me, O God, and know my heart. Try me, and know my anxieties; and see if there is any wicked way in me, and lead me in the way everlasting" (Psalms 139:1-24)

Jesus overcame His obstacles, giving us hope that—with His help—we can also overcome ours.

Road to Recovery

"This calls for patient endurance on the part of the people of God who keep His commands and remain faithful to Jesus" (Revelation 14:12)

"He (Jesus) was chosen before the creation of the world but was revealed in these last times for your sake. Through Him you believe in God, who raised Him from the dead and glorified Him, and so your faith and hope are in God" (1 Peter 1:20-21)

Satan is behind every abusive action.

Just Listen

No one wants to listen
No one likes to hear
No one tries to help
Nothing left but fear

Should I run away
Or live here on my own
While struggling every day
More abuse to condone

My mind stays in a whirl—
Misery has me bound.
I thought that I was lost
But God said, "You are found"

No reason left to fear
No one left to blame
This trial—but a season
There's hope in Jesus' name

© *Phoebe Leggett*

Excluded

I was excluded
And left confused
Always ignored
Often abused

Forever rebuked
Then left on my own
I was condemned
I was a pawn

Somewhat conflicted
My life disputed
I had no place
Was not included

Now all has changed
I'm not the same
I have no fear
I share no blame

All is forgiven,
Old thoughts deleted
My life's improved
I feel completed

© *Phoebe Leggett*

God is With Me

I know that God is with me
I know He truly cares
I know He'll never leave me
I know He's always there

I know for His Spirit
Reminds me where I'm from
Assures me that I'm safe
And that I'll overcome

He brings me peace of mind
When my day falls apart
He places joy within me
And puts love in my heart

When deepest sorrow comes
That takes my sleep at night
I feel His Spirit with me.
And He whispers, "It's all right."

© *Phoebe Leggett*

Chapter Eighty-One

History of Divorce

Separation and divorce in early history created severe difficulties for everyone involved. Most faced serious consequences if they tried to re-define their lives. Divorce was humiliating as it brought shame to both families. The hatred was intense and harsh, although laughable in today's society.

Divorce created a vacuum of its own in early American history as state legislatures argued over whether it should be allowed. Religious organizations were soon caught up in the debate as many members were involved in their own divorces.

Over time, marital breakups created new interpretations of the Bible as churches became more flexible with divorce, and re-marriage. A strong deliberation is still ongoing and continues to create many disturbances within the Christian community.

In the past, fear of the unknown, apprehension of future relationships, and financial burdens were associated with responses to the word *divorce*. All created apprehension and were dreaded. Following divorce, parents often denied emotional or financial support to their divorced offspring.

"You're on your own," was said as a reprimand to their newly divorced child. And, for the most part, they were. Shunning by friends and family was acceptable and expected.

Divorce within the church arena in the 1970's was treated in similar ways, although it was more accepted than in years past. But in smaller churches, actions of separation and divorce are still shunned.

Likewise, when Jessica decided to flee her abusive marriage, both families lacked in desired support, making it difficult to move forward without incredible, and almost unbeatable, odds. The undeniable fact that she had been a minister's wife only made matters worse.

Treated as a villain, and no longer accepted or forgiven for what were conceived lies, she became the accused. Disbelief was rampant in both family and church, and reigned in unspoken contempt.

Disrespect and blame were dumped in her lap, leaving her broken and desperate. The mockery of being shunned created a challenge of survival amid an onslaught of contention pounding her from every direction. But she wasn't the guilty party.

Trey's attitude toward their last baby was another strategy of placing blame for everything wrong in his life— the infidelity, the insincerity, and the ability to mistreat his wife in violent ways. His abusive behavior was both intimidating and terrorizing. Because no one believed he was abusive, she remained in a loveless marriage while caring for his children.

Even today she carries signs of the Battered Wife Syndrome.

Most abusers are labeled as *classic* because they display similar patterns of exploitation, manipulation, and mistreatment toward their victims.

Chapter Eighty-Two

More on Battered Wife Syndrome

Repeated physical and verbal assaults on a woman by the man in her life will result in serious physical and psychological damage to her. This violence tends to follow a predictable pattern that begins with verbal abuse and escalates to dangerous assaults and cruel violence. Most episodes follow an accusation as every outburst of violence is blamed on the wife.

Over time, the severity and frequency of the battering could result in death of the woman. The longer she remains under the batter's control, the more difficult it is to make a more permanent escape from her abuser.

A divorced woman can also be called a widow. And God takes care of widows.

"A father to the fatherless, a defender of widows, is God in His holy dwelling" (Psalms 68:5)

"He defends the cause of the fatherless and the widow, and loves the alien, giving him food and clothing" (Deuteronomy 10:18)

This promise is only available to those who keep the faith. "May your fountain be blessed, and may you rejoice in the wife of your youth" (Proverbs 5:18)

Refuge

"Whoever dwells in the shelter of the Most-High will rest in the shadow of the Almighty. I will say of the LORD, "He is my refuge and my fortress, my God, in whom I trust."

Surely, He will save you from the fowler's snare and from the deadly pestilence. He will cover you with His feathers, and under His wings you will find refuge; His faithfulness will be your shield and rampart.

You will not fear the terror of night, nor the arrow that flies by day, nor the pestilence that stalks in the darkness, nor the plague that destroys at midday.

A thousand may fall at your side, ten thousand at your right hand, but it will not come near you. You will only observe with your eyes and see the punishment of the wicked.

If you say, "The LORD is my refuge," and you make the Most High your dwelling, no harm will overtake you, no disaster will come near your tent. For He will command His angels concerning you to guard you in all your ways; they will lift you up in their hands, so that you will not strike your foot against a stone.

You will tread on the lion and the cobra; you will trample the great lion and the serpent. "Because he loves me," says the LORD, "I will rescue him; I will protect him, for he acknowledges my name. He will call on me, and I will answer him; I will be with him in trouble, I will deliver him and honor him. With long life I will satisfy him and show him my salvation" (Psalms 91:1-15)

From There to Here

How did Jessica get from there to here? The only instruction she received from both parents concerning her future was the expectation of marriage. For them, children were only possessions with an inability to think for themselves.

Her father, a man of few words, required immediate compliance to his demands. Her mother, in obedience to her husband and her own personal beliefs, executed punishment for the slightest of infractions. Chastisement in the home was expected and received daily.

Growing up in the Nineteen-sixties was a difficult period for many living on farms in rural America. Jessica was raised on a farm. She was born in the mid fifty's and grew in the sixties. Both her parents were young adults during the World War II era.

After they married, they waited ten years before any children were born. Her mother was thirty-three and her father thirty-eight when she was born. Because of their poverty, clothing consisted of hand-me-downs from kind church members and distant relatives.

Her father served in both Army and Navy during World War II but returned a broken man. Physical wounds did not exist, but mental and emotional scars surfaced throughout her childhood, and beyond. But he refused to talk about the war—only sharing pictures from his tours, and a few metal awards.

Shipwrecked in the frigid ocean for many hours while his naval ship sank, was general knowledge. The remainder of his military history remains a mystery. In 1957 he decided that a public job was more than he could handle following the war.

He quit his public job and began operating a poultry farm with a hand full of chickens, and little knowledge. He was known around town as the "Egg Man', with only enough customers to eke out a meager living.

Jessica's childhood consisted of hard labor seven days a week. Every hand on the farm was needed to raise enough chickens to produce enough eggs to sell to neighbors and townspeople. Coupled with a large field of hay grown for the cow, and a small vegetable garden, her family existed mainly on eggs cooked in every conceivable way possible. Fresh vegetables, and occasional meat from half a pig, or calf raised on the farm, finished the menu.

Indifferent and uninterested, her father rarely acknowledged her existence, and only when he needed work done on the farm. For Jessica, growing up was the very epitome of hard labor, disciplinary restrictions, neglect, poverty, and imposed abuse.

Her childhood is often described as living with Amish parents in the Eighteenth century while growing up in the Twentieth. Their family was only as modern as electricity, running water, and a toilet in the house.

The downside was not receiving the same acceptance, or support, an Amish family would have provided for a child. Instead, she was thrust into a modern world by overly strict and religious parents who lived an out-of-date lifestyle.

Her father was not an affectionate man. Hugs and kisses were nonexistent, and words of praise never uttered.

Aloof and distant, he surfaced only for work and meals. As a farmer's child Jessica's help was needed for his survival. While growing up she needed his love and approval. What she didn't need, as a teenager, was a cute boyfriend. A loving father would have made a world of difference to an ignored child.

In her quest for love flirting was essential and brought many relationships to her doorstep. Yet she remained a virgin, saving herself for the one she would one day marry.

Your parents ruin the first half of your life, and your children ruin the second—Clarence Darrell

Chapter Eighty-Three

Who can I Trust?

Living in the darkness of repression keeps the light of freedom restrained. But with God's help, a leap through the darkened tunnel into the light is achievable.

"The man, who hates...his wife, says the LORD, the God of Israel, does violence to the one he should protect. So be on your guard, and do not be unfaithful" (2: 16)

"I hate divorce, says the LORD, the God of Israel, because the man who divorces his wife (or causes the divorce) covers his garment with violence" (Malachi 2:16)

Jessica's trust had been placed in parental training received as a child, and later, in the church. To remain married was the requirement, no matter the cost. It wasn't until she read a book written by Richard Roberts titled, <u>He's the God of a Second Chance</u> did she begin to hope a release from brutality was possible. But could she survive an impending onslaught of church and family rejection if she denounced her marriage?

"But He said to me, "My grace is sufficient for you, for my power is made perfect in weakness. Therefore, I will boast all the more gladly about my weaknesses, so that Christ's power may rest on me" (2 Corinthians 12:9)

Doing without food and essentials is better than living in a house with a husband who degrades, beats, and then threatens to kill you.

Where is the Love?

If I speak in the tongues of men and of angels, but have not love, I am only a resounding gong or a clanging cymbal. If I have the gift of prophecy and can fathom all mysteries and all knowledge, and if I have a faith that can move mountains, but have not love, I am nothing. If I give all I possess to the poor and surrender my body to the flames but have not love, I gain nothing.

Love is patient, love is kind. It does not envy, it does not boast, it is not proud. It is not rude, it is not self-seeking, it is not easily angered, and it keeps no record of wrongs. Love does not delight in evil but rejoices with the truth. It always protects, always trusts, always hopes, always perseveres.

Love never fails. And now these three remain: faith, hope and love. But the greatest of these is love" (1 Corinthians 13:1-7, 13)

Family History

Divorce was a rare occurrence in the past. Most who divorced during that time were shunned by society and became the topic of many sermons delivered in rural churches across the South.

Trey's parents divorced when he was small. His mother raised four children on her own, but often spoke of the stigma of an unforgiving family, and church.

Her divorce was triggered by a cheating husband who lied to cover his actions. He came out smelling like a rose, but she was left to carry the brunt of society's judgment. He married his lover but his first wife never re-married. Their emotional baggage became Trey's, whose abusive tenancies revealed distrust, and anger. In turn he heaped his rage and animosity on Jessica's shoulders, as a

341

young bride.

On the flip side, Jessica's parents spoke in serious terms of Biblical reasons a person should never divorce. Their belief brought acute confusion. Was it also Biblical to accept abuse from one's husband? Or should she remain steadfast in her desire for a positive outcome beyond the marriage relationship?

Church leadership strongly advised that only prayer would stop the abuse. Their advice could easily have caused her death.

In the past battering and molestation were ignored. If a girl told her mother she was mistreated by her husband, she was admonished to remain quiet, and never speak about it. His acts of violence were swept under the rug and forgotten by everyone but her.

Manipulation, violence, exploitation, foul language, indecent vulgarity, insults, cruelty, injuries, and swearing are now considered abuse. Today violence in the home remains a challenge. Although information is available for the abused, many women remain with their children in dangerous situations. Fear may be the reason why.

Due to a serious lack of understanding ramifications for the abused will have side effects. Women and children will be permanently damaged, both physically and emotionally, if they remain in harm's way.

Fear keeps many under the arm of an enraged abuser. "No one will ever believe you," or "When you come to the door, I'll blow your brains out." These same threats were hurled at Jessica during her marriage to Trey. Meanwhile, and in secret, plans to escape her cleric husband were well under way.

"Husbands, love your wives and do not be harsh with them" (Colossians 3:9)

When she became an adult, Jessica's dreams for a blissful marriage were destroyed, and culminated in divorce twelve years later.

Inflicted brutality was a constant threat, and systemically produced physical, mental, and emotional restraints.

The scars of abuse left a throbbing ache of residual damage long after the marriage had ended.

Some memories are best left to fade away...

Chapter Eighty-Four

Rage

A victim of abuse often struggles with eating disorders, low self-esteem, or an inability to bond with others.

Beaten by her mother during childhood and long into adolescence programmed Jessica to accept her first husband's abuse.

"Better to dwell in the wilderness, than with a contentious and angry woman" (or man) (Proverbs 21:19

She loathed the abuse but was helpless to change it. Even today she experiences self-hatred based on her powerlessness to escape her abusers. Deliverance from parental restraints, and later her first marriage, was enormous. Stepping into new-found freedom was simply unadulterated liberation.

God's Law vs. Man's Traditions

"...wisdom is supreme; therefore, get wisdom. Though it cost all you have, get understanding" (Proverbs 4:7)

"In the past God overlooked such ignorance, but now He commands all people everywhere to repent" (Acts 17:30)

"He changes times and seasons; he sets up kings and deposes them. He gives wisdom to the wise and knowledge to the discerning" (Proverbs 10:23) "For the LORD gives wisdom, and from His mouth come knowledge and understanding" (Proverbs 2:6)

"Get wisdom, get understanding; do not forget my words or swerve from
them" (Proverbs 4:5)

"Do not take revenge, my friends, but leave room for God's wrath, for it is written: "It is mine to avenge; I will repay," says the LORD" (Romans 12:19)

It's not about age, looks, or money. It's about commitment.

A Blind Eye

As a young wife Jessica embraced bad advice while ignoring her inner voice. With a blind eye she also continued to look to her parents, and the church, for guidance. But the outcome was negative as their advice required that she remain in a volatile marriage while ignoring the battering, threats of death, and physical harm that were sure to intensify if she followed their recommendation.

Twelve years after her marriage began, and following numerous assaults and death threats, ideas began to form in her head—plans to escape her darkened tunnel of death before Trey put a bullet through her head.

Over the past few years domestic violence has been exposed. Assistance is now available for women all over the world who face daily battering.

For Jessica, the great escape came when she put her complete trust in God. With his help, her tunnel of despair ended at the end of a brilliant rainbow.

"Now choose life, so that you and your children may live" (Deuteronomy 30:19)

"I will restore you to health and heal your wounds, declares the LORD..." (Jeremiah 30:17)

Seek Knowledge

And he said to the human race, "The fear of the LORD—that is wisdom, and to shun evil is understanding" (Job 28:28)

"...for God did not endow with wisdom or give a share of good sense" (Job 39:17)

"What advice have you offered to one without wisdom!" (Job 26:3)

"The mocker seeks wisdom and finds none, but knowledge comes easily to the discerning" (Proverbs 14:6)

"The wise store up knowledge, but the mouth of a fool invites ruin" (Proverbs 10:14)

"Stay away from a fool, for you will not find knowledge on their lips" (Proverbs 14:7)

"...always learning but never able to come to a knowledge of the truth" (2 Timothy 3:7)

Voice of Wisdom

On every path taken, ask God for wisdom so your decisions aren't flawed concerning your future. Refuse emotions that dictate negative outcomes.

Begin all decisions with the wisdom of the Creator, and under God's covering. He alone will reveal himself in ways never expected. But most of all, don't allow the drama of life to create your destiny. Choose wisdom and receive favor from the LORD.

"For those who find me find life and receive favor from the Lord" (Proverbs 8:35)

"How much better to get wisdom than gold! And to get understanding is to be chosen rather than silver" (Proverbs 16:16)

Fear God

"The fear of the LORD is the beginning of knowledge, but fools despise wisdom and instruction. Listen, my son (or anyone) to your father's instruction and do not forsake your mother's teaching. They are a garland to grace your head and a chain to adorn your neck.

My son, if sinful men entice you, do not give in to them. If they say, "Come along with us; let's lie in wait for innocent blood, let's ambush some harmless soul; let's swallow them alive, like the grave, and whole, like those who go down to the pit; we will get all sorts of valuable things and fill our houses with plunder; cast lots with them; we will all share the loot"—my son, do not go along with them, do not set foot on their paths; for their feet rush into evil, they are swift to shed blood.

How useless to spread a net where every bird can see it! These men lie in wait for their own blood; they ambush only themselves! Such are the paths of all who go after ill-gotten gain; it takes away the life of those who get it" (Proverbs 1:1-19)

It's not what happens in life, but how the situation is handled that makes, or breaks you.

Wisdom's Rebuke

"Out in the open wisdom calls aloud, she raises her voice in the public square; on top of the wall she cries out, at the city gate she makes her speech: "How long will you who are simple love your simple ways? How long will mockers delight in mockery and fools hate knowledge?

Repent at my rebuke! Then I will pour out my thoughts to you, I will make known to you my teachings. But since you refuse to listen when I call, and no one pays attention when I stretch out my hand, since you disregard all my advice and do not accept my rebuke, I in turn will laugh when disaster strikes you; I will mock when calamity overtakes you—when calamity overtakes you like a storm, when disaster sweeps over you like a whirlwind, when distress and trouble overwhelm you.

Then they will call to me but I will not answer; they will look for me but will not find me, since they hated knowledge and did not choose to fear the LORD. Since they would not accept my advice and spurned my rebuke, they will eat the fruit of their ways and be filled with the fruit of their schemes.

For the waywardness of the simple will kill them, and the complacency of fools will destroy them; but whoever listens to me will live in safety and be at ease, without fear of harm" (Proverbs 1: 20-30)

One can't always listen to the heart, for the heart will deceive. Instead, allow God's wisdom to be your guide. Only He can direct your path because only He knows the plans He has for you.

"Trust in the LORD with all your heart and lean not on your own understanding; in all your ways acknowledge Him, and He will make your paths straight" (Proverbs 3:5-6)

Following years of youthful mistakes, God's wisdom has proven its worth.

Seek godly wisdom, and you will travel the path of righteousness into a better life.

Without God in the equation, you're on your own.

Chapter Eighty-Five

Divine Order

God's order in the universe established the family unit from the beginning of creation. Satan deception works hard trying to destroy the order God created. When man defies God's order he will inflict abuse, cruelty, and violence on other men, women, and children. This rebellion causes the household to malfunction.

From the beginning of time God established the role of man, and the order of succession in the family. Man was placed as leader of the household just as God is head of the church.

"For the husband is the head of the wife as Christ is the head of the church his body, of which He is the Savior" (Ephesians 5:23)

A husband, or father, is the designated breadwinner, leader, and protector of his family; and has the greater responsibility in the family. The wife has the lesser responsibility, although both have significant roles in the family unit.

Husbands, love your wives, just as Christ loved the church and gave himself up for her to make her holy, cleansing her by the washing with water through the word, and to present her to himself as a radiant church, without stain or wrinkle or any other blemish, but holy and blameless. In this same way, husbands ought to love their wives as their own bodies. He who loves his wife loves himself.

No one ever hated his own body, but he feeds and cares for it, just as Christ does the church—for we are members of his body. "For this reason, a man will leave his father and mother and be united to his wife, and the two will become one flesh.

This is a profound mystery—but I am talking about Christ and the church. However, each one of you also must love his wife as he loves himself..." (Ephesians 5:25-32)

Man in the role of husband and father should never lead his family as dictator, ruler, or king. "The 'give me, I deserve', and 'you're my slave' mentality was never God's intention when He placed man as leader over the household. Neither did God intend women, or children, to be mistreated by the dominance of man.

He Who Would Be Chief

He who would be chief must first be servant...whoever wants to become great among you must be your servant..." (Josh 20:26)

Man must provide for his family, as well as lead.

"He must manage his own family well and see that his children obey him, and he must do so in a manner worthy of full respect. (If anyone does not know how to manage his own family, how can he take care of God's church?" (1 Timothy 2:3-5)

Family First

A man's wife must come first. The woman was created from a rib in Adam's body, and designed to walk beside him, not above or beneath him.

"Then the LORD God made a woman from the rib He had taken out of the man, and He brought her to the man" (Genesis 2:22).

Eve was created from a part of Adam's body which allowed her the status of walking beside him, not beneath him. She was also fashioned to be his helper, and not a servant.

"The LORD God said, "It is not good for the man to be alone. I will make a helper suitable for him" (Genesis 2:18)

When a man leads his family with the mindset that he alone rules, the family is in danger of collapsing. As leader of the family, he should reverence the role he was created for.

"For unto whomsoever much is given, of him shall much be required:" (Luke 12:48)

The man should help his family and be available when needed. Instead of indulging in his own desires, he should love, honor, and protect his wife. He should never dominate, nor dictate what she says or does.

Christ sacrificed for the church. Man should follow His example, and willingly sacrifice for his wife, and family.

"Husbands love your wives just as Christ loved the church and gave himself up for her" (Ephesians 5:25)

Sanctifying and sacrificial love are the benefits of a godly marriage. But an ungodly husband will delight in pointing out the faults and failures of his wife while refusing beneficial complements, or praise.

Most marriage vows include spoken words of promise to honor, cherish, and treasure their spouse as Christ cherishes the church. But a man who compromises his vows believes his wife is nothing more than a possession. Her attributes are ignored as is her role as helper, and companion. Men who systematically destroy their marriage by displaying unparalleled bitterness and anger are not walking in God's divine order.

A man should love his wife beyond her faults and shortcomings, and as a prized possession.

"A wife of noble character who can find? She is worth far more than rubies. Her husband has full confidence in her and lacks nothing of value. She brings him good, not harm, all the days of her life" (Proverbs 31: 10-12)

God's Gift is Family

A father should devote time to raising his children in the fear and admonition of the Lord. This *is* his God-given responsibility, and not the mother's. God never intended for a mother to shoulder this duty. The chief responsibility of raising children is in the father's hands.

Although both parents are accountable for their offspring, a father's role has the greater accountability. His children will follow his lead whether he provides spiritual leadership or not. He is responsible for leading his children to God. Children will follow the father before they follow a mother's lead.

"Why do I have to go to church? Daddy doesn't go?" To raise godly children, one must first be godly themselves. It is imperative that we take time to teach our children about God, and the plan of salvation. This responsibility lies heavily on the father. However, it's difficult to find enough time to adequately teach our children, as single parents.

Many women end up in the role God intended for man. But the result rarely turns out the way it was intended. When a man rejects his role, the family is ignored, and the children are crippled, confused by the father's rejection.

When a man ignores his wife and children, over time their world will crumble and fall. He should be the one to pick them up again when they fail. By providing love and encouragement, they can regain lost ground. But when he ignores their needs, and squashes their hopes, he pushes the family down again.

Men should re-establish their relationship in love, and not with a stick. It's best to talk things over with an injured family member, and not beat them down as a resolution.

"If someone is caught in a sin, you who are spiritual should restore him gently..." (Galatians 6:1)

For women, don't bond with another man just because you are lonely, or believe he will be your salvation. One must first be rescued from abuse.

A girl's first love should be her father. If that doesn't happen, there is an alternative.

"...I will be a Father to you, and you will be my sons and daughters, says the Lord Almighty" (2 Corinthians 6:18)

When one stumbles, restore them again in love. Man must first be a servant and provide guidance, love, and assistance to his family. A father should relate to God as he relates to his own family. Abuse and disrespect, with a lack of self-control inflicted by a husband, is one of many reasons divorce occurs. The family unit *will* break apart when man neglects his leadership role in the way that God intended.

Divorce rates continue to climb at a staggering rate. According to www.marriage101.org, the divorce rate in America is now more than fifty percent which means one in every two marriages will break up. Divorce was never God's original plan for a man and a woman.

The woman is next in leadership of the family and provides a supportive role as wife and mother.

"Wives, submit to your husbands as to the LORD. For the husband is the head of the wife as Christ is the head of the church his body, of which he is the Savior. Now as the church submits to Christ, so also wives should submit to their husbands in everything.

Husbands, love their wives, just as Christ loved the church and gave himself up for her to make her holy, cleansing her by the washing with water through the word, and to present her to himself as a radiant church, without stain or wrinkle or any other blemish, but holy and blameless. In this same way, husbands ought to love their wives as their own bodies. He who loves his wife loves himself. After all, no one ever hated his own body, but he feeds and cares for it, just as Christ does the church—for we are members of his body."

"For this reason, a man will leave his father and mother and be united to his wife, and the two will become one flesh. This is a profound mystery—but I am talking about Christ and the church. However, each one of you also must love his wife as he loves himself, and the wife must respect her husband" (Ephesians 5:22-33)

A wife should be able to trust her husband by submission and love. But in some cases, this role places her in grave danger.

"...and he shall rule over you" (Genesis 3:16)

After twelve years of respecting Trey Jessica realized he didn't deserve her respect. By then it was too late as the bonds of matrimony had been broken through assault, abuse, verbal degradation, and infidelity. Although her father wasn't always right, he did receive her respect.

A godly man apologizes when he realizes his mistakes. But an ungodly man will never acknowledge his error, and is quick to place blame on others, more specifically the wife and children.

When Jessica submitted to Trey, her first husband, the abuse began, and she became a battered woman. But the secret remained for years, and only because she refused to ruin his reputation in church ministry.

God, in his mercy, covered her with compassion, although her ignorance could have cost her life. It was years before she realized the extent of His grace and mercy.

Due to church teachings, she remained silent concerning the abuse. Even when the residual of assaults became more noticeable, it could only be spoken of in undertones. Fear was the delegated factor.

God ordained the family unit but Satan desires to destroy what God has ordained.

Over time the love and desire Jessica once held for her husband died. By the time her marriage ended all emotion was gone. It was killed with cruelty.

When the family unit is destroyed, the children's walk with Christ is also destroyed. It is the husband (and the father's) place to set the example and demonstrate the love of Christ by action. He is the leader, and responsible for his leadership.

Life is all about choices.

Chapter Eighty-Six

Family Matters

God is our example of what a father should be. But Satan's plan is to wipe out the family's existence. His unique deception is to rip the unit apart, bit by bit. A father is his point of entry.

According to the Bible, the husband is to be head of the household. He should not dictate, rule, or dominate. Instead, he should serve, as a servant, by providing and guiding his family while relying on God for leadership.

"For unto whomsoever much is given, of him shall be much required: and to whom men have committed much, of him they will ask the more" (Luke 12:48)

How to Treat a Wife

- Love her

- Do not dominate her

- Be like Christ who is head of the church

- Sacrifice for the good of her, and the children

- Don't point out her flaws

- Cherish and treasure her as Christ treasures the church

- Praise and complement her

- Don't drag her down with indecent and degrading words

- Treat her better than you want to be treated. She is your prized possession.

- Do not hate the wife of your youth

- Don't allow bitterness and anger to destroy what was once a good relationship

The benefits of love will bring sanctification to the wife and family but comes only when the husband sacrifices his life for their sake. Children, on the other hand, will follow in their father's footsteps.

"For I have chosen him, so that he will direct his children and his household after him to keep the way of the LORD by doing what is right and just, so that the LORD will bring about... what He has promised him" (Genesis 18:19)

Deception and anger will eventually lead a child away from God. To raise children that one will be proud of show by example. Learn to teach in love and not in anger. Take time with your family, and your children. Don't be so busy that they feel ignored.

As for the role of a woman, the words *submit* and *yield* in the Bible, misinterpreted by many in the church, literally means what it says. "Wives, submit yourselves to your own husbands as you do to the Lord" The key point is *as you do to the Lord.*

Because submission was wrongly interpreted, Jessica was attacked, belittled, berated, battered, and left to struggle on her own. Through experience she learned that submission in a marriage does not mean accepting abuse. It also does not mean being subservient.

As leader in the home, the husband bares the

responsibility of love by example. But many don't truly believe or accept their authority in the way it was intended.

However, its often used as an excuse to bully, and literally antagonize, threaten, and attack those placed under his protection and provision—making this scripture a stumbling block for those who abuse their authority in ways never intended by God.

"Have confidence in your leaders and submit to their authority, because they keep watch over you as those who must give an account. Do this so that their work will be a joy, not a burden, for that would be of no benefit to you" (Hebrews 13:17)

A husband's authority was put in place by God. But man demeans and destroys every aspect of that respect if he mistreats those he should love the most.

Exactly how does God look at someone who destroys the family unit? As it goes with the head of the house, so goes the family.

He does not leave the guilty unpunished; He punishes the children and their children for the sin of the parents to the third and fourth generation" Exodus 354:7)

"The LORD is slow to anger, abounding in love and forgiving sin and rebellion. Yet He does not leave the guilty unpunished; He punishes the children for the sin of the parents to the third and fourth generation" (Numbers 14:18)

"Fathers, do not exasperate your children; instead, bring them up in the training and instruction of the Lord" (Ephesians 3:5)

"Fathers, do not embitter your children, or they will become discouraged" (Colossians 3:21)

"Parents are not to be put to death for their children, nor children put to death for their parents; each will die for their own sin:" (Deuteronomy 24:16)

"The secret things belong to the LORD their God, but the things revealed belong to them and to their children forever, that we may follow all the words of this law" (Deuteronomy 29:29)

"Whoever fears the LORD has a secure fortress, and for their children it will be a refuge" (Proverbs 14:26)

As it is with the head of the house, so it is with the family

.

Wrong Choices

How is it possible that a marriage beginning with love, dreams, and great intentions end up in a trash dump like a pile of rubble?

Unrealistic dreams and youthful ignorance are often the cause of disastrous decisions. Although difficult to accept, all choices *will* produce consequences. It does not matter how old, or how young, a person is—misguided decisions will result in negative conclusions.

Wrong choices will bring sorrow and judgment just as good choices create reward and success.

"For God does not show favoritism" (Romans 2:11) "He causes His sun to rise on the evil and the good, and sends rain on the righteous and the unrighteous" (Josh 5:45)

Bad choices, unrealistic dreams, and youthful ignorance are reasons one makes wrong decisions.

Strict, religious training received as a child from her parents, and later the church, required Jessica remain married no matter the circumstance. It was the law. Divorce was sin because the Bible said God hates it.

A television program hosted by Phil Donahue, a talk show host from years past, opened her eyes to the truth: that destruction follows a child who experiences his father inflict abuse on his mother day after day during childhood.

The crux of the show made it clear that the guest's children weren't impressed by their mother's decision to stay in the marriage. On the other hand, she believed her stay was in their best interests. Now grown, the children quickly shared their disregard for her decision. Not having an abusive father, and the niceties of life, would have been a better choice. The mother left in tears.

Transformation and modification are hard to accept. People move in and out of our lives all the time, for one reason or another. Yet love in our relationships, and freedom to exist in peace, are things that truly matter.

Friendships are most often relative to jobs or common interests, and usually disappear when similarities fade. Yet, when someone close moves away, or dies, hurts will surface. Life is full of twists and turns, joys and sadness. This scenario is mentioned many times in the Bible. We are no different than others in past generations. Hurt is hurt.

It may be difficult to understand why things happen the way they do. We may even be the one responsible, and blame God when our dreams dissolve. But it's important to realize that God is still in control. He didn't promise to remove the consequence of our bad choices. He did promise to be with us during our struggles.

"Brothers, I do not consider myself yet to have taken hold of it. But one thing I do: Forgetting what is behind and straining toward what is ahead, I press on toward the goal to win the prize for which God has called me heavenward in Christ Jesus" (Philippians 3:13, 14)

Those who truly love you when you need it most should be family.

Let the Future Forget the Past

If possible, move beyond all hurt and anger created by a bad relationship. Your goal should be realistic, but also attainable. Be aware of those who want you to wallow in your mistakes. In this way they become unaccountable for their own lack of concern.

Steps to Recovery

- Take on step at a time

- Be slow to make decisions

- Accept help when offered but use caution

- Don't allow others to take advantage of your situation and pull you into another pitfall. Women are resilient and will bounce back. But remember. It will take time to overcome the pain of the past
- Learn who your true friends are

- Stay away from those who fail to understand what you've been through

As the hare soon learned, the tortuous won the race *only* because he took his time, thought things through, and remained committed to the race.

"You will keep in perfect peace those whose minds are steadfast, because they trust in you" (Isaiah 26:3)

A Trace of Sanity

Forgiveness takes time. It is the last step in the healing process. Don't beat yourself up over mistakes made. Remember. If you have repented, there is no remembrance of the past in God's eyes.

Satan desires to kill, steal, and destroy. The domino effect will be irreversible for a man who destroys both wife and family. When a man's faith in God has failed, his children are affected in negative ways, and often remain in jeopardy for years to come.

"God is our refuge and strength, an ever-present help in trouble" (Psalms 46:1)

"The thief comes only to steal and kill and destroy; I have come that they may have life, and have it to the full" (John 10:10)

"Record my misery; list my tears on your scroll—are they not in your record?" (Psalms 56:8)

Bad decisions bring sorrow and judgment just as good choices bring reward and success.

Acceptance

Accepting the unavoidable was a tough pill to swallow. What Jessica learned as a small child was tolerance that carried far into adulthood, and beyond. The ramifications of abuse run deep, but are often traced back to childhood.

- Beatings taught pain tolerance

- Feelings didn't matter, and neither did she

- Others were right but she was wrong allowing acceptance of abuse without complaint

- That she lacked value

- Others were important, but she wasn't

- Being controlled taught there was no other choice

Others made important decisions for Jessica as a child. Current decisions are now difficult to make. A lack of personal self-worth devalued her personhood and allowed acceptance for what was not acceptable.

Anger and Bitterness

"Then your Father, who sees what is done in secret, will reward you" (Josh 6:6)

"For God will bring every work into judgment, including every secret thing, whether good or evil" (Ecclesiastes 12:14)

"Therefore, judge nothing before the appointed time; wait 'till the Lord comes. He will bring to light what is hidden in darkness and will expose the motives of men's hearts" (1 Corinthians 4:5)

The rapist is another example of self-indulgence. Is there any remorse when one causes physical and emotional pain for a woman—even worse, a child? There is no justification for a lustful soul.

"Behind your doors and your door posts you have put your pagan symbols. Forsaking me, you uncovered your bed, you climbed into it and opened it wide; you made a pact with those whose beds you love, and you looked with lust on their naked bodies" (Isaiah 57:8)

"You burn with lust among the oaks and under every spreading tree; you sacrifice your children in the ravines and under the overhanging crags" (Isaiah 57:5)

"Do not lust in your heart after her beauty or let her captivate you with her eyes" (Proverbs 6:25)

Many lives have been wrecked by lust, and premediated arrogance. Decisions that were made have consequences. Not only is it unfair for the victim, but also for the families on both sides. They will suffer right along with the perpetrator.

It's a vicious assault requiring revenge. And who is our vindicator?

"Do not take revenge, my dear friends, but leave room for God's wrath, for it is written: "It is mine to avenge; I will repay," says the Lord" (Romans 12:19)

Women throughout history have been targets of exploitation by man. The female gender is often unable to ward off outrageous attacks from an abuser, or rapist. But the psychological damage created during the attack may never heal. Even physical scars are sometimes permanent.

Many abused women live an isolated lifestyle following an assault. Their very existence consists of meager moments when they can briefly push aside the horror they've barely survived.

"He is driven from light into the realm of darkness and is banished from the world" (Job 18:18)

"This is the verdict: Light has come into the world, but people loved darkness instead of light because their deeds were evil" (John 3:19)

The process was painfully tedious for Jessica as she worked through the pain of the past. Yet God gently urged her forward as the murky darkness of heartache closed in around her. And slowly, she is finding her way. The channel of confusion darkened the earlier years of her life. But when the passageway opened, she could see a light at the end of the tunnel.

"You, LORD, are my lamp; the LORD turns my darkness into light" (2 Samuel 22:29)

"He reveals the deep things of darkness and brings utter darkness into the light" (Job 12:22)

Even in darkness light dawns for the upright, for those who are gracious and compassionate and righteous" (Psalms 112: 4)

**Respect and protect the relationships
that you treasure.**

Chapter Eighty-Seven

No Regrets

When Jessica told Trey their third baby was on the way, he more than exploded. "Get an abortion!" he shouted. "If you don't, I'll tell everyone this baby isn't mine!"

She couldn't understand his words. As a minister of the gospel, he often spoke in church about the sanctity of life.

Over time it was obvious Josh had inherited his father's good looks, and charismatic personality. He was, without a doubt, his father's son. But Trey was an abusive man who detested married life. He did not enjoy parenting his first two children, and he most certainly wasn't happy about the third. It was a difficult time in family history. He and Jessica divorced when Josh was three.

As a teen, Josh struggled for identity. His father could have given him a sense of self but didn't. Birthdays and Christmases came and went, but without recognition from his father.

As a young adult, he needed serious reinforcement, and a different direction. But Trey wasn't interested, so Josh struggled alone. He was later killed in a car crash.

Could his untimely death be the result of an absentee father?

**Release the pain, forgive the oppressor, and allow
all anger and hurt to slide into history**

Chapter Eighty-Eight

Forgiveness

God will repay for the wrongs done against us. Forgiveness, however, doesn't necessarily mean relationship.

Learn to forgive—not only the person you're at odds with, but for yourself. If we don't forgive others, how can we expect God to forgive us?

Reasons to Forgive

- Because God's word says to forgive

- Faith doesn't work if we don't forgive

- Un-forgiveness is like sludge on the inside

- Un-forgiveness will bring inner torment

- Un-forgiveness will interfere with having a personal relationship with God

- Un-forgiveness takes away the ability to love others

- Un-forgiveness opens the door to Satan if one chooses not to forgive

"Do not take revenge, my dear friends, but leave room for God's wrath, for it is written: "It is mine to avenge; I will repay," says the Lord" (Romans 12:19)

"Do not be afraid; you will not suffer shame. Do not fear disgrace; you will not be humiliated. You will forget the shame of your youth and remember no more the reproach of your widowhood (or divorce). For your Maker is your husband—the LORD Almighty is his name—the Holy One of Israel is your Redeemer..." (Isaiah 54:4, 5)

"The LORD is known by His justice; the wicked are ensnared by the work of their hands" (Psalms 9:16)

"The LORD works righteousness and justice for all the oppressed" (Psalms 103:6)

How can someone do hurtful things to a loved one, and never apologize? How can an abuser believe he's still a Christian? And how can someone, as an abuser, continue serving as pastor, teacher, deacon, or member of a Christian church? Where is his conscience?

Even on their death bed some will never acknowledge the pain and suffering they've inflicted on wives and children. How can one be justified if their sin is never acknowledged? And can one be justified?

Justification comes only if sins are forgiven, and under the blood of Jesus. Some will pay for their sins while still alive. Others will reap their judgment in hell.

"These are the things God has revealed to them by his Spirit. The Spirit searches all things, even the deep things of God" (I Corinthians 2:10)

Perfect love casts out all fear

Chapter Eighty-Nine

Running From Conflict

Jessica lifted a handful of dirty dishes from the table, carried them back to the kitchen, and gently placed on the counter. But her mind was elsewhere. "I'm tired of routine chores every day, and wasting my life away in this house," she said out loud.

"I'm tired of coming home from work every evening to a sadistic husband and being battered. I'm tired of shielding the children just to keep them safe. I need to get away. But when—and how?"

In desperation she plopped down on a chair and buried her head in her hands. "I don't want to be here anymore," she said under her breath. "This is no way to live."

People are born with survivor instincts. Yet many find it easier to run from conflict than to stand and confront. Because it took time to discover the ease of running from a challenge, it will also take time to stop running, and face the issue. Some conflicts resolve by themselves. But, for the record, most don't.

Negative habits and inbred family traditions often create serious problems for children in the family. Ideas long ingrained are the hardest to break away from. Abuse, negative relationships, or busy parents who ignore family issues are repeated throughout the generations.

Bad conduct, viewed through the eyes of a child, creates fear instead of harmony. Running from conflict is a learned behavior. Nothing but time can heal negative or hurtful conduct.

Patterns of avoidance need to be reversed. One must learn how to confront, and then resolve. The only way to recovery is to stop the old pattern and create new ones. It's called *confronting* instead of *running*.

- Stop running from conflict

- Seek help from a professional

- Recognize, and name the problem

- Work through conflicts instead of running away

- Manage conflicts instead of escaping from them

There are times when God calms the storm. But there are times when He calms me

Post-Traumatic Stress Disorder

Post-traumatic stress disorder (PTSD) is a mental health condition triggered by a terrifying event, or a series of happenings. This condition releases neurological changes in the brain.

Brain damage dysfunction has been medically recorded, and is reversible with proper diagnosis, and treatment. Also labeled as an anxiety disorder, symptoms may include flashbacks, severe apprehension, or nightmares.

Women who suffer at the hands of an abuser will go through varying degrees of post-traumatic stress.

Painful or shocking events will cause some sufferers to have difficulty coping for a period of time. It's important to take care of yourself so the events causing the syndrome can recede into history, and not return to create mental chaos that may last for months, even years. If those events continue to shake your life up, making it impossible to manage, the diagnosis may be post-traumatic stress disorder, or PTSD as labeled.

It's important to seek medical treatment as soon as possible if this is the case. Ignoring the problem will create serious long-term effects. Symptoms of post-traumatic stress are similar to the warning signs of clinical depression. There are differences that need further evaluation if the problem refuses to go away.

Indications of this disorder usually begin within three months following an incredibly traumatic event. Be aware that PTSD symptoms may not appear until years following the trauma.

Re-occurring fear and rage can become explosive over time. Children and loved ones will be recipients of one's volatile PTSD symptoms. Suffering past events of terror can leave a victim with sensations of extreme danger ahead, with an inability to directly control the situation.

Reactions can be embarrassing or cause unbelievable outcomes for the PTSD sufferer. But when one feels burdensome to those around them, it's simply a cry for help. Suicide could be the end result if not treated immediately. Although selfish, the number one reason suicide occurs is simply a distorted impression of feeling unwanted, misunderstood, or being a burden.

Symptoms of PTSD are categorized as escaping, invasive memories, avoidance, increased anxiety, feeling hyperactive, or sensations of being numb. These symptoms have been grouped into three unique categories and are listed for further evaluation.

Intrusive Memories

Disturbing memories include re-living traumatic events for minutes up to days at a time. Flashbacks will occur at unexpected moments. Nightmares, or dreams recalling the event, can be powerful symptoms of this disorder, and needs treatment in order to overcome them.

Symptoms of Intrusive Memories

- Flashbacks, or re-living the trauma repeatedly for days at a time
- Nightmares related to a traumatic event

- Tightening in the chest wall

- Panic over even the smallest of infractions

- Feelings of dread when confronting even the simplest of situations

Avoiding the Facts

A victim often avoids talking about or recalling a traumatic event. At times emotional numbness will surface with just the mention of a specific, distressing event. Avoiding activities once enjoyed or experiencing feelings of hopelessness concerning the future are also symptoms that need monitoring.

The injured party may have difficulty concentrating on any one thing, and experience problems in maintaining close relationships.

Anxiety

A victim of PTSD will become frightened in an instant or startled at any unexpected moment. They can have trouble sleeping. Over time they may become self-destructive by drinking too much or refusing to socialize. But a serious danger is isolation from others.

This disorder carries an overwhelming sense of shame, or guilt, concerning the trauma. The victim could see and hear things that don't exist. Most will instantly become irritated, or angry.

Symptoms of PTSD will come and go, but at unrelated times. But when things in general become more stressful than normal, or reminders of a recent trauma surface, the emotional outcome could have overwhelming consequences.

It's normal to harbor negative feelings and emotions following a traumatic event. If the aftermath ignites problems with getting things back under control, then it's time to talk with a health professional. If symptoms of this disorder become too severe, emergency services may be required.

Don't be afraid to ask someone for help if emotions of post-traumatic stress become too difficult to handle on your own.

Mood swings and flash backs are considered PTSD related. Don't underestimate the relationship anxiety and stress has on any disorder. It's not uncommon to learn that a dread disease has surfaced long after an abusive relationship has ended.

Although symptoms of PTSD, anxiety, or emotional numbing come and go, most occur when things are very stressful. Incidents can also occur that accentuate the experienced trauma. You may hear noises that reinforce negative thoughts or see a news report such as rape or battering, and suddenly be overwhelmed with memories of personal assaults.

Symptoms of Avoidance or Emotional Numbing

- Feels numb emotionally

- Avoids activities once enjoyed

- Inability to remember important things

- Hears or sees things that don't exist

- Has problems sleeping

- Feels hopeless concerning the future

- Has trouble concentrating

- Struggles with emotional anxiety

- Tries to ignore recent or extended trauma

- Has difficulty overcoming guilt and shame

- Struggles with close relationships

- Maintains self-destructive actions such as drinking too much

- Is easily frightened, or startled

- Feels enraged and out of control

Medical Treatment

It's normal to have a wide range of feelings and emotions following a traumatic event. Fear and anxiety will surface under these circumstances. But an inability to focus on everyday life, feelings of sadness, sleep deprivation, unusual eating habits, or depression could exhibit as spells of crying.

Nightmares, or an inability to stop thinking about a recent trauma, is not unexpected. This alone does not mean a diagnosis of PTSD. But if these events continue for more than a month or two, it's time to seek medical treatment for help in getting back on track.

If diagnosed with PTSD, treatment will be necessary to stop symptoms from controlling your life. If post-traumatic stress becomes severe, immediate emergency care may be needed. Call 911, contact a doctor, or have a family member do this for you.

The after-effects of stress could cause the victim to mentally re-live their trauma again and again although the situation has long passed. PTSD can also surface in unusual ways under normal circumstances.

"The LORD makes firm the steps of the one who delights in Him" (Psalms 37:23)

"You will keep in perfect peace those whose minds are steadfast, because they trust in you" (Isaiah 26:3)

"The prayer of a righteous person is powerful and effective" (James 5:16)

Jessica suffered the effects of this disorder for years. Her perception is exceptional. Having lived through it, she understands PTSD and knows it is survivable.

Panic Attacks

Panic Attack Disorder can be a serious condition if not treated properly. The ratio for persons having these attacks is one out of seventy-five. There could also be a genetic pre-disposition. If someone in your family suffers from this disorder, you may be at risk.

Panic attacks that follow an event, or series of events, will keep a person under extreme stress, and duress—often without a way to escape the pressure. Stress is the deciding factor.

A panic attack usually begins with a sudden surge of overwhelming fear. Panic seizes a person's ability to think in a rational way. These attacks will also come without warning.

Severe panic attacks followed Jessica's divorce from Trey—fear that he was lurking in the shadows watching, and ready to pounce when she was least prepared.

The will of God will never send you where the grace of God cannot protect you

Symptoms of Panic Attack

- Difficulty breathing

- Feelings of terror

- Paralyzing fear

- Racing heartbeat

- Sudden bouts of sweating

- Trembling or shaking

- Dizzy or lightheaded

- Feeling nauseous

- Cold chills, or hot flashes

- Chest pain, or racing heartbeat

- Tingling in extremities

- Feeling out of control without a remedy

- Blackouts—time lapses

Symptoms of panic will also occur while asleep. The attack seems to come from nowhere and causes different levels of panic to the stricken. There's no way to stop an attack from transpiring. Symptoms could pass in minutes, or last for hours. Some re-occur at unspecified times.

The event could be fierce and lingering, although not physically dangerous. Feeling out-of-control is normal for someone who experiences panic on a regular basis. This disorder can be scary and make one feel as if are going crazy. It also creates a social stigma if the attacks are witnessed by others.

There have been instances when a person under intense pressure blacks out, and is later unable to recall places, things, or people she has met. Certain blocks of time will vanish without a trace. Although seemingly awake and cognitive to others, time and events happen that simply cannot be remembered—even later.

Time lapses are common for someone who steps beyond the premise of reality into a semi-conscious state of mind. Again, stress is the instigator of panic.

For some, fear of the unknown is cause enough for

panic. If this is the case, stay away from things that cause severe stress to avoid another episode. If panic attacks are increasing, perhaps it's time to seek medical treatment. A licensed therapist can provide a complete diagnosis if you are suffering from Panic Attack Disorder.

The aftereffects of stress will cause a victim to mentally re-live their trauma again and again although the situation has long passed. Just as PTSD, panic disorder will surface in unusual ways under regular circumstances.

A person under extreme stress will act out of frustration. Impulsive behavior can be embarrassing and later cause regret after the episode has ended. It's not unusual for someone to fold under the pressure of an event, or excessive trauma.

Victims of abuse, spousal or other, will suffer from PTSD, and panic attacks. A person can be apprehended with these disorders again and again, even years following the initial cause of stress. Seek medical treatment if new bouts of anxiety are overwhelming, or symptoms of either disorder surface.

Out-of-control spurts of rage, memory lapses, blocks of missing time, and delayed reaction to normal situations are all part of Panic Attack Disorder. Extreme weight loss or excessive weight gain are the after-effects of someone suffering from this disorder.

Manic depressive disorder, days and weeks of utter turmoil, and moments of insane panic and fear are also normal. Time delays for reactive response can happen but could be serious if not addressed by a practiced physician.

Many will act out their aggressions on others, not realizing the consequences of their actions—or maybe they do

Chapter Ninety

Role Reversal

To better understand both sides of gender relationship, this equation is broken down for easier evaluation.

Recover, salvage, rescue, reclaim, and take back

Biblical Role of a Husband

"Now as the church submits to Christ, so also wives should submit to their husbands in everything. (Ephesians 5:24)

"Husbands, love your wives, just as Christ loved the church and gave himself up for her" (Ephesians 5:25) "In this same way, husbands ought to love their wives as their own bodies. He who loves his wife loves himself" (Ephesians 5:28)

"Husbands, love your wives and do not be harsh with them. (Colossians 3:19) Then they can urge the younger women to love their husbands and children (Titus 2:4) ...to be self-controlled and pure, to be busy at home, to be kind, and to be subject to their husbands, so that no one will malign the word of God" (Titus 2:5)

"Husbands, in the same way be considerate as you live with your wives, and treat them with respect as the weaker partner and as heirs with you of the gracious gift of life, so that nothing will hinder your prayers" (1 Peter 3:7)

"Husbands, love your wives, just as Christ loved the church and gave himself up for her" (Ephesians 5:25)

Biblical Role of a Wife

"Wives, in the same way submit yourselves to your own husbands so that, if any of them do not believe the word, they may be won over without words by the behavior of their wives.

For this is the way the holy women of the past who put their hope in God used to adorn themselves. They submitted themselves to their own husbands" (1 Peter 3: 1-3)

"Jesus replied, "Moses permitted you to divorce your wives because your hearts were hard. But it was not this way from the beginning" (Matthew 19:8)

"Have nothing to do with godless myths and old wives' tales; rather, train yourself to be godly" (1 Timothy 4:7)

The love of God removes all fear

Chapter Ninety-One

Medical Battle

Symptoms of disease often surface during and after the devastation of serious assaults and battery. Multiple Sclerosis was Jessica's personal disorder to battle.

This disease includes weakness, extreme lack of energy, partial blindness, an excessive number of migraines, cognitive issues, with an inability to function normally on a regular basis. Indicators are highly aggravated under extreme duress. Warning signs generated from stress accelerated by her first husband prior to their divorce has continued many years following.

When Jessica turned thirty-nine the secret of all unexplained symptoms was finally revealed. Her diagnosis brought feelings of relief instead of fear.

Learning more about the disease allowed an understanding that most, if not all, MS attacks were directly related to undeserved trauma brought on by an unstable and uncaring husband. The brutality she suffered was highly problematic and generated more stress in the home than was necessary.

Trey's anger would culminate into physical battering and verbal assaults but excelled in frequency over time. These strongholds created detrimental effects on every aspect of Jessica's life. Severe stress connected with his actions was a direct re-activation of her disease.

As a child Jessica was taught to do what she was told, and never ask questions. What she learned carried over into adulthood.

As an obedient wife, she obeyed her husband; believing the promises in their marriage vows were sacred, and to be honored.

The result was the necessity of escaping just to

survive.

Lingering effects of an abusive relationship leaves scars one may never completely recover from. The solution may take a short amount of time, or a lifetime to resolve, depending on the nature of the abuse and the will of the abused.

There is hope for renewal. When we make mistakes in our relationships, God can pick up the pieces of our lives, restructure them, and then orchestrate our future if allowed.

Five Steps to Freedom

- Recovery

- Salvage

- Rescue

- Reclaim

- Take Back

"God heals the broken hearted and binds up their wounds" (Psalm 147:3)

Recovery from physical, emotional, or material damage following a violent relationship, or break-up, will take longer than one realizes. Broken bones, fractured minds, and the loss of cherished possessions are difficult to accept.

It's imperative, as in first steps, to care for the physical as soon as possible by seeking medical attention. Wounds created from an assault, or multiple assaults, may need more attention than first realized in order to heal properly.

Manipulation, misuse, exploitation, insults, verbal abuse, swearing, name-calling, foul language, molestation, injury by assault, misuse, ill-treatment, sexual abuse, and physical harm are only a few of the agonies one may have suffered at the hands of a perpetrator.

Don't be afraid to address the reason these injuries remain. Doctors and medical professionals need to know the truth to understand the entire situation and provide everything that's needed to complete the healing process.

As for material goods, salvage the remnants, and be thankful for what remains. Reclaim what you can and let go of the rest. Understand that some things may never be recoverable. Although difficult to accept, it's best to forgive the one who stole from so you can move ahead with your life.

Nothing more can be done, at this point, if the damage is beyond repair. Accept what cannot be changed and move forward with peace in your heart.

In the future, address anger when it surfaces—and it will surface from time to time. Be aware that abusive memories sometimes take longer to fade than physical scars.

Good vs Evil

There was some concern for Jessica's safety on the part of her ex-in-laws, but not enough to reach beyond the *blood is thicker than water* barrier. For her, escaping with her life, and her children, was all that truly mattered. Many hurtful things had to be released, and this was one of them.

God desires all creation to enjoy their life without the possibility of an untimely death. Freedom to exist in safety was only a dream as long as Jessica remained under the same roof as her abuser.

To completely recover, leave your baggage at the door, and step inside. God will meet you there.

A Loving God

God will take away your care
Have no fear
He'll meet you there

Once you step inside the lair
It's then you'll find
He's everywhere

© *Phoebe Leggett*

Never Give up

Try to enjoy every aspect of your life even if the aftereffects of violence are recent. We weren't designed for mistreatment, or rejection.

"...God, who richly provides them with everything for their enjoyment" (1 Timothy 6:17)

"...that it may go well with you and that you may enjoy long life on the earth" (Ephesians 6:3)

Refuse to surrender to the pressures of others who desire that you remain a frightened woman running from an abusive man. In the eyes of most, he's the one who's been done wrong.

Ignore what others see, believe in yourself, and step forward into an oasis of liberation, freedom, and independence from your oppressor. Trust yourself to bring about the change your heart desires and deserves.

Remember, God does heal and restore.

Be strong. Be encouraged. And be a survivor.

As painful as they may be, hurts from the past need to be released to obtain the freedom that needed to move ahead with your life

Chapter Ninety-Two

The Police

A serious lack of compassion from local law enforcement allows criminal intent, violence, and assault to occur on a regular basis without dispute, or fear of arrest.

Can Small Town Police be Trusted?

Often labeled as the good old boys from locals, rural policemen repeatedly cater to their own offenders. From North Carolina to Georgia to Tennessee, small town police instigated negative stains over Jessica's life. As observed and experienced, local enforcement can't always be trusted with circumstances entrusted to them.

On three separate occasions while living in North Carolina local police were called following domestic violence episodes that left Jessica battered, bruised, and shaken. But their refusal to engage in assistance was bewildering.

After turning a deaf ear to her plight, they simply walked away. Their stance to remain neutral was stunning as a serious lack of involvement kept her stranded without resources concerning her safety, and the safety of her children.

Life is tough, but I'm tougher.

Georgia on my Mind

A well-known insurance carrier from a small town in the state of Georgia, the town where Daniel and Jessica moved, hired several women to man the phones for his established business. Their job was to generate lists of interested parties for salesmen to push an insurance sale. But none were compensated for time spent while in training—which was illegal.

Two weeks after Jessica was hired, Mr. Shyster began laying off his new employees, one by one. He then called her home and told Daniel she was fired.

The following day she went to work as scheduled, deciding this coward needed to fire her in person.

Mr. Shyster was stunned when he saw her. "I told your husband you were fired," he said. "What are you doing here?"

"You didn't tell me," she said.

"You're fired," he said. "Now get out."

After returning home, she called the Better Business Bureau to report the man. Following their instruction, she contacted the Georgia Department of Unemployment. From them she learned Mr. Shyster had broken the law by not compensating his employees for time spent while in training. He was then contacted, fined, and required to pay everyone for their time.

A few days later, as she walked through the parking lot of a local grocery store, Mr. Shyster recognized her and accelerated the speed in his truck to drive her over. Realizing who it was, she was able to dodge the truck and preserve her life. He screeched away, leaving her frightened, shaken, and on the verge of collapse.

She knew better than to contact the police as some had purchased insurance from the man. Since its common knowledge that local businessmen befriend police departments, she realized they wouldn't believe her anyway. Instead, she contacted her husband for assistance.

Daniel agreed it was best not to contact the police but promised to take care of the assault himself.

The following day he became Jessica's knight-in-shinning-armor. After confronting her aggressor at his place of business Daniel challenged him with these words, "Don't you ever come near her wife again. If you do. I'll take you out."

Mr. Shyster cowered at his desk. His only comment, "That's a dangerous woman."

Jessica never saw the man again.

Tennessee Recall

Local police in another town generated yet another chronicle. Shortly after their move to Tennessee, Jessica ventured out on a busy four-lane highway still under construction. But recently installed signal lights gave her pause, so she continued with caution. Her driving record was immaculate, and she wanted to keep it that way.

After navigating at a snail's pace through workmen, sign holders, and concrete boulders, she stopped at the light, which was red in color, and waited for the green arrow turn signal. When it turned green, she guided her car left as indicated.

Seconds later several small-town policemen surrounded her car, lights flashing and sirens screeching, and she was instructed to pull over.

A robust officer glared at her through her now opened window. "What do you think you're doing?" he asked.

"What did I do wrong?" she asked. "Was I going too fast?"

"You just ran a red light, lady," he said. "Plain as day."

She was stunned. But noting the officer's arrogance, she decided to hold her ground. "I turned left only when the green arrow lit up," she said.

"There's no turn signal there," he said, fingering his holster. "You ran a red light. Don't you know how dangerous that is?"

"I'm sure the turn light was green."

"Lady, you ran a red light," he said. "Let me see your license and registration."

"We just moved here," she said, and handed him the required documents. "My license has my old address."

"You can't run red lights here," he said, and handed the license back. "But since you're a new resident, I'll only give you a verbal warning."

Meanwhile the other officers had sauntered back to their cars, turned their flashers off, and driven away.

"Just make sure you never run another red light," he said.

After calming down, Jessica retraced her steps. Due to road construction the officers must have been confused. The installed lights beside the turn signal did not function with the turn light, as normal. But the light with the arrow was exactly as she had said it was and turned from red to green as before.

Police ignorance is often the instigator of deception. Is it any wonder many don't trust small-town police? City cops—maybe. Small-town police—never.

And use caution. Never trust without reservation. Ask for assistance *only* from proven policemen, and protectors of the peace, who aren't labeled as good-old-boys.

God will provide. He has—and He will.

Chapter Ninety-Three

God Is My Helper

Many moments gave Jessica serious doubt of survival following her court-ordered separation from her then husband Trey. Following their separation money was so tight every penny counted for something. But her anchor was her relationship with God. Without him on her side, hope for survival, and a better future, would never have been realized.

As a victim of domestic violence, it was obvious her abuser would ultimately cause her death if she remained in harm's way. His threats could easily have been executed as her struggle was ignored by those around her.

Her encouragement came from deep within. By faith she believed God would protect her, and her children, and keep them safe from harm. And He did.

Brutal Existence

Most refuse to believe, much less admit, that one of their own is an abuser. It's much easier to ignore a victim's pain than to acknowledge that someone they love is a perpetrator.

"He causes His sun to rise on the evil and the good and sends rain on the righteous and the unrighteous" (Matthew 5:45)

Trey had a fierce passion for preaching the gospel. He also had a dark side that manifested in cruelty to animals, as well as family. But it took years of time following her divorce before Jessica could piece together the truth as it was.

When Trey stood before church congregations her hope was always renewed. What she couldn't understand was his compassion for others, but none for her and their children. This burden, although oppressive, was shielded, and pushed deep inside; remaining until forced into the open.

Her inability to comprehend the truth kept her engaged in mental battles of hope that he would repent, and change. Yet improvement never came, and she remained chained to the darkness of fear, dread, and the anticipation of another battering. Although this chapter in her life was long and treacherous, the result was victory.

Why me?

You may ask, "Why me? Why did I make such horrible mistakes when choosing a mate?"

Realize it isn't God's fault. He gave us freedom of choice from the beginning of time to make our own decisions.

"And the LORD God commanded the man, "You are free to eat from any tree in the garden..." (Genesis 2:16)

At this time in history, God gave us the freedom of choice.

But why did Jessica, as a Christian, make such huge mistakes when choosing a marriage partner? And is it God's fault?

No. It is, without a doubt, directly related to ignorance and inexperience in decision-making as a young adult. Childhood restrictions from parents and the church, mixed with youthful enthusiasm, were to blame.

To believe a Christian doesn't make mistakes while attending church is a misnomer. Trusting leadership can also be a mistake. Although now subdued, religious dogma in the seventies created a strong relevance to restrictive doctrine in churches and was believable.

Yet again, the Bible explains that God is no respecter of persons.

"For God does not show favoritism" (Romans 2:11)

"He causes His sun to rise on the evil and the good, and sends rain on the righteous and the unrighteous" (Matthew 5:45)

Realize God's wisdom is far greater than ours. We don't understand why we make the choices we do. Perhaps it's because we were raised without good direction as a child. Or perhaps we were too stubborn to acknowledge a bad relationship before it evolved into a more serious commitment.

It's important to realize that God is in control even though we may have lost ours. His promise to be with us during hardship and struggle is our only hope.

**When most memories are horrible,
the good ones are easily forgotten.**

Chapter Ninety-Four

True Wisdom

"Jesus replied, "If anyone loves me, he will obey my teaching. My Father will love him, and we will come to him and make our home with him" (John 14:23)

Because her family was poor, Jessica instinctively knew college was out of the question. For her, setting goals was simply a waste of time as they would never be unattainable. Other important elements in childhood were also missing—guidance for achievement, and praise for accomplishment.

But she did learn about God. And that relationship has carried her through the twists, turns, and heartaches life has thrown her way. The wisdom of this world could never teach the depth of wisdom she learned at the foot of the cross.

When she realized that Jesus would be with her when she died, living for Him was worth more than all the wisdom this world could provide. Instructions coated with love from above are found on the pages of His guidebook, the Bible. His word provides all the direction needed to live in perfect harmony with others.

What's most important in life is making room in our heart for Jesus. When allowed joy and peace that passes all understanding will be ours. God will thebe with us through every trial and heartache that tries to beat us up.

True wisdom will be ours because Jesus cares that much for us. Living and working among people who appreciate, accept and trust is another huge step toward restoration of body, mind, and soul.

Chapter Ninety-Five

Angel

The bed where Jessica slept as a child was slammed hard against the wall, allowing more space in the tiny room. But during the winter months it was more than cold. Small puffs of air would rise above her head with each tiny breath and cloud the room.

One night, after her mother tucked her in bed, she climbed in beside her; and they both fell asleep. Early the next morning when she awoke, her eyes instantly rested on the wall. An angel was up against it.

He smiled at her. Blonde hair framed his face, and he was dressed from head to toe in a robe of white. Calm and fearless, she returned the smile. She knew, in an instant, this was her own guardian angel.

As a four-year-old Jessica's knowledge of angels was limited, although she could recite the Christmas story from memory—when angels announced the birth of Jesus to the world.

On the wall in another room a small picture portrayed two small children crossing a bridge with missing wooden planks. That angel was dressed in colorful clothing. Her angel was dressed in sparkling white.

Turning away she glanced at her mother, who was still asleep beside her. When she glanced back at the wall, her angel was gone. But Jessica knew that this angel was real. This was a divine appearance, and one she will never forget.

Angels have facilitated many escapes from dangerous events in her life. What more evidence is needed than the fact of survival?

"He who dwells in the shelter of the Most-High will rest in the shadow of the Almighty"
(Psalms 91:1)

Utopia is a place of perfection. When battered and broken, search for that perfect utopia, a place of solace—in the arms of God.

Chapter Ninety-Six

Biblical Encouragement For the Abused

"...Whoever sows to please their flesh, from the flesh will reap destruction; whoever sows to please the Spirit, from the Spirit will reap eternal life. Let them not become weary in doing good, for at the proper time we will reap a harvest if we do not give up. Therefore, as we have opportunity, let us do good to all people, especially to those who belong to the family of believers" (Galatians 6:7-10)

"We are hard pressed on every side, but not crushed; perplexed, but not in despair; persecuted, but not abandoned; struck down, but not destroyed" (2 Corinthians 4:8-9)

"We are therefore Christ's ambassadors, as though God were making his appeal through us. We implore you on Christ's behalf: Be reconciled to God" (2 Corinthians 5:20)

"For we must all appear before the judgment seat of Christ, so that each of us may receive what is due them for the things done while in the body, whether good or bad" (2 Corinthians 5:10)

"The LORD is slow to anger, abounding in love, and forgiving sin and rebellion. Yet he does not leave the guilty unpunished; he punishes the children for the sin of the parents to the third and fourth generation" (Numbers 14:18)

"Oh, the depth of the riches of the wisdom and knowledge of God! How unsearchable are his judgments, and his paths beyond tracing out!" (Romans 11:33)

"For the wisdom of this world is foolishness in God's

sight. As it is written: "He catches the wise in their craftiness" (1 Corinthians 3:19)

"The angel of the LORD encamps around those who fear him, and he delivers them" (Psalms 34:7)

"Fear the LORD, you his holy people, for those who fear him lack nothing" (Psalms 34:9)

"...the eyes of the LORD are on those who fear him, on those whose hope is in his unfailing love" (Psalms 33:18)

"As a father has compassion on his children, so the LORD has compassion on those who fear him" (Psalms 103:13)

"He fulfills the desires of those who fear Him; He hears their cry and saves them..." (Psalms 145:19)

"The LORD confides in those who fear him; He makes his covenant known to them" (Psalms 25:14)

"Surely the righteousness will never be shaken; they will be remembered forever. They will have no fear of bad news; their hearts are steadfast, trusting in the LORD. Their hearts are secure, they will have no fear; in the end they will look in triumph on their foes" (Psalms 112:6-8)

"But you, LORD, are a shield around me, my glory, the One who lifts my head high" (Psalms 3:3)

"The secret things belong to the Lord our God, but the things revealed belong to us and to our children, forever..." (Deuteronomy 29:29)

"Now what I am commanding you today is not too difficult for you or beyond your reach." (Deuteronomy 30:11)

"This day I call the heavens and the earth as witnesses against you that I have set before you life and death, blessings and curses. Now choose life, so that you and your children may live" (Deuteronomy 30:19)

"...to proclaim the year of the LORD's favor and the day of vengeance of our God, to comfort all who mourn, and provide for those who grieve...to bestow on them a crown of beauty instead of ashes, the oil of joy instead of mourning, and a garment of praise instead of a spirit of despair.

They will be called oaks of righteousness, a planting of the LORD for the display of his splendor" (Isaiah 61:3)

"If anyone, then, knows the good they ought to do and doesn't do it, it is sin for them" (James 4:17)

"Blessed are those who find wisdom, those who gain understanding, for she is more profitable than silver and yields better returns than gold" (Proverbs 3:13-14) (NKJV)

"You will keep in perfect peace those whose minds are steadfast, because they trust in you" (Isaiah 26:3)

"The LORD will strike ...with a plague; he will strike them and heal them. They will turn to the LORD, and he will respond to their pleas and heal them" (Isaiah 19:22)

"Even to your old age and gray hairs I am he, I am he who will sustain you. I have made you and I will carry you; I will sustain you and I will rescue you" (Isaiah 46:4)

"Do you not know? Have you not heard? The LORD is the everlasting God, the Creator of the ends of the earth. He will not grow tired or weary, and his understanding no one can fathom.

He gives strength to the weary and increases the power of the weak. Even youths grow tired and weary, and young men stumble and fall; but those who hope in the LORD will renew their strength. They will soar on wings like eagles; they will run and not grow weary; they will walk and not be faint" (Isaiah 40:28-31)

"The LORD is my rock, my fortress and my deliverer; my God is my rock, in whom I take refuge, my shield and the horn of my salvation, my stronghold" (Psalms 18:2)

"Scorn has broken my heart and has left me helpless; I looked for sympathy, but there was none, for comforters, but I found none (Psalms 69:20)

"Surely God will crush the heads of his enemies, the hairy crowns of those who go on in their sins" (Psalms 68:21)

"Blessings crown the head of the righteous, but violence overwhelms the mouth of the wicked" (Proverbs 10:6)

"Weeping may endure for a night, but joy comes in the morning" (Psalms 30:5) (KJV)

Good for All

"Brothers and sisters, if someone is caught in a sin, you who live by the Spirit should restore that person gently. But watch yourselves, or you also may be tempted.

Carry each other's burdens, and in this way, you will fulfill the law of Christ. If anyone thinks they are something when they are not, they deceive themselves.

Each one should test their own actions. Then they can take pride in themselves alone, without comparing themselves to someone else, for each one should carry their own load. Nevertheless, the one who receives instruction in the word should share all good things with their instructor.

Do not be deceived: God cannot be mocked. A man reaps what he sows. Whoever sows to please their flesh, from the flesh will reap destruction; whoever sows to please the Spirit, from the Spirit will reap eternal life.

Let them not become weary in doing good, for at the proper time we will reap a harvest if we do not give up. Therefore, as we have opportunity, let us do good to all people, especially to those who belong to the family of believers" (Galatians 6:1-10)

New Strength

"We fix our eyes not on what is seen, but on what is unseen. For what is seen is temporary, but what is unseen is eternal" (2 Corinthians 4:18)

"But the fruit of the Spirit is love, joy, peace, patience, kindness, goodness, faithfulness, gentleness, self-control" (Galatians 5:22-23)

"Now to HIM who is able to do immeasurably more than all we ask or imagine, according to His power that is at work within them, to HIM be glory in the church and in Christ Jesus throughout all generations, for ever and ever!

Amen" (Ephesians 3:20-21)

"Do not be anxious about anything, but in everything, by prayer and petition, with Thanksgiving, present your requests to God. And the peace of God, which transcends all understanding, will guard your hearts and your minds in Christ Jesus" (Philippians 4:6)

"I can do all things through Christ who strengthens me" (Philippians 4:13)

"Now Faith is the assurance of things hoped for, the conviction of things not seen" (Hebrews 11:1)

"So take a new grip with your tired hands, stand firm on your shaky legs, and mark out a straight, smooth path for your feet so that those that follow you, though weak and lame, will not fall and hurt themselves, but become strong" (Hebrews 12:12)

"...by His wounds you have been healed" (1 Peter 2:24)

"And this is the confidence that we have in him, that, if we ask any thing according to his will, he heareth us: And if we know that he hear us, whatsoever we ask, we know that we have the petitions that we desired of him" (1 John 5:14)

A Warning against Hypocrisy

"Then Jesus said to the crowds and to his disciples: "The teachers of the law and the Pharisees sit in Moses' seat. So, you must be careful to do everything they tell you.

But do not do what they do, for they do not practice what they preach. They tie up heavy, cumbersome loads and put them on other people's shoulders, but they themselves are not willing to lift a finger to move them.

"Everything they do is done for people to see: They make their phylacteries wide and the tassels on their garments long; they love the place of honor at banquets and the most important seats in the synagogues; they love

399

to be greeted with respect in the marketplaces and to be called 'Rabbi' by others.

But you are not to be called 'Rabbi,' for you have one Teacher, and you are all brothers" (Matthew 23:1-8)

"...not lording it over those entrusted to you, but being examples to the flock" (1 Peter 5:3)

The Beatitudes

"He said: "Blessed are the poor in spirit, for theirs is the kingdom of heaven. Blessed are those who mourn, for they will be comforted. Blessed are the meek, for they will inherit the earth.

Blessed are those who hunger and thirst for righteousness, for they will be filled. Blessed are the merciful, for they will be shown mercy.

Blessed are the pure in heart, for they will see God. Blessed are the peacemakers, for they will be called children of God.

Blessed are those who are persecuted because of righteousness, for theirs is the kingdom of heaven. Blessed are you when people insult you, persecute you and falsely say all kinds of evil against you because of me.

Rejoice and be glad, because great is your reward in heaven, for in the same way they persecuted the prophets who were before you.

Brothers, I do not consider herself yet to have taken hold of it. But one thing I do: Forgetting what is behind and straining toward what is ahead, I press on toward the goal to win the prize for which God has called me heavenward in Christ Jesus" (Philippians 3:13, 14)

An abuser is someone once trusted who later violated that trust again and again until nothing remained but numbness of heart.

Chapter Ninety-Seven

A New Life

Jessica has been married over twenty-four years to Daniel, a man who loves unconditionally, and enjoys doing things for her. She also survived childhood abuse and neglect as well as an abusive first marriage.

She survived three major surgeries—one of which was directly related to the abuse suffered at the hands of her first husband. The removal of her left ovary in 1992, residual from Trey's final battering, was devastating; but also revealing as death had been averted.

In 1997 she was diagnosed with Multiple Sclerosis—a disease she had battled many years without a diagnosis. An accurate conclusion for walking with a limp, staggering to the side, partial blindness, severe weakness, and other un-explained problems was a blessing although physically and mentally challenging at times. Problems assimilating information while struggling to understand instruction are common.

Her entire life she was told she could never accomplish anything. Instead, she chose not to believe bad instruction. By then she had learned to trust in herself, just as she learned to trust in God.

During her marriage to Daniel, his employment transferred them to different locations. Learning different perspectives and living in different states allowed exposure to unique aspects of life. But she is still the same person she always was.

Through every twist and turn on life's highway, God has been with her. Although recovery from abuse is still ongoing, she is learning how to move beyond deception into forgiveness. In the process she has salvaged what was good from the past, reclaimed her health, and taken back much of what the devil had stolen.

Recovery from childhood abuse, and again as a battered wife, has been a challenge. There are times when she again feels like a small girl struggling as a casualty of abuse. Although her parents meant well, generational ignorance is a difficult cycle to break.

Emotional wounds, bullying, and name calling from others was also significant. The blotched mindset placed on her as a small child escalated far into adulthood by way of her own ignorance, and wrongful trust.

Wounds of mistreatment are permanent reminders of just how far she had to travel to escape all the mental, physical, and emotional violence that once dominated her life.

Her one desire was to be loved without struggling to survive. Today she and Daniel are testimonies of love in action. The past has been conquered, and the future is sunny and bright.

Nothing Hidden

"Nothing in all creation is hidden from God's sight. Everything is uncovered and laid bare before the eyes of him to whom we must give account" (Hebrews 4:13) (NIV)

"For there is nothing hidden that will not be disclosed, and nothing concealed that will not be known or brought out into the open" (Luke 8:17) (NIV)

"All my longings lie open before you, Lord; my sighing is not hidden from you" (Psalms 38:9) (NIV)

"Therefore, judge nothing before the appointed time; wait until the Lord comes. He will bring to light what is hidden in darkness and will expose the motives of the heart. At that time each will receive their praise from God" 1 Corinthians 4:5) (NIV)

"For rulers hold no terror for those who do right, but

for those who do wrong. Do you want to be free from fear of the one in authority? Then do what is right and you will be commended" (Romans 13:3)

"Yet I am writing you a new command; its truth is seen in him and in you, because the darkness is passing, and the true light is already shining" (1 John 2:8)

The past sins of an abuser *will* be revealed. Hope will surface, and life will be fulfilling if we place our past in the hands of a loving God.

Exactly what does this bring?

Peace and happy feet, tranquility, and the ability to sleep at night because joy comes in the morning. (Psalms 30:5)

Where you have been hurt, others will be healed.

Chapter Ninety-Eight

Moving Forward

Jessica's escape from domestic violence into freedom was the most uplifting day of her life. Shattered in body and emotionally fractured, yet she was exuberant in spirit. At long last she was free, and finally on her own.

But times were hard—both financially and physically. She often struggled with starvation as money was tight, and food kept only for the children.

During that time, and lacking proper nutrition, her nails began to peel, and her hair to fall out by the handfuls. Coffee, often her only nourishment, and at times dry saltines, helped to squelch the growls of hunger that caused embarrassing moments at inappropriate times.

A gripping fear of the unknown followed her escape and remained as persistent as did her hunger. A lack of money was also a serious factor in maintaining her independence. Freedom had its drawbacks.

Although starved and thin, no longer was she a battered wife. Struggling alone, and doing without to obtain that freedom, was worth more than all the tea in China.

Injustices and Forgiveness

"...forgive your brothers the sins and the wrongs they committed in treating you so badly..." (Genesis 50:17)

Reasons to Forgive

It's best to forgive, even if it's difficult.

- A lack of forgiveness is like drinking poison and then believing someone else will die

- The key to freedom from the past is forgiveness

- Internal offences need to be forgiven

- Unintentional or perceived sins need to be acknowledged, and forgiven

- The essence of freedom is forgiveness

Making Decisions

- Think carefully. You may be one decision away from ruining your life.

- Don't run with fools.

- Don't run around

- Adultery is poison

- Don't run your mouth

- Don't accept foolishness over wisdom

The greatest love of all inside of you...words from a popular song by Whitney Houston that taught how the best love of all comes from deep within.

The Corner

Retreat from life
And calm my fears
Sweet camouflage
Replace my tears

When things get rough
A place to hide
My safety net
When threats collide

A spot to flee
From danger's zone
A corner patch
For me alone

Protected place
At last, secure
My corner world
The only cure

© *Phoebe Leggett*

On Sunday-School Day

To church we all go
To learn and to grow
On Sunday school day

God's lessons we hear
We learn not to fear
On Sunday school day

Then take time for fun
To play and to run
On Sunday school day

Its days we enjoy
To each its own glory
On Sunday school day

© Phoebe Leggett

Me and My Three

Resilient, happy, free
Happy as can be
No more conformity
Just me and my three

© *Phoebe Leggett*

Forgiveness

How do I overcome all the injustices served to me over a lifetime?

Forgiveness is the first step to re-thinking and re-designing our lives. Mercy for others is essential for healing, and forgiveness. After we forgive, we must also forgive ourselves. Only then will the weight of guilt melt into sheer freedom.

"So, if the Son sets you free, you will be free indeed" (John 8:36)

And whatever effort it takes to achieve that freedom will have value beyond measure.

Conclusion

Accepting advice from well-meaning people could be a mistake as wrong choices will be made, but for the right reasons. Jessica was set up early on to believe that all the spiritual, physical, and mental abuse she had suffered her entire life was all in God's will.

From experience she learned that man's control was the driving force to this insanity. The rigidity of Christian dogma from parents, church, and others all but strangled the life out of her.

Betrayal on any level is harsh. Due to an element of secrecy, all the verbal and physical abuse she endured her entire life remained a secret for years.

In the beginning of her marriage to Trey, she believed he would benefit if she remained silent about the abuse. His ministry was going strong, and people had great respect for him as church pastor, and evangelist. Many were converted to Christianity under his ministry.

But truth has a way of exposing itself. Once uncovered, it thunders forth; and deception is no more.

Looking back over a lifetime of injustices, heartache, disappointment, mistakes, regrets, and wrong decisions will make one re-think their objectives, and goals.

It's important to take account of yourself, and purge your heart of un-forgiveness, animosity, bitterness—even hatred toward others.

Who can recognize you error? Who can know you hidden thoughts?

"But blessed is the one who trusts in the Lord, whose confidence is in Him. They will be like a tree planted by the water that sends out its roots by the stream. It does not fear when heat comes; its leaves are always green. It has no worries in a year of drought, and never fails to bear fruit.

The heart is deceitful above all things and beyond cure. Who can understand it?

I the Lord search the heart and examine the mind, to reward each person according to their conduct, according to what their deeds deserve" (Jeremiah 17:7-10)

The End

Prayer of Salvation

God desires to have a close relationship with everyone. If you are broken, despised, or hurting, you are a perfect candidate for his redemption.

Everyone is equal at the foot of the Cross. No matter what has happened to you, the brutality you may have accepted, or what you have done to yourself—all can be forgiven.

"...for all have sinned and fall short of the glory of God" (Romans 3:23) Acts 16:31 says,

"...Believe on the Lord Jesus Christ, and you will be saved, you and your household." (NIV)

"If we confess our sins, he is faithful and just to forgive our sins, and to cleanse them from all unrighteousness" (1 John 1:9)

I believe that Jesus Christ died and shed His blood on a cross for my redemption. I also believe He arose and is alive and sitting at the right hand of God the Father; ready to make intercession for me.

I'm sorry for my sins and I repent of them all. Please forgive me. Come into my heart and live in me. Save me, clean me up, and make me a child of the living God. And now I accept him as Lord and Savior of my life.

Deliver me from the oppressor.

In the name of Jesus, I pray.

_____   _____
Sign name   Date of conversion

"...I will forgive their wickedness and will remember their sins no more" (Hebrews 8:12)

"Jesus said, "You have now seen him (God); in fact, He is the one speaking with you" (John 9:37)

Acknowledgments

To Ann Tatlock, a friend and mentor who helped to guide me into the world of professional writing. Without her continual support, this book would not have been written. Our friendship is ongoing, and a testimony to how God works out the details of our lives through others. www.anntatlock.com

To Cathy Baker, an award-winning poet and friend, who delights in writing, journaling, and blogging. www.cathybaker.org

To Pamela King Cable, a mentor who provided needed guidance that led to the publishing of this book. She is the author of *Southern Fried Women* and *Televenge—the dark side of televangelism.* www.PamelaKingCable.com

To Pam Zollman, a talented mentor and children's author, speaker, freelance editor, and writing instructor. www.pamzollman.com and www.thewritersplot.com

To Vonda Skelton, a friend and mentor, who teaches the fundamentals of basic writing through critique. She is also the Author of *Seeing through the Lies: Unmasking the Myths Women Believe*, and a coveted Conference speaker. www.VondaSkelton.com

Resources-Vows & Lies

Abbreviations

MS. Multiple Sclerosis
PTSD Post Traumatic Stress Disorder

Bibliography

Battered Wife Syndrome, information collected from www.divorcenet.com Walker, L., the Battered Woman (1979) See Walker, L., the Battered Woman Syndrome (1984) p. 95-97.

(www.Merriam-Webster.com) copyright © 2011, 2012 by Merriam-Webster, Incorporated.
All scriptures NIV unless otherwise indicated
www.biblegateway.com

New International Version, ©2011 (NIV) Copyright © 1973, 1978, 1984, 2011 by *Biblica* Zondervan Bible New International Version Copyright 1973, 1978, 1984 by International Bible Society® The Zondervan Corporation Grand Rapids, MI 49530 U.S.A.

Credits

All scripture in *Vows & Lies* was taken from the New International Version of the Bible unless otherwise indicated

Domestic Violence Resources

Domestic Violence Hotline at 1–800–799–SAFE (7233) or TTY 1–800–787–3224
Find help for domestic violence or abuse

Where to Turn for Help

In an emergency: Call 911 or your country's emergency service number if you need immediate assistance or have already been hurt.

For advice and support:

- In the U.S., call the <u>National Domestic Violence Hotline</u> at 1-800-799-7233 (SAFE).
- UK: call <u>Women's Aid</u> at 0808 2000 247.
- Canada: <u>National Domestic Violence Hotline</u> at 1-800-363-9010
- Australia: <u>National Domestic Violence Hotline</u> 1800 200 526
- Or visit <u>International Directory of Domestic Violence Agencies</u> for a worldwide list of helplines, shelters, and crisis centers.

Call 911 or your country's emergency service number if you need immediate assistance or have already been hurt.

Crisis Hotline: South Carolina   800-291-2139 or 800-273-5066,   North   Carolina   888-997-5066, North Carolina 222-997-8128

- Australia: <u>National Domestic Violence Hotline</u> 1800 200 526
- Or visit <u>International Directory of Domestic Violence Agencies</u> for a worldwide list of helplines, shelters, and crisis centers.

Find a safe place to stay:

Call your state's branch of the National Coalition Against Domestic Violence or another local organization.

For contact information, visit <u>State Resources</u>
What if someone I know is in crisis? If you are thinking

about harming yourself, or know someone who is, tell someone who can help immediately.

Call your doctor.

Call 911 or go to a hospital Emergency room to get immediate help or ask a friend or family member to help you do these things.

Call the toll-free hotline of the National Suicide Prevention Lifeline at 1-800-273-TALK (1-800-273-8255); 1-800-7994TTY (4889) to talk to a trained counselor

Safe Harbor, A safe place to start a new life ~ 24-hour crisis hotline - 800-291-2139
www.safeharborsc.org

North Carolina~ 888-997-9129

www.thehotline.org/get-help/help-in-your-area
www.womenindistress.com

Resources –Survivor Guide

Abuse: http://www.abusesanctuary.blogspot.com/

American Psychological Association: www.apa.org
Ann Landers, Fifteen Ways to Leave your Lover, newspaper article,1978?

Blood Banks of North Carolina - bloodbanker.com/banks/city.php?city=Asheville&state= NC

Book: He's the God of a Second Chance 1985 -Richard Roberts-http://oralroberts.com/about/their-history/richard-roberts

Book: Mending the Soul, on understanding and healing abuse by Steven R. Tracy, Professor of Theology and Ethics at Phoenix Seminary in Phoenix, Arizona
Book: When Love Goes Wrong: What to Do When You Can't Do Anything Right by Ann Jones and Susan Schechter

Divorce: www.Divorcenet.com

Declaration of Independence:
http://www.themhistory.org/declaration/document/index.htm

Domestic abuse, Amy Bonomi, associate professor at The Ohio State University

Depression and Posttraumatic stress disorder: 1998-2011

Domestic Violence Statistics
http://domesticviolencestatistics.org/domestic-violence-statistics/

Mayo Foundation for Medical Education and research Division, produced by ABA Publishing as a benefit to Division members. 321 N. Clark Street, Chicago, IL 60654

Divorce support: www.aboutdivorce.com

Emotional Abuse, Cathy Meyer, Certified Divorce Coach, Marriage Educator and Legal Investigator, www.about.com

Panic attack disorder. 2011 American Psychological Association, 750 First Street NE, Washington, DC 20002-4242

Divorce support: www.aboutdivorce.com
Domestic Violence Statistics
http://domesticviolencestatistics.org/domestic-violence-statistics/

Emotional Abuse, Cathy Meyer, Certified Divorce Coach,

Marriage Educator and Legal Investigator, www.about.com
Endometriosis www.Wikipedia.org the free encyclopedia

Endometriosis is a gynecological medical condition in which cells from the lining of the uterus (endometrium) appear and flourish outside the uterine cavity, most commonly on the ovaries.

The uterine cavity is lined by endometrial cells, which are under the influence of female hormones. These endometrial-like cells in areas outside the uterus (endometriosis) are influenced by hormonal changes and respond in a way that is like the cells found inside the uterus.

Symptoms often worsen with the menstrual cycle. Endometriosis is typically seen during the reproductive years; it has been estimated that endometriosis occurs in roughly 6–10% of women–Symptoms may depend on the site of active endometriosis. Its main but not universal symptom is pelvic pain in various manifestations. Endometriosis is a common finding in women with infertility.

Family Black Sheep ~The New York Times
www.nytco.com

History of Divorce:
http://www.history.com/encyclopedia.do?articleId=20769
http://www.allacademic.com//meta/p_mla_apa_research
citation/2/6/8/9/2/pages268925/p268925-1.php

The Judges' Journal, published quarterly, is the magazine of the American Bar Association Judicial
Mayo Clinic: Learn more about depression
Multiple Sclerosis www.nationalmssociety.org
Oh, Be Careful Little Hands, Christian Hymn Lyrics Online

Contributors

Cathy Baker, an award-winning poet who delights in observing God at work in the nuances of life, and sharing those observations through writing, journaling, and blogging. An experienced Bible teacher, Cathy leads a Bible group in her church, as well as a community Bible study for women. She and her husband Ayden live in South Carolina with their answer to the empty-nest syndrome—a pampered pooch named Rupert.

Cindy Sproles, Christian Devotions Ministries - P.O. Box 6494 - Kingsport, TN 37663, www.christiandevotions.com, www.iBegat.com, DevoKids.com, www.DevoFest.com, devocionescristiano.com,blogtalkradio.com/Christian-Devotions

About the Author

Phoebe Leggett is an author, poet, and free-lance writer. She lives near Greenville, South Carolina with her husband and two demanding felines.

In 2007 she was presented two awards for her work at the Blue Ridge Mountain Christian Writer's Conference in Ridgecrest, North Carolina. As poet and writer, articles, stories, and poetry have been published in adult and children's Christian literature as well as online. Also, a bi-monthly poetry contributor to Critter Magazine.

Other works published in Slate & Style, Shemom, Harold and Banner Press in Primary Pal, Pacific Press Publishing Association in Our Little Friend, MS Focus and MS Connection Magazines, Who's DANN? a monthly magazine, Gospel Publishing House in LIVE, a weekly journal, the Pentecostal Evangel—an Assemblies of God publication, Heartland Boating, Christiandevotions.us Assistant Editor-www.devokids.com, and the Upper Room magazine.

More Books by this Author

Seasons of Courage Series:
It's my Time to Grieve

Hidden Treasures Series:
Southern Charm
Southern Fantasy
Celestial Wonders
Southern Attitude
Sand Dunes Ocean Waves
Cats, Cats, and More Cats
Over the Hill

Christmas in Appalachia-Piper's Dream
Up 4 the Challenge

Made in the USA
Columbia, SC
06 May 2022

59803322R00269